D0437888

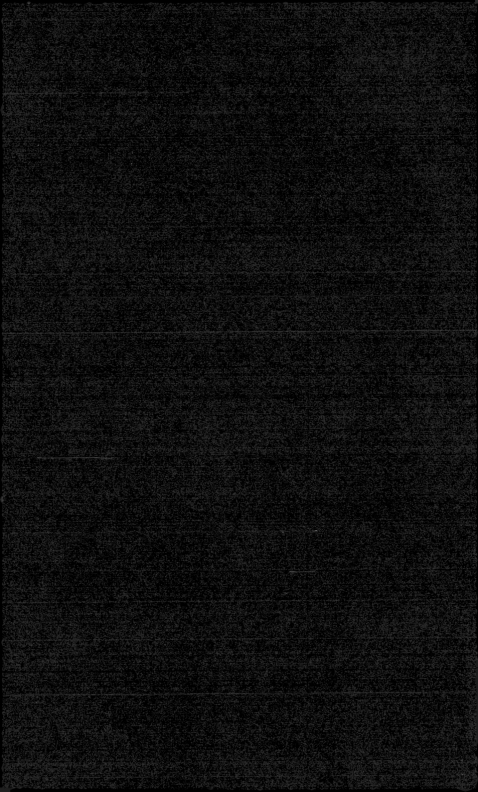

RADICAL

RADICAL

E. M. KOKIE

Candlewick Press

First edition 2016

Library of Congress Catalog Card Number pending
ISBN 978-0-7636-6962-1

16 17 18 19 20 21 BVG 10 9 8 7 6 5 4 3 2 1

Printed in Berryville, VA, U.S.A.

This book was typeset in Goudy.

Candlewick Press
99 Dover Street
Somerville, Massachusetts 02144

visit us at www.candlewick.com

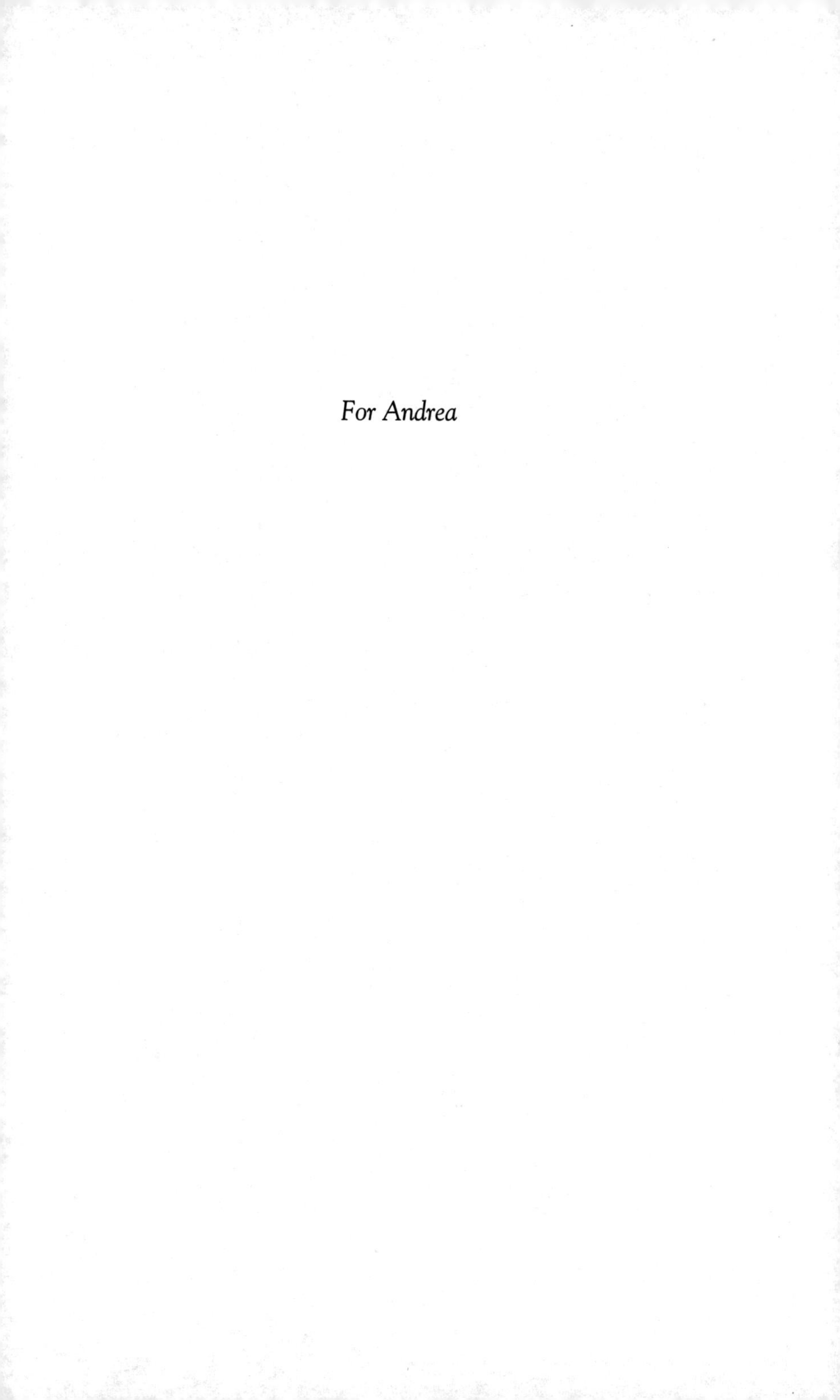

For Andrea

CHAPTER 1

They can die in their beds for all I care. All of them.

Especially Mark.

Mom's always been hopeless, but now Dad's checked out, too. He spends more time thinking about baseball than what we need to be doing to prepare — like knowing game stats of rich guys who wouldn't spit on us if we were on fire is going to matter at all in a grid-down scenario.

Then they give me crap for trying to prepare on my own.

Well, fine. Screw them.

My boot catches on a root, and I almost go down, grabbing the tree to save myself from a header into the trunk. My face scrapes down the bark until I get some purchase and stop the slide. The weight of the pack shifts to the side, pinning me against the bark with the rifle in its sling between me and the tree. I focus on the arm that's keeping me upright and turn just enough to brace my body against the tree until I can get my footing.

Once I can peel myself off the tree, I assess the damage. Stings, scrapes, aches, but nothing serious.

Before moving on, I adjust the shoulder straps on my assault pack and tighten the waist belt to make sure it won't shift like that again.

If I knocked myself out, I'd never hear the end of it. Instead of just being restricted to Uncle Skip's land, I'd probably be housebound, too. Maybe roombound. That would make them happy: me "safely" locked inside. Like keeping me from training will make me safe.

At least before he gave up, I had Mark. He rolled his eyes at all my plans and would never train seriously, but I knew that if we needed to bug out, he'd be there, right beside me, helping me get them out of here. With both of us, we might have a chance. Dad would rally. Uncle Skip would be another armed man, if we could get him to leave. Mom would need help, but with all of us, she'd be okay. But without Mark, it would be just me. They never listen to me.

I could survive by myself if I had to. Hook up with a good Mutual Assistance Group. Or form my own MAG. But that's only if I would go and not look back.

What kind of person leaves their family behind? What kind of person even thinks about leaving their family behind?

Thinking it is giving up.

I won't give up.

We should *all* be preparing. But until I can make them see what's coming, I will keep preparing on my own. And then we'll be that much further along.

Because it's only a matter of time until we will have no choice but to fight.

My phone vibrates, and I drop to my knees behind brush as if evading a scout. I work deeper into the brush and then pull the rifle to ready while I go prone. A perfect transition. Sweep the area. Acquire my target: a knothole on the tree. Sight and hold, as if waiting to engage. Dry fire, work the bolt to load the next imaginary round, and scan the area for other hostiles. I'm pretty sure I would have hit the knothole. With dry firing, it's hard to be sure, but it felt right.

When the phone buzzes again, I take it for the all clear and sprint for the pond, ignoring stealth. Sprinting all out like I'm being pursued.

They say that the difference between getting away from danger and not is the ability to sprint for three minutes. If I was ambushed—or even now, if someone tried to jump me on the street—the energy exertion to break away from the initial threat would be like sprinting all out for two to three minutes. I might not be able to outfight a grown man, or a trained soldier, or a bunch of hostiles, but I will be able to outrun them, outthink them, and hide, especially in wooded terrain. I could last a long time in dense woods.

At the pond I sweep the area, as if the dirt berm we use for shooting could be shielding hostiles. I sight on a fragment of clay disk still stuck in the dirt, steady, sight, and pull the trigger. I know I would have hit it.

It would be better if I could be sure, but Mom would go ballistic if she heard live rounds. Dad isn't crazy about me shooting alone, either, but he'd be most pissed at the "wasted" ammo, especially with Mom's ban on unnecessary spending. Like anything is more necessary than ammo. We don't have near enough on hand. I can only squirrel away so much without Dad noticing. The message boards and forums say you should have at least a thousand rounds for each armed member of a unit. If our family is a unit, we are nowhere close. We couldn't each carry a thousand rounds, but what we have is not nearly enough if we have to defend ourselves here or fight our way out.

If I were already eighteen, then I could stock up whenever there's a deal on ammo, but we don't have two years and

I can't get Dad to see reason. The government is restricting guns and ammunition already, cataloging us with permits and paperwork. Supply is already disrupted, and if the online warnings are right, supply could be cut off at any time.

With every incident—protest or shooting or whatever—the pressure builds. I watch the news and the sites. I stay on high alert, everything packed and ready to go. We are one rancher standoff or police shooting or massive protest away from all-out chaos, followed by a military state.

In the forums and message boards, people are sharing leads, talking about what they're hearing. The guys in Texas are freaked. Their governor is mobilizing the National Guard, in case those army training exercises end up being cover for something more.

Some people think it's the multinational corporations turning us on each other and distracting us with foreign problems and culture wars so we don't have time to watch them take over everything. Some think it's the government stirring up all this unrest so they have an excuse to declare martial law. I think it's all related. Dad loses his job because some rich guys decide to send the jobs somewhere else, and then we lose the house because the banks get paid either way. The rich guys and their corporations own the government. They won't be happy until they own everything else, too.

Whatever sparks the chaos, the result will be the same. It will be us against everyone. We'll need to be ready.

Government forces. Militarized police. Foreign hostiles. So-called patriots. Fellow survivors of whatever plague or catastrophe hits first, maybe gone feral or just competing for scarce resources until society rebuilds. We could trap and fish and forage. We've done it before. But getting somewhere safe and defending ourselves will take more than that.

Why can't Mark at least see it? I get that Mom isn't clued in to this kind of stuff and that Uncle Skip and Dad think it's all paranoid "wackos" with "conspiracy theories." But Mark reads the same sites I do, or he used to. He used to be right there with me and Dad on survival skills weekends and deep-woods camping trips. It's like when we lost the house, they all gave up. Even Mark.

Every time I try to make them see the urgency, I get in trouble.

They're probably sitting at the kitchen table right now, Dad reading the box scores, Mom wishing he'd focus on the want ads. If they're thinking about me at all, they're pissed that I'm out here training instead of obsessed with useless crap the way my cousin Hannah is.

I like it out here by the pond. A breeze and a stump to sit on and no one bugging me.

I dig into my pack for a protein bar.

Everything I'd take if we were making a break for it on foot is in this pack — my bug-out bag.

Most guys think the bigger the better. Like a four-wheel-drive vehicle stocked to the rims is the bare minimum. They think dragging as much as they can physically carry is better than maximizing efficiency.

Even Mark. He doesn't know what we would really need, or how it would feel to pack it, carry it, go for days on what was in that pack strapped to his back.

I do.

I've been training with my pack for months. And before that, I used my regular backpack, weighted down with whatever I could get my hands on.

I raided what I could from our camping supplies — compass, D rings, paracord, fishing line and hooks, a first-aid kit, the firesteel and scraper, and the aluminum tent stakes and military surplus poncho, which I can strap to the outside of the pack and use to build shelter pretty much anywhere.

But I can only add new things one item at a time, quietly, so as not to draw Mom's attention. I need a better water-purification system and a space blanket. A portable chain to cut wood (much smaller and safer to carry than a hatchet or chainsaw). A better knife sharpener, because if ammo gets scarce, or it's too dangerous to go where the ammo is, the fixed blade strapped to my thigh might be my best weapon.

I have a visual in my head, the pack with empty spaces where items still to be acquired should be. The written lists freaked Mom out, and the mental image plays double duty—shopping list and preparation exercise—as I visualize the contents of my pack before I fall asleep and when I wake up, so I can organize it and find what I need without thinking in a crisis.

Until my pack is complete, a couple of water bottles and boxes of bolts keep the weight and bulk right for training and acclimation. Bolts and washers in the pockets of my vest stand in for ammo. A large wrench strapped to my belt simulates the weight of my Glock, because even on our land, I don't carry a handgun. That is Dad's line in the sand.

My phone buzzes. Text from Mark. *Leaving in 40.*

Mark's coming to the range? All right, then. He hasn't wanted to shoot with me in months, not since we set off the pipe bomb and Mom went ballistic. He's shot plenty of hostile beer cans with his idiot friends, but that's not going to help him improve his accuracy or his readiness on the move.

I take a different trail back, closer to the road that runs along the far perimeter of our land, until I get to the old barn.

This hasn't been a working farm in decades. Dad and Uncle Skip grew up down the road. When Uncle Skip bought this place, he converted the barn into a workshop, with built-in workbenches and shelves for his woodworking tools, and a storage area for all our collective junk that doesn't fit in the house. In the back of the storage area, under some boxes and a tarp, half behind a standing mirror, is an old trunk, with a combination lock added by me. I spin the dial, pull it open, and push my pack inside. I'll bring my pack in later, when everyone's asleep. Or tomorrow. If I bring it in now, and Mom's itching for a skirmish, she might just try to take it away. Dad might actually change the combo for the gun locker instead of looking the other way.

I survey the house from the barn, make sure no one is looking out the kitchen window or door, and then move low and fast to Dad's truck. I stow the rifle in its soft case, which I put in the back of Dad's truck earlier so he'd have no reason to look for the rifle in the locker.

"Where have you been?" Mom says before I'm even through the screen door.

"What? I went for a run. I'm not even allowed to run on our own property anymore?"

Mom slaps the counter with the hand holding a dish towel, giving me that look, the one that says I'm trying her patience, that I'm not too old to be put in time-out, dragged there by a good grip on my ear like when I was six.

I stand my ground, staring back at her. We've been having this fight for weeks. They can refuse to do anything to prepare themselves, but they can't stop me from training.

"I don't like waking up to find you gone. Sneaking out while it's still dark, running around the woods doing Lord knows what."

"I had to get a run in before we left." She stands there, staring. She isn't backing off. "Fine," I say. "From now on, I'll wake you up on my way out, however early that is."

Dad pauses midbite to give her a look that says he's not in favor of early wake-up calls.

Mark says something unintelligible around half-chewed eggs and toast, double-fisting the fork and toast like a toddler.

"Swallow," Dad says. "And you." He looks at me. "No more sneaking out. If," he continues, putting up his hand to stop my response, "If you plan an early run, you make sure we know the night before."

"Fine," I say.

Mom stares at him for a long pissed-off beat and then turns back to the dishes, pan clanking off the edge of the sink.

Mark forces the food down. "We're gonna be late."

"For what?"

"We're dropping Mark off on the way," Dad says. "His truck died. Again."

Mom slams the pan against the edge of the sink louder.

"Dropping him where?" I ask.

Mark mumbles a response, food getting in the way.

"Where?"

"Clearview Sportsmen's Club," Dad answers, like he can't believe it any more than I can.

"A *sportsmen's* club? Are you kidding me?" I can't get either of them to train, but Mark's going to a snooty gun club full of wannabes and rich losers? "Since when are you the joining type?"

"Daniel Trace invited me to check it out."

"This is a joke, right? With what money? You can't even afford to keep your truck running."

"He's going as a guest," Mom says from the sink. "A free guest, right?"

"Yes. As a guest. For free," Mark says.

The way Dad won't really look at Mom makes me doubt it's really free. Mom's back is tense and angry. Dad's looking guilty. Of course Dad's giving Mark money. Never mind that neither of them is earning anything steady these days, or that

Dad said I had to pay the range fees today out of my money. If Mark wants something, then by all means.

"Why does he get anything he wants and he doesn't even have to—?"

"I don't get anything—"

"Enough!" Dad yells. He can't stand talking about our current financial condition.

By the time I've cleaned up and changed, Dad and Mark are waiting outside, ready to go.

Mom grimaces at my clothes—my too-long-and-baggy-by-her-standards cargo shorts, my layered shirts. Even the bandanna over my hair.

"Mom, we're going to the range. No one you know will see me."

She grunts and turns back to the sink. I am dismissed. I grab an apple on the way out the door.

It's already getting hot, and three of us crammed into Dad's truck makes for a sticky, sweaty ride.

"The rifle will be back in the locker as soon as we get home," Dad says. "And it will stay there unless we are going to the range."

Crap. "I was just dry firing."

"I don't care." Mark's pretending he can't hear us. "You know better."

"What good is practicing tactical movement without at least being able to sight and dry fire?" Dad gives me a look. "Only on our land, I promise."

"Skip's land," Dad corrects. "It's Skip's land. We are his guests."

"But I need to—"

"Not when you're home alone, or like this morning, when no one knows where you are. End of discussion."

Mark's still quiet. Usually he'd be giving me crap or sucking up to Dad. But today there's nothing.

He showered. He shaved what little facial hair he has. Clean clothes. New boots. Well, newer than his old ones. He doesn't look dressed for a snooty club, but he definitely put some effort into this.

The snotty, sulking Mark we've had to deal with since moving out to Uncle Skip's place is gone. Maybe he's finally waking up again.

Daniel Trace and his dad used to camp and do survival skills weekends with us. Mr. Trace is the one who taught me to set snares. I can't believe they've gone club. Clubs are for wannabes and poseurs, and they always cost money.

"It's really free?" I ask.

"Yeah," Mark says. "For now."

"Why just for now?"

"Because right now I'm a guest, checking it out. They're just getting started."

"And later?" I ask. He looks at me. "When it stops being free?"

"I'll work it out."

"How exactly are you—?"

"Leave your brother alone," Dad says. "It's his business. Not yours."

Of course. Because he's a boy. No, a man now. I'm still just a girl. And not even good enough at being that.

CHAPTER 2

"There, on the right," Mark says. "There."

Dad slows to a crawl and then turns onto an unmarked road.

"Are you sure?" Dad asks. There's no official sign marking the entrance. Just NO TRESPASSING signs on trees here and there.

"Yes." Mark seems amused by Dad's skepticism, like he's in on some secret joke we don't know.

After we pull off the main road, we drive for at least a mile on a country road before turning onto an even smaller one. I'm not sure two trucks could pass in some places. More NO TRESPASSING, PRIVATE PROPERTY, and NO HUNTING signs as we go deeper into woods. Then DANGER: SHOOTING RANGE signs start to appear. Then the road widens and the trees recede, and there is a metal cattle gate, with a fence extending from the road into the woods. But it's not "gated" like where Aunt Lorraine and Uncle Nathan aspire to live, with the manicured lawns and friendly attendant in the booth to wave you through. There's no booth. Just a card reader and a keypad. A building on the other side of the fence could accommodate guards, in a shit-hitting-the-fan scenario.

Dad slows as we approach the gate.

"Go through. It's open," Mark says, but Dad's look is asking again, *Are you sure?* "It's okay, Dad. We're allowed."

Dad pulls through slowly, as if waiting to be ambushed.

After another half mile or so, an open space emerges. A large gravel parking lot. A few benches and a picnic table next to it. Beyond that, some grass and then a gravel road. A large post-frame building with wide doors for equipment. A smaller building that looks like it could be offices. Poles in the ground for something else next to it.

There isn't even a sign like these snooty clubs usually have.

Dad pulls in next to some other trucks. Maybe twenty cars and trucks parked around the gravel lot. Plates mostly from Michigan, like ours.

Dad's looking around, dipping his head to see past the cars and trucks. He's starting to look more and more skeptical about leaving Mark here.

"Daniel," Mark calls out the window before he even has

the door open. "Daniel," he yells again, louder, adding a wave as he jumps out of the truck. Daniel and the two guys he's walking with turn around. They don't wave. The two other guys start walking again, but Daniel holds up at the edge of the lot.

"Hey," Dad calls to Mark. He motions Mark over to his side of the truck, and when Mark doesn't move says, "Come here."

Mark rolls his eyes and lurches around the truck and over to Dad's window.

"Thanks, Dad," Mark says, to forestall any lectures. "I'm pretty sure Daniel or one of the others can give me a ride home. So . . ."

Dad looks hard at Mark, then across at the buildings again, around the lot, squints at the trees behind the buildings, then back at Mark.

"Dad," Mark whines.

"Where are the ranges?" Dad asks.

Mark points back toward the buildings.

All I see are trees.

Where *are* the ranges? Screw the ranges—where are the sportsmen? Where are the poseur wannabes in their expensive shirts and stuff? Where's the clubhouse? We may not have seen a lot of sportsmen's clubs, but this doesn't look like *any* kind of club, let alone a snooty gun club.

If there are ranges here, they are well hidden.

A guy walks by the truck in full tactical gear.

Dad turns off the truck and opens his door.

"Come on," Mark gripes, but Dad gets all the way out of the truck. Then he puts his keys in his pocket.

"I just want to check things out," Dad says.

Mark looks over his shoulder. Daniel is standing with some guys on the path near the buildings. "Look, there's Daniel's dad. Okay? You know Mr. Trace wouldn't be involved in anything weird."

Daniel's dad is standing next to a man wearing a polo shirt and khakis. He's the first country club–lawyer type we've seen here. *He* looks like he could be in a sportsmen's club.

"Dad," I say, "I want to get to the range before it gets crowded."

"You're embarrassing me," Mark says, trying to block Dad's path.

Dad stares until Mark steps back. "I want to say hello to Mr. Trace. That's all."

Mark groans, but he follows Dad across the lot toward the men.

When they get there, Mark does introductions. Daniel walks over, and his dad puts his hand on Daniel's shoulder while Daniel shakes Dad's hand. Like they're saying, *This is the boy that sprang from my loins. I see your son is a boy as well. We have sons, and they are grand.* Don't mind the girl waiting in the truck—who can shoot better than either of them.

Another man walks up. Handshaking all around. Mr. Country Club does that thing where he reaches out with his nonshaking hand and draws Dad closer.

Mark is grinning and nodding so hard he looks like a bobble-head doll. Then he bumps fists with Daniel and they head over to where the other guys are waiting, and the whole group starts down the path toward the trees. And still Dad is talking to the two men.

At this rate we'll never get to the range before the wait is three deep. I reach over and lay on the horn. Dad turns and waves me off, then goes back to the talking and smiling. Daniel's dad crosses his arms. Country Club guy touches his chin like he's got a great idea. More talking and now gesturing. Dad looks back toward me, and then Mr. Country Club is motioning toward the truck and over. Dad is nodding. And then all of them turn their backs on the lot and more gesturing and nodding, now toward the buildings.

Ten more minutes and they're still talking.

A car pulls up next to the truck. The driver takes off her

sunglasses and tilts the rearview mirror so she can see herself. She likes what she sees. She takes her time gathering her long dark-red hair behind her head, and then puts it up in a ponytail. She smooths the hair on the side of her head until it's just right, and then adjusts her ponytail and studies herself in the rearview mirror. She wipes at the side of her lip, like her lip gloss got smudged. She gets out of her car and pulls a vest on over her tight black T-shirt. Then pulls her range bag out of the trunk. Her vest is nice but far from new. Same with her bag.

She looks at me as she fastens her vest. I turn my face, pretend I was just looking around. But when I glance back, it's clear she knew I was watching her the whole time. Stupid. I should have just held her stare, like I don't care at all what she thinks.

She walks by slowly, her hips swaying in camo shorts, and then follows the same path Mark took. There are girls in this sportsmen's club? Well, *a* girl, at least. A girl who feels like she needs to primp before she goes to shoot. Maybe she doesn't even shoot, just strikes a pose and squeals at how good the guys are. I've seen girls like that at the range. These clubs never take girls seriously. Maybe they hold a basics class for wives and daughters, or even a pink-themed ladies' session, but never more than a condescending nod toward their skills, never as equals.

Dad and the men are still nodding and pointing. And now moving toward one of the buildings. Did he completely forget about me? Screw that.

The gravel crunches under my shoes until I step over the wood divider and onto the grass.

I can't really make out what they are saying until I get close, and then I can hear Mr. Country Club talking. "Eventually, yes. But for now, the course, and some kind of accommodations out by the camping area." He waves toward the far right, where I can just make out a camper behind the trees.

"Sure, sure," Dad says. "What are you thinking in terms of timing, budget?"

"Why don't we go into the office and look at the plans. I—"

"Hello, Bex," Daniel's dad says when he notices me.

"Hello, Mr. Trace." The others turn around.

"Why, hello," says Mr. Country Club.

"Oh, right," Dad says. "The range." He looks at his watch. "Uh, this is my daughter, Bex. Bex, this is Mr. Riggs and Mr. Severnsen."

"Hello," I say, reaching out to shake their hands.

"Nice to meet you, Bex," Mr. Riggs says. His hand is soft and smooth. He doesn't work with his hands.

"I promised her we would go to the range. Uh"—Dad looks at his watch again—"maybe I could come back after. Drop Bex home and . . ."

"Why doesn't Bex just join the others at the range here?" Mr. Trace asks. He looks at Dad and then at Mr. Riggs.

"That's a wonderful idea," Mr. Riggs says. "We can consider Mark's guest pass a family pass. You can all see the facilities."

"No, we couldn't," Dad says.

"Why not?" Mr. Riggs asks. "Bex can check out the ranges. Meet some of the other young people. I can show you both around on the way out to the range, and then we can go into the office and look at the plans."

I try to give Dad the head shake no, but he's not looking at me.

"We have range rifles," Mr. Severnsen says to me, and then he turns to Dad. "There's adult supervision. If you're comfortable with her shooting without you there, she can use a range rifle."

"She has a rifle," Dad says.

"Yeah, but . . ." Dad's look shuts me up. This isn't what I wanted. I wanted Dad, to myself, at the range. I want to shoot my rifle *and* my Glock. Here I'll be restricted to a rifle unless Dad stays to supervise me.

"Great," Mr. Trace says, with a big grin. Mr. Riggs nods with a smile of his own.

Dad hands me the keys. "Get your stuff out of the truck."

As we walk away from the buildings and toward the trees, we move into shadows, and the sudden chill makes me shiver.

Riggs points out places, some with stakes already in the ground, where they plan to build this and that. A "proper" education center. Places for people to sleep and eat and clean up. Eventually. He chatters to Dad about other families, and about membership and how they're still figuring things out. He points to where the indoor training facilities will go—again, eventually. And waves toward the left, where other things will go. But right now there's not much beyond the buildings near the lot.

I glance at Dad. He's nodding, smiling, but I have a feeling his mind is on whatever "plans" they were discussing and whatever work that may mean for him. If there are no lines for him to supervise or tool-and-die work he deems worthy of him, maybe he can at least make some money here until something better comes along.

We pass the beginnings of a couple of trails, different

colors marking the start of each trail, and then an area that's been cleared for construction, with pegs in the ground and string. Riggs points out a squat, square metal building, which he says they're using to store their guns and stuff. But he also details his plans for a proper "armory" and then for more. I bet they're handing out free passes like Halloween candy. You need paying members to fund all this.

From the highway, if you didn't know they were here, you'd never guess. The sportsmen club label makes sense for ranges and trails, but they're talking about a lot more than that. Almost like a compound, but of course he doesn't call it that.

Riggs seems a lot younger than he must be, strolling along with his hands in his pockets. But he moves smoothly, fluidly, like he could break into a sprint or execute a roll at any time, drop to prone and pop back up again just like that.

His clothes are expensive. Expensive watch, too. Like he's dressed to work in a fancy office somewhere.

"We're hoping to have an indoor range in place by year three," Riggs says, looking from me to Dad and back again, "and after that maybe a pop-up range. But for now we have two ranges and some cleared training grounds. Once we get an organized training schedule set up, we'll reevaluate our needs. Maybe in addition to the tactical courses, we'll need to add some pistol bays."

So they want Dad to help them build tactical courses, and maybe more. But is this help or work? Unless that's how they get people like us in — let us work off our fees. Mom will never go for that. Mark and Dad need to be doing actual, money-paying work or we'll be broke and living with Uncle Skip forever.

The path widens and blends into the area behind the first range. "This is our pistol range," Riggs says. "Target boards at twenty-five yards on the right"—he motions to the firing points to the right of us—"and at fifty yards on the left, so you can also sight in rifles."

Maybe twenty firing points with wooden tables behind them. Stools for those who want to sit and space between the tables for kneeling or going prone. The range is cold while two men are packing up their gear and another is getting ready to shoot. The others are talking or checking their targets while they wait to continue.

"You know," Dad says, looking at the guys waiting to continue with their shooting, "if you added a concrete wall in the middle, one group could stay hot while the other side is cold."

Riggs smiles like Dad is a genius. "It's been requested, along with overhead cover, but we haven't gotten to either yet."

It's Dad's turn to smile, and now I'm sure that at least *he* thinks he's getting paid for whatever "help" he offers them with all these plans.

"What do you think?" Riggs asks, and it takes me a beat to realize he's talking to me.

"Nice," I say, but it's better than nice. I could spend all day here.

"You'll have to be tested before you can shoot outside of group training sessions or scheduled one-on-one times with an instructor's supervision," he says to me, leaning around Dad. "We're going to put together a posted schedule showing when teens are allowed individual practice. Always supervised, mind you. Sixteen?" he asks, but before I can answer, he says, "We have some other active young shooters. Their parents drop off their firearms and ammunition, or we'll supply what you need to shoot here."

For a fee, I'm sure. Fees. Ammunition. Money. But to be able to shoot whenever, with actual targets, in this range, would rock. And that's at least three times he's said *training*. Could they be doing more than shooting?

We move on back into shade and trees. Riggs is still talking.

When the path widens again, we come around a bend and there they are. About fifteen kids are standing around, with two adults talking near the firing points. They've already set up metal freestanding targets and wooden target frames in front of three or four of the shooting tables on one side of the range. Off to the left are additional targets, barrels, and obstacles, ready to be used. The obligatory dirt berm forms a wide U around the whole area and seems high enough that no rounds should leave the range.

On closer look, some of the kids could be adults, too. At least nineteen, like Mark, or maybe even twenty.

We follow Riggs down front to where the two men in charge are talking.

"Randy, Carl, hope we're not interrupting," Riggs says, even though it's obvious they haven't started yet.

Some laughter filters through like a breeze through the trees.

"This is Bex Mullin, Mark's sister," Riggs says, turning slightly and looking for Mark in the group. Mark scowls at me. "And their father, David. Bex is going to join you all for today. And may attend some of the open sessions. As our guest," he adds, maybe for Dad's benefit, maybe for Randy's and Carl's, some sort of communication about how much I belong. Like I'm not entirely trustworthy, or maybe making sure they know I'm just a guest.

"Welcome, Bex," Randy says, not very convincingly.

Carl just smiles and dips his chin.

“Are you all set to start?” Riggs asks, looking around for someone.

“Yes,” Randy says, “but we can hold off a few minutes.”

“Great.” Riggs turns, and somehow I’m turned with him. “Ladies,” he calls out. Some girls who are hanging near the far end of the range look at each other. The redhead from the parking lot is in the middle of the group. Riggs waves and they start toward us, reluctantly, as if only because they have been ordered to do so.

“Ladies,” Riggs says again, waving them close, his hand between my shoulder blades so I can’t bolt, “I want you all to meet Bex Mullin. Bex, these are some of our core girls. Karen Severnsen.” A tall girl with a dark-blond mullet clenches my hand in a hard shake.

“Hi, Bex,” Karen says. Her arms are defined, strong, and her hand crushes mine, but her smile is real.

“Trinny and Rhonda,” he says. A girl with pigtails and a short, soft girl both say hi.

“And Delia.” A girl with dark skin and braids smiles and says hey. It’s good to see her here; it means they’re not into all that racial-purity crap.

“Stacy,” says a girl with a long brown ponytail, offering her own name when Riggs doesn’t immediately come up with it. Then he acts like he knew it all along. I can't tell if her sour look is for me or Riggs.

The redhead is the only one left, and she hasn't moved.

"Cammie," Riggs says, like it's her rank more than her name.

She walks forward and extends her hand.

The queen. Or maybe lieutenant. Maybe lieutenant of the Apron Brigade—that's what some of the guys on the forums say, as if women would only need to use the guns in their apron pockets if their men fell. Is that what this is? Because if Riggs felt the need to introduce me to "the ladies," his "core girls," then he sees us as different from all the guys he's not bothering to introduce.

"Welcome," Cammie says, but her look is a challenge. Her nails are short but still sharp. One pinches into my wrist as we shake hands, like she's daring me to squirm or pull away.

"Hi," I say. My voice sounds funny.

Cammie doesn't let go of my hand.

"I'll leave you all to get acquainted before the training starts." Riggs walks, brisk and formal, back the way we came, all that easy looseness gone. "Come on, David," he says, gathering my father without breaking stride. "The girls will take care of her."

Sure they will. I refuse to rub at the stinging indentation on my wrist. The girls are already moving back to the end of the range where they left their stuff, all of them together, separate from the guys.

"Okay, everyone," Randy says. I turn to watch and find myself near Mark, who is glaring again.

"Wasn't my idea," I whisper.

He just mumbles, "Whatever." But it's clear he's blaming me.

"Basic weapon handling," Randy says, staring at a few still talking in back, "takes a lot more than hold, point, and shoot. I know most of you have been shooting for years, but since we don't know you all personally, we're going to start slow, checking the basics. Today, in small groups, you'll take turns shooting. That way we can monitor everyone, make sure everyone is handling their firearm safely, and focus on perfecting the building blocks, so that once we are working with higher-caliber weapons, moving from the ranges to tactical maneuvers, we can be sure a sound foundation is in place."

"And we *will* be moving toward tactical maneuvers," Carl says, maybe seeing that Randy has lost some of the older guys. "Holding positions. Attack and retreat. Flanking. Defensive positioning. Maybe even some squad work, if all goes well," he says, glancing at Randy.

Squad work. Tactical maneuvers. Holy crap. Thank God Dad left already—this stuff would freak him out.

"Right," Randy says, "but we're going to start with range rules and safe-handling tips before we move on to monitored shooting."

A lot of groans, and then someone says, "Come on," but I'm impressed. This isn't just about safety, but actual proficiency.

"Let's break into three groups," Randy says. He motions to indicate some of the older guys in back. "You guys are with me," he says. "The rest of you split into two groups. One with Carl at firing point five and the other with Karen at firing point eight."

Four or five older guys filter through the group from the back and follow Randy, all looking a little resentful to be here. "I know, I know," Randy says, waving off their grumbling. "We'll do a quick run-through and then get you guys shooting." He leads them toward firing point two.

I'm right near Carl, so I join his group. He has his handgun holstered, but he places a rifle on the table, muzzle toward the targets. Then he just sort of looks at me.

"Bex," Mark says.

"What?"

Mark, Daniel, some mouth-breathing skinhead-wannabe

loser, and the other three guys in my group are all glaring at me. And then I look over at the other group, which is clustered tight around Karen. Karen's with the girls. The guys are here with Carl.

Mark jerks his head toward Karen's group.

Apron Brigade for sure. Well, screw that. I turn so I'm facing Carl and wait.

Carl stares for a few beats and then says, "Okay," and he turns to place his handgun on the bench.

He runs through the basic safety fast. Everyone here is experienced, but he still goes over the first-day-at-the-range basics, like how to always point the gun toward the targets or down, never leave a loaded gun on the table, finger off the trigger until you are actually in position, all guns unloaded until ready to shoot, et cetera.

"What about open carry?" one of the guys asks. "I mean, we can carry out there, but we can't carry here?"

Carl takes a deep breath and looks over at Randy, but Randy is in the middle of explaining something to his group. "If you're eighteen or older, and the firearm you're carrying was legally purchased and is registered in your name, it's fine to carry it on the land. But we're encouraging everyone to exhibit some basic courtesy by the ranges. That means keeping handguns holstered and unloaded, and keeping long guns unloaded and open unless you are actively shooting."

"Bullshit, man," the guy standing next to Mark says. "If I can carry out there, chambered and ready, I'm not disarming myself here."

"Well, you can take that up with Mr. Severnsen, who's in charge of the ranges, or Mr. Riggs."

"Talk to Riggs about carrying?" one of the others says. "Yeah, right."

"Anyway," Carl says, directing us back to the range rules.

Then he makes each of us step forward and run through safety checks using his rifle and pistol. After each guy goes, Carl pulls him aside to make corrections or offer advice without tipping off the rest of us who have yet to be tested. The guy before me is a little too casual about it, and, from the looks of it, he gets more of a chewing-out than simple corrections.

"Bex," Carl says. I step forward. The doofus left the handgun pointing sideways on the bench with the magazine in *and* the action closed. Pretty much a what-not-to-do if you're trying to show you know how to safely handle it. I pick up the pistol, point it downrange, remove the magazine, and put it on the table. I pull the slide back and hold it open, look in the chamber, and then hold it so Carl can also see that the chamber is empty. He nods his approval, so I let the slide slam forward on the empty chamber. I pick up the magazine, show him it's empty, and slap it back in. I check that the safety is disengaged, sight on a target, and dry fire. I lock the slide back, remove the mag and put it down, and then set the pistol on the table with the muzzle pointed downrange and the action open. Carl smiles. I run through the checks on the rifle, then shoulder it, sight, and dry fire toward the target. Then recheck and lay it down.

"Good." Carl doesn't correct anything, and seems surprised not to have to. "Under eighteen? The rule for all the under-eighteens is that you can participate in dry-fire drills and live long gun drills with your parent's consent. But you do not touch a loaded handgun without a parent present. Understood?"

"Yeah." I was hoping they'd be more lax on that. If Dad consents, what do they care?

"I know," he says, "but it's the law. And we will be following all laws and regulations." Carl looks over toward Randy and then leans closer. "At least for now," he adds. "Once we get more organized, get to know everyone a little better, we'll be talking about squad work and how to best accommodate the training schedules."

Meaning maybe they're just being sticklers until they

know if there's a plant around who will run to the closest law enforcement to report any infractions or violations.

I glance around the group as I step back. I don't know any of these guys, but I can't imagine any of them are federal agents or informants.

"We going to shoot anytime today?" Karen asks from her table.

"Yeah," Carl says, but he turns and waits for Randy to finish.

"You ready?" Randy finally asks. "First shooters up. The rest of you, fall back to give the shooters some space. Eyes and ears, everyone."

I get my eye protection and earmuffs from my range bag and put on my vest.

Mark, Daniel, and the other guys in our group all step to the right so they can see the skinhead-wannabe loser getting ready to shoot. I hang to the left so I don't have to deal with them. Mark, mostly.

Even before he can fire the first shot, Carl is stepping in to give the wannabe some direction.

The short girl is up first over at table eight. Karen is working with her. She's using a range gun and is still pretty timid. She's probably a beginner. Cammie is watching, one step back, like she's the one in charge.

All three are readying to shoot, so I put my muffs over my ears.

Trinny, the girl with the pigtails, has on a unicorn shirt. It sparkles. So does the stretchy band to keep her hair out of her face. Her earmuffs are pink and covered in star stickers that I bet glow in the dark. I hope she has a different pair for maneuvers.

If we're still here by the time they're doing maneuvers. When Dad figures out that they're in to more than shooting ranges, he'll probably bail. Or our guest passes will expire, and they'll want money, which we don't have, not for this.

One of the older guys starts shooting. He's using a Sig Sauer with night sights. From the way the older guys looked to him, I figured he was the alpha of that group. Maybe of the whole group. Seeing him shoot, and his choice of weapon, gives me hope. He's serious but not a show-off, no tactical gear or drama. He has a solid firearm, and he handles it well.

The rest of the older guys are still grumbling or talking. Not even bothering to look at the guys in my group, let alone the girls. As far as they're concerned, they're already their own group. Men, not boys.

In my group, Wannabe is getting frustrated. Probably because he was strutting around before, but he's shooting like a beginner. He even clips the empty target holder in front of firing point four.

Delia's up in Karen's group. She's using a range rifle, too, but she's pretty good.

Mark and the two guys who were going on about open carrying are joking around, mostly about Wannabe. But I think some of it's about me, or maybe the other girls. Maybe Delia. Something jerky.

Daniel is standing apart from them, acting like he's watching Wannabe but really watching the older guys. He wants to be over there, not with Mark and these clowns. He probably should be, and if Mark and the others weren't here, he probably would be. Wonder if he's realized that recruiting these guys seems to have worked against him.

After Delia, Trinny shoots. Her rifle has a pink tiger-print grip. It would be pathetic if it wasn't so clear she didn't care what people think. Or if she didn't handle it so well.

Daniel does fine. When he's done, he looks over to see if any of the men noticed. They didn't.

Mark does well enough, and after him, the less mouthy of the open-carry guys does okay, too. Better than the sulking Wannabe. Then Mr. Open-Carry-You're-Not-Disarming-Me goes. For all his talk, he's only about at Mark's level. Nothing special.

I wait for my turn, watching Mr. Open Carry reload.

When he's done shooting, I step up. Cammie is getting ready to shoot at her table, but I force myself to focus front. I unpack my rifle and ammunition. I run through my checks, load up, and then pull a stool over to get in position.

After Carl signals me, I let everything else fade away. It's just me and the rifle. I ignore the steel targets placed at handgun distance and focus on the paper targets on the fifty-yard target boards. After the first five shots, I put the rifle down with the bolt open and pick up my binoculars to check my shots. I have a good group, maybe an inch and a half to two inches, about two inches below the bull's-eye. I don't want to adjust my sights, so I'll just aim higher for the next five shots. Carl taps my shoulder and holds out his hand for the binoculars, so I hand them over. He checks my target and hands them back with a smile and a thumbs-up. I half hear him and half read his lips as he says, "Good shooting."

I load the next magazine and shoot again, holding a little higher this time. When I check again, the group is about the same, but now centered nicely in the ten ring. While Carl checks my shots, I lean back to see where the others are at. Cammie and the guy in Randy's group are both ready to go with their other guns. Rather than reload, I clear the rifle and hold. I'm a guest, and figure it's better to leave Carl impressed by my corrections.

Cammie is still shooting. Looks like a Glock, newer than mine. Her form is perfect. She takes out the metal targets in order, slow but deliberate and in rhythm, and then focuses on the humanoid target. Nice clusters. In the target zones of head and chest.

She's good. And she knows it, by the way she ejects the magazine and checks clear.

Once the range is called cold, Karen runs down and gets Cammie's target. She studies the clusters and then hands it to Cammie. Karen high-fives her and then slaps her butt. Cammie smiles, then sees me watching and stops.

Carl hands me my target. I get another, more pronounced, "Good shooting." When I look up, Cammie and Karen are inspecting my target. Karen nods her respect. Cammie checks out my rifle on the table.

"Hey, Carl," Karen says. "Do you need to spot my turn?"

Carl gives her a *don't be stupid* look and shakes his head.

Karen grabs her own range bag while Cammie resets her targets.

Ready and focused, Karen looks fierce. Hard-edged and serious and not to be messed with. She lifts her pistol and focuses downrange. Cammie moved the targets back some, and Karen still efficiently knocks over all of the metal free-standing targets, and then readies for the paper target. She glances over her right shoulder at Cammie, and the right side of her mouth turns up. I move over to get a better look, just as Karen nods and Cammie starts calling the shots. Heart. Right temple. Neck. Nipple. Kidney. Pinpoint shots, including one last one down low, near the edge of the target, and it's not hard to guess where she was aiming.

"Excellent," Carl says, bumping fists with Karen when she's done and clear.

Maybe not *just* an Apron Brigade.

Laughter and a squeal off to my right. One of the older guys is lifting Stacy off the ground.

"Cut it out, Trip," someone says, but Stacy's only playing at being upset.

Karen and Cammie roll their eyes. Not impressed.

But I am. Not with Stacy or that crap. But with the ranges. The trainers. Tactical training. Finally, other people who get it. *This* is exactly what we need.

CHAPTER 3

"How was it?" Mom asks as soon as Mark is through the screen door and into the kitchen.

"Awesome," Mark says, heading straight to the fridge—to drink something from the carton, I'm sure.

She's at the table, the bills and her notebook of financial info in front of her. Serious stuff, usually. But she's always got time for her precious boy.

"The range is so cool," Mark says. "So much better than the indoor range. And the trainers said we're going to be working up to"—he catches Dad's warning look—"uh, longer distances. Today was mostly about safety and skills checks." He takes a huge glug of juice. "Next week we're going to do more actual shooting. And then—"

"Mark, get a glass," Dad says, more to shut him up than anything else.

Mom looks from Mark to Dad, and then to me. "And how

about you?" Mom asks me. "Did you have fun at the range with your dad?"

"It was okay. Like Mark said, they've got a good setup."

"You went to this club, too?" Mom stares at Dad.

"I wanted to check things out before I just left Mark there," Dad says, like that should earn him points. "Steven Trace was there, introduced me to some of the organizing committee. They showed me around, while Bex joined the other kids at the range. Looked nice," Dad says, looking to me to confirm. I nod. We're on the same side, for now.

"Can I borrow your car?" Mark asks Mom. "Just for a few hours?"

"What for?"

"I told the guys I'd come back out and meet up with them."

Mom puts down her pencil. "I thought you were just going for a visit." She looks at Dad. "We can't afford for you to *join* this club, Mark."

"It won't cost anything," Mark says.

"How does it stay in business if there are no membership dues or other fees?" Dad and Mark don't answer. "Who's paying for whatever this ends up costing?"

"I said I'd try harder to find a job," Mark says. "I've been looking. There's nothing!" He waits for Dad to back him up.

"It's important," Mark says. Mom sucks in her lips. "I'll only be gone a few hours. Promise."

I can see Mom wavering. She looks at Dad. "I haven't gone to the grocery store yet," she says, meaning either Dad gives Mark his truck or he drives her to the store.

Mom and Dad have one of those silent conversations, and then Dad picks up his keys off the counter. "I'll take him back."

"Really?" Mom asks.

"Yeah. I was going to go out there tomorrow anyway," he says. "Riggs, the head guy, mentioned there may be some work for me, since they're just getting things off the ground and still building the facilities. I was hoping to have a chance to talk to him one-on-one. I'm sure he'll still be there."

"Can I come?" I ask.

"You have schoolwork to do," Mom says.

"I can do it later." It's distance learning. I can do it anytime.

Dad hesitates. "School first," he says, looking at Mom like that will win him more points. "Next time." And they're out the door.

"Nice to see him excited, making new friends," Mom says, like Mark's happiness is all that matters. She scowls at me. My face must be showing just how much Mark's happiness does not matter to me.

"I don't need a lecture right now. I've got to clean my gun and put it away. And then I'll do one of the lessons," I add as an afterthought.

I get the rifle and my cleaning supplies from the workshop and set up on the porch.

Once all my supplies are laid out, I pull the bolt back and double-check that the magazine is empty. Then I activate the bolt release and pull it to the rear and off the rifle. It would be better at the kitchen table or the workbench in the workshop, but there's no breeze in the workshop, and I'm not going back in the house, where Mom will nag me about school.

She's inside at the table, crunching numbers and paying bills, but mostly she's making stacks of the bills we can't pay and recording figures in her grand-plan notebook, always calculating how long it will take us to be in our own place again. Today she's muttering too much. If Dad gives any money to Mark for the club, she's going to lose her shit.

I clean the bolt face with hand sanitizer and a toothbrush. One of the preppers on YouTube did a video on off-the-grid field hacks, and hand sanitizer was one of his tricks. It works so much better than the expensive stuff, and you can find it everywhere for cheap. If we were on the run, we might have nothing better than soap and water. Lubricant might have to be oil or transmission fluid pilfered from an abandoned car, or a bit of industrial grease scrounged along the way.

I put the bolt face on the towel next to me and grab a rod and patch to clean the bore.

"Dammit," I hear Mom say in the kitchen.

I wait for more, for the sound of erasing or any indication if that was a "dammit" because the math got the best of her, or if the magic line she's racing toward is creeping away again. I hear Mom's deep sigh and more shuffling paper. A not-enough-money "dammit."

I put the rifle and all my supplies on the edge of the porch and brace myself before going inside.

She's shuffling the bills. Moving things from one pile to another, until three bills remain. She puts two into what are obviously wait-for-next-paycheck, or maybe the paycheck after, stacks. She rubs her eyes like they're full of sand. One last bill sits on the table in front of her.

We canceled everything we could before giving in and moving out here. They should just cancel Mark's truck insurance, since his truck is always busted. Other than that, there's not much left to cancel.

She's looking at our cell phone bill. We wouldn't have phones at all, but when Mom said they had to be canceled,

I agreed to pay half. But it looks like half is still pushing it. I can't lose my phone. It's my most reliable Internet. The only one that's really private.

I go upstairs and close the door to the room I'm using as quietly as I can. The starched and ironed curtains have flowers in faded pinks and yellows and blues embroidered around the edges, faded nearly white in the folds that get more sun. Aunt Gracie made them. She made the quilt on the bed, too. The room still sort of smells like her. She's been dead for years, but, even though Uncle Skip hasn't slept in here since she died, I think he only cleaned out her stuff so I could have this room. It's like him to hang on to things, to the bits of people who are gone. Grammy's sewing machine is in the barn, too.

There are still outlines on the mirror where Aunt Gracie stuck photographs into the frame—twenty years of dust leaving a cloudy ring to memorialize their absence. Behind the mirror is a key, taped as far back as I can reach.

Under the loose floorboard in the closet, pushed back as far as it can go, is an old lockbox I found at a secondhand store. I unlock and open it. I count out enough for the whole phone bill, count what's left, and add a little more to the phone-bill stack. Then I put everything back, hide the key in a new location, and then I'm standing in front of Mom.

I don't say anything. I just put the money on the table,

over the phone bill. Enough to pay what we owe and then some.

She should be grateful. Instead she looks at the money like I just spit on the table, or like I'm trying to make her feel bad.

I leave it there and go back out onto the porch. She'll take it. She has to. We need our phones. Especially Mom and me.

It hurts to give her my money. But it would hurt worse not to.

I sit on the porch, legs hanging over the edge, recalculating my purchasing order for my pack. Dad never stops feeling like a guest here, so we'll go as soon as Mom says we can afford it. Probably to an apartment. In a crappy neighborhood. I stare at the trees beyond the barn, listen to the birds. Feel the breeze, cool across my bare arms. I hope it takes years.

I listen to Mom in the kitchen while I use the rod to run a patch with solvent through the bore. Then a few swipes with the brush, followed by clean patches until one comes through looking near as clean as when it went in. And finally, one last patch lightly soaked in oil to preserve the bore.

We've got other guns, better guns. But when it comes down to it, I like the feel of this old Remington best. It's not going to take down a deer or anything bigger than a squirrel at long range. But I love this gun. I trust this gun. She jams for

Mark and Dad, but she works for me like she trusts me. Maybe because I baby her, or because I can feel how she moves.

I wipe my fingerprints off the bolt, reinstall it, dry fire to make sure everything works, and then start wiping down all the exposed metal with a clean rag. Toxic fingerprints can eat away at the metal. An old T-shirt is perfect to get in deep, make sure it's well cleaned.

Dad's truck comes down the drive.

When he gets out of the truck, Mark's not with him. I'd make a joke about it, but I don't feel much like joking. Mark hasn't done anything in months. He doesn't work. He doesn't train. He doesn't help out around here. But he wanted to go to the club, so we went. And now he wanted to go back to the club, and Dad took him.

Dad stops with his foot on the bottom step and looks at the rifle in my hands.

"Just cleaning it before putting it away."

He holds out his hand for the rifle. Giving it to him feels like the last time I'm going to hold it. He opens the bolt, uses his thumbnail near the chamber to reflect light in, squints down the bore. He nods approvingly. "You take good care of it."

My throat closes around the lump of pride and anger and frustration all balled up there. I've been waiting so long for him to wake up and take this seriously, take me seriously. If I'd found Clearview, there's no way Dad would have agreed to go out there. But Mark emerges from hibernation and he immediately gets what he wants. Whatever he wants. Dad always chooses Mark. They both do.

"When you're done, put your rifle away. Then give your mother a hand with dinner, okay?"

My rifle. He's never called it that before. "Okay." He barely touches the back of my head as he walks by, just enough for my head to follow his hand and leave me leaning when he's gone.

"Where's Mark?" I hear Mom ask.

"Daniel will drop him off later."

"Haven't seen him excited about anything in a long while," Mom says. "But I spent half the afternoon trying to figure out how to pay the bills. The extra gas, his insurance and truck repairs, all of that adds up. He's going to need to find *something*."

I can't make out what Dad says, but Mom responds, "I'm busting my butt at temp jobs, staying with Lorraine all week, and then coming home and busting my butt here on weekends."

"You're not the only one busting your butt. I'm out there—"

"What? You're what?"

"For crying out loud, Charlotte!" That's Dad's all-encompassing response when he's frustrated.

Mom slams a cabinet, her response when Dad goes for the *crying out loud*.

I can hear their voices, their movements through the house, and a door slams upstairs. Another fight.

My Glock could use a good cleaning, too.

I break it down and start with the solvent.

I can still hear their voices now and then through an open window upstairs, but not what they're saying, not from this side of the house.

Eventually Mom comes back downstairs, back to the kitchen, starting dinner, from the sound of it. Mainly she's slamming stuff around the sink. No way I'm going in there.

I've got the Glock almost back together when a truck comes down the driveway.

Mark, Daniel, and some other guy.

"Hey," Mark says, bounding up the steps past me as the truck pulls away.

"Want me to leave this stuff out for you?" I ask.

He pauses with his hand on the screen door and looks over his shoulder. "Nah, I'll do it later."

No, he won't. His gun will continue to collect crud

because he's lazy. Lazy and irresponsible, but he's a boy, and that's all that matters.

I put all the cleaning stuff back in the workshop and then head into the house to lock my rifle and Glock back in the gun locker.

"Wash up," Mom says, before I've even got my boots off. She hates the smell of the oil and solvent. On days when Uncle Skips lets me work on cars at the station, she makes me strip down in the laundry room and put everything right in the washer. The laundry room soap smells like cheap pine, a manly smell Dad and Mark won't balk at using. Instead I just go upstairs and take a fast shower.

On the way back downstairs, I can hear Mark yammering away at Mom and Dad.

Mom hands me the knife, and I take over cutting up the vegetables for the salad. It looks like the rest of dinner is almost ready.

"And Daniel said he can pick me up this week so I can start right away," Mark says. "As soon as I can, I'll pay the insurance on my truck. But until then—"

"It needs more than insurance," Dad says. "Better talk to Skip about the repairs when he gets home. Maybe you can work off some of it."

Last week Mark would have sneered and sulked at that

suggestion, but today he's all eager beaver, ready to agree to anything.

Mom takes her usual seat across from Dad. I put the salad on the table and fall into my place. Dad says grace, and then the conversation continues as if it never paused.

"So, he wants to join," Mom says, nodding toward Mark. "What about you?" she asks Dad. He just shrugs and eats his dinner. But Mom's waiting for an answer.

Eventually he puts down his fork, takes a sip of his iced tea, and looks directly at Mom. "I'm not sure yet. Right now all they're asking is that I consider it and maybe help them build the tactical course."

"I don't even know what that means," Mom says. She shakes her head, taking a bite of her chicken. She probably knows she won't win if he's already made up his mind, but she's not giving in yet. Not without some face-saving concessions.

"It's like an obstacle course, with different targets you have to shoot," Mark says. "They're going to build one in wooded terrain, and one that simulates close urban combat. And then maybe—"

"For what? To train people to be killers? I don't—"

"No." Dad gives Mark a *pipe down* look. He didn't plan on giving her enough info to nitpick the details. "It's like a fancier range."

"And members can work on survival techniques or hike the trails. It's so cool. And they're going to organize into . . ." At Dad's glare, Mark stops talking.

Mom stares at Mark, then at Dad. "And they want you to build these tactical training courses?"

"Maybe. If I want, and if we can agree on the plans," Dad says. "And the price."

"I'm joining." Mark helps himself to more of pretty much everything. "I don't care what you do, but I'm in."

Mom leans back in her chair and crosses her arms. "With what money? Whatever this ends up costing," she says, ignoring his repeated protests that there are no fees, "you'll also need gas, ammunition, truck repairs and insurance, and whatever else."

"I'll make money. More than enough."

"How?" Mom asks.

"Daniel's been working steady for one of the other members. Landscaping. Construction. Painting. Sometimes other stuff. Good money."

"Oh, well," Mom says, "if Danny Trace says so . . . Isn't he the little genius who talked you into lighting your farts on fire?" I stifle a laugh. Mark set his pants on fire and then couldn't sit down right for a week.

"He said a few of the other members hire guys from Clearview, too."

When Mom doesn't change her position, Mark says, "I'm an adult."

Mom just snorts at that. "You think we should let him join," she asks Dad, "before checking it out more?"

"Steven is a good man," Dad says. "I trust his judgment. He has his son there."

Mom's not won over yet.

"Can I eat, please?" Dad asks, meaning he doesn't want to discuss this anymore in front of us.

No one asks if I want to join. No one even seems to acknowledge the possibility. And, unlike Mark, I could probably pay my way. Not that I would.

After dinner, I would normally be on cleanup, but Mom sends me off to do some "homework" so she and Dad can talk without me there. I get the workbook and go out to the side porch, just around the corner so they won't see me if they open the screen door.

"They seem genuine about building something good," Dad is saying. "They're all part of the organizational committee. I would be, too. They're still working out what this will be, and we could have a say in that."

"We?" Mom asks.

I can't hear Dad's answer, assuming he said anything at all.

"And what could this be?" Mom asks.

"Friends, work, maybe more. A fresh start. Can't hurt to be better prepared."

"Prepared for what?" Mom asks. When Dad doesn't answer, she asks, "Am I going to have to start sniffing *your* clothes for bomb residue, too?"

I let my head fall back against the house to keep from yelling. It was one time. One pipe bomb. For fun. And Mark was there, too. But every time Mom wants to make a point about how much she hates me training, she acts like I'm some kind of pyro, blowing stuff up every day.

"*If* I'm interested," Dad says, "I'm in it for the work. For the hope that it leads to more work."

"But?" she prompts.

"But . . . they make a lot of sense. Things *are* getting worse. Unemployment, tensions. More taxes, and no one looking out for us." I can't hear what Mom says, but Dad says, "Charlotte, I'm just suggesting, maybe it's time to be a little more serious. It couldn't hurt to be better prepared, just in case."

"In case what?" Mom asks.

"In case . . . whatever," Dad says.

Shivers crawls up my spine and down my arms. This is what I've been saying for a year.

It's quiet for several seconds, and then Mom says, "I don't want to see you get your hopes up and then find out it's a scam. Or not a scam, but not something we can afford. Not now, anyway." I can't hear anything, and then Mom says, "It just sounds too good to be true."

A bang, a cabinet slamming shut or something. "Why is it so damn hard for you to accept that maybe, just maybe, someone thinks I have value? That *we* have value?"

"How much value?" Mom asks eventually, and even I can hear the softening in her voice, maybe because it's clear Dad's already made up his mind. Or maybe because it's been a long time since Dad had any leads.

"I don't know yet," Dad says. "I need to see what all they have planned and put in a proposal, but Jim Riggs said they'd rather a member did the work. So I think it'll go hand in hand."

They must have moved, because I can't hear them. I inch around the porch, closer to the screen door.

"Then if it is a bust or too good to be true," Dad says, "we say no thank you and we've lost nothing. But if it means work and more—a support system—I don't think we can pass up the opportunity."

"Not a penny to them," Mom finally says.

"Fine," Dad says.

"If it gets weird, you're out."

"Of course."

Weird for Mom means anything beyond shooting and camping. For a while she was convinced I was going to run away and join some kind of radical survivalist cult or, like, fall in with white supremacists. If she knew anything about anything, she'd know that none of them would want *me*, and I sure as hell wouldn't want anything to do with *them*. I'm about the prep, not the politics or racist bullshit.

"And Bex?" Mom asks.

Crap. Maybe she's not done fighting.

"They've got girls, too," Dad says.

"Really?" Mom asks. "Girls?" she asks, meaning *girls who look like girls*.

"Some of them were there today," Dad says. "Seemed like a nice group of girls," he says, meaning *yes*, *girls who look like girls*.

"We agreed to start trying to redirect her interests back to normal things, things that will help her integrate back into a normal school," Mom says.

"Bex is fine," Dad says, but even I don't believe that he means it. "Maybe it would be good for her to be around other girls. To see that they shoot and camp, and still . . ."

Look like girls is what he wants to say. Act like girls. Want to do girl things, and date boys.

"I want her to come to the city with me," Mom says.

"There's a summer program. She'd be back in a classroom, around normal kids. And then if she wants to do this stuff on the weekends, at least she'll have both."

No way.

"Hannah is in a program at the same place. They can go together. It will be good for her."

No freaking way.

"What does it cost?" Dad asks. "It's a valid question," he adds, in response to whatever face or gesture Mom must have made.

"Don't worry about that. I've got it covered." Nice. Dad will love being reminded that Mom's making the money right now. "We will have to pick up a few things for her. She can't go looking like she's wearing her brother's hand-me-downs. Just a few things to start, until she can see what the other girls are wearing. I can take her to the outlets next weekend."

I can only imagine what Mom would make me wear. And I'd have to deal with Aunt Lorraine every day, and Hannah.

"What about the station?"

"Skip will have to find someone else for during the week."

Mom doesn't like me working there any more than she likes me training. I can't win. I let my hair grow out the way she likes. I pay for everything for myself. I give her money.

And still all that matters is that I'm not like Hannah, all girly and interested in "normal" things.

She'll never let me train for real.

She'll never let me really join Clearview.

She won't stop until I look like she wants me to look and act like she wants me to act.

CHAPTER 4

"Phone's already ringing," I say as Uncle Skip unlocks the door to the station. It's not even seven yet.

"Everyone with a weekend problem'll be champing at the bit."

He flicks on the lights in back and in the service area. I head straight to the front.

"Hey, Bex, what's shaking?" Mike asks, leaning over the counter reading the paper.

"Not much. Coffee?"

I start filling the pot. Uncle Skip hollers from the back, "Go ahead and open. Bud's coming by."

"Better be bringing doughnuts," I shout.

Bud does indeed bring doughnuts, and his own coffee because he says ours is weak as spit, but I'm busy taking the messages from the voice mail and just wave a thanks as he goes by.

"Mullin's Service Center," I answer the phone, shuffling the messages in order of emergency. "Depends what it is. . . . Yeah, we can handle that. Yeah, no problem."

"Whatta we got?" Mike asks, already three-quarters of the way through a doughnut, powdered sugar all in his beard.

"Two won't-starts, blown tire, a weird clunking noise, Sanford seeing if you have time for a quick oil change and once-over this morning, a guy named Ben who says he's calling about the camper?" I ask, and he takes that one. "And Mrs. Presley, twice. She says it's shimmying again." I waggle my eyebrows, and he laughs. Mrs. Presley has a thing for Uncle Skip.

"Call Sanford and tell him to come on over," he says. "I'll take the rest."

It's a steady stream of calls, cars and trucks at the pumps, lost tourists, regulars stopping in to see who's around or to get a pop or gas. A lot of equipment, lawn mowers, and ATVs to be gassed up. Deliveries. Parts, pop, the supplier servicing the kerosene pump. Monday.

Late morning I go out to help Mrs. Johnson at the pump so she doesn't have to get out of her car, and then do a once-around, checking the pumps and picking up trash.

Mr. Hirsch, Mr. Hoff, and Mr. Henderson (three of the Four Hs) play cards at the picnic table, drinking my coffee and talking, like they do most Mondays.

"How's tricks, Bex?" Mr. Hirsch asks.

"Fine. Where's Mr. Heinman?"

"Prostate," Mr. Hoff says, and the others grunt. "Gin!"

I don't ask for clarification on whether Mr. Heinman is dead, dying, or merely off getting probed. I hope it's the last one, but I don't want the details.

Uncle Skip calls around to track down a part, and then he hands the phone off to me, "his girl," to handle the order and shipping details. We have a deal: I don't give him shit about being "his girl," and I get to learn something new every time he says it. By then Mike has some things that need to be ordered, too, but those we get from a supplier. He and I work the computer for a while, reading part numbers and checking prices.

By noon things quiet down out front. Uncle Skip and Mike are both working on cars, but nothing I can help with. There are too many cars and trucks and customers waiting to hang back there and watch. I snag my lunch from the office and settle in to play around online for a while. I check for any good rebuild prospects. I need my own truck, especially now that we're all the way out here. Uncle Skip promised to help me fix one up. I have to find the truck, pay for it, and learn how to do all the work. He'll supervise. But so far I've found nothing remotely interesting in my price range.

Then I check into my usual sites and forums. The group in Washington has their new training schedule up and a recap of their latest event. If they were closer, we could join them. They already have their shit together. The Second Amendment newsgroup has a few new posts. I copy one and e-mail it to myself to read later. I check into my message boards, at least the few left that haven't gotten all riled up about gay marriage. They don't know about me, but I don't need to read their bullshit. I leave a reply to one of the guys looking for info on a site in Michigan and the new permitting requirements here. Yet another argument over prepper versus survivalist versus whatever. And it's the usual suspects, too. I sign in so I can quote the main arguments and respond, "Who cares what people call themselves? I'm not a prepper. I'm not a survivalist. I'm a realist who plans to survive." I post replies in a few other threads, and then I check the chat rooms, but no one is around. There's a new post up from the guy in Virginia recruiting for his Mutual Assistance Group. If I were closer, I'd be tempted to apply. Of course, I'd have to fudge the application, at least as to age. And getting from Michigan to Virginia, or the meet sites, would be near impossible in a grid-down situation. I've thought about suggesting a few northern sites as their backups, but it's not worth disclosing them to a MAG I'm unlikely to join.

I answer a few direct messages and e-mails. Delete a few

without answering, like Kelly back home, wondering what I've been up to. Last time we hung out, she played hot and cold all night, and then the next day tried to pretend the hot was all because of half a can of beer.

More calls. Then I ring up a few gas customers. By the time I check back on the forum, there are several responses to one of my posts. Some agreeing with me, but a few calling me a bitch or stupid, sometimes both.

Another customer comes in, and so does Uncle Skip, so I close the browser.

"Did you get ahold of Mrs. Presley?" Uncle Skip asks, flipping through the work orders. He runs his hand through his graying hair and then puts his cap back on. Salt-and-pepper stubble dusts his chin and upper lip, standing out on his red-tanned face.

"Yeah." I hand the customer his change. "She's going to bring it in Wednesday, when her daughter can follow her and take her home."

The alert dings, and I glance out the door to the pumps.

"Best thing I ever did was getting those new pumps," Uncle Skip says behind me.

We both watch a guy in expensive clothes and expensive glasses wash the windows of his expensive car. Guys like that don't bring their cars here for service unless they have no other choice. Especially now that the fancy dealerships and big places are expanding out this way. When I was little, I wanted to work here when I grew up. Now I just hope it's around long enough for Uncle Skip to follow through on teaching me how to do rebuilds and restores, and to keep me employed until I figure out something else to do. Long enough for Uncle Skip to work as long as he wants, then sell it and retire. Maybe someday I can still have my own place, even if cars are different in the future.

I watch the guy buff a spot on the side of his shiny car. Will you need a college degree to work on cars when they're all electric, or whatever else they think up? Assuming the world hasn't imploded before then.

Some of the guys on the forums think you should avoid newer cars — too many computer components in newer models make them hackable and susceptible to electromagnetic pulse. And soon there may even be non-nuke EMP weapons. Safer to stick with an older model.

"Where's your brother?" Uncle Skip asks. "He said he wanted to barter for some work on his truck today. I was going to have him run into town to pick up a few things."

"He went out to Clearview."

"Right." A lot of meaning in that one word. I don't comment.

It's not like I have anything to say. Dad and Mark have been out there a bunch of times since we visited, acting all father-son chummy, like they are so proud of themselves. For what, a club and some part-time work? Every time I ask when I get to go back, Dad makes excuses or says not today. I'm not going to stop asking, but I have to be careful about Mom. If I push the issue at the wrong time, Mom will dig in her heels on taking me to the city. I need to strike at the right time so that Dad is willing to back me up, or else I need to make Mom change her mind.

"How's he swinging that, without a truck or cash?"

"Daniel Trace, I guess."

I can feel him wanting to say something. I know how Uncle Skip feels about "the militia stuff." Even if this isn't anything close to militia, it's close enough for Uncle Skip.

He rubs his jaw, a scratchy sound of contemplation, and the look on his face gets the better of me.

"What?"

"Seems like a bad time to be spending money," he says.

We're staying in his house, mostly for free, so I guess he gets to have a say, but it doesn't mean I have to like the criticism.

The alert dings again. Customer. I move over to the intercom so I can turn on the pump if it's a regular who wants to pay cash.

The oldest piece-of-shit station wagon I've ever seen actually running is parked at pump two. Old wood panels and so much rust and primer and splotchy paint, I have no idea what color it's supposed to be. But next to it is a girl. Dark hair, dark sunglasses, red T. She pushes her sunglasses into her hair and leans over to pop the hood. Perfect-fitting jeans. Denim faded in all the best ways. Even better from the front. I watch her walk across the lot.

"Bex." Uncle Skip waits for me to look at him. "I didn't mean it like that."

Whatever.

"Just forget I said anything, okay?"

"Sure."

She blocks the sun through the door for a moment, and then she's inside, blinking in the dimness, looking around. "Oil?" she asks.

"Shelf," Uncle Skip and I say in unison, both pointing.

"Well, I'm going to run into town and get the parts, then," Uncle Skip says.

"Yeah."

The girl ducks down to look at containers of oil. Uncle Skip's keys jangle. I look at him.

"Mike's in back if you need him," he says.

"Sure."

She's got some oil and is moving toward the drink case.

Maybe she'll need help. I stand up a little taller.

She has the oil in the crook of her arm, a bottle of something in one hand, and a bag of sunflower seeds in her other hand.

She looks up. Dark eyes. A birthmark near her jaw. One corner of her mouth turns up, and I slouch against the counter, playing it cool, waiting to see if I get a smile.

She puts the oil on the counter and digs her hand into her jeans pocket, looking for cash, smiling up at me while she does.

I'm free to look, and she takes her time.

She can dig all day as far as I'm concerned. Her breasts push in, her T caught between them, lifting her shirt. Her waistband's fraying above the button, soft threads begging to be touched against soft belly.

"Anything else?" I try to sound cool.

"Yeah," she says. She counts her money. "Twelve, no, thirteen, on pump two." Her voice is like honey.

She can have twenty dollars on the house. She looks older than me but not by much. She has to be at least sixteen to drive alone, but I doubt she's much more than eighteen. Straight girls sometimes think I'm younger than I am. Queer girls usually get me on sight. Not that I see a lot of queer girls out this way. Or any, really.

She sorts through the lollipops in the bin on the counter.

I would sell her anything. Even some of the local booze Uncle Skip doesn't know I know he has in back. But I stop myself from telling her that.

"Um." She doesn't laugh, but it's close. She's staring at me, at my face. She has a great smile. Her lollipop's already on the counter next to the rest.

"Sorry." But I'm not. Is she actually flirting with me, or just being friendly? Or does she think I'm acting weird? I ring up the oil. "And . . . thirteen dollars in gas?"

"Yup," she says, playing with the pens in the cup on the counter, trying to look so cool.

I take her money. Count out her change. Hope I got it right.

When I hand it to her, my fingers touch her skin and I drop the coins.

She laughs and covers her mouth with her balled-up hand.

"Sorry," I mumble. I can't get the dime off the counter. It slides. My nails are too short to get under it. "Sorry."

She laughs harder and leans over, pushing my hand in an exaggerated way.

"Ha! I've got it," she says, jumping back with the dime pinched between her fingers.

She smells good, like oranges and something spicy. Her lips look soft, not bare but none of that thick, sticky gloss.

"You need any help with that?"

Her eyes crinkle, confused, and I point at the oil. "Ah, no," she says. "*This* I can handle all on my own. But thanks." She gathers up her stuff and swings toward the door. One more look over her shoulder. I want to freeze that look for later.

Outside she gasses up and then uncaps the bottle of oil and pours it in, bending over, her shirt pulling tight across her back.

She tosses the empty bottle into the trash, replaces the cap where she poured in the oil, turns it tight, then a little more for sure, and then closes the hood. She wipes her hands down her thighs. I watch her get into the wagon and then pull away.

One taillight blinks into the turn.

The afternoon is so slow, I have plenty of time to think about her—if she was just passing through, and where she might be staying, since she didn't sound local. And if she was actually, seriously flirting with me.

"Hiya, Bex," Mr. Henderson says, coming in carrying his wife's old vacuum cleaner. "Mary says it's got that smell again, the burnt-rubber smell, and is hardly sucking up anything. Can you take a look at it?"

"Sure. I'll take a look now. Want me to call when I'm done?"

"Nah, I'll be here Wednesday, and she can live two days without vacuuming."

I check with Mike, and then pull the folding table out from the back so I have room to work. As soon as I've got it pulled apart, I can see the issue. I call Mr. Henderson, and then get Mike's okay to order the new belt and another part that is looking ready to go. Then I put it mostly back together and store it in back until the parts arrive. Mr. Henderson will reimburse us for the parts, and then we'll go through our usual dance of him offering me money in addition to the brownies from Mrs. Henderson, and I'll decline, and he'll eventually shove it into my hand. Much less than a pro would charge, but fun money for me. I always use the repair money for a splurge.

At five thirty, Uncle Skip turns off the pumps and locks the door. But he has a few things to do, so I snag some more computer time.

I run another search on Clearview. Not much online, not even a website yet. Just a few hits on land auction and public notices. I watch a few videos of tactical courses and competitions, thinking about what Dad might build for them. He should make sure they can reconfigure regularly or the course will lose effectiveness. And if he does an indoor course, he should do more than the boxy rooms most of these courses use. He should make one at least that looks like what we would see. Farmhouses and trailers and schools and warehouses. Stores, with glass and shelves and crazy sight lines. Factories. How much land do they have?

Not that he's asked what I think.

I check out the dykes who hike site. I like to read their trail reports, but I don't post there. Too crunchy and liberal. And the queer sites are even worse. A lot of the teens are obsessed with proms and GSAs, school stuff. And they're going out, to clubs and on dates. I don't get that stuff, and they'd never get me. But I can't stop myself from reading, even if I don't post. I feel like I know some of them. I like the pictures. One girl in particular is always posting pics of her and her friends. I like to look at those. I *really* like the one she posted today. But every time there's a shooting in the news—so, like, every week—doesn't matter the circumstances, every thread on every site becomes about how guns are bad and people who disagree with them are bad or crazy, too.

I clear the browser history, and then sign in to YouTube and check my videos. There are some more comments. Most of them junk and assholes, guys who only want to see a girl shoot if she's Militia Babe Barbie in Daisy Dukes and a threadbare tank, showing off her boobs. A few of the regulars left encouraging comments. BigBob critiques my grip, like always, but he does it with love. The video of the pipe bomb is up to two thousand likes. The girl in the Philippines has a new video up. She's getting good. The sidebar shows a new video labeled "Urban Bugout Simulation." I click on it, but before the intro ad even finishes, my phone buzzes with a text.

You around? Boyd. Haven't heard from him in a while.

I text back, *Yes but leaving soon.*

ETA 3.

In back.

I pick up the trash that was waiting to go out with us and head for the door.

"Where you going?" Uncle Skip asks from his office.

"Taking the trash out. There's two trips' worth."

"I'll be ready in about ten minutes."

"Okay."

I close the door behind me and take the trash over to the Dumpster, pulling open the gate to heave it in just as Boyd's car pulls up.

"Hey," he says, not even bothering to shut it off.

"What's up?" I ask, because this doesn't feel like he's just dropping by to chat.

"Not much," he says, but he's looking around, squinting.

Boyd, his brother Willie, and his dad used to be part of the deep-camping crew. But then his parents got divorced and his dad moved away. Boyd came with us on his own once, but then he stopped.

He's still looking around, like he's watching for an attack. More paranoid than usual.

"I heard about Willie," I say. "Sorry." I knew Willie was messed up, but I didn't think he was stupid enough to start cooking meth.

Boyd shrugs. "Bound to happen. Listen." He clears his throat. "I'm thinking of taking off for a while. Going out to Montana to see my dad, maybe see if he can get me a job." He looks away from me. "I need to get out of here for a while." I can imagine things are shitty at home without Willie around to run interference with his mom's boyfriend. "But I need cash."

I like Boyd. And he's always been good about helping me out and not charging a crazy markup when I need ammo on the sly. But I'm not just giving him money. I'm starting to shake my head when he says, "You still interested in a Bobcat?"

"You serious?" I ask, already picturing how the subcompact pistol fits in my hand.

"Willie's not going to be using his, and I can't leave it behind." Not with his younger brothers still at home and his mom a mess. "You always loved to shoot mine, so I thought maybe you'd want it."

Dad would kill me, but . . . "How much?"

We haggle for a while and then arrange a time for him to come by. He'll get his quick cash, less than he'd get from a proper dealer, but he knows me and can trust me and I won't be recording the sale anywhere. I'll get the Bobcat, holster, and whatever he's not taking of his ammo, mostly .22s, the ones the Bobcat likes best, but some .44 VOR-TX as a bonus, because he's not going to find many buyers for those. All in all, I got the better deal.

He's barely out of the lot, and I'm already nervous, thinking about where I'll hide the Bobcat and extra ammo, especially the .44s—Dad will know he didn't buy those. Dad would kill me for real. I almost call Boyd to tell him I've changed my mind. But I don't. I want that Bobcat.

I go back to the office, but Uncle Skip is shutting down his computer and packing up. He's already turned off the lights and computer out front. "You ready?" Uncle Skip asks, but he seems weird.

It's normal for him to be quiet. Sometime we don't talk at all in the truck. But today it's like I can hear him trying not to talk.

"You know," he finally says, trying to be all casual, "those guys who are always obsessing over the doomsday scenarios, you know most of them aren't playing with a full deck, right? It's fear talking. Paranoia." He glances at me before turning. "It's not real."

Crap. I must have left the video up.

"No wonder you're freaked out all the time," he says, sighing like I'm not even here.

"I'm *not* freaked out." He looks at me. "I'm focused."

"Those videos, those men—"

"Not just men."

"People," he corrects. "All those people, posting those videos . . ." He seems to try to figure out what to say and then gives up. "Nothing is going to happen, Bex."

I wonder how many times in history people have said that, right before the shit hit the fan.

"Something always happens." I look at him, wanting him to understand. "You can choose to be ready or not."

CHAPTER 5

There are a million things I could be doing right now that would be more useful—or more entertaining—than sitting at the table, eating some cereal, with a stupid book open randomly next to me. Every other bite, I turn the page. In between, I survey Mom and Dad when they're not looking. They're very lovey this morning. I wish they'd stop. And leave. Mark will probably sleep half the day. Uncle Skip went to the station. Just Mom and Dad to go. Then I can get down to business.

Mom taps the open book. I guess I haven't turned a page in a while. "I expect you to be further along by the time we get home. Your aunt Lorraine is going to send me the links for the quizzes that go along with the summer reading list."

"Can't wait," I say. Like I'm taking any quizzes or working my way through the eleventh-grade summer reading list for a school I have no intention of going to.

"I'm sure Hannah would be happy to talk about the books if you have any questions. Or she might have some ideas about which books were most helpful in her classes."

Mom's smile is so hopeful. She thinks she has me snowed, that I don't know she's been plotting to dump me with Aunt Lorraine and Uncle Nathan. Within weeks, if I'm not careful.

Aunt Lorraine always looks at me like I'm defective or will get dirt on her furniture. Mom used to defend me. Now she just wants me to be like Hannah.

Perfect Hannah can keep her perfect ideas inside her perfect drone head. All her books and grades and perfect clothes aren't going to help her when the world goes to hell. These books can't save us.

I will never live with Aunt Lorraine.

"Charlotte," Dad says from the door. He's been ready to leave for fifteen minutes.

Mom drops a kiss on the top of my head, stroking my hair down to my shoulders. "We'll be back in a few hours."

She's so happy my hair is "growing out." It's like she thinks since I gave in on my hair, she can dress me in some new clothes, park me at summer school, and I'll stop being me.

I eat another bowl of cereal and scroll around on my phone to kill time until I'm sure they're really gone.

Maybe I'll go ahead and build another pipe bomb, this

time with a timer. I swiped a cell phone from the station's "lost" box months ago. Then Mom got all freaked out about the first pipe bomb, so I just packed it away in my trunk in the barn. But maybe I don't care anymore.

Building it wouldn't be the hard part. The hard part would be making sure it didn't blow up accidentally in transport to one of the abandoned subdivision lots or somewhere else I can set it off. I can't set it off here, and not just because of Mom. Mrs. Hoepkin said she'd call the sheriff if I set off another one anywhere near the property line. Which is ridiculous, because we shoot on the land out here all the time, and people set off fireworks. A little pipe bomb's no different. And it's not like her yappy dog was even hurt. She got it out from under the house.

Mark almost screwed up the video of the one we set off by the pond. If I hadn't made him show me the test video, all he would have recorded would have been me setting it up and then a frozen, squiggly image of me walking back. But with a timer, I'd be able to build a pyramid with junk lying around the lot—like maybe an old TV or minifridge or something—and take the video myself. I wouldn't even need Mark. I'd need a truck or car or something, though.

"Mom and Dad leave already?" Mark asks, stumbling into the kitchen, scratching his stomach like a monkey.

"Yeah."

"I wanted to borrow her car."

"Then you should have gotten up earlier."

Mark opens the screen door and leans in the doorway, lighting a cigarette. He takes a long drag and blows the smoke outside.

Mom will kick his butt if she catches him smoking. And Dad's, too, if he's providing the cash for Mark's cigarettes.

He offers me the cigarette, but I wave him off. I like my lungs. If he's serious about training, he better cut those out, too.

He leans back against the frame, exhaling smoke through the door.

He smokes and I scroll through the search results on my phone. Then he stubs it out and flicks it into the yard. Because of course he can't see that anyone will know it's his.

He grabs the phone off the wall, stretching the curly cord to the fridge and then to the cabinet. "Hey. Can you guys pick me up?" He pours some milk into a glass and drinks a gulp before saying, "They're waiting on a part. Should be done next week, they said." Who is he kidding? He hasn't even worked off the cost of the parts yet. "Yeah. Yeah, I think we have some. Sure." He hangs up with a flourish, like he's slam-dunking the phone back onto the receiver, except he misses and it hits the floor.

He makes himself some toast and eats most of it but leaves the crusts on the plate.

"Who do you think will clean that up?" I ask when he moves the plate to the counter and leaves it there, crusts and all. He flips me off on his way upstairs.

Boyd texts and we go back and forth, scheduling a time to meet. He's in a rush, but not so much of a rush that he'll meet today. It'll have to be before work some day this week.

Half an hour later, Mark's back down the stairs. I can hear him at the gun locker. He's getting more than just his gun. He comes back into the kitchen with his range bag and several boxes of ammo.

"Did Dad say you could take that?"

He ignores me and pulls out his wallet, checking his cash. He shouldn't have any cash, which means Mom or Dad gave him some. Figures.

"Once I'm working, I'll restock this," he says. "But I can't look like a jerk in front of the guys. They don't need to know just how broke we are." He's serious. "I've been downplaying how bad it is."

"Mark." He looks at me. "Are they for real?"

"Yeah," he says. "They're for real. The club's just the first step, to make it private. Down the road they'll have barracks, everything we'd need in a crisis."

Plans for a compound. "We don't need a compound," I say. "We need to be mobile." If not one big MAG, maybe an array of smaller ones, which could network in a crisis. Not a bunch of sitting ducks hiding behind a fence.

"Yeah, but if it's on private land, then the government can't regulate the guns kept there," Mark says. "So it has to have some shelters, a community. That's why members have to have a share, like a cooperative."

If they're focused on a compound, they won't be mobile. They'll hesitate to move when the first crisis wave hits. They'll ignore key training.

"Did you know," Mark says, "that during the Revolution only three percent of the able-bodied men actually fought to free us from tyrannical rule?" He pauses for effect. He holds up three fingers. "Three."

I've read this stuff online, usually from scammers who want you to give them money, or guys who are half off the grid.

"We'll need other patriots to support those who can fight," Mark says. He's parroting someone. This isn't how Mark talks. "We need to be organizing that support now, and talking with the other groups around the country, so we have a network of support and refuge. We're one spark away from all the dry tinder going up."

"Sure, but we should be focused on mobility, not this stuff."

"Clearview is just getting started," Mark says. "They're looking at what others are doing and taking the best bits. But they're not scared of ruffling feathers or thinking there's a fed behind every bush. They're *really* preparing—legal protections against disarmament and tactical training. We'll be getting in on the ground floor, before it will take money to join. I thought you'd be all in."

I should be. But Mom's right that getting all this for free does seem too good to be true.

"All that and they'll give us work, too." He nods, enthusiastic puppy again. "So why invite us? Why immediately, after what, ten minutes, start involving Dad in their plans and offering him work?"

"They're looking to add members. The right kind of members."

"And we're the right kind of members? We're broke, and who knows how long we'll be living out this way." I can always tell when Mark's lying. I wait for him to give it up.

He blows out a breath. "Daniel's dad is on the committee. And he's close to Riggs," Mark says, dipping his head. "I told him Dad hadn't been able to find work." Dad would be mortified if he knew. "They need someone like Dad. Dad needs work. We need to get in now, as part of the organizational group, before there will be buy-in costs."

"That doesn't mean Dad would want you telling people his business."

We can both hear a truck on the drive, and then a honk.

"You'll see," Mark says, picking up his bag.

Maybe. I'm never going to be a full member if I can only go on weekends.

I put my bowl in the sink and take Mark's crusts outside and toss them into the yard for the birds. This is starting to feel like home, with the quiet, the trees and land. Working at the station with Uncle Skip. Learning how to fix things. And now Clearview, maybe.

Maybe Mom and Dad can move to the city and I can just stay here.

But they'd have to want to let me stay here. *Mom* would have to want to, starting with this summer. Shipping me off to Aunt Lorraine's has to be eliminated as a viable option.

I assemble my tools in the bathroom and take a few deep breaths to calm my pounding pulse. If I do this, there's no going back. Mom and Dad will know I'm never going to change, never going to become the good girly-girl they want.

I dampen my hair, part it off-center, and comb it until it hangs straight down, barely resting on my shoulders. Then I pick up the hair bands to section it like in the YouTube video I found. But before I can do that, I stop, because with my hair like this, I really do look like Hannah. I can see exactly why Mom thought she could pull it off if she dressed me in Hannah's castoffs and sent me to Hannah's school. Growing out my hair was just the first step. Aunt Lorraine is ten times as stubborn as Mom. Maybe Mom thought that with them working together they could make me into a real girl who giggles and goes to dances and isn't fighting like hell to save all of our lives. One who will grow up and marry a guy who will take care of her and go shooting with Dad. One who will have babies, and gossip and laugh with Mom. Someone I will never be.

But pretending doesn't work. People stare. Even with my hair this long. They look at my face, and then my chest, and they wonder. A kid in a bathroom asks if I'm a boy or a girl, or some asshole grunts "dyke" when I pass. My hair's never going to be long enough to stop that. I'm still going to look like I look. Be how I am. And I like how I look, except for the hair. So why am I letting them force me to be uncomfortable, when it's not working anyway?

Maybe *they're* the ones who need to be made uncomfortable.

They don't see *me*.

I bundle my hair into four sections: a ponytail on each side and one in the back, and a messy bun on top. Then I take a deep breath, position the scissors on the left side of the band holding the right ponytail, and cut it off. What's left of my hair springs back free. I drop the ponytail in the sink. I do the same with the one in back and the one on the left. Then I go to work cutting what's left of my hair as short as I can with the scissors, trying not to cut my scalp where I can barely see it in back despite using the mirror over the sink, the mirror on the door, and my phone's camera to try to see. When I'm done with the back and sides, I pause to rub my fingers over the soft, bristly hair, loving how it feels on my fingers. And how my fingers feel on my sensitive scalp.

I undo the top section and comb it again, figure out where I want the sharp line between crew cut and long hair to be, and cut off everything to the right of it. I comb the long layer several different ways before I figure out how it will hang. Then I cut it on a diagonal so that the hair makes a point near my chin and then angles up toward the back of my head, revealing the crew cut underneath. I wet the long layer, comb it again, and then trim it in sections to get as straight a line as possible.

When I'm done, I turn from side to side, admiring my

work. It's patchy in places, and clippers would have probably been better, but it still looks cool. Not at all like Hannah now. It's amazing what you can learn to do on YouTube.

The one long layer is somehow more daring than just cutting it all off. It makes a statement. It demands attention. It can't be ignored. And Mom always says she likes a little hair around my face.

If people are going to stare, I'll give them something worth staring at.

If Mom and Dad want to pretend they can't see me — see who I really am — then they can look at the side with hair.

I clean up the hair and take a long cool shower. After, I use some of Mom's gel to get the long layer to hang straight and sleek. It takes forever to get it completely dry and like I want it.

I find the box of random earrings in my drawer and dig through them until I find the small hoops. I use one of the posts to reopen the piercings in my right ear and force the hoops through both holes. Then put the post in my left ear. I shake my head. The hoops swing free, with no hair to get in the way. Maybe I should add a few more holes up that ear.

In the full-length mirror, it's even better. From one side, my hair is sleek near my cheek, with just the small stud earring, but on the other, the hoops in my ears swing free with no hair to get in the way. Maybe I'll pierce my eyebrow on the right, too.

I'm contemplating how to add a third hole in my right ear when I hear a truck on the drive. Dad's truck.

They're back.

The screen door squeaks open and slaps shut. Their voices in the kitchen. Mom's laughing. A twisted tangle of anxiety knots in my stomach. Best to face it now, head-on, without delay.

I step into the kitchen. Dad inhales loudly, and then seems to forget how to exhale. His mouth flaps open and closed like a fish just pulled from the water.

"We found some great watermelon at—What did you do?" Mom screeches, dropping the ears of corn she was holding on the floor. Coming at me fast.

I hold my ground. "Cut my hair."

"What did you *do*?" she screeches again, turning me, grabbing my head, tugging at my hair.

"Ow." Her hand crushes my right ear, which still hurts like hell from forcing the earrings through.

"Why?" She examines my arms, turns me like she's looking for wounds or missing parts. "Why? Why would you do this?" She's hysterical. "What happened to you to make you—?"

"Charlotte!" Dad shouts.

She doesn't stop, her nails digging into my head and cheek, examining my hair from too-close range, making noises, garbled and distant, through her hands over my ears.

Dad gets a hand between us and she backs off, across the room, shaking. I knew she'd be angry, but this is something else. Her whole body is vibrating. Dad stays between us, watching her. I'm afraid to move, like if I turn my back, she'll attack.

She rests her hands on the counter, taking deep breaths. Then she sort of laughs, but not really.

"What am I going to do with this?" Mom turns her head to look at Dad. "Are you going to say anything?"

"What do you want me to say?" he asks. "It's not like I can glue it all back on."

"You let her get away with whatever she—"

"Enough," Dad says. "Just . . . enough." But he's not on my side. "Go to your room."

I walk through the living room, but I don't go upstairs. I'm out the front door and halfway to the tree line before I hear him yelling my name.

I stay away for hours, until I'm hungry and thirsty. I don't have anything to purify the water from the pond, and chewing on foraged greens isn't cutting it.

When I get back, they're all sitting at the table. They don't say anything when I sit down and join them. Uncle Skip stares, wide-eyed, at my head, but once the initial shock wears off, he sort of smiles. He quickly wipes the smile away before Dad can notice, but it's enough.

I fill my plate in silence.

"You look like a freak," Mark finally says. No one acknowledges that he's even spoken. "Can't you see how stupid she looks?" he asks Mom and Dad, looking from one to the other. Uncle Skip just eats. I wait, surprisingly curious about their response. "You're not going to let her go to Clearview like this, right?" Mark asks. When Dad doesn't answer, Mark starts to sputter. "Da-ad, everyone's going to—"

"We can see how she looks, thank you," Mom says, a little too calmly. Her being calm is not a good sign.

Mark retreats to his room as soon as he's done chewing.

Uncle Skip excuses himself with "Delicious, Charlotte," and goes out to his workshop.

I'm on cleanup duty. I'd have had to clean up even without the haircut, but now it's got the added weight of punishment.

Mom is on the phone with Aunt Lorraine. I can't hear what she's saying, but the murmur of her voice bleeds through the ceiling from upstairs. Anger. Anguish. Something else that makes dinner churn in my stomach.

I take my time wiping down the counters, drying the dishes and putting them away, feeling the tension build. Mom and Dad are sitting in the living room, talking too quietly for me to hear. I catch my reflection in the window over the sink. I like how I look. Enough to smile.

It's time to get whatever is going to happen over with. Anticipating the worst is making my stomach hurt.

When I walk into the living room, Mom stops talking midsentence and leans back. Dad turns to face me.

"Why?" Mom asks.

I shrug.

"That's all? That's all you think we deserve, when you . . . I don't even know what to make of this. Because we want you to look nice? To fit in, and . . ."

I step closer but don't sit down. I'm not sure I'm supposed to sit down. "I'm not like Hannah or—"

"You don't have to be like Hannah! There's a world of difference between her and *this*."

She doesn't understand. Or maybe she does.

"Well," Mom says, "you can shave your whole damn head. Dye it blue while you're at it. I don't give a fig anymore. But this was selfish, and it was childish, and it was disrespectful."

"It's my hair!"

"You don't think how you look reflects on this family?

That people won't judge us based on this?" She gets up from the sofa and walks toward me, turning me toward the mirror on the wall. "Look at yourself. Is this who you want to be? Someone who people stare at? Who people think is, is—?"

"What?" She doesn't respond. "What, Mom?"

Just when I think she's not going to answer me, she whispers, "Damaged. People will think you're damaged."

"I'm not damaged. Or confused. You don't have to fix me." I don't look at her, or at Dad. "You can't change me," I say, looking at her in the mirror.

We stare at each other.

"Well?" Mom finally says, but it's not directed at me.

Dad clears his throat, looks at me until he can't anymore, and then says, "What do you want me to say?"

Mom looks like she wants to hit him. "Nothing, David, as usual." Then she turns to me. "I can't bring you to Lorraine's like this. Can't fix it," she says.

Nope. I bite my cheek to not smile.

"I can't even send you to Arizona looking like this."

Gran would have another heart attack.

"Go," Mom says. "I can't look at you anymore."

Mission accomplished. So why do I feel like crap?

CHAPTER 6

I changed my mind about the Bobcat every five minutes, and I had more than a week to debate it. But when Boyd finally called to set up a time to meet for the exchange, he caught me in a *yes* frame of mind. Which is how the Bobcat and ammo come to be in my backpack by my feet, within reach of Uncle Skip, who would seriously wig out right now if he knew.

When Uncle Skip and I pull down the drive, Dad and Mark are over by the grill. Talking, sipping beer. They've been a little boys' club lately. For the past few weeks, Mark's been out to Clearview nearly every day, and Dad's been out there or at meetings about Clearview almost as much. Mom hasn't totally warmed to the idea of their joining. I get the sense it's her pressure on Dad keeping me out. She gave up on me going to the city, but she's pissed and so won't give in on me going to

Clearview. I should have acted like I didn't want to go; then she'd probably make me.

Dad and I used to talk all the time, on the porch, in the truck when we went to the range or when he picked me up from work. I'd even sit through baseball with him sometimes, for the talking in between any action. I wonder if he even realizes he's swapped one kid for the other.

Uncle Skip is ahead of me when we go in, but I can hear the radio on, Mom singing along. Inside, the table is already set.

"Oh, good," Mom says to Uncle Skip, wiping her hands on her apron. "You're just in time. Wash up." She did her hair and put on lipstick. This is an event. "You, too, Bex. Dinner's almost ready."

Ribs outside. Potato salad. Biscuits. Pie on the counter. My mouth is watering, but this much effort has me on edge.

"I'm going to go change," I say, keeping my backpack slung over one shoulder.

Mom turns and looks at me. "You're fine," she says. "Just wash up."

"The ribs have arrived," Dad says, coming in the door carrying the platter.

I put my backpack in the laundry room, behind the hamper, where no one's likely to mess with it, and then scrub my hands and arms in the laundry-room sink, using the brush to get the oil out from under my nails and the wrinkles at my knuckles and wrists.

Leaving my backpack there, with the bundle of stuff from Boyd inside, makes me crazy nervous, but I have to play it cool. The last thing I need is for Mom or Dad to try to take it from me or to move it and feel the weight.

Mark puts two more cans of beer on the table, and Dad just smiles. A few weeks of Clearview bonding, and it's totally cool for Mark to drink out in the open now.

"Looks wonderful, Charlotte," Uncle Skip says, pouring himself some tea from the pitcher and then reaching for my glass without asking.

"Thank you, Skip." Mom is beaming.

Dad's grace is shorter than usual, maybe because he's as hungry as the rest of us.

Dad and Mark pretend to fight over the ribs.

Plates and platters are passed. Uncle Skip, who doesn't usually say much at dinner, is telling them about the guy who thought he could haggle the price of his repairs down today.

I open two warm biscuits and slather them with butter, then look for the honey. I always put honey on my biscuits. But it's not on the table. I have to get up and get it from the shelf. Before my hair, Mom would have put it next to my plate.

"In the morning we did some painting—I worked on the porch—and then he bought the whole crew lunch," Mark says. "Then this afternoon we finished marking the section of trail we started the other day." Smiles all around—like I haven't been working for almost a year.

"Make sure you're done on time tomorrow," Dad says. "We need to leave early. I told Jim that I would go with him to check out some equipment."

"Sh'okay," Mark says with a last mouthful of potato salad. He swallows it down before saying, "Darnell says he can use us all weekend helping him turn around a rental that needs to be ready by Monday. I'm going to crash at Daniel's tomorrow night, and maybe Saturday if the job goes to Sunday."

"Which one's Darnell?" Mom asks.

"The black guy," Mark says. Dad gives him a look. "What? He is!"

"And he's a member of the club?" Mom asks, skeptical.

"Yes," Dad says, as if it was a stupid question. "Darnell and Frank served in Iraq together. Darnell's the one who went with me to look at the prefab structures."

I bet Darnell is Delia's father. Most of the younger members have parents who are involved in the organization. Delia probably gets to go to Clearview all the time. "When do I get to go out to Clearview again?" I ask.

Conversation stops.

Dad looks at Mom and then at me, and then says, "Soon." From Mom's look, that wasn't the right answer. "They're coming up with a schedule for training sessions now. We'll get you back out there before they have the schedule set so you're ready to go."

"Everyone ready for pie?" Mom asks, getting up and clearing dishes, obviously changing the subject.

"Dinner was wonderful, Charlotte," Uncle Skip says, taking some of the plates to the counter.

With Mom away from the table, Dad gives me a small smile and a wink. Then shakes his head at my smile, nodding toward Mom. I swallow it back but still look at Dad. He's already decided to let me go back. And soon.

Once everyone has pie, Dad says, "Okay, Charlotte, out with it. Is this a celebration?"

"It's nothing big," Mom says. "At least not yet. But the new placement feels like a good fit. The office manager said I've caught on real quick, and he heard I was taking those online Excel classes and said they might be able to use me full-time when the lady I'm covering for comes back from maternity leave."

"Well, that's great," Uncle Skip says when the rest of us don't immediately respond.

"Yeah, great," Mark adds.

"Real proud of you, honey," Dad says.

Everyone looks at me. I try to make my mouth work, but my brain is running in another direction. "Full-time? So you'd stay with Aunt Lorraine, like, permanently?"

"Well, no," Mom says. "If it works out, we'll find someplace of our own, soon, somewhere closer to the city."

None of us wants to move down by Aunt Lorraine and Uncle Nathan. Well, none of us but Mom. The silence drags on.

"Well, that's great," Uncle Skip finally says again. "Sounds like a great opportunity." He takes a sip of his iced tea. "But you know, you're all welcome here as long as you like," he says, looking around the table. "There's no rush."

That's my plan. Just have to convince him to let me stay even if they go.

"We know, Skip. And you've been so generous, but if we could get settled before the fall, Bex could start at the high school in September," Mom says, like that's a selling point.

"I'm all caught up," I lie. "You said if I stayed caught up, I could keep doing the distance-learning program."

"I said we'd discuss it if we were still out here," Mom says.

"And there's no need to make any decisions now," Dad says. "Let's just wait and see. Might be getting worked up for nothing."

Mom's face falls.

"I mean about the school," Dad adds. "The job sounds great. Here's to being a dual-income family again"—he lifts his glass—"soon."

"Really?" Mom asks.

Uncle Skip stares at Dad. "When did that happen?"

"The meetings have been going well," Dad says, looking at Mom more than the rest of us. "Frank, Norman, Jim, and I met this afternoon. We're hoping to present the plans to the organizational committee at the end of the month for preliminary approval. If all goes well, we'll start building the first tactical course later this summer."

"Well, great," Mom says, but she has the same forced excitement we did about possibly moving to the city.

Mark asks Uncle Skip about fixing his truck, and Dad chimes in about the insurance, and Mom adds her two cents, and I just pulverize my piece of pie. No way I'm going to the city. Maybe it's time to be less picky about finding a truck. If I'm going to stay out here on my own, I'll need a vehicle.

Uncle Skip excuses himself as soon as he's done and heads out to the workshop to sand wood and listen to the baseball game in peace.

Mom gets up and starts to clear the table.

"Let the kids do that," Dad says, waving us to take over

and then shoving Mark when he doesn't immediately jump up to help.

"Come on," Dad says to Mom. "Let's take our iced tea outside and sit on the porch swing. They can handle this mess." He waggles his eyebrows at her. "Maybe I'll try and get fresh with you."

"Gross," Mark says.

Mom shakes her head like she's exasperated, but she touches Dad's cheek, and he takes her hand, leading her toward the porch.

"Oh, Bex," she says at the door to the porch, "Lorraine sent more books. Some of the ones Hannah read in her ninth- and tenth-grade classes, so you won't be lost if they come up next year. I put the bag near the stairs."

"Why do I have to read all these books if we're waiting and seeing?"

"Reading a few books won't hurt you," Mom says.

"Far from it," Dad adds.

"And then if you do enroll in September, you won't start off any more behind than you already are."

"But . . ." I scramble for a viable reason to wait.

"Hey," Dad says. It's an all-encompassing *Stop, do as your mother says, and I'm tired of the chatter.*

As soon as Mom and Dad leave the kitchen, Mark backs through the doorway and into the living room. "Have fun," he says, turning and heading upstairs.

"Mark!" I yell after him, but it's no use.

I put away the leftovers and wash the dishes, piling them high on the drain board to dry. Sometimes slamming a cabinet or drawer just to feel better.

I can hear Uncle Skip join Mom and Dad on the porch, and smell his pipe after a while.

When Uncle Skip comes inside, he gets a glass out of the cabinet and some ice out of the freezer.

"You're going to join this Clearview, too?" he asks.

"Maybe."

He hands me the glass to fill from the tap. "I know that you're worried about the future. That you think there's going to be some big war or plague or something. I know the training is important to you. Just don't be so ready to throw your lot in with strangers, okay? At least until you get a better idea who they are."

"Okay." I smile at his grumbly face.

"I don't like it. Not one bit."

"I know," I say.

"You be careful."

I just nod.

When I'm about done, Mom comes back inside. I know I'm sulking, but I can't make my face stop.

"Look," Mom says, grabbing my arm before I can leave the kitchen. "When training was you and your father and Mark camping out and shooting some, well . . ." She thought it was like Girl Scouts. "But the sneaking around, the packs, the . . . blowing stuff up. It's scaring me. *You're* scaring me. But I'm trying to understand. I'm trying to see what about this, the training, makes you happy. Your father says there are nice girls in this club. That would be nice, right? Having girls who like what you like?" She rubs my arm. "You've been isolated out here, no friends, not even school with the distance learning—maybe this will be good."

I want to rant at her about how this isn't for fun, it's not what I "like"—that this is serious and that maybe, hopefully, those girls are more like me than Hannah. That I'd take strong over nice.

"So, we'll give this a try," she continues. "And I'll try to keep more of an open mind." I stare at her face, waiting for the *but*. "And since I'm meeting you partway, I want *you* to keep an open mind about school. And read the books. Deal?"

"Deal," I say, and she pulls me into a loose hug.

Upstairs, I unpack my backpack, carefully unrolling the shirt I used to wrap up the bundle from Boyd.

A lot of people probably think Boyd's a loser. But he's never treated me like a kid, or a girl. He talks to me about stuff and listens when I talk. He has skills. I had him on my unofficial MAG list, if the shit hit the fan and I had to assemble one on the fly.

Now he's headed to Montana. That's one less person who might have my back. One less person who might help me get my family to safety.

Maybe my last friend.

I take a few minutes to look at the Bobcat properly. To hold it in my hand. I wish I could carry it all the time, the weight of it just enough to be a comfort at my hip or ankle. Not yet.

I double-check to make sure it's unloaded and then wedge myself between the wall and the dresser so that I can slide the boxes of ammo and the Bobcat behind and under the dresser. No one else is small enough to get back there, even if they go snooping. It's fine for now.

Tomorrow, when everyone's out, I'll hide them under the floorboards in my closet, with the rest of my stash.

CHAPTER 7

Clearview has been busy. There's now a sign, small but official, just before the turnoff. And there's a new gate. A stronger, more serious gate, one that is closed across the road. And now there is barbed wire on top of the gate, and on top of the fence from the gate to where it disappears into the trees. Dad punches a code into a keypad in the center of a metal box and waits, staring at the gate. When nothing happens, he tries again. Still nothing. After a few clicks and a beep, static, and then, "Yeah?" an annoyed voice says.

"Uh, hi," Dad says, leaning toward the metal box. "I tried the code, but—"

"Name?"

"David." He leans a little closer and looks up, where I see a camera pointed toward the car. "Mullin. David Mullin," he says again, friendlier. When still nothing happens, he says,

"Oh, and my daughter, Bex. Rebecca, but she goes by Bex. I'm supposed to—"

A loud buzz and then the metallic clanking of the gate slowly sliding open in front of us.

"There we go," Dad says, smiling at me. "Thank you!" he shouts toward the box.

After we drive through, the gate closes behind us. Locking us in.

There are more cars and trucks in the large gravel parking lot. And someone has added two more picnic tables. And a gazebo. White, with big open arches and low railings, like for parties. Kind of cheesy, really, especially next to the other buildings, including the new one that was just poles in the ground last time I was here.

Dad waves to someone. Two women walking into the new building pause and wave, but they don't look very friendly.

Outside the truck I can hear some shots off in the distance, from more than one gun, different guns. Voices from somewhere nearby.

And another new sign, this one big and fancy. Carved wood, snooty enough for any rich-boy club.

We cross the grass, and by the time we're walking across the road, I can see there are also more trucks and campers parked on the other side.

"Are there people living here now?"

"Camping out. Families on vacation. Members who've driven in for a few days. Some of the young people who have the summer off. Work crews. We hope to have some shelters up by winter. It's starting to come together."

He smiles like he had a part in it. Not like he just got here less than a month ago. On a guest pass. A charity pass.

"You were the one saying we needed to train harder, right?" Dad asks. "Take preparation more seriously? I didn't get it until Jim laid out their heightened response plans. You were right," he says, glancing at me. "We *do* need to be more serious."

Serious is good. But are they *really* serious? Serious about training, about being organized and prepared? So far this is all still just buildings and talk about squads and organization and more serious prep. And Dad talks about Riggs and the other men like they're his friends. Mark, too. The guy with the MAG in Virginia says screw friendship—select your members based on maximum survival, for what each can offer the group. How does Clearview choose? Can anyone buy in if they have enough money? And if membership *is* about money, and we don't have any, then what do we have that they want?

We walk past the first building. Dad says hellos to the

people we pass. They mostly nod or say hello back, but it's forced. They're distracted by my hair.

"Good morning," Riggs says, coming out of one of the buildings and walking down the steps. Dad stands up straighter, grins bigger. His new best friend.

"Hello, Shelley, Myrt," Riggs says to two women passing by.

Then we're just standing there, Riggs smiling, waiting for what, I don't know. "So, Bex," he says, "I'm glad you're here."

Usually when Dad goes anywhere with me, he looks down or to the side and keeps a body's space between us. He doesn't look at my head, except when someone else does, and then he's embarrassed all over again. But now he has a hand on my shoulder. I'm Riggs-approved, and he's proud. I'm not sure how I feel about that.

"Are you going to the open training session?" Riggs asks me.

"Yes," Dad says. "I was going to walk Bex over and then check in with Steven."

"I know where it is," I say.

"You sure?" Dad asks.

"Yeah. I can find my way there."

"I'll meet you back at the lot after," Dad says.

"Excellent. Then we can get to work," Riggs says.

By the time I make my way out to the range, they're already readying to shoot. Most of them are clustered around the first six firing points, with Carl and Karen supervising. But Randy has a small group all the way at the other end of the range, guys and girls.

"You're with Randy," Carl says when I start toward his group. Karen gives me a welcoming nod, but Cammie looks through me like I'm not even there.

In a lot of ways, it's just like last time I was here, at least for my group. Randy makes everyone start with rifles and prone, even though a few of them are over eighteen and last time we were allowed to stand or sit. I glance at the other firing points. The others are shooting more or less independently, with Carl and Karen offering only tips and corrections. They're upright and selecting their own targets. But there are more of us now. Maybe Randy's nervous at the numbers, or maybe someone made him nervous at one of the sessions I missed.

"We're going to be moving on to other weapons and exercises in the coming weeks," says Randy. "I just want to be sure everyone is ready."

So Randy *is* evaluating us. When it's my turn, he gets close and watches every move I make. Even more intent than Carl was last time.

I take a deep breath and then smoothly run through my

safety checks and setup. I'm confident in my skills. He needs to see that I know what I'm doing. Once he gives me the go-ahead, I try to block him out and shoot. Maybe not my best accuracy, but smooth, easy, and better than the rest of them. After prone, we repeat sitting, kneeling, and standing. When I show clear on my last round, Randy gives me a curt "Good."

There's one more to go in my group. Instead of watching him, I inch over so I can watch Cammie shoot. And then a girl with short hair. Karen steps in to give her some correction, but it's about accuracy, not safety. Karen's good: encouraging but correcting. And she can flat-out shoot. Maybe I should have just joined her group last time. I assumed the girls wouldn't be as serious. They are, or at least most of them are, and they probably don't ever have the wannabes to deal with.

"Bex."

Randy's standing there with two of the others. I walk back over to them.

"You three are cleared for all of the open training sessions. Bex," he says, holding me up as the others go over to where their friends are, "there are a few sessions and drills that will use handguns. Those will be marked on the schedule. You can have a parent attend, or you can observe. We'll work you in as much as we can with a long gun or at least positioning, once we move on to maneuvers. Understand?"

"Yes, sir," I say. The "sir" was a good move. Randy's pleased.

"Good shooting today. See you next week." From Randy, that's like a personal invitation.

A group of the older guys, with Daniel at the front, intercepts Randy as soon as he moves away from us. Lobbying, I'd say. I can't really hear, until one of them says, "But we can start that *now.* We don't need this stuff," he says, pointing toward the rest of the group. "We can train as a patrol unit now, and then patrol the land, look for trespassers, and map—"

"We already have surveyors and—"

"Then on a trial basis," one of the others says.

"Hey," Randy says. "You can take it up with Riggs if you want, but he was clear. Under twenty-one, you're here. At least for now." Again with the "for now."

"But we shouldn't have to be with the children," one of them says.

"And you're not," Randy counters. "Sixteen and older, and there are at least two sixteen-year-olds who could probably outshoot half of you. Now, you want your own sessions? Recruit more members. But for now, it's this or you're on your own."

"Sucks," I hear Mark say behind me.

"Only three percent," I hear Wannabe say, just like Mark.

He's even using that stupid three-finger gesture. "The next time, we're going to need . . ."

He parrots the same spiel Mark's been doing lately. Wannabe drones on and on about how no one is telling him what he can shoot, and how not even Riggs is telling him he can't carry—next year, when he's old enough for a permit—and police states, and how the next "war" is going to start with someone like him stepping up and blah, blah, blah. These guys don't know anything. Not about what would really happen if the shit hit the fan. Yet here they are, talking their bullshit about how they will "light the match." Like they would know what to do once the world was on fire. And then they think what, they're just going to come here and hunker down? Total BS.

"What did you say? Hey," Wannabe says. "Hey!"

I look up. He's pointing at me.

"What?"

"What did you say?"

"Nothing."

"Come on, Zach," one of the others says, trying to pull him away.

"Bullshit, nothing," Zach says, moving closer. "You said 'Total BS.' "

I look at Zach, at the guys around him.

Mark's not there anymore. He's over by Daniel, not paying any attention.

"Too chickenshit to say it to my face?" Zach asks.

Okay. "It's bullshit to think your big survival plan is getting here."

They stare at me.

"Right now, there's nothing here to sustain more than a few people long-term. No shelters. No food. No organization. This place isn't remote enough to be safe long-term."

"So we go somewhere else," Zach says.

"How?"

"We've got trucks."

"Damn right," the tall kid says. "Fully loaded. Or will be."

Will be. Typical. "When? You can't know when a crisis scenario will erupt. And if a massive four-wheel-drive truck stocked to the rims is your 'bug out' plan," I say, with finger quotes, "then you're done. Roads might be barricaded, clogged, or unsafe. And trucks are loud. Especially when the ambient noise dies down. There'd be no finesse or stealth to them."

"Who needs stealth?" Zach mocks. "We'll have power."

"The extra weight will give it extra ramming power," the tall kid says. The others laugh at his "ramming" motion. "Ram our way through. Full provisions, ammo, the works."

They probably see themselves as action heroes, kicking ass and taking names, probably with a harem of women they collect on the way.

"Where are you going to fuel once the grid goes down? Most gas pumps these days run on electricity. Those massive trucks are guzzlers. And what about food, water?"

"Hunt," Zach says, "raid stores and businesses. Whatever, until we could get somewhere defendable."

"What place could you defend with the number of people you could fit in a truck—along with everything else you'd be carrying? Assuming, of course, that you're not killed for that truck in your first confrontation with a hostile group."

"What do you know?"

"I know that none of you could make it on foot, and it's unlikely you could make it long in a truck. You couldn't possibly carry enough provisions and people to defend yourselves. You could maybe fit three or four of you in that truck, but that would be it, unless you started pitching your provisions. And then how are the four of you going to defend any site worth defending, alone?"

They don't argue. Zach and the tall guy are red-faced pissed, but I'm on a roll.

"What you need is to be mobile, and in a small-enough unit to move efficiently. A three-day assault pack, holding just what you absolutely need to defend yourself and make shelter and find water and food, and then the skills to survive. If you're relying on a truck full of crap, you'll be dead in a month. Sooner if it's winter."

"Won't need any of it when this place is ready," the tall guy says.

"Maybe," I say. "But a compound is a refugee magnet. And there's trying to defend it with the number of people it could support. But, again, how are you even going to get here if the crisis hits without warning and the roads are closed or blocked? If what we're facing is the police state you were just talking about?" I ask, waving toward Zach. "You four are going to all fight through the barricades and forces to get here? Without bringing the hostiles with you? You think *that* gate is keeping anyone out who really wants in?"

The two guys in back look at each other.

"Assuming you keep the truck gassed up, stocked, and ready to go, and the crisis scenario doesn't hit until you are fully prepared, there is still no guarantee you'll be able to get here. We need to be doing more than shooting. Survival skills. Foraging and shelter. Scouting and evading."

"You're not even a member," Zach says. "But even if we keep your family on," he says like that's in doubt, "we'd have a better chance than you would."

I smile at him. "No, you wouldn't. Because I could get here, or wherever else we decided to go, on foot. We'd be mobile. Adaptable. We wouldn't need a truck or a compound to survive. I know what it's like to live out of a pack. To find food and water and build shelter. Do you?"

"Sure."

I feel the smirk creeping up my face. "Really?"

He advances. "You think you could really take any one of us?" he asks, and then he pushes his finger into my chest, daring me.

I smack it away and spin, moving to sweep his legs, and then someone yells, "Hey!" and I pull back. Zach stumbles, and then one of the other guys has Zach by the arms. "Cut it out," the guy yells, like we were goofing around.

I hold my stance in case Zach comes at me again.

"Come on, dude," one of the others says.

"She's not worth it," another says.

Finally Zach shakes him off and falls back.

"No, *it's* not," he says. "Stupid dyke," he adds, just loud enough for me to hear.

I watch until they seem to be moving away, Zach included, and then I turn to get my bag where I dropped it.

I'm shoved out of the way by someone moving fast.

"Oh, I know you aren't that chickenshit," Karen says,

advancing on them. Zach looks like he just sucked on a lemon, caught readying to hock a loogie at my back. "Go ahead," she says, "swallow it down."

Zach looks trapped, and the others shift their feet, putting a little distance between them and Zach. Instead of swallowing, Zach pulls back and lobs a huge gob of spit into the dirt off to the side.

"Nice." Karen shakes her head in disgust. "The way you shoot, you should do less talking and more watching. You might learn something."

"You gonna teach me a lesson?" Zach asks.

"Sure." Karen smiles, and then says, "I could whoop your ass any way you want. Any day. You just name it."

"Really," one of them says, stepping up beside Zach. He grabs his crotch. "You got a dick after all?"

"No, you little pissant, which is why it would make it all the more satisfying when I kicked your ass. And let me tell you," Karen says, "you whip that thing out around me, you better make sure you came to play. I have no issue with slapping you—or it—down."

"Bring it in," Randy yells over from where he and Carl are waiting to dismiss the others. It's clear Randy knows something is up, but not what, and that he's letting Karen handle it. I walk over, not really knowing what to do. But Karen walks up front as if none of that just happened.

"Hi," the girl with the sparkles says, sitting down beside me at the back of the group. "Trinny," she reminds me.

"Trinny, yeah, hi."

She's just so happy, in her sparkly shirt and sparkly headband and weird rubbery belt.

"I like your hair," she says.

"Thanks," I say, but I'm not sure she means it. Her braids are very girly and old-fashioned.

"Don't worry about those guys," Trinny says. "They're just jerks. Are you coming next week?"

"Maybe," I say.

"Good," she says. "You did good." She is up and moving toward the path before I can even register that Randy is done talking. She catches up with one of the older guys and they walk on together, looking very friendly.

Mark's already gone.

I have a dilemma. I can run ahead and put some distance between me and Zach and them. Or I can stick close to Randy and Carl. Either way, those jerks will know I intentionally took a defensive posture. I'll have to watch my back forever around them. Or I can attack and go on the offensive, and maybe get double-teamed and marked as a troublemaker. Or I can hang back and let the chips fall, but not be the aggressor.

"Are you ready?"

"What?"

Cammie gives me a *duh* look. "Are you ready?" she asks. "To go back? I'm heading that way." She looks at Karen and rolls her eyes. Karen nods. Karen appointed her my bodyguard.

"Oh, yeah, right." Good. This is good. "Yeah, I'm ready."

I want to thank Karen before we go, but Cammie says, "She has to take the range guns back to the Box for her dad."

"Box?"

"Armory," Cammie says, like I should have known that. "We call it the Box. And I don't have all day, so . . ."

"Right."

We walk in silence for a while. Not because I don't want to talk, but because pretty much everything I've said in front of her thus far has made me sound like an idiot, and I don't know what to risk next.

And Cammie doesn't seem to want to talk.

"Karen's really good," I finally say. "I mean, you're good, too, but, I mean . . ." I stop talking.

"Thanks," she says, dripping with sarcasm. "And yes, she is. She should be officially on the training staff."

But she's young and a girl. "Yeah."

"Think you can find your way from here?" Cammie asks. I look up to realize we are at the main path that runs behind the buildings and near the trails. "Just around that bend it will open up to the lot. Okay?"

"Yeah," I say. "And thanks. And tell Karen—"

"Bye." Cammie turns and heads off down the path toward the buildings, one of which I know is the armory—the Box—without looking back.

I make it to the lot without incident and then cop a squat on the rail of the gazebo to wait for Dad. I scroll through my phone while I wait, but it doesn't get great reception out here.

"Hello."

Riggs is crossing the grass.

"Don't get down," he says when I start to climb off the railing. "I hoped I might find you."

He comes over and sits down on the top step, facing out toward the lot and the administrative buildings. He's so tall it feels sort of like we're sitting next to each other, even with him sitting on the step.

"What did you think of the training session?"

"It was fine." He just looks at me. "Good, I mean. It was good."

"I know we're starting slow, with the basics, but we think it's important to . . ."

I nod, because we already heard all this from Randy. And Carl.

"Anything I should know about?" he asks.

"What?"

"About training, anything you think I should know?"

"About?"

He studies me and then smiles. "Okay," he says, looking back toward the lot.

He knows something—I just don't know what. I can't believe he would be down here about Zach, but maybe Cammie ran right to him? Or one of the others? Karen? Or maybe he thinks *I'm* the problem, like I shouldn't have provoked him? Or maybe Zach went right to him, saying I was talking trash about Clearview? Crap. Dad will kill me if I've made Riggs think he's the one being critical.

He waves to someone in the lot.

"You're right about the survival skills."

Someone did run to him.

"We're planning to integrate foraging, trapping, scouting and evasive techniques, finding water and shelter"—he waves his hand—"all the basic survival skills, into the training sessions. But when you're building something like this from the ground up, you have to start with the basics, and with the areas of highest interest."

Meaning they don't have any confidence the guys would show up for hiking and survival skills. Or they really are making all this up as they go along, and they hadn't really thought through the immediate survival needs.

"I heard that you're handy," he says, finally twisting on the step to face me. "That you can fix things. That you're learning auto mechanics from your uncle. Those are valuable skills."

"Yeah?"

"Maybe we can find you some work around here."

For fees? Or free labor? Because I don't think either Mark or Dad has gotten a single cent for what they've been doing around here. Yeah, no. But Riggs is waiting for a response, looking like he's just made me some great offer.

"Maybe," I say, because I don't know what else to say. "But I'm not sure how much time I'll have between working at the station and training. And I need to be earning money. Things are tight. I can't work for free. I mean, if there are fees or . . ."

"Of course," he says, smiling wider, like I said exactly what he thought I would say. What he wanted me to say. "I appreciate your focus. Your father said you were loyal," he says. "To your uncle, I mean."

I look at the buildings, wishing for Dad. Or that Riggs would just go away.

"Well, I should get back to work, but I wanted to check in with you." He gets up from the step, brushes off his pants. "It's important that these sessions run smoothly while we're getting organized. You have good ideas, Bex," he says. "And from what I hear, strong skills. But it's going to take some time for everyone to gel and buy in, so that we can all benefit from each other's strengths and evaluate our weaknesses."

Weaknesses like my big mouth?

Weaknesses like fighting?

Or weaknesses like they really only want Dad's free labor and then we'll be out?

CHAPTER 8

I break from the last bit of tree cover and sprint full-out for the back door. Once my feet hit the cement, I check my watch, gulping air, while I do the math. Thirty-two minutes from the kitchen door to the station, without going on any roads and without being seen. At least I don't think I was seen, and I cut across several private stretches of land, so I'd have heard a holler if I had been.

Next week I'll try for thirty minutes. By the end of the summer, I want to be under twenty. And still not seen. That's the real goal. If something happened, something bad, being able to get clear of people would be the first crucial step. It doesn't much seem like anyone else thinks about the first hours, when getting away from town, from roads, unseen, would be the biggest obstacle. The one thing that makes out here better than home is how much easier it would be to get away clean. Here we could conceivably get to open woods on foot if we had to.

I clean up and change in the cramped, grimy bathroom in back, shoving my sweaty workout clothes into a plastic bag and then putting them in my pack.

I start the coffee, flip on the computer, check the messages, and then it's time to get to work for real.

The morning is quiet. It's storming again, and that keeps away most of the regulars who come by just to talk. Mike finishes the two repairs early and then goes off to pick something up, and probably take a long lunch.

Uncle Skip's been hovering. He clearly wants to say something, but you can't rush Uncle Skip. He gets there when he gets there. He watches me sort through some invoices and then get the clipboard to restock the snacks and note what needs to be ordered. All the while, he stands there by the counter, having some kind of conversation with himself, or maybe me, in his head. It's almost annoying, but I know better than to ask.

When I've finished restocking and I'm making the list to reorder, he clears his throat.

"I don't mind you using the workshop," he says. I put down the clipboard and turn so I'm facing him. It sounds like a serious conversation. "And I look the other way at the amount of shooting you're doing," he says. "Lord knows your father and I did the same. But I can't look the other way about other stuff."

"What?"

"You promised no more blowing stuff up."

"I'm not. I haven't." I don't know what he's talking about.

"You put everything away," he says. I keep myself from confirming or denying by not moving at all. "But you didn't throw it away." We stare, neither of us giving anything up. "I'd prefer it if you got rid of whatever is still around."

So he suspects I've got somewhere to hide stuff but doesn't know for sure. "Fine."

"It'll feel like lying to your mother if I see anything like that again and don't say something. Understand?"

Is this about the Bobcat, somehow? "Yeah, sure." What did he see? "It was just one time."

"Keep it that way."

Is it Clearview that has him all worked up? Because he hasn't brought the pipe bomb up in months.

"Feel like helping Mike with a brake job this afternoon?" he asks.

"Sure."

"There's something wonky with the diesel pump. They're sending a guy down to look at it, so I can watch the front while I deal with him."

"Cool." I think this is his way of making things okay after the mini-lecture.

"It's Jarvis's car, so it'll be a good one for you to work on. But he'll probably supervise," Uncle Skip warns. Yeah, supervise and talk our ears off.

I finish restocking and then Google around my sites.

My cell rings. Mom. I watch it ring. She's been nagging at Dad about Clearview, about when he'll start being paid. He's stopped looking for any other work. Two beats after my cell stops ringing, while I'm still waiting for the voice-mail alert, the station phone rings. Somehow I know it'll be Mom. I could let that go to voice mail, too, but it might be a customer. It's probably better to just get it over with. But then it stops. I feel only a slight twinge of guilt. I'll check the voice mail right away, in case it's a customer.

"Bex," Uncle Skip yells through the service-bay door, "it's your mother."

Crap.

"Hi, Mom."

"Hi," she says with too much happy in her voice. "I was just having lunch and thought I'd call and check on you. How are you?"

"Fine."

"Your father said you've been having a good time at the club?"

"Yeah." I've been out there twice while she's been staying in the city. I thought maybe she planned to never ask.

"He said the girls seem nice. Are they?"

"They're fine."

"What do they wear for practice?"

"It's not practice, Mom."

"For the meetings, or trainings, whatever they're called. What do the girls wear? I could pick you up a few things. If you're going to be going out there more than once a week, you need more things."

"I don't need anything."

She launches into a "talk" about "this Clearview," and how much it means to Dad to make a good impression, and how I had better be on my best behavior. Like it's a tea party, not training. And how I need to look presentable.

"I look fine. Seriously, they don't wear anything fancy."

"Still, you could use some new things."

"I don't want anything." At least nothing Mom's going to buy me. I could use new hiking boots. I'd love a new range vest.

I hear her exhale into the phone. Probably trying not to yell or something if other people are around.

"Are you reading?"

"Yes."

"Really?"

"Yes, I'm reading. I'm three-quarters through *The Color Purple*." Well, I've started it, anyway.

"Good," she says, surprised. "Do you like it?"

"It's okay."

"I've never read that one. Maybe I should."

"Maybe." Yeah, no, this book would freak her out. I'm actually kind of shocked Aunt Lorraine let Hannah read it, or that Hannah gave it to me.

She talks about work and Hannah and Aunt Lorraine, and I say "yeah" several times like I'm listening.

There's silence.

"Well, I should . . ." I say, trying to remember what she was saying.

"Bex," she says, introducing whatever she really called about. "It's been a while since you tried to break into a new group of girls. Just . . . if they're being standoffish, or distant . . . Just give them some time. It might be hard for them, with . . ."

Hard for them. Because I'm such a freak.

"Don't worry, Mom. I'm making extra sure everyone knows I'm a girl."

She lets out a long breath. I want to hang up, but I know it would just piss her off more.

"You don't have to throw up these walls to shove everyone away." Another long silence, something whispered to someone else.

"Mom, I have to—"

"I don't . . . What is going on with you?" I swallow the hurt but don't trust myself to speak. "Just . . . promise me you'll try. Just try to be who I know you are, down deep, under all the hostility and, and . . . Be nice. Wear something nice, those nice shorts I got you. And a shirt that actually fits. Try to make friends. Okay?"

Nice.

"Bex?"

"Fine."

"I'll be home this weekend. We can talk some more."

Yippee. "Bye, Mom."

Be nice. And make it easy for them. Because it's still all about how *I'm* the problem.

After lunch, Uncle Skip and I trade spots, and I put on a work shirt in the back to keep the worst of any grease and muck off my clothes.

Jarvis does talk at us the whole time, but it's easy to ignore after a while and concentrate on Mike. Mike's sometimes even better to work with than Uncle Skip, because Mike just tells me what to do, instead of adding in all kinds of other stuff that might happen on some other car sometime.

We're done, and I'm ringing Jarvis up for the work, when a familiar patchwork station wagon pulls up to pump two. The girl with the dark hair gets out and goes to the pump and chooses the option for cash. I'm supposed to make her prepay—anyone but a true regular has to—but I flip the switch and use the intercom to say, "Go ahead. You can pay after." I watch her, hoping Jarvis will take the hint and leave.

I take Jarvis's money and hand him his copy of the work order. "See you later, Jarvis. Say hey to Betty."

"Will do, will do," he says, scratching his chin, staring at the receipt. "You going to work your way up to full-time tech?" he asks, like he's just trying to find any reason not to leave yet. "Stay on here with Skip?"

The girl walks through the door, pushing her sunglasses up into her hair in the dimmer inside light.

"Maybe," I say, but I'm watching her.

She glances my way, does a double take at my hair—looks surprised but not repulsed—pivots with flair, and heads to the drink case.

"Could do much worse, you know." Huh? "It's good work," Jarvis says. "Skip's a good man. Could teach you well."

"I know," I say. "Thanks, Jarvis."

She's studying the drinks, like there's a wider selection than last time. Touching her hair, or her neck, scanning the small selection of snacks next to the case. Her hair is curlier than last time, shinier, which makes it even darker. Before she moves from chips to candy, she looks up and smiles at me. I don't stop watching her, and she keeps looking, smiling more, until she gives up and walks over to the counter with just a can of pop.

"Hi again." Her voice is nice, deeper than I remembered. There's just a bit of twang to how she talks, the "hi" stretched out in the middle. She laughs and I snap out of it.

"Yeah, uh, hi . . ." I ring up her drink.

She scoops a handful of the plastic rings out of the bin on the counter and picks through them, putting some down on the counter and dumping others back in the bin.

"Your hair looks cool."

"Thanks." I touch the choppy bit at my neck, suddenly self-conscious at how hacked up it looks. I tried to clean up the choppy parts, but without clippers, there's not much more I can do.

"I stopped in Saturday," she says, scooping out more of the rings.

"I don't work Saturdays usually," I say.

"Yeah," she says, "I've noticed. I've been by during the week, too."

"Really? I've been here most days."

"So, my bad timing, then, huh?" She smiles at me, glancing up but continuing to sort through the rings.

I can't figure out what she's playing at. "Where are you from?" The twang, I can't place it.

Her hair flutters around her face when she moves. "I was born here, but we moved to North Carolina when I was little."

She dumps the remaining rings in her hand back into the bin and turns all the rings on the counter to face her, their incomplete circles facing me. Then she goes back to the canister, like maybe she needs one more.

"So . . ." I say.

"So . . ." she says, "what am I doing up here?" Her dark eyes crinkle when she smiles. "Staying with my grandparents."

Maybe it's their piece-of-shit car. That would explain the local plates and why I hadn't seen her around before last time.

She takes a deep breath and lets it out, like she's in some TV show. "I usually only come up for June, but I had to get out of town early this summer."

I nod like I get it, even though I don't.

"I broke up with my girlfriend." She waits for reaction. "She got all our friends in the split."

I can't believe she just said it, like it was no big deal. I glance around to make sure Uncle Skip and Mike are in back.

She looks at my book by the phone. "Have you met Shug yet?" she asks.

"What?"

She leans over so she can tap on the book, putting her breasts on display over the counter and her hair all in my space. "Shug Avery. Has Celie met her yet?"

I shake my head.

"God, I love *The Color Purple*. Love," she says, like I might not have understood that the first time.

I pick it up and look at the cover again, just to make sure we're talking about the same book. "Really?"

"Oh, it's brutal, I know. But stick with it, at least until Shug arrives. Trust me," she says.

I flip ahead, scanning for *Shug*.

"Which one?" She holds out two of the rings: a plastic-gem flower and a red peace symbol. She makes them dance in front of me, all playful, her face as flushed as mine feels. She pushes them closer. "Pick one!"

"Neither," I say. She looks at them again and agrees, tossing them into the bin and digging deeper, scooping rings up by the handful, sifting through them and letting them fall through her fingers onto the counter.

"What part of North Carolina?" I ask, to prolong the conversation.

"Mom and Dad teach at UNC," she says, like that answers my question. She holds out a glitter star and I shake my head. "What about you? I come up here every summer. I'd have remembered seeing you before."

A flutter in my belly. "It's my uncle's station. We're staying with him for a while." And I didn't start until July. A few weeks earlier, and maybe I'd have met her last summer.

"I'll be with my grandparents until August. Then Mom and Dad are driving my stuff up here so I can start at the University of Chicago in the fall."

So she's eighteen, or close to.

"So, what do you do, besides work here?"

"Not much."

"Maybe we could hang out sometime."

"Yeah," I say. "Sure, that'd be great." My face gets hot, but she's still smiling, and I can feel that smile from the top of my head down to my toes and plenty of places in between.

She's making me dizzy.

"I'm Lucy." She holds out her hand, and I reach across the counter and shake it.

"Bex."

Her hand is almost the same size as mine, and warm, and just a little clammy.

"Bex." I like the way she says it.

Touching her, even just her hand, is like touching more of her. My knees and stomach go funny, and I fight the urge to squirm against the counter.

She finally takes her hand back, and she does have to take it back, because my hand is not letting go. My blood is fizzing with wanting to touch more of her. I've never really flirted like this before. Out in the open, clear about the flirting.

She puts a ring down on the counter next to her pop. A black plastic skull with silver outlines of eye sockets and face and teeth. I ring them up, and she hands me the exact amount, her pop cradled against her body as she counts out the coins. I look up from putting the coins in the register, and she's backing toward the door. The ring is still on the counter. I pick it up and say, "Wait! You forgot—"

"That's for you. Until next time, Bex."

She puts her sunglasses on and then opens the door with her back.

I'm left clinging to the counter, holding the ring in my hand. Only later do I realize I never rang up her gas.

CHAPTER 9

I hit the trail at a run just past the Box. Dad was pissy on the drive over, even though his having to come get me was Mark's fault, not mine. Uncle Skip wasn't happy, either, since he thought I'd only be training on weekends.

I blow past the pistol range and hook to the left, going off trail to cut the angle at the widest curve in the path. I don't stop until the trees thin and the rifle range is in sight. They haven't started yet. Carl and two of the older guys are dragging mats off the ATV and positioning target stands of various heights at the far end of the range in front of the dirt berm. Most everyone else is talking in groups behind the barriers marking the firing points for today.

As usual, I can feel the looks bouncing around me — not all are unfriendly, not anymore, but every time there are new faces, or faces I've only seen at maybe one other training, I have to weather their once-overs, always with a long pause on my head. My hair's getting long already. I need to get some clippers or try trimming the sides and back with scissors.

Karen, Trinny, and a few others at least acknowledge me as I drop my range bag and cool down after the all-out sprint. Cammie acts like I'm crashing her party. There's some laughter, too, as usual, and I can imagine the witticisms being shared by Mark's mouth-breather friends. Zach spits, not near me, but like he's proving something.

"Where were you?" I ask Mark when he wanders closer.

"What?" he asks, his fake innocence all about showing off for his friends.

"Dad said—"

"I told Dad," he says. "I had stuff to do." Oh, big man with "stuff." "He's not paying for my insurance anymore. So I'm not running his errands."

Selfish shit. He smirks.

"If I were you," he says, "I'd start thinking about how you're going to get here when Dad's working most days again. Maybe you need to finally spend some of that wad you've been saving for wheels of your own. Because I am not ferrying you around."

Jerk. I make a face and lean closer to him. "When's the last time you did laundry?" I sniff at him. "Because you stink."

Two steps away and I hear the razzing. The idiot actually sniffed himself.

But the problem still stands. How am I going to get here if Dad's working or in meetings or wherever, if Mark won't pick me up? And Dad would have to transport my gun and ammo for me even if I found a way here on my own. Complications I don't need.

"He was in full tactical gear," one of the new guys says. I can't remember which one he is. "Full visor and everything. We got the whole thing on video. The geezer who runs the range nearly shit his pants when he saw him. It was awesome."

"It was stupid," Karen says. "They could have arrested him."

"For what?" the guy asks, turning away from the older guys and toward Karen. Despite the requests that we not open carry at the ranges, his pistol is holstered at his waist and he has a semiauto strapped to his back. Knife at his belt. A little much for a range day. "What did he do that was illegal?"

"Well, you said he was breaking range rules, for one," Karen says, continuing to check the club's semiauto rifles, one at a time, on the back of the ATV. "That's private property. Range owner gets to make the rules. Disturbing the peace. Brandishing, since he had the rifle loaded and in patrol position. Harassment, since he was there to get a rise out of the owner for having him booted. Any number of things."

"None of them would stick. He was open carrying. That's legal in this state," the guy's friend says.

"On private property, prohibition posted? No, it's not," Karen says.

"Yeah," the first guy says, "it is. Second Amendment trumps some stupid poster."

Karen gives this new idiot a look and hands yet another safety-checked AR-15 to Carl. Then she looks at Zach. He invited these two.

"Never would have stuck," the first guy says.

"But why draw the attention?" Karen asks. "What did he gain?"

"You have to exercise your rights if you want to keep them," the guy says.

"And they need to know they can't mess with us," Zach adds. "We're not pushing back enough, making enough noise, if you ask me."

"No one's asking you," says Karen. "If you all think you're going to go play *scare the sheeple* and then come here and strut around, we're not impressed."

"And you get to decide who comes here and who doesn't?"

Karen doesn't answer but stares the guy down. She may

not have the say of Randy or Carl, but she has more than most. Her father practically *is* the armory, and he listens to her, and Riggs listens to him.

"Devon," Zach says. The guy looks at Zach, but he doesn't move away. He stands there, fingering the strap across his chest, as if he actually thinks he and Karen are in some kind of competition.

Karen doesn't. She grabs the next AR-15, removes the mag, pulls the bolt back, locks it to the rear, and checks the chamber. Then she hits the bolt release and applies the safety. Then moves on to the next, almost like she could do it in her sleep, until she hands the last one to Carl and hops down from the ATV.

A lot of the guys have their own semiautos. They line up and grudgingly let Carl and Karen see that their mags are out and chambers are empty to make sure the rifles are unloaded. At the same time, Karen and Carl are eyeballing the weapons themselves for illegal modifications or accessories.

"No foregrip," Karen says.

"What?" Devon asks.

"Can't have a foregrip on an AR-15 pistol. Angled grip only," Karen says.

"Says who?"

"The ATF," Karen says.

“That’s bullshit. I’ve been using this for a year.”

“Then it’s been illegal for a year,” Karen says. “You can use another firearm or a range rifle, but you’re not shooting that here.”

He’s ready to argue, looking around for his backup.

“And while we’re at it,” Karen says, looking at his friend’s AR with a slide stock, “no bump fire, either.”

“Oh, come on!” Devon shouts. “You’ve got to be shitting me. There is nothing illegal about using a slide fire stock. Neal shoots it all the time.”

“No bump fire in group training,” Karen says.

“You’re seriously saying I can’t use a completely legal weapon here?” Neal asks.

“Yeah,” Karen says. “That’s what I’m saying. So you can swap out for a regular stock, get another rifle, or you can leave.”

These guys were a pain in the ass last time, giving Randy trouble about shooting prone. Neal’s not moving to swap out or accept Karen’s directive, and she’s not moving an inch until he does.

“Carl?” Zach says. “Bump fire is totally legal. And a foregrip doesn’t change anything about his pistol.”

Carl steps closer to Karen and crosses his arms. He answers to Randy, and to Riggs, and to Mr. Severnsen. No way is Carl undermining Karen.

"No illegal weapons," Karen says. "And no bump fire in training."

"Also no green tips," Carl says, pointing to the box in Zach's vest pocket.

"What?" Devon says, leaning around Zach. "Why not?"

"Well, for starters, because we said so," Carl answers. "When you're here, you do as we say. But second, range rules. No green tips."

"Not even in rifles?" Zach asks.

"No." Carl moves on to the next person. "We can give you some range ammo if that's all you have."

"This is bullshit," Mark says, stepping up next to Zach and his friends. "They're legal in rifles."

"In rifles, maybe," Carl says. "But that armor-piercing stuff chews up the metal targets. So it's not allowed on the land."

Mark looks at Daniel and the older guys, waiting for backup, but it's not coming. None of them are happy about these assholes Zach brought. No one but Zach and Mark.

The standoff doesn't last long. Karen and Carl clear the others' weapons and then move over to the firing points with the range rifles the rest of us will take turns using.

"We should be learning what they can do," Devon says. "At what distance they can cut through tactical gear."

"And stocking up before they try to ban them again,"

Neal says. "All the police departments and sheriffs have military-grade tactical gear. They say it's for riots, or anti-terrorism."

"Crowd control," Mark scoffs. "And no one is questioning it."

Daniel and some of the guys walk away, but four or five are listening.

"It's just a matter of time," Devon says now that he sees his audience, "before they come up with some reason to bring out the militarized units and declare martial law."

"Are they really armor piercing?" Trinny asks, suddenly at my elbow.

"Not really," I say, but quietly enough not to draw the guys over. "They're made for rifles, but when shot from handguns, at close range, they can cut through body armor. But so can a lot of other bullets."

They're not wrong about militarization, about the pressure building, but green tips aren't the answer. The open-carry and tactical gear demonstrations aren't helping, either. We don't need to be drawing that kind of attention.

"They are banned from the range," Randy shouts, making everyone jump a little. He steps right up to Devon and Neal. "End of conversation. We catch anyone using them here, and you will be asked to leave. Don't even bring them here."

Trinny and I join Cammie at firing point four, but we hang back until our turns. Cammie has her own rifle—obviously optimized to her preferences. She sights down to the berm with the empty rifle, slides into stance, and then relaxes. Her motions are so smooth, from the muscle memory of sliding into stance and relaxing a million times. She's as good as any of the older guys—maybe better—but she's not agitating to move beyond the rest of us. Cammie doesn't cheerlead like Karen. She doesn't tell any of the girls how great they're doing or try to puff up their confidence. But she acts like she's their leader. Encouraging them in her own way. Karen's as nice to me as she is to the others, but Cammie doesn't talk to me at all. Not since Karen made her walk me to the lot after that second session. She doesn't even look at me if she can help it. She sights the targets ahead of her, dry fires, and adjusts her positioning. She glances over her shoulder, catches me looking. Again.

I wish I could take one of the range AR-15s and get a feel for it, practice sighting, figure out how to move with it around obstacles and go from prone to upright. But today I'll just get to use one when it's my turn to shoot. I've only ever held one of these once or twice at a show. Dad says we don't need assault rifles for hunting or defense. I wonder if he's changing his mind.

"This is awesome," JoJo says, grinning ear to ear. Cammie glares; JoJo waves her off. "You can be cool all you want," JoJo says. "This is totally awesome."

JoJo's been around awhile, maybe nearly as long as Trinny and some of the other girls. But she wasn't at the first few trainings I went to. When she showed up, she was extra hostile, like I was trying to take her place or something. And now she's using some stuff to make her hair sort of spiky, like she's trying to compete with me. She's no competition. But her spiky hair matches her personality, like a porcupine.

Trinny is wearing a Team Jacob shirt today, and not ironically. Her twin braids are decorated with a stack of different-colored rubber bands at the end of each. She looks even younger than usual. I hope she's homeschooled. Public school would eat her goofy-elfin self alive. Well, unless she put the hand-to-hand to good use. Dropped a few preppy girls on their butts.

Delia wipes her sweaty forehead on her shirt, showing several inches of fit, toned, dark-skinned abs. Mark is always staring at Delia. So are some of the other guys, but I don't think *they're* admiring the view like Mark is. There were some racist comments the first time the open-carry guys came. They got an earful from Carl about how Clearview does not tolerate the kind of shit they were saying. They didn't kick them out, but at least we don't have to hear it anymore. And they leave Delia alone. But that might have more to do with Karen and Cammie and most of the older guys having Delia's back.

Randy is watching the first shooters like a hawk, ignoring the grumbling from the guys about shooting prone.

I've seen enough YouTube videos to know that for a lot of wannabes and backyard warriors, guns like these are just a fun way to waste ammo. But to be tactically ready takes work. Especially if they are already thinking about movements and maneuvers. Going from prone to patrol to combat, and in group movements, armed, takes a serious amount of trust and preparation. The guys can grumble all they want, but I'm not. I don't trust any of them with live ammo outside the range yet. We're far away from that. Very far. Especially the newer guys. I barely trust them at the range.

"Clear downrange," Randy calls, followed by: "Eyes and ears." Cammie relaxes her shoulders, takes a breath, and fires. She adjusts her positioning and fires again. And again. Then smoothly, with no hesitation between shots. No break in the flow. Total concentration, fluid, like the gun is part of her.

The distant *pop-pop-pop* of the first shots bleeds through my earmuffs. *Pop-pop-popopop-pop*. The overlapping shots sound like popcorn kernels. I watch Cammie shoot.

"Might want to wipe your chin," Mark says. "You're

drooling," he adds, like I didn't understand what he was implying.

I ignore him.

"She's *really* not your type."

I glare at him.

I don't care which of the guys she's dated. I just like to watch her shoot.

Mark, Zach, and both of Zach's friends are in the next group.

"No green tips," Carl says to Zach.

"I heard you," Zach says.

"Just making sure." Carl watches him load his magazine.

Mark jerks on his first shot, and his second, and Carl steps in to correct his positioning. Some of the others get corrections, too, between rounds. Karen is spending a good amount of time with JoJo.

When it's my turn, I take my place, load the magazines, and lay them aside until I'm ready to shoot. Carl and Karen are helping some of the others, so I take the opportunity to get comfortable with the rifle.

I brace the butt of the AR-15 against my chest, the gun turned at an angle, and check that the chamber is empty, just to be sure. Then I can sight and dry fire and get a feel for it.

It's lighter than the last one I held. Or maybe I'm just stronger. It's also smaller than Cammie's or Karen's, and doesn't have any of the scopes or laser sights a lot of the others have. Still, it's a nice AR-15—sixteen-inch barrel, collapsible stock, looks practically new. And Dad is so wrong—I really need one of these that I can trick out the way *I* want it.

"Problem?" Cammie asks, right next to me instead of back by the others, maybe because Karen is sticking close to JoJo.

"Actually, yeah," I say. "I can't get my left arm right."

She studies me. "Give it here," she says. She takes the rifle, pushes the stock in a notch, and then hands it back. "Try that."

I adjust my firing hand, move my left hand back a little, and try again. It's better. Not quite there yet, but better. "Thanks," I say.

She barely acknowledges it and steps back. Not all the way back, but enough so she's not right on top of me.

I shake them all off and just practice. I focus on my hands and arms, sight down the barrel at the uppermost target, and pull the trigger. The snap doesn't have the force of an actual shot. I pull back the charging handle and then sight on a different target, again adjusting my arms and body, sighting and then pulling the trigger. Over and over, different targets, focusing on how it feels. I look up and Cammie is watching me, with no smirk or sneer, and then just a twitch of a nod.

"Ready?" Cammie asks.

And then Randy calls, "Clear downrange."

I insert the magazine and slap it home. Then I slap the bolt release to chamber a round and pull back on the charging handle just enough to see the chambered round. I get my elbows and arms and all in position, sight down to the targets, adjust, and then wait for Carl's okay.

I glance over at JoJo, to my right, to see if she and Karen have their earmuffs in place, and then down the line to the others. We're all ready. The signal comes from Carl, and the pops start around me. I take my time, focus on the targets, and everyone else fades away. It's just me and the sight down the barrel at the first target, nearly level with me and straight ahead. I squeeze off my first round. There's almost no kick at all, and I squeeze off two more, but I can see they were way off. I adjust my body, then reposition to shoot. I adjust my support hand and then concentrate on the largest center target. This time the feel of the shot and recoil is familiar, and I focus on the targets. One, then another. I run through my mag without interruption, eject it, and slap in the second. Then Cammie hands me a third, already loaded. When we break to reload, Cammie resets some of my targets to give me different angles and distances, just like she and Karen do for each other.

When I'm done, I hold position with the gun pointed down toward the dirt while the others finish. When Carl calls the range cold, I eject the last magazine, check the chamber, and engage the safety. Karen collects my rifle and checks it again, to be sure, before moving over to the storage locker on the back of the ATV.

I put my gear away and then pour some water over my neck and the side of my head, use the water to slick my hair away from my face, and wipe my face and hands with a bandanna. I'll need a shower as soon as I get home.

"Good job," Carl says. "All of you."

Cammie and Karen are walking back to get their lunches, and it's easy as anything to just fall in beside them.

"What are you doing Monday?" Karen asks. "Bex?"

"Oh, me?" Karen nods, while ignoring Cammie's look. "I have to work."

"How late? Some of us are meeting out here around six to try the new crossbows," she says. "Just us, not all the idiots. Come on out, if you want."

"I don't think I can get a ride."

"Where do you work?" Karen asks. "I can probably swing by and get you."

I tell her, and we exchange numbers.

"Stop pouting," Karen says, bumping Cammie's shoulder while we walk. "One more won't make a difference. You can have the compound bow, and the rest of us can share the others."

Karen's playing with a green-tip bullet she found near the table, nowhere near where those guys were told green-tips are banned.

"I wish they'd get rid of those guys," Cammie says. "It was better before they started recruiting all these jerks."

"Why don't they?" I ask. "I mean, at least Devon and Neal."

"Riggs," they both say.

"He's big into giving people a chance," Cammie says. "Building the membership."

I can't help but feel she's got me, and maybe my whole family, lumped into that category.

CHAPTER 10

"What happened?" Uncle Skip asks, grabbing my arm so I can't get away.

"I'm fine," I say.

"Like hell." He touches my jaw with one finger, turning my face to look at the scratches and bruised cheek. "Your dad seen this?"

"Yeah." I pull free and continue to the front counter.

"And?" Uncle Skip asks, following me.

"And what?" I say, sitting down and getting ready to take the messages off voice mail. "I tripped during training. No big deal."

Except I tripped over Zach's foot, so, not so much of an accident. But to call him out would be to play right into his hands. Besides, I beat all those assholes on the timed hike and successfully evaded them on the scouting exercise. All in all, I'm fine with it.

"I'm fine. Really. Just training." Serious training. If only they focused more on survival and mobile readiness, it would be perfect training. But it's better than nothing, and Riggs does seem to be adding more skills training.

"Just be careful." I roll my eyes, but he catches my sleeve. "I'm serious. I don't like you out there messing around with those wackos. Whole lot of them are wackadoodle, if you ask me."

"Is that the technical term?"

"You know what I mean."

I know he thinks they're crazy or dangerous. I've heard him and Dad, what passes for heart-to-hearts between brothers who have spent a lifetime mastering nonverbal communication with each other. But the people at Clearview aren't crazy or dangerous, not even Devon and them. They're not afraid to think practically about ammo rationing and regulations, to be planning now for the next phase of disarmament, or to organize into training units. I would be happier if they were primarily about mobility, but I get that for now they're focused on getting the club ready and recruiting. Not sure I like that people—maybe whole families—can just buy in if they have enough money, without any proof they have skills or can learn. Every good MAG and group out there says to be wary of leeches with money. But more paying members means more facilities, more equipment, better ranges, and better preparation. It makes sense, so long as you don't take on more dead weight than you can handle.

Dad's happy to have Riggs's attention. Stupid happy, like he's got a new best friend. More and more meetings he has to go to. More and more certain that a paycheck—a "good one"—is right around the corner. Riggs's hand on his shoulder when they walk together.

Mark's all in. He looks more in every time I see him, which is only when we run into each other out there, since he's crashing with some of the guys now. Puffed up with how cool and in he is—and I'm not. He acts like he doesn't even know me. Like he's finally, finally moved past me, or like he's won.

People still stare at me when I'm out there. I can feel them watching sometimes, even when I don't see anyone, like on the walk from the parking area, past the buildings to the trails.

I know there are probably training sessions happening beyond the open sessions. I'm not sure when or where, how official they are. For all I know, none of the girls are allowed. Maybe that's how they're placating the guys.

The bell rings and I look up. Another shiny tourist SUV and two over-dressed richies out for an afternoon drive. Inside, they blink in the dimness, look around like they were expecting some big fancy store. She needs the bathroom. He needs directions. She comes out, scowling, coating herself in hand sanitizer like even the soap and water were dirty. He studies the drink case. She browses the snacks. She's scrutinizing the labels, frowning and muttering. He's ready to go.

Ultimately she decides on Twizzlers, which makes no sense after whining about the "additives" in the granola bars. They continue to talk like I'm not there. He prepays for gas, and I can't imagine what this leisurely drive will cost. They're miles from home, and that thing gets no more than fourteen miles per gallon highway. Less in the city, where they probably live.

I watch them drive away, knowing they are asleep. By the time something wakes them up, it'll be too late. Their money will be useless. That shiny SUV will be an albatross. Their fancy clothes and need for comfort and fear of hunger will cripple them. They'd last a week if they could hide at home. Less if they're caught out.

For the first time, I don't feel like I'm in this alone, like I've got to research and plan because no one else is. Clearview may look like a club, but at least some of them are thinking like a MAG. Maybe better than a MAG.

While I'm on hold with one of the suppliers, trying to find

a part for Mike, the bell dings. I'm all ready to be helpful until I see Mark and Zach.

Mark struts in like he owns the place. Every time I seem him, he's strutting harder—makes me want to trip him. His too-cool routine is getting old.

"Where's Skip?" Mark asks.

"*Uncle* Skip is under the Chevy in the first bay. Why?"

"None of your business." Mark puffs up bigger, like whatever he's here for is important, like he's on a mission.

"What's your problem?"

"No problem," he says, but he looks smug, like he knows something I don't know. He wants me to ask. He used to do this when we were kids, pretend to know some big secret, but refuse to tell. Made me nuts. He knows it makes me nuts.

"Zach, have a pop or something. I'll be right back."

Zach makes like he's going to jump at me, and then snort-laughs like he's hysterical. He wanders around, picking up one thing and then another.

"You going to buy anything?" I ask.

He knocks a whole row of snacks off the shelf. "Oops," he says, stepping over it all with a slight hesitation, like he was going to step on them.

I can hear Mark in back, but the supplier comes on the line, and I have to pay attention to ordering the part. I try to keep an eye on Zach and watch the door. Mark's been back there too long, given that Uncle Skip's in the service area.

Mark comes out with a bag and hands it to Zach. There's a six-pack of pop sticking out the top, but also probably some of the beer Uncle Skip has in back for poker night and when he and Mike have to do paperwork after hours. "Take this out while I talk to Skip." Maybe something else, too. The bag is bulging and heavy, not just two six-packs and snacks. It's solid and full. Mark takes a cold can of pop from the case, opens it, and takes a gulp.

"You gonna pay for any of that?" I ask, playing along like it's just pop and snacks.

"Shut up." Mark pretends to toss the can of pop at me, and then laughs when I react. He laughs all the way to the service bays.

Fifteen minutes later, Mark bursts back through the door, slamming it into the wall. He forces a smirk when he sees me looking and resumes his strut, but it's for show. For Zach. He's pissed.

"Yeah, no problem," he says into a cell I've never seen before. "It's handled. I . . ."

When did he get a new cell? He's out the door, still talking, but I can't hear. He stands there in the parking lot for another few seconds and then flips the phone the bird before shoving it in his pocket. He climbs back into Zach's truck. Zach stares at me through the window, letting me know he can see me watching them, and then he guns the engine and peels out of the lot.

Mark's whole "handled" bit leaves a weight in my stomach. What was in the bag? I could ask Uncle Skip what Mark wanted, but he's back under the Chevy, so not now.

A few people come by to pick up their cars and trucks, and then Uncle Skip pulls me in back to look up parts and codes so we can get stuff ordered before closing. When the bell rings that there's a customer at the pumps, I jump up to check if they're paying cash and see a familiar station wagon in the lot.

It's like the air changes when she comes in the door, hot and cold and thin all at once, leaving me lightheaded. She's wearing those perfectly worn-in jeans with a crisp white cotton shirt. She glances at the counter and then oh-so-casually around until she sees me and smiles. Not even hiding what she's doing.

"Hey," I say, wiping my hands on a towel as I walk toward the counter.

"Hi." She touches her hair and then smooths her shirt down over her stomach. She's soft under the shirt, breasts and curves and belly. I want to touch her, to run my fingers over her skin and see if my hand fits as perfectly above her hip as I think it will. "I'm gonna," she says, pointing to the snacks. She touches candy bars and chips and, in between, her hair or her hips.

The more I watch, the slower she moves, the more her body moves over her legs, like the start of a dance. I should feel weird watching her. I should feel nervous, but I don't. It's like she gave me permission. Or I didn't need it.

Finally she picks up some candy and walks back toward the front, even slower than before. My nerves kick in all at once.

She seems quieter, less silly than last time. But the way she looks at me, tucks her dark, curly hair behind her ear, it still feels like we're doing something here.

"I have a burned-out taillight. What would it cost for you guys to fix it?"

"Not much. Uncle Skip would probably cut you a break, but he'd have to charge something for the labor. You could get the bulb at any automotive store, and you could probably change it yourself."

She shakes her head. "I wouldn't even know how." She starts fiddling with the lighters by the register, sorting them by color so that each row in the display is all the same color, in rainbow order.

"I could do it if you want. Then all you'd have to pay for is the bulb."

"Really?" She continues to sort the lighters but looks up in between placing them. "Do you know how?"

"Sure." If she tells me the make and model, I can figure it out. I watch her straighten the sorted rows.

"I'd need it fixed before Monday."

"We could do it Sunday. In the afternoon? We're closed, but you can meet me here. It won't take long." And if I can't figure it out, Mike can do it first thing Monday morning.

My heart pounds. Uncle Skip would probably do it cheap. But the thought of getting to see her alone is too much to resist.

"That'd be great."

A car pulls up to the pumps.

I give her a piece of scrap paper to write down the make and year of her station wagon. When she hands it to me, I stare at her handwriting. It doesn't look like I thought it would. I don't know what I expected—maybe loopier.

"Well . . . should I just come by or . . . ?"

I shove the paper in my pocket. "I could give you a call when I know when I can meet you."

She pulls out her cell and hands it to me. "Give me your number—then I'll text you so you have mine." Her cell is fancier than mine, and I fumble with the buttons. She takes it back, pulls up the right screen, and hands it to me. I can barely type with her watching me. My fingers keep hitting the wrong places. But I get my name and number entered and hand it back. She looks at the screen and smiles. "Great."

"Great."

We're just smiling at each other like idiots. "Well . . ." she says. "So you'll call?"

"Yeah, as soon as I know," I say, trying to be cool.

"See you." She leaves without taking the candy.

Uncle Skip is quiet when he comes through a few minutes later, but I don't look at him, hoping he didn't hear me with Lucy. It isn't until I'm getting ready for bed that I remember I was going to talk to him about Mark.

It can wait until tomorrow.

CHAPTER 11

I had a lie ready to go—different lies, in fact, for Mom and Dad and Uncle Skip, so that I could meet Lucy at the station without anyone wondering where I was. As it turns out, all that planning was completely unnecessary. They're all vacating the house, unusual on a Sunday, but it means no one will miss me until dinner.

"David!" Mom yells up the steps. "We're going to be late!"

Mom rechecks her hair for the third time. She's wearing a dress and her nice heels. Must be more than brunch with Aunt Lorraine and Uncle Nathan; must be brunch at "the Club," and when she and Aunt Lorraine say it, they mean country, not Clearview.

"Who will be supervising?" Mom asks, referring yet again to trying out the crossbows tomorrow night. I shouldn't have told her.

"One of the adults, I'm sure," I lie. "But Karen is practically one of the trainers anyway."

"But she's not."

"Because she's a girl," I say. "A woman, really."

Mom narrows her eyes. "Mom." I close the book but keep my finger in to pretend to mark my place, like I can hardly wait to get back to it. "It will be totally safe." She's still looking at me like it's a bad idea. "Isn't this what you wanted? Me, making friends?"

"I'd hoped for friends who wanted to go places, do things, *normal* things," she clarifies.

"Yeah, well . . ." Dad already said I could go. He's thrilled, in fact, that I'm "in" with Karen and Cammie. I'd think he asked their parents to put them up to it, if he hadn't been so clearly shocked when I told him they'd invited me.

"Well, just be careful."

"I will," I say, holding eye contact, making her see that it will be okay.

"There's some leftover potato salad and chicken from last night," Mom says. "I made a double batch of chicken. Plenty of sliced turkey and cheese for sandwiches. And a casserole for tonight, good for a few days of leftovers as well. That should get you through the week."

"We'll be fine." Her mouth turns down and her lips suck

in. She needs us to need her, and to thank her, so she can go to Aunt Lorraine's without feeling guilty. "What kind of casserole?"

"Cheesy chicken and broccoli."

"With the crunchy top?"

"Mm-hmm."

I give her a real smile. "Thanks, Mom."

"Well, I figured you'd mostly be the one eating it. There's some vanilla ice cream and fresh strawberries, too."

For that she gets an even bigger smile.

"You have everything?" Dad asks, still buttoning his cuffs as he comes into the kitchen.

"Yes." Mom pats the plastic-bag-covered clothes hanging over the chair, her small bag next to it.

"Bex," Dad says, "I should be home by dinnertime. Stay out of trouble."

"Of course."

Mom and Dad both give me a look. I cross my heart and hold up three fingers, even though I got kicked out of Brownies for roughhousing.

Uncle Skip left hours ago to go fishing with Sanford and Mr. Johnson, and I'm sure they'll stop for lunch on the way back.

No one will miss me until tonight.

I wait an hour, just to be sure Mom and Dad are gone, and then I text Lucy.

In the bathroom at the station, I strip down to my tank and quickly wipe off the grime and sweat from riding my bike over. Maybe instead of a truck, I could just get a moped. I put on fresh cargo shorts. I layer up on top — leaving on the tank but adding a gray T and then a dark-blue polo. I step back far enough to be able to see in the mirror and try to decide whether to tuck in the T or leave it hanging loose underneath the polo. Eventually I decide to leave it loose and concentrate on combing my hair so it's neat but not too neat. It can't look like I've fixed it just for her. In fact, I pull on a clean work shirt and leave it open. Like I'm ready for the work, not like I'm ready for her.

I keep the lights off and stay in the service area, with only the back service-bay door open. From the street, no one would even notice we're here.

The bulb for her taillight is ready and waiting, and so am I, a full half-hour before she said she'd be here.

I don't turn on the computer. Too much chance of giving away that I was here. Uncle Skip's emergency set of keys will be back where they belong, hopefully hours before he even gets home, and then no one will be the wiser.

Nothing to do but scroll through my phone, trying not to

worry that maybe she won't show up. Or, alternatively, that she will.

I've never been so nervous in my life.

Well, maybe the first time I tried to kiss a girl, but I was eleven then, and pretending to be a boy named Jake, and not wearing a shirt (best disguise for pretending to be a boy). And I wasn't sure she would let me kiss her no matter who she thought I was.

But it's the good kind of nervous, like the first time I shot a rifle all by myself.

When I hear a car pulling up around back, I hop off the counter and spit out the gum I've been chewing to keep my breath minty fresh.

Lucy. My head spins and sweat breaks out on my neck. I gulp some water from the bottle in the side of my backpack and try to talk my heart rate down. Could very well be that I'll change the bulb, she'll leave, and I'll go home and think about what might have happened if she'd stayed.

I pick up the bulb, still in its package, and wave her through the service-bay door.

She carefully pulls in, intent and serious, inching in until she starts to trust me. Then she just focuses on me, waving her forward. There's a flutter in my chest at her trusting me, following my directions. I like the playful, flirty Lucy, but she's even more interesting when she's serious.

Once in park, she smiles, relieved. By the time she's out of the car, all that hip-swishing front is back in place.

"Hey." She takes her sunglasses off the top of her head and fluffs up her hair, looking around. "It's okay we're in here on a Sunday?"

"It's fine."

"Really? I don't want to get you in trouble."

"Don't worry." I pick up the stuff I'll need and walk around the wagon. "But don't touch anything, and my uncle'll never know."

I give her my bravest smile, and she hesitates for a second before smiling back, still wary. Then she notices the stuff in my hand, and I can see her get more nervous.

"Are you sure you can do this?"

"Yes." I put the rag, tools, and the bulb down and grab the printout from my back pocket. "Here are the pages from the owner's manual I found online. We're going to do exactly what it says. Unscrew a few screws, pull the casing out, switch out the bulb. Piece of cake."

She's still uneasy, glancing from the screwdrivers to the car, sort of rocked back on her heels like a rabbit ready to flee.

"Read it." I put the stuff down and hoist myself up onto the counter. "Go ahead. We won't do it unless you say it's okay."

Her face goes weird and then she cracks up. I replay the last bit in my head. "Totally not what I meant."

"Sure it isn't," she says. "But good to know." She looks up at me over the pages, a look that says we're both feeling it. I'm glad I cleaned up.

She reads. I check her out. I don't really have a type; I don't usually go for slathered in makeup and perfume, but I can't say I wouldn't go there for a while. If I had a sweet spot, though, it would be Lucy. She's got curves and she's not afraid to show them off, not ashamed of the bit of belly or soft thighs. In fact, she's soft in all the places I like soft. Her sundress looks old, blue cotton, pockets, straps that cross in back, and a neckline high enough that there's not even a hint of cleavage, which makes me want to see all the more. Loose enough to allow access, but she could wear it to a church picnic if she wanted. Nice legs. Really nice. And short boots, well broken in and worn at the sides. I'd have looked even if I wasn't thinking about touching.

I realize she's been watching me watch her. I don't even try to pretend I wasn't checking her out.

"You really know how to do this?"

"Yes." I try to exude confidence. Truth is the flutter of

anticipation of what comes next has been chased away by nerves. I don't want to screw this up, be forced to tell her I can't do it, that I'm all talk. But mostly, I want this part done.

She looks over the instructions again. I hop down and pick up the stuff, because I know she's going to let me fix it.

"Look," I say, walking toward the back of the station wagon. "You hold on to the instructions. Read along with me and we'll do this together. If at any point you want to stop, we stop and you can come back tomorrow and Mike can do it." Mike would do it and not ask questions.

She nods yes and then squares her shoulders, like she's all ready to assist.

"Great. Pop the back and we can start."

She pushes the key cylinder button to pop open the rear window and then swings the rear door open. There are some boxes near the backseat and a smaller box, shoes, a few bags, and some trash near the bumper, where we need to be.

"Sorry," she mumbles, pushing stuff over to make a clear spot for us to work. "I guess I didn't think about how you get at the bulb."

"It's fine."

I help clear a bigger area, moving a box of books and a pair of sneakers to make a spot for her to sit. She climbs in and then pushes the stuff even farther back, so she can scoot back until only the ends of her legs dangle over the bumper. I go ahead and unscrew the screws that hold the taillight assembly in place, but once that's done, I wait for her to look at the next step.

"It says to remove the housing that covers the spare tire."

I fiddle around with the panel and the area that I think is the housing. It doesn't seem to want to budge, and I don't want to break anything. The wagon may look pretty worn on the outside, but the inside is in good condition. "It doesn't say how, does it?"

"Nope," she says, turning the pages over and then back. "At least, not in this part of the manual."

Crap. I didn't think we'd need more of the manual. If we get stuck on this stupid step, I'm going to feel like an idiot.

"Try pulling it." She leans over a little to see, and then lies on her side so she can reach over and pull at the panel. I can feel it wants to give.

"I've got it," I say as it comes off. "Thanks."

I put the housing to the side and wipe my hands on my shorts. She's propped up on her elbow, hand in her hair, stretched out in the back of the wagon. Visions of blankets and her without that dress pop into my head. From the look on her face, she's thinking along the same lines. I wonder how often she's gotten comfy back here.

"Next it says to . . ."

"Unscrew the wing nut, right?" I ask.

"Right."

I unscrew it and look at her, our eyes almost level. She grins at me. I could just climb on in there and we could finish this later. "Next?" I know the steps, but it's her call.

She leans over to look at the pages. "'From the outside of the vehicle, carefully pull the taillamp assembly away from the body.' How are you going to get it off?"

I smile at her face when she realizes what she said, but instead of going for the joke, I say, "Panel pulls," and hold up the plastic tool.

Once I have the taillamp assembly loose, I wait for her next instruction.

"'Press the bulb housing release lever and turn the housing a quarter-turn counterclockwise to remove it.'"

I look at the inside of the assembly, careful not to pull it too far away and break something. "Press the . . . ?"

"'Bulb housing release lever,'" she says, and I can hear her move, and then she's sitting on the edge of the bumper so she can see what I'm doing. "There?" She points to it, and I press the release. "'Turn the housing a quarter-turn counterclockwise to remove it.'"

I turn the housing and it pops out. I use my thigh to hold

the assembly near the car and remove the burned-out bulb. Lucy reaches around to find the replacement bulb and starts to open the package.

"Careful," I say, stopping her and trading her the old bulb for the new package. "You're not supposed to touch the bulb. Hand me that rag?" I open the package carefully, using the plastic to hold the glass end of the bulb in place. Then I slide it free and into the clean rag so I can install it without touching the glass.

Lucy watches, looking more impressed than she probably should, but I like how it feels: her watching my hands, me being proficient. I pop the assembly back in place and then retrace our steps. Screw in the wing nut. Panel in place, screws in and tightened. Done.

She jumps out, slides into the driver's seat, and turns the wagon on. I give her the thumbs-up. Light all fixed. She turns it off and walks back around.

"There you go," I say, tossing the screwdriver into the air. I try to catch it, but I misjudge the distance and it hits my hand and bounces to the ground. "Crap." I chase it as it rolls under the car in the other bay. Lucy laughs. I can't reach it with my foot. I have to lie down and reach under to get it, ruining any cool points I just earned.

"Well, it's done anyway," I say, placing the screwdriver on

the counter, then gathering up the rag, the old bulb, and the cardboard and plastic from the new one. "I'll toss this stuff in the trash later. Otherwise . . ." She's sitting in the back again.

"Someone would see it," she says, leaning back, this time on both elbows, her legs dangling out of the wagon. "You've thought of everything."

My face goes hot at that, so I busy myself with pushing the trash into a neat pile.

"Come here." When I don't move right away, she sits up a little more and tilts her head. "Come on."

I push my hands into my pockets, stupidly nervous. The hard part is over. This is supposed to be the fun part. I lean on the edge of the car, my shoulder against the open back, right above the newly replaced taillight.

I imagined this part, fantasized every night since we made the plan—her flirty *What do I owe you* and my *Don't mention it* and her *Well, the least I could give you is a kiss* and fade to the obvious conclusion. But now that seems silly and stupid. She's real. And I'm more nervous than I've ever been around a girl before. Ever.

"Thanks for doing that," she says. She's picking at something on the floor of the back of the wagon, closer to the serious-faced Lucy who pulled in than the flirty one who's been helping me while stretched out like a cat in the sun.

"And for letting me help. I feel like next time there's something that needs fixing, maybe I could even do it. I never would have tried, but now . . ."

I like knowing I taught her something, that somehow she will remember this, me, whatever happens. "I should wash my hands."

"Come *over* here," she says again, and scoots closer to the edge of the wagon.

My heart's pounding. I'm so glad I put on extra deodorant. She reaches for my hand, pulling me a little closer and then tugging me down until I'm leaning in and she kisses me. Just a touch of her lips on the side of my mouth. She pulls away a little, looks at me, then does it again, more directly over my mouth. On the third kiss, I kiss her back. Then her hands are on my arms and my arms are reaching for her, making us almost topple, and I pull back, both of us laughing.

Climbing in there feels like too much, too fast. I tug her hand and she stands up and I close the rear door and window. She swallows and snaps her mouth closed and starts to dig her keys out. She thinks I'm rejecting her. I stop her hand in her pocket and walk her back until she is leaning against the wagon. Then *I* kiss *her*.

I've kissed other girls, but none who weren't nervous

about kissing a girl. Weren't testing it out one kiss at a time. Lucy is all in. Egging me on.

But our teeth keep hitting until I pull back and take a breath, and then try again.

We bump noses, both trying to lead, until I push my hands into her hair and hold her still so I can kiss her for real. A beat, two, and then I'm in. Tasting the inside of her mouth, feeling the soft wet tease of her tongue.

Then we're taking turns. Small kisses. Then deeper kisses. Not all of them perfect, but all good.

She rubs my arms, encouraging me, humming into my mouth, a happy sound that I can feel.

I push a little closer, and her hands slide down my sides. Her mouth opens and I kiss her deep, feel her give under the kiss, her hands holding me close.

Her fingers knead my hips and sides, but I keep mine in her hair and just focus on kissing her, on all the ways it feels to kiss her and let her kiss me.

There's nothing hesitant in how Lucy kisses.

When the kisses slow, she kisses my neck, and then her mouth is open and hot, sucking. I pull away. I can't risk a mark. Not when she's a secret I plan to keep. She seems to get it and kisses my neck again, soft and teasing, and I let her.

We kiss for a long time, until my lips feel puffy and a little chapped. After the kissing we just stand there, feeling good, until we're leaning there hugging and not really moving.

"I should go," she says.

"Do you have to?" I kiss her jaw.

"Yeah," she says, but not like she's sure.

She looks at the scratches on my cheek, but then she's kissing me again. One long kiss and I pull back, disentangling us. My legs feel like I've hiked five miles. Uphill.

I push my hair back and then look around for the stuff I need to clean up for something to do while she straightens out her dress.

"Free tomorrow?" she asks, untangling her hair where my hands made a mess.

"No, not tomorrow. Sorry." I'm not bailing on Karen and them, not even for this.

"After that I'm in Chicago until Friday," she says. "But I should be back by dinnertime."

"I have to check. If my mom's around, I might not be able to go out." Mom goes overboard on "family dinners" when she's home on weekends. And I don't need her asking *where* and *with who* and everything.

"We can figure it out later. I'll text you."

I don't think she means just about where to meet up next weekend. She steps closer and wraps her arms around my neck, one hand scratching at my short hair. One more kiss and then she's getting into the car, backing out, and leaving.

I think about the kisses all the way home, and then carefully shut Lucy away in the back of my brain during the walk from the barn to the house. Dad's home, and Uncle Skip. No way I can be thinking about Lucy around them.

CHAPTER 12

Lucy texted to say *Thanks again*, and *See you Friday, maybe, hopefully*, and I texted back *No problem*, and *Yeah*, and *I'll try*. I wish I had something better to say, anything to say, so I had an excuse to text her again. But I can't think of anything that doesn't sound stupid or make too big a deal out of this afternoon. Make any deal out of this afternoon. She acted like it happens all the time. Maybe for her it does. Maybe she goes around kissing whatever girls she wants. I'm still caught between disbelief and waiting for her to pretend it was an accident, like the fumes in the service area made her woozy.

I put the casserole in to heat midway through the baseball game, knowing Dad and Uncle Skip will come wandering in looking for dinner as soon as the game is over. Then I scroll around, checking my boards and forums. There was a dustup in the women's area of the prepper forum. The mods locked the threads. I subscribe to the thread so I can weigh in when it reopens.

Just as I'm putting on a load of laundry, I hear a truck on the drive. Then Mark's voice. Great. There goes half the food that's supposed to last us this week.

He dumps a duffel near the laundry room and goes straight to the fridge.

"Casserole's in the oven."

He wrinkles his nose and continues looking.

"I have three more loads to do. Mom's orders. You can do yours later."

"Whatever." He bends over, digging through the containers and bottles until he comes out with the potato salad. He grabs a pop and a fork on the way to the table, not bothering to get a plate, then straddles a chair and starts right in, eating the potato salad from the container. Shoveling it in—two, then three forkfuls.

"That's disgusting." I grab a plate from the cabinet and a serving spoon from the drawer and shove them across the table to him. "We don't need your spit all over the potato salad."

He looks up at me, licks both sides of his fork, and then shoves it into the potato salad, stirring it all around.

"Gross."

He grins around another mouthful of potato salad, letting it squish through his teeth.

I go back to the laundry room, staking my claim before he can sneak in and start a load. I hop up on the counter so I can see the timer for dinner.

Once I'm out of the kitchen, he slumps forward, losing some of his swagger. He pulls his fancy new phone out of his pocket, looking at the screen. I checked out our bill. I don't think it's on our plan. He puts his phone down and shovels in more food, touching the new bruise blooming around his eye with his non-fork hand. The latest in a series, coming from somewhere other than open training sessions. He wears it like a badge.

His phone makes sounds now and then, texts or messages or something, and then it rings.

"What? No, not yet." He takes another gulp of pop and then burps. "Yeah, well, that's my only option, so . . . No. Okay, I'll call as soon as I know. 'Kay. Later." He hangs up and chugs the rest of his pop.

When he gets up from the table, he sees me watching. He puts down the container of potato salad and makes a big deal of licking all over the clean, unused plate. Then he puts the container back in the refrigerator and drops his fork and plate in the sink with a clatter.

"I'm not washing them!"

He flips me off over his shoulder.

I'm not washing them. They can sit there all week and Mom can be as pissed as she wants, but I'm not cleaning up after him.

I move the clothes from the washer to the dryer and then put in a load of my dark clothes. My training clothes really stink. I add a little extra detergent. Next week I'll do a midweek load. Maybe I should add even more detergent and do an extra rinse? But then it will take longer.

"How's it going?" Dad asks from the doorway, making me jump.

"Dinner's ready whenever you are. Might want to avoid the potato salad—Mark might as well have spit in it." Dad makes a face. "And he left his dishes in the sink. I'm not doing them."

"You don't have to," Dad says, sounding tired, maybe tired of us. "What time do you have to be out to Clearview tomorrow?"

"After work." He rubs his forehead. I can almost hear the gears grinding, him thinking hard. The wrinkles on his forehead double. "Karen's picking me up," I say, in case that's his worry, how to get me out there.

"Oh," he says. "Good." Bingo. "That's great." He's so

proud. "I'm glad you're making friends. Your mother is, too."

I snort and close the washer a little too hard. She wouldn't be if she met them, especially Karen. And JoJo. Trinny, Delia, and Cammie look girly enough, but maybe even they aren't girly enough for Mom.

"She is," Dad says. "She just worries." He watches me set the washer. "I assured her you would be supervised tomorrow."

"Mr. Severnsen wouldn't let us use the crossbows unless he was comfortable."

"That's what I told your mother," Dad says with a smile, like he should get points for sticking up for me. He always backs Mark up without expecting demonstrations of gratitude.

I hit start, and the washing machine's noise fills the small laundry room.

I push past Dad and back into the kitchen so I can pull plates from the cabinet for me, Dad, and Uncle Skip. Dad watches me set the table. He's working up to something. I wish he would just spit it out.

"What?" I finally ask when I have to move around him for the second time.

"Maybe we should have some of the girls over for dinner." He pauses, and then says, "On a weekend."

I stop and stare at him.

"You could even invite them to stay over. There's plenty of room." Big smile.

"Is this Mom's idea? She want to vet my friends? Make sure they're actually girls?"

"No, it's my idea. I think it would be nice."

Nice. To have Cammie and Karen and them over for a sleepover. Maybe we could do each other's nails. I'm talking to him about training and he's thinking about slumber parties. Did he think Mark should have his "little friends" over for pizza and video games?

"It's training, Dad."

"Right," he says. "Jim said you were the one who suggested some of the new training sessions, the survival skills and foraging."

"Yeah."

I don't like Riggs and Dad talking about me. Even good talking.

"Well, I think it's great," Dad says. "I'm glad to see you really fitting in out there."

The timer goes off. Uncle Skip comes into the kitchen, and I dish up casserole for the three of us. Saves me from having to talk anymore about Clearview, since we don't really talk about it in front of Uncle Skip.

After dinner, Dad and Uncle Skip retreat back in front

of the TV. I clean up our dishes, then put Mark's back in the sink. I stay at the table, reading more of *The Color Purple*. Since it's gotten good, I've been reading slower.

Lucy finally sends me another text during the last load of laundry, and I hop up on the washer and we text back and forth while it jerks and spins.

Dad and Uncle Skip went to bed a while ago. On my way upstairs, I get a glass of water from the kitchen. Mark's dish and fork are still in the sink. I turn off the light and leave them there.

I turn off the lights in the living room, too. If Mark actually comes downstairs to do laundry, he can turn them all on again.

I'm in bed, texting Lucy, when I hear Dad and Mark down the hall.

"How much?" Dad asks.

I can't hear Mark's response.

"*How* much?" Dad asks again. "Are you crazy? We don't have that kind of money to spare!"

"But it's not to spare. I'll be the only one who doesn't have his own."

"You won't be the only one, I'm sure."

"Dad, do you really want me to tell them that we can't afford to equip me?"

"No," Dad says, "I expect you to tell them that *you* can't afford to buy your own equipment."

A burst of sound from Mark and then, "I've been training so hard. It's been really hard to get up to speed and, and . . . I work, as much as Darnell can use me, but . . ."

"You're an adult now, as you keep reminding us. You have responsibilities. Gas costs money. Maintenance on that truck costs money. Insurance. Food. And equipment costs money. So you need to make more money. More than fun money. We can't float you."

"It's not fair! I don't have time to—"

"If you need equipment, gas, food, then I suggest you start looking for a way to earn it. A real job."

Mark stomps past my room. His bedroom door slams.

The texts backed up while I was listening, and Lucy texted good night.

I reread her texts and then replay every bit of this afternoon. Mostly, I think about how it felt at the end, standing there smushed together. I let my mind, and hands, wander, thinking about next weekend.

"Hey, we need some parts," Mike says loudly, obviously, leaning on the counter, blocking me so I can shove my phone under some papers before Uncle Skip comes into the front and catches me texting for a third time.

"It's not like we're busy," I say, only loud enough for Mike to hear.

He hands me the codes, and I start looking them up.

My phone keeps vibrating against the desk, under the papers, making more noise than if I'd kept it in my hand or shoved it in a pocket.

Uncle Skip comes up behind me, looking at the parts that need to be ordered. "Put that thing away when there are customers in here," he says, heading back to his office. He can't stand waiting for someone to do something because they're "playing" on their phone.

"What's in this?" asks a girl, the kind with too much makeup and her nose in the air.

"Beef jerky." I text Karen to let her know I'm almost done.

"I know that." She rolls her eyes. "I mean: What. Is. It. Made. Out. Of. It doesn't have its ingredients listed." She studies the noncommercial plastic wrapping.

"It's beef jerky, babe," a guy wearing a too-loose tank top says, putting a couple bottles of water and three energy drinks on the counter. "Low carb."

"Oh, good." She grins up at him and puts two sticks on the counter next to the drinks.

"And twenty-five on pump one," he says, pulling out a wad of cash, but when he starts to peel off bills, they're mostly ones. I ring them up. Then they're gone. Too bad. I wanted to watch her take a bite and then tell her the jerky is made by a very hairy guy who dabbles in both food dehydration and taxidermy, when not checking fishing and hunting licenses. The fact that he wrapped it in plastic was a victory for food prep everywhere.

I'm explaining the work and costs to a new customer when Mark saunters in like he owns the place. He grabs a bag of chips off the shelf and opens them, shoving some into his mouth, dropping crumbs. Daring me to stop him. I don't. But I *will* talk to Uncle Skip about Mark's thieving. At least about the chips and lighters and easy stuff. I'm not sure how to bring up the beer and whatever else he grabbed from the back without getting me in trouble, too. Mark probably knows that.

When the clock hits five thirty, I lock up and head back to tell Uncle Skip I'm leaving. I can hear Mark's voice through the partially closed door.

"I'm sorry, Mark. But my answer is no."

"I'll pay you back. Promise. I just haven't been able to find something steady that pays enough for all my expenses, that won't interfere with my responsibilities."

"Responsibilities?" Uncle Skip scoffs. "And anyway, I thought you *were* working. That they would find you work. Isn't that what you said, what your father said, for why you all were—?"

"Okay!" Mark pushes the door open. "Forget I asked."

"That'll be a buck twenty-five." Uncle Skip doesn't move from behind the desk, but it feels like he's stood up. "For the chips."

Mark freezes mid–storming out and looks at the bag in his left hand, and then at Uncle Skip, and at the bag again. His right hand sort of flinches toward his pocket but doesn't make it all the way there.

"Forget it," Uncle Skip says. "But it's the last time. You want something, chips, gas—*whatever*—you pay for it. I agreed to let you work off the costs for your truck, and you haven't even done that. From now on, you're a paying customer."

Mark leaves without answering. The door between the office and storage area slams open.

"I was going to mention that," I say.

"And his rooting around back here, too?"

I stare at my shoes.

"I don't want him hanging around here. No more mooching off the shelves or anywhere else." I nod to show I get it. "You lock up?"

"Yeah. Here's the deposit." I hand him the pouch and pick up my backpack, bulging because of the change of clothes. "If you don't need anything, I'm going to change."

"Okay. See you at home."

"Dad's going to be late, I think, and I'm going out with some friends for a while." He grunts, which means he knows where I'm going.

I change out of my work clothes and into a clean pair of cargos and T-shirt, a long-sleeve shirt tied around my waist in case it's cooler under tree cover.

When I walk around front, Karen's waiting.

"Hey, Bex," she says through the open window, over the loud radio.

"Thanks for picking me up," I say, getting into the car.

"No problem. I had to work, too, so it was more or less on my way." She pulls out of the lot and turns down the radio.

"Where do you work?"

"Home Depot. I know," she says with a self-deprecating grin. "Corporate. But it's a good job."

"I thought you'd work for the Club, for your dad."

"Nah. I don't mind helping out. But that's not a career. I need a career. I'm gonna work my way up. Become a manager." She tilts her head back and forth, like she's continuing the conversation by herself. "I'd be a good manager."

She would be. She has that easy way of getting people to do what she says, sometimes with just a look.

"Clearview's great, but it's not my whole thing." She glances my way a few times, in between watching the road, then shrugs. "I just like to shoot."

I thought Karen would push for a leadership position at Clearview, and maybe speak for the women in the group.

When we get to Clearview, Karen swipes her access card and the gate opens. Some of the guys think the cards are a bad idea because they record who is coming and going, and when. I think that was maybe the point.

Cammie, JoJo, Delia, and Trinny are waiting at the lot.

Cammie looks annoyed, as usual. The only time she doesn't look annoyed is when she's shooting.

We head out to the cleared area that's being used for archery and other nonshooting training, while Karen brings the bows and arrows from the Box on an ATV. She unloads a couple of crossbows and a compound bow, and three quivers of arrows. She immediately hands the compound bow and one of the quivers to Cammie.

Cammie looks over the compound bow. She already has her arm guard, glove, and release strapped on.

It's like none of us are here anymore. It's just Cammie and the bow and the targets.

She nocks an arrow and brings the bow up, facing the targets. Her body is curved slightly, and her shoulders opened, as her right hand pulls back near her cheek. She holds her form while she sights through the scope, and then lets the arrow sail. It hits the second ring. On the second arrow, she seems to hold her form longer, sighting more carefully. That one hits the far edge of the center circle. Three and four hit closer to the center.

"Who's next?" she asks.

JoJo's game, but after Cammie shows her how, JoJo's first arrow lands far short of the target. I start to feel a little less pressure, watching Cammie work with JoJo.

"We usually just use crossbows," Trinny says. "But Cammie says we need to know how to do it this way, too."

"You never know what will come in handy," Cammie says. "Plus, the guys won't bother. So when we do archery, you'll all be ahead of them."

Cammie turns, finds Delia, and crooks her finger, motioning Delia forward. While Delia is putting on the arm guard, Cammie says, "Practice until you can hit the target right out of the gate." She stares into Delia's eyes. "When the time comes, hit two or three good ones. Then let them saunter up and miss by a mile."

That would show the mouth-breathers, the ones who

think that Delia shouldn't even be here. I can't wait to see Devon's and Neal's faces.

"What if I can't?" Delia asks.

"You can." Cammie hands Delia a glove and release. There is no question about *can't*. Cammie won't allow her to fail in front of those guys.

Cammie shows Delia how to hold the bow, and I move a little closer to listen. I try to commit the lesson to memory.

Delia and Cammie are like chess pieces, light and dark, but both tall and curvy and strong.

Delia is really struggling to follow Cammie's directions. But Cammie just starts over again, until Delia shoots an arrow that actually hits the target—not in the colors, but still, on the target. When Delia makes ready for the next one all on her own, Cammie steps back, next to Karen.

"You up for it?" Cammie asks over her shoulder, but I know she's talking to me.

"Sure," I say, walking up to stand closer to her and watch. "I've never used a compound bow before."

Delia lands two in the rings and then hands off the bow with a grin.

Cammie helps me get the release on my right hand and shows me how to nock the arrow and connect the release to the loop attached to the string.

"Okay, now, stand like you are in the batter's box. Open your hips a little more," Cammie says, touching my right hip. She keeps her hand on my hip as I pull the bow up, pull the arrow back, and rest my hand near my cheek. "Use the sights." I line up the arrow like she tells me and take aim. It feels awkward, but I know I'm holding it right. I sight along my arm and let it fly. The arrow lands on the white part just outside the largest ring.

"Relax your arm," Cammie says, and then she's closer. She hands me another arrow. I nock it, connect the release, and pull back. "Relax," she says, almost into my ear, tapping my extended arm, holding the bow. This is the Cammie who shoots, all serious and focused. But focused on me. "There," she says, touching my arm. "Don't force it. Take your aim, and then a clean release, but hold your form until the arrow hits."

My pulse is pounding. I breathe in and out to try to calm the waves of tremors moving through me. In. Out. In again, and on the exhale I let go.

"Better," Cammie says quietly, not as close but still nearby.

She hands me another arrow. I pull back and line up the shot, try to relax my arm, adjust the sight a little to the left, breathe in, out, and let go. Not center, but in the colors.

Cammie's withdrawal is respect. She's leaving me to work it out. But I can still feel her behind me, focused on me.

I let a few more fly, until one just nudges the center circle.

"Good," Cammie says from behind me. "Stop on that one."

My arms feel tight and heavy, nerves flowing down and out through my fingertips.

"Now for some real fun," Karen says.

Everyone takes turns with one of the crossbows. They're harder to load, especially the bigger one, which even Cammie has trouble getting cocked and loaded on her own. But they're easier to shoot, with sights, stocks, and triggers like a rifle.

My aim is way better with the crossbow, and yet I'd like another shot with the compound bow sometime.

Instead of taking a second turn with the crossbow, Cammie moves to the far position, steps back another ten feet, and sends arrow after arrow into the target with the compound bow. Like it was made for her. I can only imagine what she could do with one that actually was made for her, to her exact measurements and preferences.

I feel Karen next to me, but I don't stop watching Cammie.

"Amazing, right?"

I just nod.

I glance back, and the others are gone already.

"She'll go all night if we let her."

"I don't have anywhere I need to be," I say.

"Neither do I."

We just watch Cammie.

"She's *really* good," I say.

"Yeah," Karen says. "She used to compete."

"Why'd she quit?"

"I had better things to do," Cammie says, resting the bow and making Karen smirk and my face flame.

But it makes me wonder if her better things are like my better things. MAG kind of better things. Cammie and Karen and I make a good team.

An ATV on the trail gets Karen's attention. We don't hear them that often.

"Hey," Carl says, pulling up next to the ATV Karen drove out here. "Hey," he says again, out of breath but looking relieved.

"Hey," Karen says back, but I feel like I'm missing something. "What's going on?"

"Nothing," Carl says, but I don't buy it any more than Karen does.

"What?" she asks, holding his stare.

Carl looks at Cammie and me, and then I guess decides we're trustworthy. "Ferguson had a team out marking and clearing the red trail extension. They heard shots and maybe a small detonation out near the perimeter, past the end of the blue trail. Randy and your dad are going to check it out."

"And you wanted to make sure we were where I said we'd be," Karen says more than asks.

His lopsided smile says it all. "I just wanted to be sure."

"Well, we're here," Cammie says, annoyed and dismissing him.

"Just Dad and Randy?" Karen asks.

"Frank's with them, and I'm going to follow. I just wanted to check here first."

"Do you need me to go with?" Karen asks.

"Nah, we got it."

"Be careful."

"Will do," he says, heading out on the trail.

She turns and looks at Cammie, like she's waiting for Cammie to say something. Cammie scowls, like Karen shouldn't have to ask.

"He was just checking," Karen says.

"He should know we're not stupid enough to shoot off-trail in the blind." Cammie puts the compound bow on the ATV and starts removing her gear.

Their chill remains all the way back to the Box. Cammie hops off the ATV and heads for the lot before we're even parked, leaving Karen and me to carry the bows and quivers inside.

"My dad back yet?" Karen asks the guy inside, who takes the bows from her.

He shakes his head. "Not yet. But radioed in. They're heading back."

"Everything okay?" she asks.

"Yeah, just some idiots screwing around." He shakes his head.

"Without permission or logging where they'd be?"

"Apparently." He glances at me and doesn't offer anything more.

Karen curses under her breath. "Who?"

"Two guesses," he says.

Karen looks at me, and I don't know how, but I know it was Zach and them. "Mark?" I ask. "Uh, Mark Mullin?"

"Her brother," Karen adds, and then nods to him, like *Go ahead, tell her.*

"No Mullin," he says.

Thank God.

Karen is quiet all the way to the lot and until we pass through the gate.

"Mark should stay away from Zach," Karen says, breaking the silence.

"No shit." Not that I could tell him that. It would make

him run to Zach all the faster. But maybe I should say something to Dad.

"Cammie and I meet at the range on Wednesday mornings for a few hours. You should come."

"Can't," I say. "I have to work." But I'm already calculating the loss of a few hours' pay compared to shooting, with friends—or whatever we are.

CHAPTER 13

As soon as Mike locks the front door, I bring Uncle Skip all of today's paperwork and deposits, and then duck into the bathroom to clean up. My hair looks like crap. The ends are starting to curl, the long layer is too long, the sides are patchy, and the back is a hacked-up mess. I brought some gel so I can try to make the layer hang straight, but I need to cut it again. Or cut it different. Or maybe just buzz it all.

I brush my teeth with my finger and then pop in some gum. I've kissed a lot of girls. Felt up a few. Gotten horizontal with two, though with both of them, my hands stayed above the waist and clothes stayed mainly on. Before Kara moved, we were inching closer to more, grinding against each other until I swear I could feel her through both our clothes. But I didn't work up the nerve to touch below her waist.

Lucy's texts have been melting my phone. She's not going to red-flag me, which actually makes me more nervous than if

I was sure she would. With the others I didn't have to think about it, because someone else was in charge of drawing the line. I could just go with it. But tonight, I think that line is on me.

And as much as thinking about making out is making me sweat, it's the not-making-out parts that have my stomach all twisted in knots. What if she wants to go to the movies and hold hands and be all obvious?

I hear Mike and Uncle Skip talking in the office and quickly repack my stuff. I said I'd meet her at the church lot, instead of her coming here to get me. Best not to give Uncle Skip any reason to ask questions or to mention her to Dad. As long as Dad thinks I'm hanging out with Clearview girls, he doesn't ask questions. In fact, I think he'd encourage me to go out as much as I want if he thought it would help cement his position at Clearview.

I stash my work clothes in the storage room and walk quickly to the back door.

"Bex?" Mike leans out from the office. "Where are you going all cleaned up?"

"Out with friends."

"Which friends?" Uncle Skip asks, standing in the doorway to the office. "Girls from out there?" He follows "out there" with a little shake of his head.

"Uh, yeah," I say. "See you later."

I don't give him a chance to ask any more questions.

It takes no time at all to cut across the back field, hop the fence, and get to the service road, then I cross another stretch of grass to the road the church is on. At the curve before the church, a horn sounds behind me, and I turn to see Lucy's wagon pulling up.

"Hey, need a lift?" Lucy flips her sunglasses up on top of her head. I get in, put my backpack by my feet, and buckle the seat belt. When I look up, Lucy is rebuckling her seat belt. She would only have unbuckled it so she could reach me. So we could kiss. I start to unbuckle mine again, but she's dropped her sunglasses down over her eyes and is pulling onto the road, heading west.

"Where to?" she asks. "Did you eat?"

"Dinner? No." I run through the places we could go and not be seen. I calculate the odds of pissing her off if I suggest somewhere no one will know me. "Did you?"

"Nope. And I feel like pizza. I know a great place."

Please not Gino's. Please not Gino's. Please not—

"You don't mind a drive, do you? It's about a half-hour away but worth it."

My stomach crawls back down into my gut and my heart slows. "I never mind a drive," I say, smiling at her.

"Great." She gives the wagon some gas and changes lanes.

She starts singing along to the radio, the wind through the windows whipping her hair around, and that confident smile on her face. Maybe I should pinch myself.

As we drive, my muscles relax. First my legs. Then my arms and shoulders. My neck. We don't really talk, just comment on things we pass or songs on the radio. I can't believe I'm here with her.

"Rough day?" she asks, finally pulling off the highway.

"No. Why?"

"You've been quiet, and you just let out a big sigh like you were finally shaking off the day."

"I didn't mean to be quiet or, well . . . Did you want to talk? We could've talked or . . ."

"It's fine. I didn't mind. I just wondered." A few turns and we're in the heart of a small town, on a side street where she pulls up next to a pickup and lines up to park.

"I don't think it will fit."

"That's what *he* said." Lucy laughs at her own joke.

She eyes the car behind her and then backs up slowly, cutting the wheel and sliding into the spot. Then she turns around and uses both hands on the wheel to slot the car right in between the other two. She doesn't even have to correct forward.

She is so pleased with herself. She's probably pleased with herself a lot.

Out of the car, I get a look at her. Another dress, but this one is newer, with little sleeves and pockets. And she's wearing sandals instead of boots. When she twirls onto the sidewalk, the skirt poofs out a little. Her eyes glitter with mischief. On impulse, I take her hand, but then I see an older couple walking toward us and I let go.

The place looks like a bar, but Lucy banks left when we walk in, and there are booths and tables, paper place mats with maps of Italy. She slides into a booth near the window. I scan the other tables. No one's looking at us.

She quizzes me about how I like my pizza, and I let her order.

When they bring her iced tea, she dumps in four packets of sugar, takes a sip, adds another packet, sips again, and then nods approvingly.

"I miss sweet tea," she says. "That's about all I miss, but I miss it a lot."

"What about your parents?"

She shrugs. "We text. And I'll see them in August." She stirs some more, then takes another sip.

"Any siblings?"

"Nope. Just me. No cousins, either. At least unless

Uncle Trevor and Dennis decide to get his-and-his matching designer babies."

I look at the other tables.

"But, frankly, I don't see that happening. They like to travel and party too much. Too much linen and silk and cashmere in their wardrobes."

"So he's . . ."

"A photographer. And his husband is a makeup artist. They met on some commercial shoot twelve years ago."

I look around again. No one else seems to have heard, but I lean in a little closer so I can talk more quietly, so maybe Lucy will, too.

"Your grandparents are okay with that?"

"With him not having kids?" Lucy asks, louder than necessary.

"No. With him being . . ."

Lucy stares, confused, but she can't really be. "Gay?" she asks, way too loud. "Now they are. I mean, they're not all PFLAGed up like my parents, but they're fine with it. Aren't yours?" I squirm in my seat. "It's okay if they're not." She looks at me. "Or . . . if you're not . . . out?" she asks, but I'm not sure it really is okay.

The pizza arrives before I can say anything, and there is a mess of shifting glasses and napkins and a back-and-forth with the waitress about hot-pepper flakes and more tea, and more sugar, before I have to answer.

I take a large bite of pizza to buy time, scorching the roof of my mouth, gasping in air, and trying to peel the molten cheese off. I swallow the bite, still scalding and nearly whole, and then gulp my pop, trying to cool my mouth and throat.

"It really is okay," she says. "I mean, I just assumed they'd know because . . ." She takes another bite and chews, using her pizza to motion to my hair and the rest of me. "But if they don't know, that's okay. I don't care. Not like some of these dykes who make it all political."

I force myself to swallow the pop without choking too bad. I can't believe she just said "dyke." Not even whispering.

She looks at me, and then around the restaurant, and then back at me. "Are you okay?"

"Yeah." I pick up my pizza and take another bite. I chew and swallow, watching her do the same. I glance around. No one is looking at us. No one cares. The pizza really is good. "This is great."

"See?" she says, relaxing. "What'd I tell you?"

The waitress brings us more to drink, and we talk in between devouring most of the pizza. As we slow down to picking at our respective last slices, I realize that at some point I stopped feeling on display. I forgot that anyone else might be listening in. Lucy tells me about North Carolina and her parents and some of her friends. About college and her grandparents. And I forget to be worried. About this. About being seen. About anything.

I pay, leaving what I hope is a nice-enough tip, and then we're on the street, walking back to the ice-cream place we passed on our way from the car.

Inside, the AC is cold enough to raise penguins, and there's a crowd. We take our place in line and wait. Lucy is bouncing up and down, rubbing her arms, freezing in her little dress. I shrug out of my button-down and hold it out to her. My bare arms prickle up fast, but everything else feels real good watching her shrug on my shirt. She tries to pull it closed across her chest, which is far from happening. We both laugh.

"I'd be mortified if I wasn't so cold." She laughs some more and hangs on my arm.

I rub my palms on the rough sides of my cargo shorts, and then realize that what I'm feeling is a stare from the right. A couple sitting at one of the few tables is looking at us, dissecting us. Dissecting me. They're staring at my chest, trying to figure out what I am. Lately, people have been staring at my head instead.

When I turn to look at the menu board above the heads of the scoopers, I notice the guys up front jostling and laughing, checking out Lucy. They barely look at me, but their girls do. One stares, a disgusted look on her face. I want to leave, but Lucy is already picking out flavors.

One of the guys says, "I'll warm her up," and the others laugh, loud and ugly. Lucy turns to me too deliberately and says too brightly, "What kind are you getting?"

She knows they're talking about her. She knows. "Not sure." She's aware of it all. "What about you?"

"Mmmm," she says, drawing it out and studying the case now that we're close enough to see in. "I'm intrigued by the key-lime pie, but that could be a mistake if it's really fakey lime with bits of cardboardy crust. I could get coffee chip or chocolate marshmallow. I'm not sure." She takes my hand. "They all look good."

I'm afraid to move. Afraid to look at them. Afraid to look at her and let her see my eyes. But I also can't let go of her hand. It's like she's asking me to stand here with her, and I can't say no.

"Sick," one of them hisses.

I don't look but I feel the group moving past us, their space pushing at ours.

"You should ditch that and come with us," says one of the guys. Without even turning, we both know they're talking to Lucy. "You can sit on my lap." Laughter.

She doesn't react at all. I stare at the mint chip and brace for impact. If I have to fight, I will. But I'll have to get Lucy behind me. Maybe the old couple will keep them from doing anything, at least in here. But in here would be better than later, outside. The bell on the door jingles and jingles, and then there's quiet. Quiet enough to hear the whir of the AC and some music on somewhere in the back. Lucy squeezes my hand and then lets go.

"The chocolate marshmallow. Definitely. Two scoops?" she says to the girl behind the counter. "In a cup. With sprinkles." She's pleased with her choice. "Bex?"

"Strawberry," I say, without even thinking about it. "In a cone." Just like I'm five.

We stand there in the shop, both taking our first tastes. Lucy makes yummy sounds. I scope out the scene outside, checking if any of those guys are still there. I walk over to the trash can near the door and take my time throwing away a napkin and getting another, and another, scanning the street.

"Want to walk?" She looks so happy with her ice cream, so at ease. Even the old couple seems to have forgotten about us. "Come on," she says, moving toward the door.

Outside, it's warmer, but Lucy keeps my shirt.

I scan the street in all directions and look toward where

the car is parked to see what's ahead. I glance back behind us as we start to walk.

"They're gone," Lucy says, and so is her overly bright giddiness. She takes another heaping spoonful, tilting her head to catch the sprinkles falling off her spoon.

"How do you know?" I ask, still scanning the street.

"Jerks like that are all talk." I stare at her, wondering how she knows that, how for sure, and then her serious face breaks. "And I saw them drive off heading out of town in the opposite direction."

"I didn't think you saw them at first." I lick around the bottom of the cone to keep it from dripping.

"They were looking when we came in. That's why their girls were pissed. But then they figured it out." She pauses to eat a huge spoonful. "They were embarrassed for getting caught looking. The rest was cover."

"You don't seem fazed at all."

"I'm used to it." She takes a seat on a bench. "I had boobs at eleven. By twelve I looked sixteen. You get used to being looked at, to shit being said. When I started dating girls, it got weirder, more hostile. But most of the time it's all talk."

I realize I'm still staring at her chest, and look away. "Most of the time?"

She takes a big bite of ice cream, works it around in her mouth, swallows. "Yes."

She doesn't want to talk about it, but there's a slip in her "I'm cool" cover. They did freak her out, more than a little.

I push the ice cream into my cone with my tongue and start biting around the rim of the cone.

"What about you?" she asks.

"What?"

"Come on," she says. "You get shit, too. You have to."

I shrug and keep eating.

"Fine." She tosses the nearly empty cup in the trash, a little harder than necessary.

"Sure," I say. "But not like that. Mostly it's people trying to figure out what I am, sometimes a mumbled 'freak' or some guys might drop 'dyke' or whatever. But not like that. Not like they're checking me out or anything." I finish my cone and get up to throw away the napkins in the can on her side of the bench. "Guys don't look at me that way."

Guys have never looked at me the way those guys looked at Lucy, which is fine by me. Now it seems like it's always the ones who would stare at girls like Lucy who go out of their way to be nasty to me. I've thought I might have to fight before, but that was a hundred times scarier.

I hold out my hand. She takes it and we continue walking toward the car, hands swinging between us.

"But the 'What are you?' crap sucks," she says, like she knows.

"Sometimes." She gives me a look, like *fair's fair*. "Yeah. When it's a kid or just a double take, whatever, fine. But it sucks when people get mad. Like it's suddenly my problem that they feel uncomfortable or whatever." Like my being in the next stall while they pee is dangerous to them. "They act like I'm doing it on purpose just to screw with them. Or like I'm cheating or something."

She nods. "My friend Jenny transitioned in ninth. People got really weird about it. Some of the lesbians worst of all. Like a straight trans girl was an affront to everything ever."

Straight trans . . . Wait. What?

"Can I ask you something?" Lucy asks, stopping me before I can get in the car. I feel the heat in my face already. I don't even understand what she just said, and now she's going to ask me something I don't know how to answer and think I'm stupid. "What happened?" She reaches out and touches my cheek where the scrapes were.

Oh. Okay. I touch my cheek. "It was nothing." I walk around the car to get in. After she is in, she sits there, waiting for more. "Really," I say, hoping we can postpone this conversation until later. I have no idea what she would think about Clearview or how much to say. We haven't really talked about politics or anything that would tell me if she would even understand training, or if it would weird her out. And I still don't really get if Clearview is supposed to be a secret or not, or how much of it is supposed to be a secret.

She's quiet. Not making any move to drive. She's looking at me like she thinks someone has been beating on me, like I need protection. If only she knew.

"I would have protected you." I didn't mean to say that, but now that it's said I don't take it back.

"From those guys?"

"Yes."

She looks dubious. "From three guys who are bigger than you. And their girls."

"Maybe not all at once, but good enough to get us away, or get you away, anyway. I've been training."

"Training? Like fighting?"

"Defensive tactics. Hand-to-hand. But, yeah, fighting."

"That's what the bruises and scratches were from?"

"Yes."

She thinks it over. "You'd really have taken them on?"

"I wouldn't have started it," I say. "And if there was any

way to just defuse it and leave, I would. I'm not stupid." She nods. "But if they tried to touch you?" I wait for her to look up from under a curtain of dark brown hair. "Then yes. I would have put myself between them and you. And they would not have touched you."

"I can take care of myself."

I can't tell if she's mad or impressed or something else. "I'm sure you can. You did, in fact. But I just wanted you to know that. I was being cautious, making sure they were gone, because I wasn't looking for a fight. But if they'd tried something, I would have protected you."

She takes a deep breath and lets it out. I'm not exactly sure what it means, but it feels important.

I scoot across the seat, duck under her hair, and kiss her. Just a small kiss, and then another, and then she turns toward me and opens her mouth, and this is where I've wanted to be all day, all week. Forever.

We kiss for a few minutes, just kissing. Last time I was so nervous, and then it was all almost too much, and hours later I couldn't remember all these things I wanted to remember, to relive. I try to focus on the details of kissing her, how her mouth feels, how soft her lips are, the sounds she makes. I slide my hand into her hair and let my other hand rest on her leg, over her dress, just keeping us connected. I can smell her skin. She touches my arm, holding me close, and we take turns kissing until we both lean back. I know we should go, and not keep kissing in a car, on display here. Maybe she does, too.

She puts the key in the ignition and tucks her hair behind her ears, smooths out her dress, like she's trying to make herself presentable. I shift around until my baggy cargos aren't all twisted and bunched, then fasten my seat belt.

I love kissing her. And how she smells.

"Where to now? Unless you need to go home?"

"I don't really have a curfew." Not when Mom's staying with Aunt Lorraine and Dad thinks I'm out with Cammie and Karen or whoever.

"My grandparents are out. Won't be home until late. We could go there?"

"If they wouldn't mind," I say, testing if that's what she wants.

"Nope." She smiles and her face flushes. "They won't mind."

I hold her hand across the seat while she drives.

Lucy's grandparents' house is about as far east of the station as Uncle Skip's house is west. Like Uncle Skip's place, it's surrounded by what used to be family farms, but her grandparents obviously sold off parcels a while ago, because you can see other houses from their porch.

Lucy leads me in by the hand, showing off the pictures of her all over the place. The mantel. The walls. Pictures of her mom and dad, too. Her uncle and his husband, and it still feels weird to hear her say that.

Her fingers are perfectly entwined with mine. And so smooth.

Her room is in the back of the house, displaying bits of her from every summer. Trophies and camp crafts and fair prizes. If we had met last year—at the station or wherever—would she have even seen me, looking like Mom wanted me to look? Lucy kicks off her sandals and sits down on the side of the bed.

I walk around the room, looking at this picture and that, asking questions, trying to figure out what I'm supposed to do and what I want to do and if my stomach is rejecting the pizza and ice cream, or if I'm just freaking out.

"Bex," she says when I'm getting ready to start lap three. She leans back on the bed, her elbows propping her up, legs slightly spread. I can see the outline of her legs through her dress. The soft curves of her belly and hips. Her breasts, but I try not to stare.

Am I supposed to just get into bed with her?

All my nerves are jangling and snapping.

She slowly smiles and then sits up. Then she stands up. "Want to see if there's a movie on?"

"Yeah. Sure." The butterflies calm down, replaced by disappointment, as I follow her to the living room. And then frustration, at myself and what a coward I am.

She hands me the clicker, points at the couch, and says, "I'm getting some tea. Want some?"

"Does the tea have sugar?"

"Yes," she says, like my question was insulting *and* stupid.

"Then water. Please," I add as an afterthought.

I check my phone, trying to ignore the sweat breaking out on my palms and neck and the backs of my knees. Relieved sweat. Disappointed sweat. You're-an-idiot sweat. I could have gotten into bed with her. Or at least *on* the bed with her. She probably thinks I'm stupid or a baby. Or not that into her. Which is amazingly wrong.

After she puts our drinks down, she takes the clicker from me and goes straight to the menu option, scrolling fast, until she finds something she deems worthy. I don't know what it is, and I don't care.

We watch for just a few minutes. Sipping our drinks and then putting them back. I can't get comfortable on the itchy tweedy couch. She crosses and uncrosses her legs and taps her hand on her knee every few minutes.

Maybe she's nervous, too. Or maybe she's bored. Or maybe she thinks I am.

I reach over and put my hand on her hand, just as she was getting ready to tap again. She looks at our hands and then at me. And then she smiles and turns her hand over so we are holding hands. It's nice, for like five minutes, and then it's awkward again. And my palm is sweaty. We both lean forward for our drinks at almost the same time, and our hands sort of pull between us. It's funny and stupid and weird and nice. We both put our glasses back on their coasters and then look at each other. The light from the TV flickers blue-green and then light across her face.

She turns so she's sort of facing me and mutes the TV.

I wish I had put on more ChapStick.

We both lean forward at the same time, hesitate, and then lean closer. Our mouths hit, and it's only sort of a kiss. She pushes forward and grabs hold of my hip so we can kiss longer.

When I shift closer, she does, too, and then I can get my arm around her shoulders and she's leaning into me, and we can relax into each other.

She's kissing me harder. Her fingers grip and regrip at the sides of my shorts. Too hard. I pull back, to swallow and breathe and find that good place again.

Her hands relax, I turn a little more, so does she, and then it's like we slot into place. Her chest against mine. I can feel myself smiling at her, at how it feels to feel her pressed against me.

Her face is pink and blotchy from the tweedy couch and my face and my hands, her lips puffy and red. She doesn't look at all interested in stopping. She pulls me closer until I'm sort of leaning over her, bracing my weight with the arm trapped between her and the back of the couch.

"Wait. Ouch." She turns, twisting, and I have to grab the couch not to topple to the floor. She yanks on my shorts to keep me with her until we can get situated on our sides, face-to-face. "Better," she says, and then she kisses me again.

But now we are lying down, pressed together, as much so I don't fall off as to be close. Her leg is between my knees, and she turns just enough to hook me closer.

She pushes and pulls and breathes into my mouth until I slide my arms under hers and lift her closer. This is very good. All of it. How warm she is where we touch, almost too warm with the summer night and the tweedy couch itching my neck and arm and leg, and the heat coming from her where we are tangled. How her mouth feels. How we take turns being in control and then it's like no one's in control, and I'm touching her, her back, her hip, and she's pushing against my leg, and it's all very, very good.

Until the bright lights shine through the windows and sweep around the room, a car coming down the drive, and we are scrambling to right ourselves and move apart and turn the sound on and act normal before her grandparents come through the front door.

CHAPTER 14

"What?" I ask, putting my phone down under the table. After weeks of no Mom and preoccupied Dad, I've gotten used to texting Lucy as much as I want.

"I said, where were you last night?" Mom asks.

"Out. With a friend."

"One of those girls?" Mom asks.

"No, I made a new friend, not from Clearview, while you were away, in all my free time between training and work at the station and cooking Dad dinner and doing the laundry."

She gives me that *watch your mouth* look, but it shuts her up. And I didn't lie.

"What did you do, with . . . ?"

Crap. "Stacy." Crapcrap.

"With Stacy," Mom says.

"Went for pizza, walked around, got some ice cream, hung

out . . ." I shrug as if it's no big deal. If no big deal is Lucy and me and full-body, all-in kissing.

Lucy would have been too easy for Dad to check out, if Mom pressed him. There aren't *that* many girls. And I couldn't say Karen or Cammie without Dad maybe bringing it up with their dads and finding out they were somewhere else last night, maybe even Clearview. But Stacy only comes sometimes, and her dad isn't in the inner circle. Hanging with Stacy wouldn't be impressive enough for Dad to care. At least I hope not.

So far I've been able to just dodge Dad, making sure I get home before him once in a while, so he won't ask where I've been. And he's been so obsessed with impressing Riggs these past few weeks, it hasn't been hard. But Mom's not as easy to dodge, at least when she's here.

"Bex? Get a move on!" Dad yells across the upstairs.

"I'm already downstairs," I yell back.

"Please," Mom says, rubbing her temples. She hasn't brought up wanting to meet any of my "friends." Dad hinted last night in front of Mom, and she left the hints hanging there.

She's got to be at war with herself: happy I have friends, worried about who they are, wanting to meet them and make sure they are "the right kind of girls," kind of afraid they're not.

Knowing Mom, she'll make some kind of rule like I have to bring them by before we can go out next weekend. Maybe she'll say I have to be picked up here, so she can meet exactly who I'm going out with and ask questions. There is no way Mom can meet Lucy. Mom's not stupid, even if she pretends to be. Lucy would be too much to ignore.

"You could come with us today," I say, keeping my face blank. "Meet some of the girls, see me train. Some of the other parents might be around. We can wait, if you change fast."

Do not smile. Innocent face.

She turns around to go pour Dad a cup of coffee, pretending to think about it.

Do not smile.

There is no way Mom would go out to Clearview, but now it's on her if she doesn't want to meet my "new friends."

My phone buzzes in my hand. Another text from Lucy. My face flames. I shove my phone in my pocket. It vibrates again. I can't read these in front of Mom.

Cammie gives me the nonverbal signal to advance. I sight around the barrier, check the position of my other team members, and then move low and fast, in an irregular line, to the next obstacle. I scan the area in front, sight on Randy, and then get ready to cover, keeping some space between me and the barrier as if I were holding my rifle. I signal Cammie it's clear.

She has so easily slipped into command of this team.

Without even really talking about it, Cammie, Karen, JoJo, Delia, and I, and sometimes Stacy or Trinny, have become a team. A unit. With Cammie clearly in charge. Sometimes they break us up or some of the guys will be paired with us, and it's fine. But it's not the same.

I hold my position as I hear movement, and then Cammie is at the other end of the obstacle, parallel to me. Intensity radiates off her, like it's not just a positioning drill.

She makes eye contact, and for a second my stomach drops like this is for real. I'd follow her into hostile territory. I'd follow her anywhere. She signals eyes forward, and I realize Randy has shifted position. I adjust my body to keep the barrels and boards as cover from Randy's sight lines. Cammie adjusts at the other end of the barrier as Randy steps to the left and looks her way.

Cammie checks me and then signals Karen. I can hear Karen advance forward to the set of obstacles behind us, and I cover her, keeping Randy in my sights but my body covered. Cammie waits for my signal, and then I shift to the left to keep him engaged as Cammie advances to the barrier forward and left. I hear movement, probably Delia taking position parallel to Karen.

Then nothing. I want to look back, but I can't. I'm their cover.

"JoJo," Karen says behind me, and JoJo advances to take

Cammie's place parallel to me behind the barrier. Karen shouldn't have had to say her name. And now JoJo is hugging the barrier too close. If she were holding a weapon, it would be pushed up against the barrier. And even then, she's too close. It's not giving her any cover from Randy. He tells us to hold so he can correct JoJo's position and show her how to adjust to targets in front of her but keep the barrier as cover.

"Good," Randy says. "That's it for today."

I relax my body, stretch out my tight muscles from holding position for so long.

We are a far cry from simulations, especially doing anything with weapons or live ammo, but it's a beginning. Drills going from prone to kneeling to standing. Moving while tracking a target. Actual organized maneuvers. Advance and retreat. Scouting. Eventually, defending against an ambush. Then, in real terrain. Eventually, armed. Cammie and Karen, JoJo, Delia, maybe Trinny or Stacy, maybe even some of the guys. Maybe a squad. Or squads.

This is what I wanted. What *we* wanted. Each group looks like I feel. Even Daniel and the older guys. Their group actually moved at near full speed, with coordinated communication. They've obviously done this before, enough to be beyond basics. But they aren't looking bored and above it all, like they usually do. Maybe even they can see that eventually we can all do this. They think they'll be in charge, and we can deal with that later. But we're moving toward readiness.

And none of the open-carry idiots were here to snark or argue about everything. No Zach or Mark, with their bullshit, trying to show off. The other guys are more focused without them.

The group runs better without them.

But where is Mark? He's supposed to be here. Dad thinks he's here.

"Bex," Cammie says.

"Oh, sorry, I . . ."

"You want to go to the range for a while?" Cammie asks. She never asks. She shows me respect in training, but she's not friendly. Karen is always the one to ask me to do things. But Cammie asked me this time. Is it because of the drills? That I did well? Or are we actually becoming friends?

"My dad found me a really cool engraved Colt forty-five," Karen says. "One round each, except for me. I have three to overlap. Loser serenades us at lunch." Like making her overlap her shots is enough of a handicap. She sees me hesitate and says, "No one's going to be around. It's fine." I hadn't even thought about that, that I'm not supposed to shoot a handgun, and Delia's probably not supposed to, either, not without a parent present.

"Seriously," Delia says. "No one cares." She nods encouragement.

Riggs does, I'm pretty sure. And maybe Randy. But if Delia thinks it's okay, maybe. But the real problem is Mom and her sudden need for "family time."

"I can't." Dammit. "My mom's expecting me home."

"Next time," Karen says, but it feels like the others think I'm scared or something. Or I don't want to.

Maybe Dad would cover for me, say he needed to stay for a meeting.

"Hey," I say. They turn around. "Let me check if my dad is still in a meeting. If he is, I'll meet you there."

"Will do," Karen says, and Cammie nods. Not a smile, but acknowledgment. Actual reaction. Maybe I can go for just a little while.

I don't get a signal out by the training ranges, so I watch my phone as I run to the lot, where I'm supposed to meet up with Dad. As soon as I have any signal, I text him. I take a seat on top of a picnic table and watch the lot, and my phone. Then I text him again. And again.

We're already late. How much worse could it be? I could just text Dad and tell him I'll be late. He can wait for me for a change.

"Waiting for your father?"

Riggs. Great. "Yes, sir." He's coming from the lot, one of those leather notebook holders under his arm, looking even more like a country-club lawyer than usual.

"I thought so. He should be here any minute. We left about the same time."

Two other members of the executive board continue on to the admin building.

So today's meeting included Riggs and some of the exec board. No wonder Dad was nervous.

"Want half?"

"Huh?"

He holds out half a sandwich. "Go ahead."

I accept the sandwich because it feels rude not to, and he takes a large bite of the other half, chewing slowly, like people do in commercials. Like he's going to turn my way, flash a huge smile, and the voice-over will praise the quality of the bread or the mayonnaise, or maybe some drug for old guys so their hearts don't explode. That would make me his commercial daughter. Great.

He takes another bite of his half and looks at mine. It's too late to give it back, and it would be rude to throw it away or put it down on the table. And Dad still isn't here.

My stomach gurgles. I take a small bite. Not bad. I take a larger bite, then dig my water bottle out of my bag. If it were

Karen or Cammie or even one of the guys, I'd offer them a swig from the bottle. But this is Riggs. It's weird enough to be sharing his sandwich.

"Training going well?"

"Yes," I say, but it feels like he wasn't really expecting an answer.

He nods as he chews, swallows, and then says, "Randy and Carl have been very pleased with your efforts in training."

"Thank you."

"They've actually been very pleased with the entire core group that has been coming consistently. Randy has nothing but praise." He means about me specifically, I think. "And that means something, coming from Randy."

Yeah, no kidding.

I shiver as a breeze brushes over my arms and neck.

"How is Mark?"

I choke on my water and sputter to clear it. "Fine."

"Good." He takes another bite. Chews. Swallows. "I ask because I haven't seen him around lately." Another bite, chewed and swallowed. How long can he nurse half a sandwich? "Darnell said Mark found another job?"

What? He's watching me. "Oh, yeah." He's still looking at me. "A good one." Shut up! Just shut up. I take a huge bite and chew. Chew fast, and then slow down, because he's looking at me like as soon as I swallow, he'll expect to hear more about Mark's good new job.

"I'm glad to hear he's doing well."

If Mark's not working for Darnell, and he's hardly at trainings anymore, then where is he?

We sit there in silence, but I can practically hear Riggs thinking something while he's chewing his last bite. He leans slightly forward and clasps his hands, studying the cars and trucks in the lot. I glance at my phone. Dad should have been here by now.

"You're smart, Bex." He doesn't turn his head, but he's looking at me out of the corner of his eye. I can feel it. "The way you shoot. The way you watch people and take it all in. You think for yourself. I like that." He turns his head and smiles at me. "We're trying to build something real here. And sometimes that means working hard to integrate all kinds of people, to form something stronger than the parts." He measures his next words. "Sometimes we have to give people time to see if they can find a place within the group, and embrace those who choose to stay and commit. Help people fit in where they can find the most satisfaction, for the greater group."

We *are* starting to gel. Even better without Mark and them. Is that what he is saying? Is he going to kick them out?

"Not everyone is going to see things the way you and I do,

but we have the chance to work to bring them around." Huh? "And *we* might not agree on everything," he says, motioning between us, "but I think we can learn from each other. Or at least listen to each other."

He pauses. Waiting. I nod.

"Some of the young men believe strongly in demonstrating their commitment to Second Amendment rights. We don't dictate what our members do when they're not here, but we discourage the kind of demonstrations Zach and his friends favor. Not because we necessarily disagree with their beliefs but because we don't believe they are constructive or serve our long-term goals." He pauses, waves to someone in the lot. "Zach is taking some time to think about whether he wants to be part of the organized training."

Wow. His dad has a stake. Are they buying him out? And does that mean the others are out, too?

"We were hoping that with fewer distractions, Mark would refocus his efforts and attention in training. Perhaps find a new place as training units begin to form."

I swallow.

He's waiting for me to say something, but there is nothing I can say. "Please let Mark know that he was missed at training, and we hope that his new job won't keep him away from training for long."

I nod. And I will. Maybe he'll start hanging with Daniel again and get back on track.

"Should you have any further trouble from Zach or . . . any of the others, please let me know. I don't want anyone committed to being here to feel disrespected. Understand?"

"Yes. Thanks."

Dad's truck rounds the curve and turns into the parking area.

"I hope that you *all* feel comfortable coming to me if there are other concerns, anyone else causing problems. My door is always open. I hope that if you hear of any problems brewing, or anyone who is maybe going down a bad road, you will encourage them to come to me. I can help. Or if they won't come to me, that you will come to me yourself. In confidence, of course."

I nod, because my mouth is dry and my tongue is tied and I don't know what to say.

He smiles and waves at Dad, and moves to get up from the table. When he turns his back to the parking area to pick up his discarded lunch bag, his face is all serious.

"I knew I could count on you," he says, but what he means is he expects me to be his spy.

CHAPTER 15

It's one of those super-slow summer days when working here is nearly mind-numbing. It's been storming off and on, so not even the Four Hs are hanging out. The few cars and trucks from today's repairs were picked up hours ago. The phone hasn't rung much. I've already stocked the shelves, helped Mike inventory the parts and supplies we keep on hand, and even cleaned up a little.

Only a few people stop by for gas or diesel, and they all use credit. Most everyone else probably went to one of those bigger places with the large canopy covers that stretch almost to the door of the fancy store to keep the customers dry.

It's so slow that Uncle Skip didn't say a word when he came through earlier and I was surfing around on my phone. I took that as an invitation to surf around on the computer, too.

I check to see if that girl with her own YouTube channel has a new video up—it's been a while since she posted.

Nothing but a few shout-outs to her from some of the other YouTubers, wondering if anyone's heard from her. Maybe they finally did it, went off the grid. Lucy and I text back and forth for a while. Mom calls to check on me, and to tell me about some thing Hannah is going to and do I want to go. No. *But it will be so much fun*. No. *The school* . . . No. *Have you read* . . . ? No. *See you Saturday*. *Love you*. Bye.

I wander back to the office. Uncle Skip and Mike are deep in conversation, and it stops just before I reach the office door.

"Still slow?" Mike asks.

"Dead."

"Why don't you go ahead and get out of here," Uncle Skip says.

"You sure?"

"We can handle it if anyone calls or needs something in the next hour," Mike says.

"Great. See you later."

I text Lucy that I'm done early.

We've timed it. She is exactly seventeen minutes away from our usual pick-up spot, and it takes me about eight minutes to walk across the back lot, across the field, and down to the church parking lot.

I'm halfway across the field when the phone vibrates in my pocket.

"Hi," I answer, knowing it's Lucy.

"I'm here, so . . ."

"I'm almost to the road."

"I'll get you there."

By the time I clear the field, Shelby—Lucy's wagon—is pulling onto the shoulder.

"Hey." She pulls the emergency brake, undoes her seat belt, and leans across the seat for a kiss. A good kiss. One that makes me squirm closer.

My stomach flips as she puts the wagon back in drive and pulls out onto the road. We've been out for pizza, ice cream, movies, to the lake. We've driven around for hours. Sunday night we parked behind the station for a while. We've talked. We've kissed. We've made out. But the only time we've had any real privacy was the night we went back to her grandparents' house. There's only so much making out either of us are going to do in the car, in public, even by the lake or behind the station. Tonight will be another night of filling time before making out as well as we can in the wagon. And still, I can't wait to get to the making out. The dinner, movies, ice cream, whatever, is all fine, but the making out is the best part. The part that I replay over and over when I'm by myself, and then imagine the next steps.

We slide into our regular booth at the pizza place and

order the usuals, plus breadsticks because I'm starving and they're fast.

"Do you like mushrooms?" Lucy asks, doctoring her tea with multiple packets of sugar.

"They're okay."

"I want to make you this chicken dish. It has mushrooms, but it's really good. My dad asks me to make it all the time."

"Okay." I can't really see Lucy cooking, for me or anyone else.

"Good," she says, breaking her breadstick up and dousing it with Parmesan cheese and red-pepper flakes. "Friday my grandparents are going to dinner with friends and then to a concert. They'll be gone until at least midnight. I'm going to cook for you."

Hours alone at her grandparents' house. "How long does the chicken thing take to make?"

I love the way she laughs. "It's easy. And there'll be plenty of time for after dinner." She pretends to be scandalized, but her face is just as flushed—and happy—as mine.

We eat our pizza slowly and then get ice cream. Drive back the long way.

"I thought my grandparents were going to go out tonight, but they didn't," she says, mirroring what I was thinking. "Anyone at your place?"

No, right now no one's at the house, but I can't risk it. "Yeah," I lie, leaving it vague.

She sighs, and I try to ignore the idea rattling around my head. But it's hard to ignore with her so close and so ready. I look at my watch, try to listen to the good Bex on my shoulder, but the bad one wins out.

"The station should be empty by now." She glances at me quickly, turning back onto the main road.

Parking behind the station is safer than the lake or somewhere else.

She holds my hand while we drive, her fingers playing with mine, and I feel that goofy grin on my face. And the heat rises as we pull up to the station.

"Stop." I can feel my heart hammering in my chest. There are two trucks parked behind the station, and the back door is propped open.

"What's wrong?"

"Someone's still working," I say. "Just, let's get out of here. Go."

"Are you okay?"

"Just go. Back up and, yeah, good," I say, when she's pulling out of the lot.

My heart won't slow down.

"I didn't think they'd be working this late," she says.

"Yeah. Me, either. I guess there must have been an emergency repair or something," I lie. "Or maybe paperwork?"

We drive around and then park by the softball fields for a while. Back behind the far field, the lot is empty. The making out is great, but it's also kind of frustrating, since it's clear we both want more. And I can't concentrate just on her.

Eventually I make up an excuse about being tired so we can call it a night.

When I get home, Dad and Uncle Skip are watching the game.

"Have fun?" Dad asks.

"Yeah," I say, and move to go upstairs before he can ask more.

"Hey," he says. "Your mom wants me to go with her to some thing on Saturday, so Mark's going to pick you up for training."

"No, he won't, Dad." He doesn't take his eyes off the TV. "Dad? Dad." He finally drags his eyes away from the game. "He won't show up. Just like last time."

"Yes, he will. He promised."

"But . . . is he sure he's going to training?"

"Yeah, why wouldn't he?"

"He's missed some," I say.

"I know," Dad says. "But Darnell is away this week, so he

won't need Mark and them for the extra shifts they've been working."

That's what Mark told Dad? That he's been working extra for Darnell?

Maybe I should just tell Dad about Mark skipping training, about Riggs asking about him. But Mark would probably just lie anyway, and Dad always believes him.

"Bex, what?" Dad asks, annoyed to be distracted from the game.

"Nothing. 'Night, Dad."

I'll just text Karen. See if she can come get me on Saturday.

It takes forever to fall asleep, and not because I'm thinking about Lucy. What was Mark doing at the station, and who was he with, beyond Zach, whose truck I recognized? They must have heard Lucy's car. The only question is whether they saw that it was us. Me. And how do I tell Uncle Skip without explaining why I was there and who I was with?

CHAPTER 16

I've written a hundred texts to Mark, but I've deleted them all. Can't exactly text, *Hey, what's going on? Because you've been lying and acting weird and Riggs was asking questions and you haven't been to training and I keep dodging Riggs so he won't ask any more questions and one of these days Dad is going to say something and I'm going to have to tell him. And why were you at the station?* He's probably just goofing off, but if he's not, he's not going to tell me. I can't tell Dad I think something is going on, because Dad will believe whatever lies Mark tells him. Maybe if Mark comes by to do laundry or get food, I can just ask, casually.

My phone vibrates. My heart pounds. Could it be Mark? Did I send that last one by mistake?

No, not Mark. Karen.

"You okay?" Mike asks. He's standing there staring at me. "Bad news?" he asks, pointing to the phone.

"No." I shove it in my pocket. "What do you need?"

"Mrs. Frankle's number and estimate."

"Bad?" I ask, handing him her signed work order.

"Not good," he says, walking away.

I look at the text from Karen again. *Are you working today?*

Yes, I text back. Then, *Why?*

"Need more coffee," Mr. Hirsh says, holding the empty pot up so I can see it.

I make a fresh pot and then go out to the picnic table and pour refills for the Four Hs.

"That'a girl," Mr. Hoff says, holding out his mug.

"Gin," Mr. Heinman says, slapping his cards down. He's been winning all morning and crowing about it. But the others are grumbling only halfheartedly. So either he's dying or they're just thrilled to have their fourth back.

"Eh, I've had enough for today," Mr. Hirsch says, holding his hand over his cup.

"Coffee or cards?" Mr. Heinman asks.

"Both," Mr. Hirsch says, tossing his cards into the center of the table.

"Me, too," Mr. Henderson says, adding his cards to the pile.

"Bex, how about a hand?" Mr. Heinman asks. "These old geezers have crapped out on me."

"I don't think so, Mr. Heinman. I'll keep my dimes, thanks."

The teasing continues as I head inside. It's good to see him back. They were incomplete at three.

My phone is blinking at me when I get to the counter.

We're coming by. And a smiley face.

We? And a smiley face?

OK? Karen texts.

There are only three more cars to be picked up. Even if all three come in at the end of the day, Uncle Skip or Mike can cover.

OK But I need to leave at 530.

I obsess all afternoon about why "they" are coming by. I start to get anxious at four, four fifteen, four thirty, and they're still not here. I text, *Where RU? I need to leave at 530*.

At least most of the cars have been picked up.

At twenty to five, Karen texts, *ETA 5*.

I only need seven or eight minutes to walk over to the church lot to meet up with Lucy. Plenty of time.

I'm vibrating with nerves when they pull up—Karen's out of the passenger side before Cammie's even shut the car off. Cammie.

"Hey ya," Karen says, walking through the front door, Cammie right behind her. They're in street clothes instead of workout gear. Karen doesn't look all that different in jeans and a T-shirt. But Cammie's femmed up enough that I bet some people would be surprised she trains, let alone leads. She's wearing a skirt. Her shirt is crisp green cotton, with slightly puffy short sleeves that show off her arms. Her hair is loose and curling. She's even wearing makeup.

"So . . ." Karen says, looking around the shop and then back at me, then at Cammie. "Where's—?"

"Not here," I say, looking toward the door to the service area. "I mean . . ." I don't know what I meant. I don't know why they're here.

"Wow," Karen says. "I was going to say bathroom. You do have a bathroom, right?"

"Yeah," I say. "Sorry. Over there."

"Hi," I say to Cammie when it's just the two of us.

"Hi," she says.

It's weird, like we're different people here from at training.

Cammie looks at the clock. Ten to five. "You almost done?"

"Yeah."

"You okay?" she asks, and her whole face is softer, and I can't square this Cammie with the one who barks orders and glares to wound.

"Yeah," I say again. "But I *have* to leave by five thirty."

Karen comes back out of the bathroom and detours for

the snacks. "Oooh," she says. "I love these!" She picks up two bags of Swedish Fish. "Want some?" she asks Cammie.

"That's a lot of sugar," Cammie says.

"I'll ration it out," Karen says. I ring them up and take her money. "Outlet work?"

"Huh?"

"In the bathroom," Karen says. "Does the outlet work?"

"Yeah, I think so."

She nods at Cammie.

"Okay, Mrs. Frankle is good to go," Uncle Skip says, coming through the door from the service bays. "You can . . ." He looks at them, and me, and them, and me.

"Uncle Skip," I say, because there doesn't seem to be a way out, "these are my friends Cammie and Karen." They smile at him. "And this is my uncle Skip."

"Well, hi," Uncle Skip says, big, like he's trying too hard.

Karen says, "Hi."

"Hi, Mr. Mullin," Cammie says. "You probably don't remember me, but my grandfather Ben Baxter used to—"

"Cammie Baxter. Of course," Uncle Skip says. "But last time I saw you, you had pigtails and braces. How's your grandfather?"

"Good," she says, all smiling nice girl. "He's up at the cabin for the summer."

"Well, say hello for me. I can call Mrs. Frankle," Uncle Skip says to me.

"Are you sure?"

"No problem."

I wait for the door to close behind him. "We can go outside if you want," I say to Cammie and Karen. Not knowing why they're here is bugging me.

Karen rips open the first bag of Swedish Fish. Then she gives Cammie a look, and when Cammie doesn't say anything, nudges her with her shoulder.

Cammie narrows her eyes and then says, "Come on," wanting me to follow her.

"Where?" I swallow.

"Just come on," she says, tugging on my sleeve as she passes me.

She's acting so weird, but Karen is still smiling, easy, chowing down on her candy.

I follow Cammie, very aware that Karen is behind me. When we get near the bathroom, Karen practically shoves me inside, and they follow me in.

I recover and turn on instinct, crouched low.

"Whoa," Karen says, laughing.

"Seriously," Cammie says. "Relax. It's not an ambush."

I don't like surprises. I don't trust surprises. Especially from people who may or may not be my friends. Cammie hangs her bag from the hook on the door and fishes around in it for a minute. When she turns around she's holding clippers.

"We noticed how much it was bugging you the other day," Karen says.

"And no offense, but it looks like a deranged toddler cut it," Cammie says. "With safety scissors. So I borrowed my mom's stuff." It takes me a few seconds to follow. "She's a stylist," Cammie says. I keep staring at the clippers and the small black case in her hands. She gives Karen the clippers and opens the case to show scissors. Several pairs, and other things. "I can clean it up for you if you want."

"It'd look cool totally buzzed," Karen says, turning my head so I can see the side and back in the mirror. "All this, just buzzed short."

I touch the hair near her hand. It is a choppy mess.

"She's good. Promise," Karen says. "Does mine," she says, brushing her fingers over the newly trimmed sides of her hair.

"I do what she asks me to," Cammie clarifies, like she's not taking credit for a mullet. "You tell me what you want and I'll do it."

I swallow. I touch the back near my neck.

"Or you can just trust me. Can't be worse." Cammie's ready, clippers all plugged in. "Turn around."

I give in and turn around, but I can feel how tense my shoulders and neck are. I'm poised for flight.

Cammie pulls a rolled-up towel out of her bag and drapes it around my shoulders. She thought of everything.

"Hold still," she says, and starts the clippers. The buzz vibrates over my skin before they even touch my hair.

What's the worst thing that could happen? She cuts it all off? It would grow back.

Her fingers touch my neck, and I shiver.

Karen starts to open her other bag of candy, and Cammie says, "Oh, gross, you can't *eat* in here!"

"Yeah, no," I add, shuddering.

"Fine," Karen says. "I'll be outside, eating my yummy gummy fish."

The door opens and then clicks shut. Cammie's fingers are still on my neck, and then the clippers move through the hair at the back of my neck. I shiver again, from the feel of it, from her fingers, from her breath hitting my ear.

"Hold still."

"I'm trying."

She's so close. I can feel her body behind me. Each pass of the clippers feels good. I can tell how she wants me to move from the pressure of her fingers on my neck. She moves my head, and then my body, so she can get to the left side. Just like when we're in maneuvers, I know what she wants.

She pauses. I can tell she's thinking. "Do you want—?"

"I don't care," I say. My voice sounds strange. "Do whatever you want."

She studies the side of my head.

"Okay," she finally says, and I know it will be.

Working on the long layers, she's so close I can smell her. She smells different from how she does in training. Maybe it's the makeup. Or perfume. Or these clothes. She turns me again and lifts the long layer. We're almost face-to-face, but she's taller. I'm breathing hard. She's not. She's focused on my hair.

"You're good at this," I say, catching a look in the mirror at the parts she's already done.

"Thanks," she says.

She works. I try to stay still. Curiosity gets the better of me. "How do you know my uncle?"

"My pop-pop used to bring me here. I could have as much candy as I wanted if I didn't bug him while he talked. His car was always needing something," she says. "Granma knew he was coming down here just to shoot the shit, but she didn't care. Broke my arm trying to jump from the picnic table to the tree branch out front when I was seven."

She lifts the long layer and tilts my head, bringing my nose an inch from her arm. It's definitely her skin that smells so good.

"Hold still," she says. She has a pair of scissors close to my cheek.

She cuts in sections, then uses her fingers to shake it out.

She stares at me and then smiles before going back to cutting. Slowly. Deliberately. Everything slows down.

"There."

I'm afraid to look.

It's me, only better. The long layer is more defined and falls to a sharp, sleek point at my cheekbone. The rest, clean and perfect. What I wanted but didn't know how to do.

"Thanks." I touch the place on my neck where her fingers were.

And then we're just standing there in the grimy bathroom.

"I should probably . . ."

"Yeah," I say. "Me, too."

We walk out of the bathroom, and I'm still touching my neck.

Karen says, "Hey, let me see." She jumps up from her perch near the door. I self-consciously rub at my neck. "Looks good! Nice job, Red."

"At least it no longer looks like a toddler cut it," Cammie teases, and Karen laughs, and the door jingles.

Lucy, standing there just inside the door, looking pissed. "Hey," I say, trying to remember to breathe. Shit, it's five forty-five. "Hey, I was going to text you," I say, and immediately realize it was the absolute wrong thing to say. "I mean, because I was running late, and I didn't want you to—"

"I needed gas anyway, so . . ."

She looks from Karen to Cammie to me, her eyes flashing when she gets back to me.

"Uh, this is Cammie, and Karen," I say. "Cammie cleaned up my hair."

"I can see that," Lucy says, more twang than usual. "Looks . . . better." She turns a sharp forty-five degrees, squares her shoulders, and shows all her teeth to Cammie. "Hi, I'm Lucy."

"Cammie." Cammie squares off, too. "Nice to meet you."

"Karen," Karen says, even though no one seems to care. Lucy looks at her like Karen just spit on her and barely acknowledges the greeting before turning back to Cammie.

Karen's bristling, working up to saying something. But Cammie's staring Lucy down, both of them puffing out their chests, looking each other over. Lucy gives Cammie another big, fake, nasty smile.

"Nice to meet you, too, Cammie," Lucy says, like it's the furthest thing from "nice." Lucy turns back to me. "I needed something, for dinner, so I thought I'd swing by here on the way back from the market. Are you ready to go?" All saccharine sweet, to hide the poison. And batting her eyes, staking her claim.

"Yeah, great, thanks," I say, trying to cover how freaked out I am to have them all here, in the station, at the same time. I should tell Uncle Skip I'm leaving, but I'm afraid to leave them alone.

I open the door to the service bays but don't step through. "I'm leaving, Uncle Skip!"

"You can leave it open," Mike yells.

"Okay." I'm ready to escape this awkward uncomfortableness. Now. "I'm ready."

"See you tomorrow?" Cammie asks, practically pushing Karen out the door.

"Yeah, tomorrow." I grab my backpack from behind the counter and hoist it over my shoulder.

“I’ll pick you up at seven forty-five,” Karen says, her look promising teasing and digging for details on the drive.

“Ready?” I ask Lucy, trying for normal and happy and not at all freaked out.

“Great,” Lucy says, but it’s hard to tell if it really is under all the fake happiness she’s throwing at me.

CHAPTER 17

Lucy hurls herself into the driver's seat and barely lets me buckle in before she's pulling out of the lot.

I don't know what to say. I don't know what she's thinking. I let her drive and brace for whatever comes next.

"I guess I should have just picked you up on the side of the road, as usual," Lucy says. She's pissed—that much is clear. Any answer seems likely to piss her off more. "I wasn't going to say anything about who I was or anything."

"I know. It's fine."

"It's just . . ." Lucy starts, and then rethinks what she was going to say. "Okay," she says. "I'm just going to lay it out there. I don't care who you tell or not. You want this to be your dirty little secret, fine by me. But it's sort of humiliating to have to pick you up on the side of the road or in some deserted lot, when your other friends come by all the time."

"They don't. They've never come by before. Cammie

brought the clippers, and . . ." I stop, because none of this is making her less pissed off. "But it's totally fine that you came by to pick me up."

"Really?" She glances at me at the four-way stop.

"Really," I say, forcing a smile. "I don't care who knows."

That was what she wanted to hear, I guess, because she relaxes back into the seat.

And maybe I *don't* care anymore.

A song Lucy loves comes on the radio, and I turn it up without her asking, just as she starts singing along, making her sing even louder. What she lacks in voice she makes up for in enthusiasm. I join in on the next song to make her laugh.

By the time we're at her grandparents' house, the station is forgotten. She has ingredients and cooking stuff laid out on the counters, and a cutting board and bowls on the table.

"Can I help?"

"Sure," she says, grabbing another cutting board and knife. "Scrub your hands, then come over here."

In the time it takes me to carefully slice the mushrooms, she dices an onion, cuts up the chicken, mixes flour and a bunch of stuff in a bowl, and then coats the chicken in the flour mixture.

When she's ready to cook, she takes the mushrooms. I hop up on the counter, where I can watch. Lucy cooking is like a different Lucy. Calmer. Quieter. Less . . . on. Relaxed, like after we've been kissing for a while and she stops trying to be so cool, only without the sexy feelings, or at least *all* of the sexy feelings.

She moves around the kitchen from sink to cupboard to stove to oven. Focused and efficient. She's someone else right now.

"Can I ask you something?" she asks, her back to me while she cooks the chicken.

"Sure," I say, and even I can hear the nervousness in my voice.

"Why didn't you ask me?" She looks over her shoulder at me. "To cut your hair? I'd have done it for you."

"I didn't really know I wanted it done." She blinks and turns back to the stove. That wasn't the right answer. "I mean, I knew it needed to be cut better, but . . . I guess I hadn't gotten around to thinking about doing it."

"But Cammie knew?"

I shrug but realize she can't see me. "I think less *knew*, more *thought it looked like crap*."

Lucy turns the chicken, moves some pieces to a dish, and adds more to the pan to be cooked.

"It's not a big deal. It gets—got—in my face sometimes, at training, when I was trying to sight. I guess they noticed."

"Sight?"

Crap. "The targets. My hair kept falling in my eyes."

"Targets. So . . . a gun?"

"Yes."

"What kind?"

I could lie. I could lie and she'd never know. "A rifle." Not a lie, just less scary for her than listing all the different guns, especially the AR-15.

"You've shot lots of guns."

"Yes."

"Do you own a gun or . . . guns? Is it even legal for you to own guns?"

"Not in my name. Can't until I'm eighteen," I say. "But . . . yeah, I have guns."

I look at my feet swinging free and then hop down from the counter in case we're about to argue about this.

She cooks and I stare at her back.

"It's not a big deal," I say. "We like to shoot."

"What do you shoot?"

"Targets, clay disks, squirrels. Whatever's in season. But for training, mostly targets."

"Here," she says, handing me the plates. "Make yourself useful."

We eat more than talk because we're both starving and

it's really good, something I tell her three times before she starts mocking me, but she's pleased. Or maybe because she's thinking. I've avoided talking about training or Clearview with her, sensing it wouldn't be her thing. I guess I was right.

"So . . . your grandparents are gone until when?" I ask, hoping to remind her of the evening we've had planned.

Lucy lets one side of her mouth creep up. "They'll be gone until at least midnight, probably later."

I look at the clock, pretend to count the hours, hoping she's still into it.

"Don't worry," Lucy says. "We'll have plenty of time." Her smile is promising. "After you do the dishes."

"Fair enough," I say, snagging a piece of chicken from her plate.

I do wash the dishes, but she dries, putting them away as we go. When we're done, she hangs the dish towel over the edge of the sink and turns. Cool Lucy is back in form, walking toward me with all the promise of what is to come.

We kiss in the kitchen, just a few small kisses, and then stop to take turns in the bathroom. I'm sure she brushed her teeth. I use my finger to push some toothpaste around my teeth, too. In her bedroom, she's turning on the small lamp by the bed, and already her shoes are lying where she kicked them off by the door.

The same quilt on the bed. Same dim lights and that smell of her. But this time we both know why we're here. This time I kiss her and let my hands wander.

She takes my hands, barely breaking the kiss, and pulls me toward her bed. And then she's leaning back, like last time—different dress, but everything else the same. Except this time I don't hesitate to take off my shoes and join her.

It takes a few minutes of shifting and elbows and legs tangling up before we have our heads on the pillows and our feet toward the footboard, Lucy lying on her side facing me.

"Hi," she says.

"Hi," I say back, our breaths puffing over each other's mouths.

By now we know how to kiss each other. Soft and deep and urgent and soft again until everything is warm and humming.

If she were wearing a shirt, I'd slide my fingers under the hem and test the waters. But her dress is tangled between us.

I trace my fingers over her bare leg just above her knee, just to see, and she pushes against my thigh. I tug at the hem of her dress.

"Yeah." She leans away and we untangle enough that I can pull it free from where it's caught. But she doesn't take it off.

She kisses me again, a small kiss, soft, all lips. And again, turning my head this way and that. I touch her over the dress, over her bra.

I've touched her before, even under her shirt, but never like this—when I can see her, and take my time, and not worry someone is going to catch us.

She rubs at the sensitive short hairs at the back of my head, encouraging me. I kiss her shoulder, her chest just above her dress. I feel the weight of her breast in my hand.

Swallowing hard, I try to be cool. But . . . being here, like this, is more than I could have imagined when I first saw her. I kiss her throat so I can hide my face, hide how big a deal this is for me.

"Yeah," she says, and I feel it against my lips. She rolls onto her back, pulling me with her.

"Touch me." She rubs my arm. "Please." She pushes my hand under her dress.

I've never done this part, not with someone else. But she's asking, and there's no way I'm saying no. I watch her face and go by touch—skin, and then elastic and cotton on the back of my hand, and then soft, slick hotness. She gasps and pushes against my fingers. I follow her sounds, trying to find where she wants me, but I don't know how she wants to be touched.

She grabs my hand, guides me until, "There," she gasps

out. "There. Just. Wait." She gets rid of her underwear, and then grabs my hand again. Putting it where she wants it. "Yeah." Her breath hisses away and sucks in and hisses away again. I try to focus, but I'm shaking with it, with doing this, with how good it feels—and she's not even touching me. Yet.

I find a rhythm; she gasps and nods, and I try to keep going steady. She grips my arm, keeping me there. She's quiet except for the gasps and little part-words. I can't stop looking at her face. I lose the spot and she says, "Higher," and groans when I'm back in the right place. I concentrate, clenching my teeth, determined not to lose the rhythm again. And then she's shaking, shoving my hand away but clinging to my arm, panting into my shoulder.

"Yeah," she finally says, letting go of my arm so I can pull my hand free. She stretches like a cat, taking a deep breath.

She's smiling and absently running her fingers through her hair on the pillow, making happy little sounds, but I don't know what to do with my hand. I hold it away from her and from me, trying not to touch our clothes. Especially mine.

"That was good." She rolls up onto her side and pulls me close for a kiss, trapping my hand between us. I let her kiss me but try to keep my hand away from my shirt.

When she pushes at my shoulder, I grab her arm out of

instinct. My fingers are sticky on her skin. She doesn't seem to care.

She kisses along my jaw, over my neck, up my ear. I can feel, inside, how I thought I'd feel, but it's like it's far away. She knew exactly what she wanted. I want her, I want everything, but what if I can't get there, if I freeze up when it's someone else touching me? I don't think I can show her like she showed me.

She leans up so we can see each other, her hair hanging in my face. "My turn?"

I close my eyes behind the burn in my cheeks.

"We don't have to if you don't want." Her hand rests very lightly on my ribs. "I've read about, like, stone butches, and about gender identity, and if you, if it would ruin this for you if I touch you there, if I . . ."

"What?" I get the words but not the meaning, and all of a sudden it's all too confusing and the room is stuffy and stifling. I pull out from under her and sit up.

She lies back with a bed-jiggling flop. "Look, we don't have to do anything. Ever. I mean, it was good, but you don't have to—"

"I liked that," I say. She peeks out at me from under her arm. "Touching you was good."

"Very," she says, nodding. "And I needed that. Been too long."

I try to process that. The "too long." Not at all something new for her. Or special. But good. Good is good. Stop thinking.

She tugs at my shirt. I lie back down on the bed, too, but keep some space between us. She stays on her back, both of us staring at the ceiling. "What do you like?" she asks. There's no teasing there. She's not whispering. So why am I ready to squirm away?

I can feel her turn over, the shift of the bed, her voice closer, her breasts brush my arm. But she leaves that little bit of space between us. "Bex?" she whispers, and she leans over, kisses my shoulder, and then pulls back.

"I haven't . . . not with someone else." I hold my breath.

I can hear a clock ticking somewhere in the room.

"So I'm your Shug Avery?"

I shake my head. "I'm no Celie. Just . . . haven't gone that far."

"Do you want to?" Her mouth is so close to my ear that her breath makes me shiver.

Yes. I didn't think I said that out loud, but then her lips brush my jaw, her fingers trace circles on my stomach.

"We haven't talked about, like, how you identify. If you want to keep your shirts on, that's okay." I open my eyes so I can see her. "I don't have to touch your chest. Or would even touching your coocher ruin this for you, or—?"

"My what?"

She blinks. Stares. Then her whole face changes. "I do not use the P word." Her hand flails out in emphasis. "Or *any* other C word."

"But . . . coocher?"

"What do you call it?" I shake my head. She's wide-eyed incredulous. "You *have* to have a word."

"Why?"

"Why? What do you mean, why? Because . . . you have to have a word. For yourself."

I think about it. When I was little Mom said *front bottom*, but . . . somewhere along the way we stopped saying anything.

"Like"—she leans closer—"what if I said, 'Can I touch your . . . vulva?'"

We both laugh, her face burying in my neck.

I think about that. About saying anything about . . . there.

"Vajayjay?" she asks, her hand trailing up my ribs.

"No way."

"Hooha?"

"Like, yeah"—I swallow as her hand moves over my

chest—"please, please touch my throbbing hooha?" She laughs again, and I feel it like she's laughing inside me. "Yeah, no."

"Then what?" Her fingers trace some pattern across my chest and then slide down, retreating and then circling around up my side, closer again, and down again, until my breathing is following her fingers, the pattern. Deep in and then held until her fingers trace away, then exhale. Over and over. Until it feels like her fingers are everywhere. "How about the good old labia and clit and vagina?" she whispers.

"Whatever you want." Don't stop. And then her hand is touching my chest. Flat on my back, there's barely anything to hold through the layers of my clothes.

She kisses my cheek, and my neck, and her hand burrows under my shirt, under my tanks.

"Do they need to be this tight? And two of them?" she asks when she can't quite get her hand under my tanks. "It's not like you need that much control," she teases.

But she's wrong. "They're more comfortable than your torture devices," I say, taking them off and tossing them over the side of the bed.

She cups my breast, barely a rise in her palm.

"I don't like any bumps under my shirts," I say.

Lucy kisses my jaw. "They just seem *really* tight."

"I like how they feel," I say against her hair.

Her lips on my throat. "Like a hug," she says.

Like armor.

"You smell good," she whispers.

"So do you."

She kisses my shoulder, my chest, and lower.

"Hey." I pull at her dress. "You, too."

She stands up so she can strip off her dress and her bra, and then waits for me. I take off my shorts and underwear and toss them on the floor, trying not to squirm when she looks me over before climbing back into bed. She's beautiful, and soft. Her skin is warm where it touches mine.

Then she's doing things to my breasts that I didn't know would feel good, despite how many times I've tested the theory. We didn't go here in the car. I'm gasping at how good nails can be. Her mouth is even better. I arch up, making stupid noises, but I don't care. I had no idea it would feel this good, that I'd feel it everywhere.

She doesn't ask for permission, not with words, but her fingers are tracing a new path, down my ribs, along my waist. She pauses, giving me a chance to stop her, waiting. I don't stop her. Not when her nails scratch over the skin of my belly, or when her fingers slide down between my legs. She pulls her hand away and moves so she's leaning over me, and then puts her hand back without any of the slow, careful seduction.

I move to give her more room and then gasp as every nerve flares.

"Yes."

"Okay." She kisses my shoulder.

Her fingers keep going, even when my whole body is moving in every direction.

"I don't think I can . . . I . . ."

"Just feel," she says.

"I can't . . ." But I can, maybe. Maybe.

We lose the rhythm, then the place, but she clamps her legs around my thigh and her fingers get there again. I stop feeling anything because I'm feeling everything, until everything goes tight and hot and I can't breathe and I let go with a wail. Loud. I cover my mouth, groaning again, but she stays there until I push her hand away.

"Too much?"

I can't talk, but she gets it, scratching her nails lightly on my skin, snuggling closer, kissing my neck. Her sticky fingers slide across my ribs to my side. I don't mind at all.

CHAPTER 18

Lucy grabs a glass of water off her nightstand and takes a sip, then she hands me the glass. I down the rest in one long swallow.

"Good," she says. "Only nine thirty." She grins and pushes my hip so she can pull the sheet out from under me and then over us. I let her pull me close and bury my face in her chest.

My hand does fit perfectly above her hip.

She touches a bruise on my shoulder.

I roll my head to look. Cammie's boot; she kicked my shoulder during the drill.

"Let me guess: training."

"Yes." I don't say more, hoping she'll just let it go.

"With them. And others."

I can feel a ripple of something and wait for whatever she's going to say next. Her lashes pet the skin near my neck, tickling me.

"Cammie should have taken the clippers to Karen's mullet while she was at it," Lucy finally says, and I don't like the sound of her voice. "She's like a bad stereotype of the militant butch."

"Actually, I think Karen's straight."

"No way!" Lucy rolls over so she can see my face. "You're serious!"

"I mean, not that I've asked," I say. "But she looks at guys." Especially Carl. She could be bi, I guess.

"Huh," she says, but there's still an edge to it.

"Karen's really cool," I say. "She can shoot anything. And she was one of the first ones to welcome me in."

"In?"

Crap. How to talk about Clearview without talking about Clearview? "When I first started going to the club, Karen was the first one to start inviting me to things, and she's picked me up a few times when I didn't have a ride. And she's really good."

"Someone should give her some soap. Show her how to get the crud out from under her nails."

"She works. Hard," I say. "And trains hard. Today, probably both."

"And I wouldn't know anything about either?" Lucy asks, daring me to say it.

I just shrug. As far as I can tell, Lucy's never had to work, outside of what sounds like silly little pass-the-time summer jobs. She's used to getting what she wants.

Whatever that was with Cammie is about me, but her nastiness about Karen is something else. Something ugly. Like the girls in the ice-cream place were about me.

I'm probably more like Karen than Cammie. Hell, Karen's family is probably better off money-wise than mine. Would Lucy still want me if she knew that my working at the station might be a permanent thing?

"And your club. Cammie's in it, too?"

"Yes."

"And you all shoot guns. A lot."

I don't bother to answer again.

"Do you carry a gun?" she asks. "Have you — when we've been out, have you been carrying a gun?" Her eyes bug out like she just realized that was a possibility.

"No," I say. "I don't carry a gun." She still looks worried. "I can't. Not until I'm older."

"But you own guns, even though you're not supposed to."

"You've never had beer? Or wine coolers? Fireworks?" I ask. "Pot?" I add, pleased when her face gives her away. "Had someone else buy them for you?"

"That's different."

"Not really. All that stuff is legal somewhere, some of it anywhere if you're a little older. Technically, the guns are in my dad's name—probably like how your car is in your grandparents' name?—but I use them, yes. They're mine."

"No one gets killed by wine coolers."

"Yeah, 'cause stupid-ass sixteen-year-olds never drive drunk. Or drink until they pass out. Or drink until the girls pass out, and then the guys—"

"It's not at all the same thing," Lucy says.

"No, it's not. Most of the people I know would never be as reckless with a gun as most people are with cars. Or alcohol."

"But you don't carry one."

"No."

She stares at my face for a moment and then seems to accept it. "Good. I hate guns."

"Have you ever shot one?"

"Yes."

"Okay."

"I don't need to do that again," she says, just in case I was wondering. "Ever."

"Fine."

"Fine," she says.

I can see her turning additional scenarios over in her mind. But I wait for her to make the next move. To keep talking or to cuddle down again or to put on our clothes.

I trace my fingers over her thigh and up her hip so it can settle in that perfect curve above her hip. I smile when I hear her exhale, giving up the talk for now.

We kiss some more. Touch some more. Nothing too serious, just touching. It's enough to be able to touch her.

I can't help but think about teaching her to use a gun. Showing her how safe it is if you know what you're doing. How good it feels to know you can protect yourself. How awesome the rush is when you pull the trigger and hit exactly where you intended.

"What are you thinking?" she asks, kissing just under my chin.

"How kickass you'd look shooting my dad's Remington."

She growls and starts to pull away, but I haul her close again. "I'm not saying you should. I'll never pressure you to touch a gun. Ever. But it's a nice image. For me. That's all I'm saying."

"Well, it's never going to happen."

"Okay." I imagine us out back near the pond, how it would feel to help her find her stance and—

"You're thinking about it right now!" she yells, but it's mostly teasing — mostly.

I shrug and lean in to kiss her neck. "It's a nice fantasy. I think if you got comfortable with holding a gun, like a light rifle, even, or our twenty-two — it's really compact and light — you might actually enjoy shooting. It's fun." The Bobcat. I put my palm against hers — she'd probably feel least threatened by the Bobcat.

"I've been hunting with Grandpa."

"Using?"

There's a long pause. "A gun."

She's shown her hand.

"What were you hunting?"

"Deer."

"Did he load two shells at a time or one?"

"Two."

"Two barrels or one?"

She pauses, thinking, and then says tentatively, "Two."

"How old were you?"

"Eleven."

I can see her. "Your arms were barely long enough, right?"

"Yes." She's not enjoying the game. "Grandpa had to help me."

"Right. That doesn't count. You would have felt totally out of control. It probably scared you more than if you'd never handled a gun."

"My position remains unchanged."

"Okay." I rub her side with my hand until she relaxes. "I meant what I said. I won't ever ask you to shoot a gun, or even to come shooting with me, if it bugs you."

"I don't want to even be around one. Ever. I mean it," she says, looking me in the eye.

"I get it," I say.

"Good." She snuggles closer, her fingers tracing a pattern on my arm. "I don't think I've ever known someone who's into guns."

"Your grandfather shoots."

"He has one gun for hunting. Keeps it locked up. Hates handguns." I can see her thinking. "It's not just shooting. You say training like . . . it's more."

Careful. She's acting too casual, but that question's been brewing for a while.

"Survival skills," I say. "Being able to survive in the woods, find water, what to eat. Shelter. Make fire. Like . . . extreme camping," I say, even though if someone else called it that, I'd take them down. "When I was little we'd go on a two-week trip every summer, two weeks of hiking deep into the forest, camping, fishing, making do with what we could find and forage. Hiking in areas you could only get to on foot." I loved it.

"And now?"

"And now . . . it's more than camping."

Lucy stares at the ceiling. "Why?" she finally asks.

"So we know how to take care of ourselves, just in case."

"In case," she repeats. "In case . . . you're attacked. Or . . ."

"Attacked. Threatened." The world goes to hell. I try to figure out how to say it. "There's some sort of catastrophe. A crisis that threatens order." She doesn't say anything, and I feel like she's waiting for me.

"Wow," she finally says, shaking her head. "If my friends could see me now." She laughs under her breath, and I get that there's a joke or something in there, one not meant for me. For stupid, backward me.

"Look," I say. "I get you don't see it. That you think this is a load of crap. That's fine. I'm not going to try to convince you. But you could show the same respect."

We lie there in silence. I want to get up, but I don't want her to watch me get dressed, and then I'd have to wait for her to get dressed. And it seems important that I hold this ground. Plus, she'd have to drive me home, which would make the storming away pretty pathetic.

She's tense beside me. Probably thinking the same thing, that it's my move. But it's not.

"I'm not trying to pick a fight," she says, and I laugh. "Hunting rifles I get. Maybe even some other kinds of guns. But, like, those automatic weapons, or semiautomatic, or whatever? Those things that hold rounds and rounds of bullets? They have no purpose except to kill people." She looks at me. "Right?"

"Having them is a strong defense. And then if need be . . . you have to know you can use them."

"That's crap," she says, sitting up again. "You don't need a fifty-round or hundred-round or whatever-capacity-bullet thing." She waves her hand dismissively. "You don't even need fifteen rounds for defending your home."

"You do if the threat has them. Or if you are outnumbered. To defend against a superior force from a distance that keeps you and your loved ones safe. Yes," I say, "you do."

"And you really think you might need to defend yourself or your family against . . . what, an army? *The* army?"

There's no way that I can answer that question without pushing her further away. I could tell her about the theories, about multinational corporations. Dirty bombs. A glass broken on a subway and a whole city goes down in hours. I could tell her about how few times in history anyone has seen revolution or invasion coming, and how much harder it will be to see it next time. I could talk about surveillance and tracking and how the phones and computers aren't safe. I could talk about the money—how even the money has electronic tracking signatures and too much of it is just data in a computer. I could talk about how close I think we are to crisis. I could mention the DHS and ATF and DEA and a host of other things short of an army that could threaten us, threaten anyone. But nothing I say will make this better.

"You do." Her eyes go wide, like she's seeing me for the first time. I don't like how the look feels.

"If we don't need them, why is the government trying to make them illegal?"

"Because they are dangerous as shit!"

"Or maybe because they are the best defense we have."

"Wow."

Somewhere in there, we both sat up. We sit there in silence, staring at our reflections in the mirror over the dresser.

"How old were you the first time you shot a gun?" she asks.

"Six."

"Six? Your were *six*?"

"It was a small pink rifle. I hated it. I wanted the camouflage one my brother got to use."

We stay there in silence, but I can almost hear her brain working.

"I will never have guns in my house around my kids."

"You want to have kids?" My turn to be shocked.

"Yeah," she says. "Someday."

Wow. I thought one of the benefits of being with girls was you didn't have to have kids.

"Here," I say, grabbing my shorts and finding my phone. I pull up YouTube and scroll through my favorites. I play her the video from the school that teaches survival skills—a woman, teaching a group of women how to protect themselves and get away from an attack. And the one from the same school showing techniques for getting out of a city and to safety on foot. And then one of the three gun competitions, with the women who look like pro golfers shooting targets around obstacles for points. Then one of my favorite videos of girls shooting, the youngest a sweet-looking kid who can pop all of the balloons on her target from crazy far. "See, not scary. Not crazy or anything. And very cool."

"I guess cool, and no, not scary, but . . . that's not really all you do, right?"

I pull up the YouTube channel for the girl in Texas who does all the training videos. But halfway through the first video, I realize this isn't helping.

“Okay, wait.” I find the video of the guy who forages and shows you how to find things to eat anywhere — even in the middle of a city. “It’s about being prepared. Like insurance. That’s all.” The video’s long and she seems to be interested, so I go to the bathroom and then get us more water, and when I get back, she’s still scrolling through my phone.

“So . . . less weirded out?”

“Yeah,” she says, but I don’t believe her.

“It doesn’t have to have anything to do with you.” She looks doubtful. “Really.” And it won’t. Soon she’ll be off to college, and then who knows, but she won’t be here.

We cuddle a little closer under the sheet, and kiss, touch a little, but that’s it. And then we get up and get dressed before her grandparents can come home and catch us for real this time.

It’s after eleven when Lucy drops me off at the house. I let her drive me all the way up to the house, because it’s not like I can tell her not to after telling her earlier I don’t care who knows.

“Door to door,” she says. She’s waiting for a kiss.

The house is all dark except for the light we leave on in the living room when someone’s not home yet, so I let her kiss me.

CHAPTER 19

It was slow for a Tuesday anyway. The whole summer's been slow, too slow. And when an inept tree guy takes out the power to the station, it means an early day for me. No sense in all three of us staring at the walls.

I run home with several contingency plans. If Lucy texts back, maybe a turn in my bed, if I can be sure Dad won't stop home. If not, then maybe some shooting by the pond, a shower, and then, hopefully, out with Lucy later.

But when I get to the house, there are two trucks parked in the driveway, including Mark's, and another on the grass, backed up to the barn.

When I'm almost to the porch, Mark, Zach, and Mr. Open Carry—Devon—come out of the house, bounding down the steps and off the porch. Laughing. With the last bites of sandwiches and cans of pop.

"Didn't I tell you?" Mark asks. He's not wearing a shirt. When did he get muscles?

"You came through, Mark," Devon says.

Mark is grinning from ear to ear, almost dancing, hyper.

Two other guys come out of the barn carrying a cooler between them and put it in the back of the truck parked near there.

"Neal," Devon yells, "my stuff's in the back of the truck. Stow it in the gear box, would ya?" Neal gives him a thumbs-up.

What he takes out of the back of the truck is a rifle. And some other stuff. Is that an ammunition belt?

Another guy comes out of the barn. I've never seen him or the guy with Neal before.

Mark jumps down off the top step, landing right in front of me, forcing me to turn and face him. When I start to look at the barn again, he moves so he's between me and the barn, bodying me away so I can't see.

Mark's smile makes goose bumps jump out on my skin.

"What's going on?"

"Go ahead," he says to Zach and Devon. "I'll be right behind you."

Zach and Devon walk around me and past me. Not ignoring me, exactly. More like making sure I know they are right there, backing Mark up. Or maybe that Mark's all that is holding them back.

"Don't dawdle, now," Devon says.

Mark just smirks. He chugs the rest of his pop and then burps, right in my face. Still that stupid smirk. Have they been drinking more than pop? And shooting? Idiots. Dad would blow a gasket.

"Where have you been? You've been missing training, and Riggs was asking me about where you were and—"

"What did you tell him?" Mark asks, grabbing my arm. Hard.

"Nothing!" His fingers dig in harder, and his eyes are wild. "I just . . . He asked about a job and said you weren't working with Darnell, and I didn't know what to tell him, so . . ."

"You keep your mouth shut. And don't worry about Riggs. He's irrelevant."

"What do you mean?" Are they trying to oust Riggs? Does Zach's dad have that much pull?

"Nothing," he says. "Forget about it." He pushes me away. "Just keep your mouth shut."

"Mark." He glances back, but I don't know what to say to him, not when he's acting like this.

He slams the door shut and starts the truck, the muffler drowning out any response I could make. But he gives me one more look, a nasty one that makes me shiver even though it's hot in the sun.

Forget drunk—was he high? Or just crazy? Drunk on his own bullshit?

Inside is a mess. Crumbs and cans on the counters. Dirty plates and knives in the sink. They ate most of the bread, all of the turkey. Some of the beer is gone, too. But there wasn't enough to get them all drunk. Unless Mark was the only one drinking.

I run out to the barn. Some scuffs in the dirt but nothing else out of place. Someone was using the workbench for something. Metal shavings near the vise. But whatever they were up to, they cleaned up after themselves. Nothing really looks out of place in the storage area, either, but I *think* things have been moved.

Every time I feel like I have a handle on things, that everything is working, something happens and I'm left scrambling for even ground again.

I thought maybe with Zach, Devon, and Neal gone, Mark would go back to hanging with Daniel and them. He's even more stupid than I thought if he's ready to throw Clearview over and follow those idiots somewhere else. Would the majority really get rid of Riggs? And if not, what line of crap has Zach been feeding Mark?

Maybe I should call Dad. If Mark's screwing up, then he needs to know. And if Riggs really is on his way out, then Dad needs to know that, too.

I sit on the porch, staring at my phone. Trying to decide what to do.

Then I do it. I call Dad. And it's ringing. I'm going to need to say something when he answers. What am I going to say?

It's ringing and ringing.

"Bex," Dad says, in a rush. "What do you need?"

"Nothing, I mean, I'm home, because the power was out at the station, and . . ."

"Fine. Good. Thanks for letting me know. I—"

"Dad, Mark was here. With Zach, and Devon and Neal, and . . . some other guys. I don't know what they were doing, but they left a big mess in the kitchen, and I—"

"You don't have to clean it up." Dad sighs. "*I'll* clean it up when I get home. Just leave it. Now I have to go."

"No, it's not that. Devon and Neal, they're . . . and Zach. I mean, Riggs said . . ."

"Yeah, Zach and the boys got in trouble, for shooting where they weren't supposed to or whatever. But Mark is smarter than that. I've already talked to him about this, and he understands."

"But, Dad, they're . . ."

"Bex," Dad says. "Look, I know you don't like those guys. Mark told me all about your getting into it with them. You don't have to like your brother's friends."

"But, Dad . . ."

"I don't have time for this right now." He says something to someone else. "I have to go. We can talk later, okay? I'll be home late, so go ahead and eat without me. Love you."

He hangs up. I stare at the phone. *My* getting into it with *them*. Always my fault. Always me that's wrong. Always.

So much for talking to Dad.

I clean up the mess.

Dad isn't that late. Early enough that I haven't eaten yet.

I put dinner on the table, but neither of us really eats it. We just push it around our plates.

Lucy calls. I ignore it. Dad's phone buzzes. He looks down at it for a minute, then pushes his plate away.

He's not apologizing. I have nothing to say.

Then Mom calls. She's tense and cranky. She doesn't even ask about the stupid book I'm supposed to be reading. I pass the phone to Dad before she can ask again about me coming to the city with her for whatever Hannah's doing. Doesn't sound like Dad's conversation with her is going much better than mine.

I clean up, scraping both our plates into the garbage, then go out to the porch so I don't have to listen to them snipe at each other. Lucy's voice mail is sort of weird. She sounds distracted and says she's going out with her grandparents. I text her, but she doesn't text back.

Aunt Lorraine's been working on Mom, even if Mom won't admit it. Mostly working the *don't you want all this?* angle, what with the country club and all. Mom's been going to church again, our old church. It means she's worried. She's not the only one. I think she's trying to get Dad to go back to church, too. Maybe he should. Maybe we all should. I miss the comfort of church before church got confusing, before I figured out that they think I'm going to hell no matter what I believe or how I pray.

Dad's not going to talk long. Not with the mood Mom's in. At one point, he looks right at me through the screen door. I know Mom's talking about me. Probably school again. I think she went and registered me at Hannah's stupid school. I'm not going.

When he hangs up, he looks exhausted. Not the time to try to talk to him, again, about Mark.

And it's not like I can talk to Mom. She's looking for any reason to say I can't go back to Clearview, to say that none of us can. Doesn't help that I don't think Dad's seen a penny yet from all the "work" he's been doing.

Plus, there's my hair. Mom flipped out when she saw it on Saturday. Then she grilled me about where I'd been so late the night before, until I told her I was out with Cammie and Karen, who fixed my hair, as the better of the possible lies.

"Fixed," she mocked. "Do they have hacked-up hair, too? Or just you? They all look nice, right?" I didn't bother to answer that. She didn't really want me to. "Right? All of you wasting your time and energy playing games."

No, I can't talk to Mom about Mark.

CHAPTER 20

When I hear Lucy's car, I say good-bye to Uncle Skip and head outside. Best not to make her wait after how many days she made me wait to see her again and how strange she sounded on the phone.

"Hey," she says through the already open window. Her hair is in a ponytail and she's wearing shorts and a T-shirt. Not dressed for a date. She gives me a very quick, tight-lipped smile. But it's barely a smile. I buckle up, trying to gauge her mood or figure out what's going on with her.

She pulls out of the lot and heads east, but she doesn't turn toward her grandparents' house.

"Where are we going?"

She takes a deep breath, forces it out, slows the car, and says, "I don't know."

"Are you okay?" I ask.

"Yeah." She looks in the rearview mirror like she's checking to merge, and I touch her arm.

"Are you back to being pissed at me?" I ask. The car swerves a little, and I realize she's really upset. "Pull over."

She drives another little bit and then pulls onto the shoulder and puts the car in park.

"What's going on?"

"This was a mistake. I should have just called."

"What?"

When she looks at me, I can see something is really wrong.

I think I'm going to throw up. "Was it that bad? I mean, I thought it was good. I thought you . . . liked it."

She stares at me and then laughs—hard, not nice.

"*That* was very good. That's the problem," she says. "I like you. A lot, but . . ."

"But?"

She won't talk to me or look at me. She just stares straight ahead, but she wants to say something.

"Lucy?"

"I've been doing some Googling around." She turns her head but stays solidly behind the wheel, like she's ready to drive at any time. "And I looked at some of the other videos you had on your phone. And the links. That group in Washington." Shit. Her face is hard. "If you think any of that is cool or, or good, then I . . . don't understand." She turns a little. "I don't understand any of it. Because those people hate us."

"They don't—"

"They *hate* us! How can you . . . ?" Her body sort of shudders, and then she hits the steering wheel with her hands. "What the fuck is wrong with you?"

I jump back in my seat.

I am too shocked to answer.

"Do you have any idea what guys like that do to us?"

"Us?"

"Dykes. Lesbos. Queers." She looks at me like she is reliving in her head everything we've ever done together. "Screw that," she says, waving her arms. "Women." She turns until her back is against the driver-side door. "Those guys, they hate women."

"You have no idea what you are talking about."

"And you're not stupid." Her face is beet red. Contorted. "If even half the shit I read is true—*half*," she says louder, "it's enough to make me run in the other direction. I wouldn't go anywhere near that. Men who think—"

"It's not like that. It's . . ." I just start spewing about Karen and Cammie and training, and Delia. "Darnell," I say. "Delia's father. He's black. He runs programs, workshops in the city for black people, to help them get permits and learn to use guns. To protect themselves. It's not about race. It's not a cult or, or . . . We're about survival. The guys I train with, they're—"

"And how many of *your* guys are pissed about people like Darnell arming black people?"

"Those are not my guys."

"Are you sure? Do *they* know that?"

I can feel the roaring in my head.

"Bex." She leans closer, starts to reach for me, and then thinks twice, pulling back her hand. "*Training* freaked me out. The bruises. The scratches. But I thought, hey, it's like hiking. *Extreme hiking*," she says, and I feel the accusation in it. "And the guns, the way you talk about the guns . . . But I convinced myself it had nothing to do with me. But . . . do you have any idea how creeped out I am? I almost didn't come to get you. I almost deleted your number!"

I'm gut-checked. Like I've been elbowed in the solar plexus and dropped hard.

"I'm still freaked out. Like they might come out of the bushes and grab us."

"No one is going to grab you. It's actually hard to get in. You have to be invited."

"Hate groups usually work that way."

"You don't know what you are talking about. There are

all kinds of people there. It's not, I wouldn't . . . God," I say, pushing on my temples so I can think. "I'm not like that. The groups I follow—Clearview—anyone who wants to train and is dedicated can join. The group in Washington, the video I showed you, they have all kinds of people. Women. That woman with the tattoos. Remember?"

"Moral turpitude," she says. "That group in Washington you think is so great? I went to their website today. Have you read it? *Really* read it? Sure, anyone, of any color, can join, who will swear their very fine-sounding oath. But did you miss the part about no moral turpitude? That means you and me. Queers."

"They mean, like, drugs and stealing," I say.

"No, they don't." I keep shaking my head, and her eyes bulge. "Look at yourself!" She waves her hand at me. "How can *you* feel comfortable with those kind of people?"

I have never felt more judged than I do right now. I swallow, try to regroup.

A week ago, I would have told her about the training, about being respected, about being part of something, finally, that was serious and mine. About girls who get it and don't treat me like I'm a freak. About readiness. About not being in this alone. But now, after this week, after Mark and Dad, and last week with Riggs, I don't know what to say to her.

"You think you can take care of yourself," she says, her voice creaky and bitter. "You think you can, but you can't. And you won't know until it's too late. You can't . . ."

I feel her breath and then her hands, and realize I'm trying to cover her mouth.

"They'll hurt you." She keeps talking even as I'm trying to make her stop. "Eventually, someone will hurt you. They'll rape you. That's what men like that do, to women who won't be like they want them to be. People who won't look like they think they should look. You can't—"

A knock, and we both jump back. A sheriff's deputy, motioning for Lucy to roll down the window. We're both breathing hard, flushed, and there are tears on her cheeks.

"You okay in there?" he asks, and she nods, gulping air, but her hands are shaking. Her whole body is shaking.

He leans down and looks at me. I clench my hands and hold still, meeting his eyes, trying to keep my face blank—calm but controlled. I'm in control.

"Everything okay?" he asks again, looking at Lucy like I might be making her not okay.

"Yeah, yeah," she says, nodding, forcing a smile and wiping at her eyes. "Yeah, we're fine."

"Why don't you step out of the car," he says, and even as she is shaking her head, starting to say she's fine again, he reaches for the door handle. "Step out of the car." It's no longer a friendly request. "You stay there," he says, waving me off.

Screw that.

"Passenger, stay in the car," he orders. He pulls her door open. "You," he says to Lucy, "step out."

Every bit of me is on full alert—my heart, my head, my gut. Every hair on end.

He motions her toward the back of the car and closes the door.

I strain to hear through the open window. Only catching a word here or there. Sounds like a laugh. I lean over the seat to see through the back windows, and she's tucking her hair behind her ear, ducking her chin, doing all the things girls do to make men feel strong and cool and in control. My stomach turns. And then there's a thud and she's against the car, and I am out the door and halfway around before he shouts at me to freeze.

"Get your ass back in that car, passenger." Lucy's eyes are huge and panicked, and he's got one hand on her, keeping her there. But I can tell, even from the other side of the car, that the other is on his gun. "I said, get your ass back in that car."

I need to figure out what to do. Distract him. Draw him

away. I could maybe outrun him. But toward his cruiser? Toward the field? He has to follow. Right? Then Lucy can get away. I look at her, try to tell her to be ready, but she's frozen. She won't go—I know it. And if he doesn't follow, then I'm not leaving her alone with him.

He turns his face toward the radio on his shoulder. Listens. Then he turns back toward Lucy. "You're sure you're okay?" She nods, another duck of her chin. He says something I can't hear and then he's moving toward his cruiser. "Move on, now." Then he's got the lights on, peeling away from the shoulder into a U-turn, and he's gone.

"What did he say to you?" I ask, but Lucy's freaked and stumbling to her door.

She's beyond shaking when she gets back in. Vibrating all over.

"Go." I put her hand on the ignition. "Just drive."

She gulps air.

"Okay. Move. I'll drive."

She pulls off the shoulder and onto the road with a gravel-spitting squeal, and drives like a maniac. She's white-knuckled on the wheel and shaking.

"Lucy," I say, and she speeds up until the car is trembling with the effort. "Lucy, we're away. Pull over. Somewhere public."

The car drifts toward the shoulder and then back. She eases off but keeps going. There are oncoming cars, and we're heading into a town. There's a parking lot on the right.

"Pull in there. Now."

She makes a sharp, wild turn into the lot and sort of into a spot, before stopping hard. I bounce back against the seat.

I reach over to touch her. "Are you—?"

"What the hell were you thinking?" She slaps me away. "You could have gotten us both . . ."

"What? Gotten us both what?"

"I don't know," she yells, throwing her hands into the air. "But he said to—"

"He had his hands on you. Screw staying in the car."

"What were you going to do? Jump him? Fight him?"

"Not with him armed. And twice my size. But I was going to draw him away so you could get out of there. I was just—"

She starts laughing hysterically. She's hysterical. When I try to touch her, she flings my hands away like she should have done with him.

"Don't touch me! What the hell is wrong with you?"

What the hell is wrong with *me*? She's the one who let him touch her and flirted and whatever with that asshole. But I'm the wrong one, again.

I can see the goose bumps popping out on her arms. The adrenaline leaving her.

"Bex . . ."

I wave away whatever she was going to say.

"I want to go home." She sounds like a little girl.

"Okay. Are your grandparents home?"

"Where do you want me to drop you off?"

I look at her face. At the streaks and dirt and fear. At how scared she still is.

I should get out and walk back.

"Bex?"

I don't want to be in this car for one more minute. But I can't. I'm so tired, and my legs are like jelly. It would be miles, and I can't call anyone to come get me. But I don't want her anywhere near the access road. He might double back.

"Home. We'll go the long way. Pull back out and go through town. We'll pick up one of the county roads on the other side. Takes us far out of Deputy Creep's way."

I don't talk except to give directions. She doesn't talk at all.

"This is close enough," I say when we near the turnoff.

"I don't mind."

I do. But she's already turning down the drive, and then I see Dad's truck.

"Here's close enough. *Really*. Stop."

She finally stops and then notices the truck. She knows I don't want her to be seen.

I don't even look at her. But I don't get out, either.

I'm sorry, I think, but I don't say it. I'm not really sure what I should be sorry for.

"Grandpa wants me to help him with some things around the house. And then my parents are coming and . . ." She scrambles for something to say. "I've got college stuff to get ready, so, so I'm not going to be around as much. And I think I'm going to head to Chicago early, to check out—"

"It's fine." We both know that whatever this was is over.

"I'll give you a call when things calm down."

"Yeah," I say. "Sure."

She won't. And I won't. But it's better than saying good-bye.

"Go home the long way," I say. "If that guy tries to pull you over, call—"

"He won't. He thought I was in trouble."

From me.

I can hear her say my name when I open the door, but it's just for show. She doesn't really want me to stay.

The walk to the house feels longer and dustier than ever. I fight the urge to look back.

I can't tell if I'm devastated or relieved. Or if any of this even happened. I can barely feel my body. Not my feet walking step-by-step up the drive. Not my arms or legs. Nothing.

The hood of Dad's truck is still warm, so he hasn't been home that long. I try to keep my face calm. I just want to escape upstairs and lie in the dark and think. If I seem tense, he'll know something's up. He might decide to care.

"Dad?" I call from the kitchen. There's a partially empty can of beer on the counter, a puddle of condensation under it. I can hear footsteps upstairs but not in Mom and Dad's room. Overhead, then toward the stairs, then on the stairs.

That's not Dad.

Mark bounds off the bottom step, stalking through the living room. He's trying to look casual, but his face is giving him away.

The hairs on my neck stand up. Goose bumps break out along my arms. Everything in me is saying run. It's like yesterday but worse. Like he's on something. The look in his eyes. It's even worse than with the deputy. But my feet are rooted to the floor, firmer with every step he takes toward the kitchen. Too late to move. If I run, he will chase me. I know he will.

He shoulders me aside on his way to the fridge. I wait for Dad.

There's no sound upstairs. I strain to hear. Nothing.

"Where's Dad?"

"Shut up, freak."

Dad's not here.

"Why do you have Dad's truck?"

He doesn't answer. He stands in front of the open fridge like he's taking an inventory of the contents, like he didn't already do that. Like he didn't already eat. The beer has been there a while.

"Why do you have Dad's truck?" I ask again.

"Mine crapped out. Again. Skip's work is for shit."

There's sweat on his forehead and the back of his neck. It's not that hot in here, and he's standing in front of the open fridge.

He closes the fridge and then turns to face me. He cracks his neck, leaning back against the counter, all pretense gone.

"What do you want?" My voice gives me away, my nerves. He smiles.

"To see you, Sister," he says with an even bigger fake smile. "What did you say to Riggs?"

What?

"You said you two had a little chat. What did you say?"

"Nothing."

"Nothing?" He squints at me, like he's trying to decide where to strike. "You had to have said *something*."

Leave. I should leave. Now. "He asked how you were, and if you got a job or . . . because you haven't been around, or not working with Darnell, or . . ." I need to leave. "I didn't know what to say, so I said you got a good job, and . . ."

That fight-or-flight thing is still sounding in my head and shooting down my spine.

"Had to be more than that."

His voice is weird, like it's not even him.

I look at the clock. I don't know where Uncle Skip is or when he'll be home. Or Dad.

"One more time. What. Did. You. Tell. Him? He said you told him 'everything.' That I could trust him." He steps toward the table, cracking his knuckles. "Kept saying I needed to talk to him."

"Nothing, I swear." Even I can hear the panic in my voice.

I edge around the table with tiny steps. As if I'm distracted, or still waiting. Anything to keep the table between us. He mirrors me. Breaking for outside won't help. It's too long across the coverless lawn to the trees, and there's nowhere safe in the workshop. The locks won't keep him out.

Stall. I need to stall. "What's going on? I can help, if you're in trouble, or . . . I can help."

"I don't need your help." He stops the cat-and-mouse around the table. He smiles. I need to run.

My only chance is upstairs. Bedroom. Good lock. Shove the bureau in front of the door. Or I might be able to climb out and around on the roof. Buy enough time for Uncle Skip or Dad to come home.

"Then let's try something else. What did *Riggs* say to *you?*"

I'll only get one chance. "Nothing. I told you, about the job and . . ." I break left and he matches me, jerks me off my feet, tries for a hold, but I don't let him get his arm around my head.

I feint left, and when he moves, I duck and move the other way. He's stronger and faster than the last time we wrestled. I deflect and slap and try to maneuver my back to the living room door.

"Your girlfriend's cute, for a dyke." Shit. "Stupid to park somewhere people might see you, though." He smirks. "I got some good pictures." One e-mail and it would be everywhere by morning.

His phone rings. I jump, and he jumps at me. Lunges around the table. I get him in the nose with the heel of my hand, but not a sharp enough hit.

"Dad would love to know about the stealing, the beer," I gasp, kicking his leg and shoving him off balance, get the table between us again. "Uncle Skip would be more interested to know about Zach's truck parked behind the station after hours. That you've all been going there, and here. That you were here. I'll tell, I swear I'll tell if you don't—"

He shoves the table into me, knocking me into the wall. He's there, hitting the wall next to my head. I almost get away, but his forearm is against my throat, pushing, pressure. His eyes. He's not stopping. I try to talk, to reason, grab at his arm, but I can't. I can't breathe!

"If you don't tell me . . ." he says, pressing harder, his eyes bulging.

I kick, scratch, claw. I aim for his eyes until he lets go. But he grabs me again. I twist, break the hold, slam my hand into his shoulder, turn, and drop him to the floor, stomp at his balls. He wails but grabs my leg, and I kick, kick until I'm free. Knocking chairs down behind me. Take the stairs as fast as I can.

I don't hear him following, but I'm not taking any chances. I lock the door, push the bureau, using my hip to get it started and then the adrenaline to shove it a few inches in front of the door. In the closet, I push my duffel and stuff out of the way. The loose boards aren't right. Shit. The Bobcat is gone. And the cash I had there. And some of the ammo. I move to the other side and pull up another board. The lockbox is still there with the rest of my cash, and next to it Grandad's revolver. I grab a box of bullets with shaking hands as I hear his feet on the stairs. Slow. He's walking.

I settle against the wall in the far corner away from the door, behind the bed. Grandad's revolver. I pop the cylinder out and load it with shaking fingers. Bullets fall around me, but I just keep loading.

I hear his steps in the hall. They stop outside the door. Too quiet. He's listening. I force myself to breathe slowly, try to calm my shaking hands. Snap the cylinder in and ready myself.

"I was just messing with you," he says through the door. "You hear me?"

Does he think he can pretend that was, what, good times? Kidding around?

"You hear me?"

I aim for the door. First shot has to count. If I miss, I'll only have maybe one more shot before he's on me, if he's crazed. If the first doesn't stop him.

He rattles the doorknob. It won't hold. If he wants in, it won't hold.

I crawl closer to the bed for more cover, up on my knees, steady my arms on the bed. Wait for my shot.

He pushes against the door, not hard, not with force, just testing. He's testing it.

"Go away," I shout. I can hear the tears thick in my throat. I wipe my face, clear my throat, and try again. "I have Grandad's revolver." I can't hear him. Creak of the door again. "I swear to God," I yell. "I'll shoot you. I will."

Creaking floorboards, but he's still there.

I steady myself, breathe, ready.

He backs away from the door, down the hall toward the bathroom. I track him through the wall. He must realize it because he moves fast in the other direction, away from me.

"Get out!" I yell. "Go! Go away!"

I strain to hear him.

His phone rings. Too close. He's right there!

"Yeah. No, not yet." He's moving away across the hall. "She won't. She won't! Because I'm handling it. No, my dad or uncle could be home anytime. I said I'm handling it. We don't need Glenn. We don't need Glenn! Just . . ."

He stops midsentence, curses, and then kicks the wall. He's down near Mom and Dad's room.

Cursing. He's cursing and muttering, "Not now. Not now. Stay cool." More cursing. Footsteps, coming back, but not like before. He's not going to try to break the door down.

"Sorry. I'm sorry," he says. "But . . . keep your mouth shut. Or else Dad hears about everything." My pulse thuds in my ears. "Bex . . ."

"Go away!"

"I'm hanging on to the Bobcat and your cash. Consider them hostages. If you keep your mouth shut, you get them back. If not, I give them to Dad. And after that, I tell them about all your lies, the skank you've been diddling. They'd never believe you anyway. Especially now that Dad thinks I'm making good money and being all responsible. You're the liar, the one who likes to blow stuff up and has guns she's not supposed to have. The defective one. So do us both a favor and keep your mouth shut."

I try to steady my shaking hands. If he comes through that door . . .

"You hear me? Not a fucking word. You say a word to Dad, to anyone . . . you'll wish you were never born."

I wait until I hear his feet retreating down the stairs. Wait until I hear the truck start. Wait until it has faded away. Wait until I stop shaking. I wait with the gun in my lap.

I wait.

Maybe he was lying about having pictures of Lucy and me. Then it would be his word against mine. When the shaking stops, I dig my phone out of my pocket and delete every reference to Lucy—her number, our texts and e-mails. Anything that could give me away if Mom or Dad takes my phone.

But he's right. They won't believe me. They never do. They just believe everything he says. They'll listen to me even less if he tells them about the Bobcat. And even if they listen, what can I tell them? They've seen us fight. They'll think it's like all the other times, or I'll sound out of control. He'll tell them I threatened to shoot him. Mom will go crazy.

He was scared. That I would tell, or something else? He was angry when I got here. Who was on the phone? Were *they* afraid I would tell something? Who's Glenn?

He was looking for my cash. Because he needs money? Or was he looking because he wanted to shut me up? And what does he think I know? Or Riggs knows? What does *Riggs* think he knows? Is this all about who's in charge? There's money involved, and Zach and his dad could have been rallying people to their side. But . . . could all of this be about ousting Riggs?

My throat hurts where Mark had his arm. No, this isn't about who leads Clearview. This has to be about more.

I should already know what's going on. Especially if they've been coming here.

But I've been distracted.

That ends tonight.

No more distractions.

No more vulnerabilities.

I can't say anything to anyone until I have some kind of proof. Something to make whatever he tells them irrelevant.

Until I know what the hell is going on, what has him so freaked out, freaked out enough to choke me. Until I know, I can't let my guard down again.

I won't let my guard down.

I look at Grandad's revolver. Feel it in my hand.

So he has the Bobcat.

I have the revolver.

CHAPTER 21

"I'm not going," I say, pretending I can't hear Mom's response and that we haven't had this argument three times since yesterday. She showed up at dinnertime with grand plans for me and her to go to Hannah's play together tonight and then stay over in the city. *We can do some shopping on Saturday. Go to brunch on Sunday, and then . . .* Never mind that I have training Saturday and would rather poke myself with sharp objects than go to Hannah's play or go shopping with Mom.

I haven't seen or heard from Mark. I have no idea where Dad and Mom think he is, but I doubt he's wherever he told them he'd be. His truck, however, is at the station. It was towed there yesterday. I have to get a look inside before he comes and cleans it out.

Thank God Uncle Skip had conscripted me into an extra-early-morning run to pick up a car or I'd probably already be in Mom's car on the way to Aunt Lorraine's.

"I'll be there to pick you up at twelve thirty sharp," Mom says louder, following me out onto the porch. "Do you hear me?"

"No. Let's go." Uncle Skip and Mike will get to work, and then I'll pull Mark's truck apart, see if there's anything in it to point to what the hell's going on.

"You haven't seen your cousin in ages," Mom says, coming across the porch so she's right next to Uncle Skip's truck.

"Fine with me."

"Rebecca Ann Mullin." Crap. I turn around and face her. "Twelve thirty sharp. End of discussion."

"Come on, Bex," Uncle Skip says, distant through the closed truck door.

"Fine," I say to Mom. I yank the passenger door open, and I'm hit with a mix of coffee, aftershave, and the whiff of oil that always clings to the inside of Uncle Skip's truck.

"I'll bring you a change of clothes," she says, like she's doing me a favor. Like I plan to be there for her to collect at twelve thirty sharp. I don't.

"Buckle up," Uncle Skip says, already in gear as soon as my door is closed.

By Thursday midday, Mark had already talked to Dad and given Dad some cash he said he earned for his insurance and to "help out." Dad made a big deal about telling Mom at dinner last night, as if it proved that Clearview was paying off. Except that Mark hasn't been working for Darnell, so that was probably my cash, or he got it some other way. Some way he's not telling Dad. There has to be something in his mess of a truck that will give me a clue. Something to explain why he was so crazed. I could have shot him. I would have, if he'd tried to break down the door. Normal Mark would never have done any of that. Something, or someone, has him out of control. I need to know what, or who. I need at that truck before he cleans it out.

"Why are we doing this again?" Uncle Skip ignores the question. "Forty-five minutes in the wrong direction, and then back, on a Friday morning, so that . . . why?"

"Courtesy for a longtime customer."

"And why are you wearing aftershave?" As soon as I say it, I realize why we're going to pick up a customer's car. As I watch, Uncle Skip's face turns red, and then redder. "Hot damn. Why didn't you say so?"

"Shuddup."

I fiddle with the radio to find something other than Johnny Cash.

"Is she the one with the hair?" I use my hands to map the

imaginary pile of hair on my head. "Or the blonde with the kickass boots?" His jaw tightens. "Those *are* some very nice boots."

"You could walk, you know. Could let you off any time."

"But then who would help you pick up your lady friend's car?" The truck starts to slow. "I was just kidding!"

Uncle Skip is looking in the mirror. I turn and see the lights, two cruisers, flashers going, coming up fast.

Uncle Skip pulls onto the shoulder to let them pass, but they slow, too, one pulling into a spin in front of the truck and the other behind. Then more cars.

"What the—?"

"Get out of the truck!" someone yells.

"What?" I hear myself say, and Uncle Skip has his hands up above the wheel.

The doors of the car in front are flung open, and the cops are behind them, guns drawn, pointed at us.

"Out of the vehicle, now!"

"Hands where we can see them!" a voice from the side says, movement in my peripheral vision, on my side of the car.

"What did you do?" Uncle Skip's eyes are huge.

"Nothing! I swear. We were just . . ."

I never told Deputy Creep my name. How did they find me? Or is this . . . What's going on?

"Do what they say," Uncle Skip says, his hands going higher.

"Keep your hands where we can see them. Out. Now."

"We're coming out!" Uncle Skip yells through the open window. "Bex, stay calm. Do whatever they say."

"Keep your hands in sight!" I can see them inching toward us, guns trained on us. "Reach through the window. Open the door from the outside!"

I start to open the door, but he yells, "From the outside!"

As soon as the door's partway open, everything happens at once. Shouting. Hands. My backpack is tangled around my leg.

Uncle Skip shouting, "She's a kid!"

"On the ground!"

"What?"

"On the ground! On the ground!"

I'm shoved down. My backpack is yanked away from me. Hands are pushing me down, pain in my back, arms pulled hard. Kicking my legs wide. Knee in my back. Someone's hitting Uncle Skip. He's still yelling, yelling about me. Then he's not, and there are voices above me, yelling, hands everywhere. Something heavy on my back.

"Clear!"

My hands are pulled lower behind my back and secured. Tight and biting. I can't breathe. I can't breathe.

"You're hurting her," Uncle Skip yells.

The weight leaves my back, but I'm still on the ground, hands bound. The guys I can see are not deputies. They're in black, or dark blue. Badges and gear. Windbreakers. FBI. ATF. They're searching the truck. I turn my head toward the truck. I can see Uncle Skip, facedown on the other side, looking at me.

"It's okay," he says.

"Quiet!"

"I'm gonna throw up. I'm gonna—" Puke, in the dirt, under my face, all over. Coughing.

I'm pulled up and toward one of the cars. Dark. Unmarked. Small flashing lights. Someone wipes my face with a towel. I spit to get the taste out of my mouth, and one of the guys from that side advances hard.

"Easy, easy," the guy who wiped my face says.

"She was just spitting out the vomit." Another voice, a woman.

Someone holds a bottle of water to my mouth. "Take a sip." I sip slowly, then turn and spit again, careful not to spit in anyone's direction. "Another sip?" I swallow this time. "Breathing okay?" I nod.

"What's—?"

"Quiet," the guy, the one who wiped my face, says.

They've got Uncle Skip up and they're taking him to the other car.

"How old are you?" the woman, the one with the water, asks.

I don't answer. Everything I've ever read says you don't say anything. Not even your name. This is how it starts. Like this. I'm gonna be sick again. It's starting and I'm caught before I could even try to get away.

"ID?" she says, and someone hands her my wallet. From my backpack.

My backpack. Fuck. They're searching my backpack.

"Rebecca Mullin." She looks at me. "Sixteen," she says. She looks at me again, long and hard, then puts me in the car, her hand on the back of my head, guiding me. It's hard to get in and upright without my hands, and she helps shift me back against the seat. "Agent Malone, sir?"

"What, Washington?" I can't see him, but he sounds pissed.

"Juvenile," she says, holding out the wallet.

He walks over and bends down to stare at me, at my face, at my body, and then takes the wallet she handed him and pulls my license out of the cover.

"Menendez!" he shouts. "Over here."

The door is closed and they talk. The three of them, and

then someone else. And then two of them are on cell phones, passing around my license. It still looks like I looked last year, young and stupid, with the long hair. The revolver. Shit, the revolver is in my backpack. I close my eyes. I can't believe . . . I'm so stupid. My eyes sting. The guys were right, those crazy guys who said never register, never let them take your name. I shouldn't have let them catalog me.

They move closer to the car, and then I can't see above their waists without craning my neck.

Stuck in the car is like being underwater—there's no air and everything's muffled. I'm going to suffocate. My heart is racing. I try to see the other car, to see Uncle Skip, but the truck is between us, still being searched.

The door is opened, and cooler air seeps in. "Rebecca," the female agent says, "where's your brother? Where's Mark?"

"What?"

Sweat trickles down my temple and my neck. A whiff of puke hits me in the face. I gag. I can't breathe. I feel the panic climbing.

"Come on, where's Mark?" the guy says over her shoulder, but she pushes him back.

"We need to find him, Rebecca. Now. Before anyone gets hurt," she says. "Where is he?"

Mark? They're looking for Mark?

"Do you know? When did you last see him? Rebecca?"

The feel of his arm at my throat. The gun in my hand. They're looking for Mark?

She closes the door again. No more air. I can't breathe. I have to calm down. Breathe slowly.

They're looking for Mark. But they arrested us. Or detained us. Whatever we are. Maybe everyone? Why Uncle Skip?

Are they rounding everyone up?

My body's shaking. I can't feel my legs. Or my arms.

I try to remember everything I've read about interrogation.

They'll try to ask me questions on the way, wherever we're going. They'll try to talk to me. They'll lie, try to trick me. If they see me freaking out, they'll try harder. I have to calm down.

I have to think, to remember. Go compliant now that they have me. Stay calm and quiet. Give them no reason to get rough. If you're injured, it's harder to stay focused.

If they try to take me anywhere but a police station, anywhere unmarked or military, go limp. They'll take it for fear or injury, and I can use the time to count doors and exits, watch for a way out. Do not drink or eat anything.

I breathe in, hold it, and then let it out slowly. Again and again. Just like in the woods, when I don't want to be seen.

I jump when the car door is opened. Front. Driver side.

The woman says, "Come on."

"Aw, hell," the guy who must be Menendez says, before opening the passenger-side door and getting in.

Ignore them. Stay still. No response. Learn what I can.

The woman agent, the one with the water, climbs in behind the wheel and turns so she can see me.

I can't look away, but I hope I seem calm.

Menendez doesn't turn around, but I can see him checking me out in the mirror. Their jackets say FBI.

My mouth goes dry and my stomach clenches.

Am I arrested, or is this it? Military state? Are we at war?

CHAPTER 22

"Do you understand these rights that I have just explained to you?" I stare at him, the agent or police officer or I don't know what he is. "Rebecca?" He waits a few beats, and then his eyes slide over to the agents standing to my right.

They keep trying to talk to me. Agent Washington, Agent Menendez, some other guys. They ask me about Mark, about weapons and bombs. About things I don't understand. About Uncle Skip and Dad and Zach and Devon and people I've never heard of, until my head is spinning and I don't even know how long I've been here. I stay quiet as long as I can, and when they force me to say something, I just say, "I don't know" or ask for Mom. Then I cry. I don't know when I started, but I realize all at once that I'm crying. They keep asking. I don't know how long it goes on. Then there's a knock on the door, and they all leave, and I'm alone. When the door opens again, different agents or police are there, in my face. It goes on and on. I have to pee, but I can't make myself ask for a bathroom. Then they make me stand up, and cuff my hands behind my back again, and then I'm in a cell. At least I'm not in here with a bunch of other people. But if there were other people, maybe I'd be safer. They could do anything to me and no one would see it.

I need to pee so bad. But I can't. I can't make myself pee knowing someone is probably watching.

I hold it until it hurts. Until I don't think I'll ever be able to let it go, even if I wanted to. Until a distant noise almost makes me pee myself.

I barely make it to the toilet, and I then I cry. In relief. In shame. With fear. I don't even know how many hours I've been here.

"Stand up. Hands behind your back."

I blink at the voice. I didn't mean to fall asleep. Again.

"Stand. Hands behind your back."

I get up from the slab bed. Step as far back as I can. Hands behind my back.

Two guards. Both women.

"Where—?"

"Quiet." The taller guard opens the gate at the end of

the hall. Eyes are watching me through several of the doors, scarier somehow than the guards when they look in.

Through gate after gate, until I'm led into a room.

The room is small, but compared to the cell, it's spacious. Just a table, bolted down, and two chairs. A camera in the upper corner. What looks like a window but is probably a two-way mirror. And the agent, the woman, is waiting for me. She and the guards barely talk, but she smiles at them and at me. She looks different. She's wearing a suit, and her dark hair is loose and sort of curled under. She's even wearing a little makeup, lipstick at least. She smiles like we're friends.

We're not.

"Hi, Bex," she says. I don't answer. They were calling me Rebecca. Now it's Bex. Someone talked to them. A different agent is with her. "I'm not sure if you remember, but I'm Agent Washington. This is Investigator Randall," she says, like I should know what that means. "Please sit."

I don't really have a choice. Seated where she wants, I face the two-way mirror. Who knows how many different people are watching me. I stare at the fake mirror. Maybe if I look hard enough, I'll be able to see them.

Agent Washington puts a bottle of water down in front of me, cap already loose.

My mouth is so dry. I've been afraid to eat or drink anything.

But I didn't see her open the bottle.

"I hear you're not eating. Can I get you something? Candy bar? Sandwich?"

She smiles again, acting like we're on the same side.

"Anything you want. I can get it for you."

Investigator Randall stands against the far wall, watching. Are other people watching, too?

"Your aunt is here. We're just waiting for her to be brought down."

"Where's my mom?"

Agent Washington ignores my question. Investigator Randall leaves the room.

I swallow hard, or try to, but my mouth is too dry. Aunt Lorraine's never been my favorite person. But my eyes sting at the thought of seeing her. Maybe she can tell me what's going on, or help me get out of here. The trembling starts in my arms again, and I hold them tight against my body. Maybe she's here to take me home. Just a little longer and I can go home.

"Go ahead," Agent Washington says, motioning toward the water.

She wants me to pick it up. Why? For fingerprints? No, they already took those. DNA? Could be DNA, but seems like they could get that any time they want. Or is there something in there? Something to make me relax, make me let down my guard? Make me talk?

"Bex, I can see you need a drink. Go ahead."

I stare at the open bottle. Debate the risks. Maybe one sip. No. That's what they want.

I cross my arms, tuck my hands in, and hold them down so I won't accidentally drink it.

Then she makes a sound and takes the bottle away. And she's gone, out the door with the water. Maybe I should have chanced it.

She gave up sort of fast.

Maybe she thought I'm just a dumb kid, easy to fool.

I'm not sure whether I'm smart or stupid. I need to drink something. My lips are too dry. But it seemed too important to her. Maybe I'm paranoid. Unless I'm not paranoid but really, really smart. You're only paranoid if someone's not trying to hurt you. They've already hurt me.

I put my head down on the table. It's cold against my cheek. Nice. I should have drunk the water. It was probably cold.

The door opens, and then stuff is falling onto the table. Granola bar. Candy bars. Pretzels. Pop-Tarts. Crackers and peanut butter. Chips.

Agent Washington puts two unopened cans down in front of me. Pop and juice.

"From the vending machines."

The cans look solid. Slick on the outside, like vending-machine cans are.

"Unopened," she says. She got it. Can I chance it?

My hand is reaching before I've fully talked myself into it, pauses, and then reaches all the way out and picks up the can of juice. Once I'm holding it, it's inevitable. I pop it open and take a quick sip. Cold and a burst of sweet, sharp across my teeth and the back of my throat. I take another sip. Then a gulp. Then chug half the can.

My mouth still sort of feels dry, like cardboard soaking in the liquid only partway. Fuzzy.

Goose bumps pop out all over me.

I didn't even realize Agent Washington was gone until she was back, with the guy—Menendez—Investigator Randall, and Aunt Lorraine.

"Bex!" She's hugging me before the agents can stop her. Then there's warnings about touching and more chairs are brought in, and she's seated beside me, hands mostly to herself.

"Are we allowed to talk in private?" Aunt Lorraine asks, big, fake, my-crap-don't-stink smile on her face.

"Sure," Menendez says, glancing at Washington.

"We'll give you a little while to talk," Investigator Randall says.

"We'll check back in a bit. And if you're ready for us before then, just knock on the door," Agent Washington says.

"That's fine," Aunt Lorraine says, still big smiles but nervous. Smiling too much. She never smiles this much.

When the door closes, she turns and looks at me. "Well, you don't look too bad. Are they feeding you okay? Do you need anything? Don't you worry—this will all be cleared up in no time. No time at all." She smiles at me, waiting, but I'm not sure for what. "Are you okay?"

Am I okay? I'm locked up. I'm pretty freaking far from okay.

"Bex?"

"No, I'm not okay," I say. "What the hell is going on? They won't tell me anything. Where's Mom? And Dad? They keep asking about Mark. About . . ." I look up at the camera. They could be taping this. "I don't know anything. I don't know what is going on," I say, loudly and clearly. "Where's Mom?" I ask again. It's burning behind my eyes.

"They're holding a whole bunch of people, including your mother, father, Mark, and Skip."

Ohgodohgodohgod.

"Who all besides us?"

"Oh, Bex, I don't know," she says. "I don't know your people." She is impatient. Looks at her watch, or where it would be. They probably made her take it off. She rubs her wrist, like I did from the cuffs. "The important thing is that we get this cleared up. Nathan said that since you are a juvenile, you should just tell them what you know and then we can get this all cleared up."

Uncle Nathan said. "But I don't know—"

"Tell them everything. Cooperate. Act in good faith, and then you'll be able to work out a deal."

Sage advice from the insurance salesman who thinks he knows everything.

"Bex." Aunt Lorraine leans closer, so close I can smell her breath. "You're a juvenile. Whatever you did, they can only do so much. But you need to get your mother out. She didn't do anything like this. I know she didn't. She couldn't. So you just tell them whatever they need to know to let her go."

I stare at her, replaying the words.

"I didn't do any—"

"You get her out!" she yells, grabbing me, shaking me. "This is all your fault. You and your brother, your father. All of you. They know you did it." Her face is crazy. "They know everything." Her eyes are bugging out. "You are in it up to your eyeballs, you and your brother. They took stuff from the house, the station. It's been all over the news." Spit on my cheek. "They know everything anyway," she says, vicious, like she's happy. "But your mother isn't involved. You need to tell them. Now."

I'm gonna be sick. Or pass out. Or explode.

"Your stupid brother." She grits her teeth, like she wants to snarl at me but remembered she shouldn't. "He tried to run away, but they found him, found him . . ." She stops, wipes her mouth, pastes on a calming look. "Honey, you know your mother wasn't involved. She was hardly even there! Working so hard to support the lot of you." Aunt Lorraine wipes at her eyes, takes a breath, pats the air in front of her like she's trying to calm herself down.

"Your mother must be terrified. And you know she would do anything for you." She gives me a sweet smile. "Bex, you need to be a good daughter and do what's right. For your mother. So"—she takes a deep breath and goes to the door—"you tell them what they need to know. You tell them that your mother didn't know anything, that she wasn't even part of this. That she's been staying with me. That's she's been *living* with us, for *months*, this whole time. You tell them." She knocks on the door.

Before I can respond, the agents and investigator are coming back in, all three of them with friendly smiles. Aunt

Lorraine smiles, too. The air is hard, pressing on my ears like hands trying to crush my skull.

"We'll be recording this," Investigator Randall says. "Okay?"

"Fine," Aunt Lorraine says. "Whatever you need." She pats my hand.

"Mrs. Blake," Agent Washington says, once they are settled into chairs across from us, "it's our understanding that you wish to act as Bex's guardian, and that her mother has asked that you be allowed to do so. There are certain formalities we need to observe. I need to read you and Bex these rights, and make sure you and she understand, before we proceed."

"That's fine," Aunt Lorraine says again, smiling, still patting my hand. "We're ready."

We. Like she's in this, too. They read her the same stuff they've read me. They ask her if she understands, and she says, "Oh, yes," like it's *easy peasy*, as she would say. Then they all look at me. They're hopeful: Aunt Lorraine gives me an encouraging nod.

"Bex, do you understand these rights that I've just read you? Again?" Agent Washington almost chuckles, like this is not at all serious.

"Bex?" Aunt Lorraine prompts.

I'm supposed to stay silent. That's all I know for sure.

Aunt Lorraine nods at me. The *go ahead* look. Go ahead and help Mom. No matter what's happening, they shouldn't have Mom. Or Uncle Skip. But you always stay silent. Always.

"Knowing and understanding your rights as I have explained them to you, are you willing to answer our questions without an attorney present?"

Does staying silent mean saying no? Or just, literally, saying nothing?

Everyone stares, and blinks, and looks at each other.

"I don't think she understood." Aunt Lorraine turns in her chair. "Bex, just say yes, and we can get this cleared up. For *everyone*."

I cross my arms over my chest.

"Do you need me to go over it again?" Agent Washington asks. Investigator Randall clears his throat, and the agents shift in their chairs.

Mom. Aunt Lorraine wants me to get Mom out.

Stay silent. Stay silent.

"Bex," Agent Washington says, a hand on Menendez's arm to stop whatever he was about to say. "If you choose not to talk with us, then we can't help you."

She and Investigator Randall drone on, tag-teaming me, all the bad stuff that will happen, state and federal and prison and how they just want to help me. Help me and Mom.

Stay silent. Always stay silent.

But . . . I didn't do anything. If I tell them I didn't do anything, they'd have to let me leave, right?

Stay silent.

"You can certainly wait for an attorney to be appointed before talking to us," Agent Washington says. "But by then, you'll be in adult court, and our hands will be tied. We've explained to your aunt," she says, looking over at Aunt Lorraine, who is agreeing with every word, "that once an attorney gets involved, your options are limited. But right now, if you want to talk, you can, and we can just figure out this whole thing. Maybe if you tell us your side, we can explain to the U.S. Attorney," she says, looking at Investigator Randall, who pauses, then nods. "But if you don't tell us your side, we can't help you."

I didn't do anything.

"And I've got to tell you, Bex," Agent Menendez says, pulling some papers from a file in front of him. "If you can clear any of this up, it might go a ways to getting you out of here faster." He shuffles the papers, like he's going to show me, but then decides not to. Then he lays a few of them down. Pictures of stuff—wires, guns, ammunition, some I recognize and some I don't. Dad's truck. Mark's truck. My ammunition, in the space under the floorboards in my room, but with the floorboards pulled up. The farmhouse and the station, both surrounded by police tape. "Because once you have a lawyer, they're not going to let us talk to you. They're going to argue and stall, and then there's no way we can avoid trying you as an adult. Going full out with all the possible charges. Conspiracy. Treason. Intent to murder people. Weapons of mass destruction." What the—? "But if you can clear some of this stuff up, then maybe something can be worked out." Weapons of mass . . . ? "I mean, you're a kid. I look at who all was involved in this, and you just don't seem to fit." He picks up the picture of the guns, and then another from the file, looks at them side by side, and then places them facedown in front of him. What do they show? "Maybe I'm wrong. Maybe you *were* in on this plan. But it feels like maybe not. Maybe you weren't really part of it. But you knew about it, or you got roped into it, or Mark asked you to do something," he says.

"And if that's true," Agent Washington says, "then it's real important that you tell your version before anyone else points a finger your way."

"The others are all adults," Agent Menendez says. "They've got a lot to gain from pushing as much of this off on you as they can."

"Otherwise," Agent Washington says, "it could be weeks before an attorney is appointed and comes to see you. Months before the attorney has worked up an initial game plan on your case. And you'll be sitting in here while he's doing whatever, maybe even working other cases, and in the meantime maybe some of the other guys cut deals, deals that put you in the mix of this."

Months. Before anything . . . I try to swallow, but my mouth's dry again. It's always dry.

"Bex," Aunt Lorraine says, "talk to them. They can help."

Please.

"Maybe we can start with something easy," Agent Washington says. "Not even about you. Let's talk about Mark. When did you last see him?"

I don't want to think about Mark. The last time I saw him, I thought he was going to choke me to death. He was so crazy. And scared. I know he was scared. *I'm handling it.* I should have told Dad. Made him listen. Aunt Lorraine said he ran, but they have him. For what? What did he do?

A loud rushing sound in my ears makes everything distant. Everything except for my too-loud heartbeat banging into my eardrums and bouncing off my temples.

What did he do?

"I've got to be honest with you, Bex," Agent Washington says, leaning on the table, her hands folded in front of her. "We just don't think you were that involved. Maybe your brother, maybe he asked you to do something. Something you didn't understand, even. Or . . ."

I miss whatever she says next. I stare at the pictures of the house, of the station. They have Uncle Skip, too. His house. His station. Could he lose his station? Could they put him in prison, because of something we did? I did so much shooting on his property. I built the pipe bomb in his workshop. Could they think he was building things? The trunk. What did I leave in it?

Or they could be lying: all of this could be lies. But why?

"Bex!"

I blink and sit up in my chair.

Aunt Lorraine glares, points for me to look at the agents.

Agent Menendez flexes his hands in front of him, to keep my attention. "Maybe you didn't know that . . ."

Something in my brain pops, and reason floods in.

They don't want to help me. They want to hurt me. Or someone else. They would never help me. That's not their job.

"No."

"No?" Agent Menendez repeats.

Agent Washington leans closer to the table. "What do you mean by—?"

"I don't want to do this, to answer questions."

"Bex," Aunt Lorraine says, grabbing my arm. "Enough

being stubborn. Now, you do the right thing. Now. For your mother," she stage-whispers. "Do what's right."

I shake her off. Take a breath. Look at the agents.

They all continue to look at me.

Agents Menendez and Washington look at each other.

"Just so we're clear, Bex," she says. "Once—"

"I want a lawyer," I shout.

Those are the magic words. Menendez and Washington sit back and start to put their papers away. Investigator Randall lets out a breath and closes his notebook.

"That's it?" Aunt Lorraine says.

"That's it." Agent Menendez grabs the papers from in front of me, takes one out from under Aunt Lorraine's fingers. "Law says we have to stop until she's had a chance to talk with an attorney."

I can see the disappointment in their faces. They're trying to hide it, but they wanted me to talk. They thought I would talk. All the more reason to stay quiet. They thought I was a stupid kid. Unprepared. I'm not stupid.

"Tell them!" Aunt Lorraine yells. "You tell them." She's unhinged. "Now! You do it now! Get your mother out!" Her nails are digging into my arms and pulling me almost out of my chair with each shake. "You ungrateful little . . ."

They pull her away from me, drag her out the door.

Then quiet. It's quiet. And then the door is open again and Agent Washington is there. She reaches for me and I spring up, low, ready. She backs off, hands up.

"It's okay. We're okay. We're—"

"Agent?" Guards, in the door.

"I'm fine. We're fine. She was just scared. We're okay. Please leave."

"Agent, I really think—"

"Leave."

"Are you okay?" Agent Washington asks. "Are you hurt? Do you need medical care?"

I assess my body, relaxing my muscles. My arm's sore, but I can turn it okay. My elbow hurts—I banged it trying to get away from Aunt Lorraine—but everything is moving okay.

"Sit down before they come in again."

"I don't—"

"I'm not going to ask you any questions. I'm just going to make sure you're okay, and give Agent Menendez a chance to settle things outside."

She retreats to her side of the table, picking up the knocked-over chairs. I pick up mine and sit down, too shattered to stand.

"Is there anyone else we can call?" she asks.

I shake my head. Gran hates me, and she's old, and in Arizona. There's no one.

We sit in silence. My juice is still on the table. It didn't even spill. I reach out with shaking hands and pick it up. Tiny sips against my shaking mouth. Maybe the room is shaking and not me.

There's air hitting my skin, wet from the sweat around my hair, on my neck; it makes me shiver.

"They won't let you take these with you," Washington says quietly, nudging a candy bar toward me. "Eat."

I'm not at all hungry. Or maybe beyond hungry.

She shouldn't be here. *I* shouldn't be here. I want to go home.

Agent Washington sorts through the pile. "Well, suit yourself," she says, unwrapping a Snickers bar and taking a big bite, chewing slowly, and then swallowing. "If we're chewing, we can't be talking."

I can smell the chocolate, and the peanuts, and even I think that bit of salt that clings to the nuts. I can't imagine dinner will be edible. I give in and unwrap a Twix bar, devouring each piece in two bites. Then I go for the crackers. They might actually have some nutritional value. Then the Pop-Tarts. Even cold, they're pretty damn good.

And then I'm in cuffs again. In another cell. In another room.

A long night, with no idea what happens next.

Then another car. And another room. A guy, a lawyer, who says stuff, but nothing I understand. A judge. Talking. I don't understand any of it, except I'm not going home.

And then another car.

Guards.

Stripped.

Searched.

They take my clothes. They take everything.

I don't know where my backpack is. I haven't seen it since the truck.

I don't think this is the crisis, not like the whole government rounding up everyone. I think this is just us. But I don't know how many of us, or why.

I can't stop the shaking.

CHAPTER 23

The cell they put me in is small. Bare. Concrete walls. Cement slab for a bed. Metal counter jutting out from the wall. Metal stool bolted to the ground. Metal toilet and sink and water fountain all in one. No bars like you see on TV. Solid walls and a solid door with a slot and a small window so they can spy on me. Blocking out all sound except for distant murmurs of life. Another small window, if you can call it that—really just mesh-glass covering the small spaces between metal slats in the wall. If I stand on the slab bed and crane my neck just right, I can see a little bit of the parking lot beyond the fences. Fences with razor wire on top.

Someone is yelling. Distant. Approaching. Louder, right outside the door. Kicking, yelling, and then moving away again. A door opening and slamming somewhere. Still yelling.

It's so hot. Sweat drips off me.

If I take a deep breath, I suck up all the air in the room and there's none left. I gasp and choke until I realize there's plenty of air, that the lack of air is all in my head. Still, I breathe shallowly.

It's a not even a room.

It's a cement box.

We made dioramas in fourth grade. I can feel the unseen audience watching me, poking at the bolted-down furniture, at me, at my clothes that are not my clothes—the too-big orange jumpsuit, dingy shirt and socks and underwear, floppy scuffs.

I have no idea when anyone will come back for me, who they will be, what they will do. They stopped as soon as I said I wanted a lawyer, but that doesn't mean some other agents or police or something won't try again. Or try something else to make me talk. I don't know whether I'm more afraid that no one will ever come to get me again and I will die here, in this room, maybe from a lack of air, or that someone *will* come and I'll wish they hadn't.

A guard looks through the window every now and then. Maybe at set intervals, I don't know. The first guard looked for a while, curious—the first time, at least. The second one just looked. The third guard sneered. I actually held my breath as I started to anticipate his return. The second time he looked, and the third, I could feel the shakes, the fear, like a deer sensing my sight through a scope must feel. Keys jingled on his fourth look, and I scurried back on the bed, scrabbling for anything to hide behind. He laughed.

The tears came then. I knew they must be watching me, even if I wasn't facing the camera, and I tried to hold the tears in. But it was either cry or scream, and I figured if I started screaming, they would definitely come in here.

I curled up and cried as silently as I could. For a long time. My muscles stiffened up, and the shame made it all worse. When I heard footsteps or noises in the hall, I curled in tighter, buried my face in the sheet, and tried to hold the shakes inside, tried to stay still.

I've read so many guides on dealing with the government, on knowing your rights and how to be strong. Guys who have been arrested—"detained"—offering tips and tactics. I've imagined the words I would say, about being a prisoner of war or a political prisoner. About demanding certain rights. I had always thought I'd be strong, like in the woods.

But when they drag you from your uncle's truck, plant you facedown, cuff you, put you in the back of a car, put you in a room, ask you a million questions, about bombs, about guns, about family, all of that leaves your head. All reason leaves your head. *You* are hardly even in your head. All speeches and plans and stands long lost in the sheer jumbled panic of your brain. How long did they talk at me, try to trick me, before my brain unjumbled long enough for me to remember the magic words *I want a lawyer*? How much longer could I have taken it without giving in if I hadn't remembered?

Until a door closes on you.

I wash my face and count the steps across my cell, from one end to the other, and then from side to side. Calming myself with the repetition of action. Until I'm so tired I need to lie down.

I curl up on the bed. For just a minute, I tell myself. So I can think, with my face to the wall, so they can't see me thinking. But I must have slept, because I wake up to the sound of the door being opened. I try to hurl myself up and away, in my mind seeing myself crouching low, ready to defend myself, like with Mark or in a drill. But I just stumble to the wall, whacking my knee on the bed, like I can't even control my muscles.

I can't control anything.

A woman guard stands in the open door, a male guard behind her, hand on a baton at his waist, but his face is calm.

"You answer when spoken to," she says. "At mealtimes

you will be given a tray through the slot. You take it. You eat it. Understand?"

I nod. Afraid to hear my voice but afraid not to respond.

The door closes and then there is a tray of food through the slot. I take it, because I'm afraid of what happens if I don't. If they open that door again. If the guy with the baton comes in here. Every muscle trembles with relief and the flood of adrenaline and the pent-up terror of the situation crashing down when they walk away.

I put the tray on the metal shelf thing jutting out of the wall. Stare at the tray. I can't eat it. Any of it. I go back to the bed.

I'm in prison. When they said juvenile detention, I pictured, like . . . rooms. Kids. Locks, but like a school or something. Not this. This is a prison.

I don't know what to do. Except to stay quiet. And try not to cry anymore.

I stare at the tray. Wondering when they will come back. Whether to trust the food.

What happens when I haven't eaten any of it? No one's going to bring me snacks from a vending machine like Agent Washington did. I'll have to eat what they give me eventually, right?

The guys on the message boards would tell me to refuse

it, that it might be drugged or tampered with. Someone might have spit in it, or worse. They'd trust no one.

I couldn't eat if I wanted to. But what happens later? I'll have to eat sometime, and drink, right? Should I flush some of it down the toilet, just so they think I've eaten?

Or are they watching me? Right now, is someone watching me? Are they always watching me? Every minute? Until I know, I should just not eat it. Strategy. Survey the landscape, and the enemy, before showing yourself or attempting subterfuge.

With my back to the wall, wedged into the corner, I can see the window in the door and most of the cell. I scan every surface, inch by inch, learning every detail, every chip, every scratch.

The wall is warm. I don't know if I am. I don't know anything.

Eventually exhaustion takes over. I sleep for hours. They wake me at times to check on me, and for meals, which I mostly ignore. Sleeping is easier than worrying about what is happening, or what might happen. Where everyone is. Where they might take me. Why any of this happened.

When I need toilet paper, I have to ask for it. Hope one of the guards is nearby. Hope they give me enough.

I still haven't seen Mom, or Dad, or anyone.

I think Mark did something. Something bad.

I keep thinking about the questions they were asking me, and the pictures of Uncle Skip's house and the station taped off as crime scenes, and replaying the last week over in my head. Then the weeks before that.

What did Riggs think I knew, or what did he already know? What did he say to Mark? What made Mark like that, made him so crazy?

Mark and Zach and who else being at the station, at night. I was supposed to tell Uncle Skip. I should have told him. I should have told Dad, when things got weird, after Riggs, after Mark. That night. I should have called Dad. Made him listen.

What the hell did Mark do?

They took all of our family. Even Uncle Skip. Is it just us, or is it bigger than that? Could it be all of Clearview? Or maybe not all, but some of the other families, too?

Maybe they really did arrest everyone from Clearview, but for what? And they kept asking about Mark. Just Mark. How long can they hold us all?

Maybe Mark didn't do anything, and they're just trying to set us all up.

Maybe someone else is setting us up. Riggs? Was he trying

to use me to set Mark up for something? Or someone else? The government? Maybe Devon and Neal and their open-carry demonstrations made the government nervous. Maybe this isn't real. Maybe they're just rattling us. Maybe they're asking Mark about me, and someone else about someone else, to mess with us all.

Is Uncle Skip okay? He hasn't done anything. Will they believe him? Did they only go after him because I was in the truck? Will he hate me?

When do I get to see Mom or Dad or . . . anyone?

Something smells awful. Has to be the food. I turn my nose into my shoulder to try to block the smell.

A tray is shoved through the slot in my door. The center compartment is full of the smell, only ten times stronger. Sloppy, gloppy, like meat stew but not good.

I take the sealed juice, the apple, and the bread and put them on my shelf for later, and then scrape the rest into the toilet and flush.

The smell lingers for a long time, making me gag repeatedly.

Maybe this is all strategy. I look at the corner where the camera is. I can feel them watching me, studying me, waiting for me to crack. Maybe this is all about making me sweat it out. Maybe they wait until I'm good and primed, and then bet I'll spill my guts not to be brought back here.

No way.

It feels like I've been here for weeks. Weeks under water. But I know it's only been days. Two? Three?

No matter what they throw at me, I'm not talking.

CHAPTER 24

I hear the keys and I'm up and standing two steps from the bed by the time the guard's got the door open. The tension falls back when I see it's Gage. It's only been a few days, but I'm figuring out how to move around the guards, how to make it clear I'm not going to be any trouble.

"Lawyer's here," Gage says. I don't know what to do, but I keep my hands where she can see them and follow her instructions, keep my head down, try to remember what to do for next time in case it's not Gage in charge of moving me.

I never call any of the guards anything. *Sir* or *ma'am* if I absolutely have to.

Gage leads me from the cell. Taggert is with her. Before I knew his name, I called him Creeper, in my head, and imagined he's Deputy Creep's cousin. He's the one who stares through the window, taunting, whispering. Like he wonders what my guts look like. He's become the thing I fear at night, in the dark, the nights I know he's on duty, the things he might do to a "traitorous little shit" like me.

I try not to think about Lucy much. She seems like forever ago. But Lucy and her aversion to the C word keep popping up, because Taggert likes it just fine.

Where is Lucy now? Does she know I've been arrested? Does she think I deserve it? For that matter, where are Cammie and Karen and the rest of the people from Clearview? There's no way for me to know what's going on and whether they've been arrested, too. They wouldn't be here. They're older.

When we get to the room, Gage takes me in while Taggert waits in the hall. There's a woman across the table, standing. Short hair. Hard eyes. Suit.

She smiles at Gage.

I don't know whether to sit.

"Hi. Bex, right?" Her voice is smooth. "Or do you actually prefer Rebecca?" I don't know if it's safe to talk to her. "I'm Joan Bryant. The court appointed me to represent you." How do I know that? How do I know she's who she says she is? "Here," she says. She motions toward the chair. I sit down. Then she sits, puts a file and legal pad in front of her, and passes a piece of paper across the table. I lean forward so I can see it without touching it. It looks official.

"How do I know you are who you say you are?"

Her eyebrows climb and tip in. Her pupils get bigger. She tosses a business card across the table to me.

I play with the card, turning it by its corner until it spins on the table. Anyone could have business cards made.

"Look," she says, leaning across the table, "if I'm not who I say I am, if I'm . . . a government agent trying to trick you," she says, like she's figured me out, "then anything you say to me would be inadmissible."

Unless she's lying about that, too.

But what choice do I have?

"You're my lawyer?"

"That's up to you."

"I get a choice?"

"Sure." She puts down the pen and leans back in her chair. "You can decline to have an attorney. If after we talk, you don't want my assistance, I'll tell the court you declined."

"So, no choice." I lean back, too. "You or I'm SOL."

"What do you want?"

To go home.

"I'm curious." She isn't mocking me. She's asking. "Who were you hoping for? Someone older? Someone who would pat your hand and tell you everything's going to be okay? A man?"

"No." I shake my head, trying to clear it. "Someone who

will fight for me. Someone . . . who can explain what's happening, so *I* can understand. Someone who can tell me how to get out of here, and what I should do."

Someone I can trust. Who will help me.

"I can explain what's happening," she says, bringing her chair closer to the table. "I can't tell you what you should do. You will have to make those choices, in consultation with your parent or guardian, if you wish. Though, given that every adult in your immediate family is involved in this in one way or another, I'm going to caution you not to discuss certain aspects of this case with any of them. I can ask the court to appoint a guardian ad litem to help guide you, to give you a second opinion, if you doubt my advice."

I don't even know what that means.

"Some things, like trial strategy, what witnesses to call, what motions to file, I will make those decisions," she says.

Trial. Witnesses.

"But the big ones," she says. "Like, should you talk to the government, should you agree to a plea deal, should you testify if this goes to contested hearing or to trial . . . I will give you all the options, the possible ramifications, and advice. But you will be making those decisions for yourself."

"And what I say goes?" I ask.

"Yes, on the big things, absolutely."

"Even if my mom or dad or someone else says I should do something different? Tells you to do something different?"

"You are my client." It hangs there. "If you so choose." I wait for the "but," or the catch. "It is your life on the line. You're the one they may try to put in prison."

"May? They might let me go?"

She holds up her hand. "I said *may* because it's still not settled whether you will be tried under state or federal law, under the criminal statutes as an adult or in a juvenile delinquency hearing. But we need to be clear on whether I represent you, and what my obligations are regarding what you tell me, before we talk about the possibilities."

"I don't even understand what's happening," I say. I start shaking again. "Why did they arrest us? Where is my family? Are they in jail?"

"What do you know of the arrests?"

"Nothing!" I feel the panic rising. "I mean, they kept asking about Mark, and bombs, over and over, and guns, and where he was, where *they* are, but then they stopped, and . . . What's going on?"

She takes a deep breath. "Your brother, Mark, and four other men have been charged by the federal government with seditious conspiracy, the manufacturing with intent to use weapons of mass destruction—explosive devices—and various weapons charges, including having illegally modified weapons, illegally acquired ammunition, and carrying and using firearms in the commission of a crime."

"Mark? And those idiots? They talk big, but . . ." But even as I say it, I can see those guys at the house. I picture Mark's face, the way he was so freaked out that I had talked to Riggs, and afraid of what I might have told him. He could have killed me. Completely out of control. "They can't possibly think they were *seriously* going to . . . to . . ."

"They did, obviously," she says. "In order for several law-enforcement agencies to have coordinated, to have obtained warrants and orchestrated simultaneous raids on multiple locations, to have acted when they did, they not only thought they were serious — they thought the threat was imminent."

I can't think.

"The indictment alleges that they planned to kill a law-enforcement officer or officers, so that they could set off explosives at the resulting funeral sure to be attended by other law-enforcement officers, in order to draw the state and federal authorities into a standoff at a heavily booby-trapped and armed location, to spark a revolution."

I can't . . . I can't even . . .

"When your brother was located, after trying to evade arrest, he almost ran over a law-enforcement officer, and he's lucky they didn't kill him right then. They would have been justified. He was armed and was found to have several weapons, including a fully automatic rifle."

Oh, my God.

"They are looking for where he, or they, were keeping the explosives—or the components they intended to use to build the explosive devices—right now."

God.

"They may have been talking big," she says, "but they took enough steps toward acting on that talk to get the attention of the federal authorities, for warrants to be issued, and to be indicted." She stares at me.

I'm shaking again. I pull the too-long jumpsuit sleeves down over my hands, wrap my arms around my body, try to stop shaking.

"Breathe," she says, and I do. Loudly. My heart is pounding in my chest and head and behind my eyes and in my ears. She waits until I'm breathing normally and looking at her to continue. "They've been criminally charged by the federal government. You have not. Not yet. Not with being part of the conspiracy."

"I don't understand. Then how can they keep me here?"

"Right now, they are holding you for possession and carrying concealed weapons—a twenty-two-caliber Smith and Wesson three-seventeen revolver, which was loaded and in your bag when they detained you, which you are not old enough to possess, let alone carry, and a knife that they allege—"

"What's wrong with the knife?" She looks at me like she can't believe I would question what was wrong with the knife. "It's a hunting knife."

"For one thing, it was concealed in your bag—a concealed weapon, so they allege. But for another, it's a . . ." She flips to her notes and reads, "Double-edged nonfolding stabbing instrument, or so they say."

"It's a *hunting* knife," I say again. "How can a hunting knife be illegal?"

"I'm not sure that it is," she says. "But the fact that you had it concealed, on or about your person, complicates things. As do the money and ammunition they found hidden in a room they assert was used exclusively by you at your uncle's house. We'll need to discuss the circumstances surrounding your staying in the house, and your use of that room, and the circumstances surrounding your arrest and the search of your bag, but for now . . ." She waits for me to argue some more, but I don't, even though it seems ridiculous. "Both the State of Michigan and the federal government have laws that govern firearms and ammunition and how to deal with acts by a juvenile that violate those laws. That means that the state and the federal government have concurrent jurisdiction." She pauses, waits for me to make any sign I'm following her. I don't. Because I'm not. "It means either of them can ultimately decide to charge you with violating their respective laws, and either can do so as part of a juvenile proceeding or charge you as an adult and try you in adult court."

"I don't understand. They have me locked up. How can they keep me if they aren't sure what they think I've done?"

"They haven't decided yet whether they have enough to charge you as a coconspirator in the larger criminal conspiracy." She holds up her hand to stop me from interrupting. "But while they continue to investigate, they have more than enough to hold you related to the weapons and ammunition."

"They can do that?"

"Yes," she says. "At least for now."

Every person who ever said to be afraid of our government was right.

"Before we talk about any of the specific evidence, and any defenses you have, any motions we may want to file, how I intend to defend you," she says, "I want to go over the case materials more thoroughly." She puts her pen down. "That is, if you want me to defend you."

I study her. She seems for real. Her hair is short. Her suit isn't fussy. Strong hands, short nails. She looks like a regular person, but she talks like she knows what she's doing. She seems smart. She seems strong. She makes a million times more sense than the guy who talked to me before the judge sent me here.

"Have you ever shot a gun?" I ask her.

"Yes, I've shot guns."

Guns. "Own any?"

"Yes."

"So you support the Second Amendment?"

"Yes, I support the Second Amendment. But more important, I support your rights as a citizen of the United States to be free from unlawful search and seizure. Your right to due process under the law. Your right to a zealous legal defense. That you are innocent until proven guilty."

"Even if you think I did everything they say?"

"Even if I come to believe you have done all of the acts you have been accused of, and more," she says slowly, "I will still do everything I can to make sure you have the best defense possible. I will make sure you are afforded every right and protection the law allows, and I will argue for your freedom."

"Why?"

"Because I believe in the Constitution." One side of her mouth turns up. "All of it. And because it's my job."

I'm afraid of the warmth in my gut telling me to trust her.

"It's a tough decision, whether to accept a lawyer's services or not. Maybe you want to see if you can hire someone yourself? Some would let you, you know, for a cut of your eventual book deals and TV appearances, or for you signing a paper allowing them to make money off of talking about representing you. You'd be on all the talk shows."

"Are you kidding me?" I don't want to be on TV at all. "I'm not doing any books or TV appearances, or any of that."

"Well, there are lawyers, experienced ones, who will take your case for the publicity alone. I can recommend some that are less sleazy than others, if you're interested."

"Are you going to want a cut?"

"No." She laughs. "This is my job. I'm compensated by the court for representing you. That's how I'm paid. But if you agree, I will be representing *you*. And I take that seriously."

I watch her, try to read her. She's the first one to treat me like I matter, to help me understand. But she belongs to them, to the government. They pay her. How can I trust her if they're paying her? Maybe if she understood I didn't do anything, maybe then she would fight for me. Maybe.

"Can you get me out of here?"

She shakes her head. "No. At least not now. As I said, they have enough to hold you in a secure facility for now.

The government is going to oppose any release terms, and the court will likely agree. I can try to get you out of segregation, but I'm not optimistic. Right now, one of the few things on which they all agree is keeping you in seg. The investigation is continuing and there's a possibility of more—and more serious—charges."

"I didn't—"

"Stop."

"But—"

"Not until we understand each other. Not until you are sure you want me to represent you. I don't want you to say *anything* until we are clear on our roles and obligations."

She talks about our roles and what I can "expect." I try to follow, but I'm tired and my head is spinning. My brain is too full. I can't sleep for more than a couple hours at a time, not even at night. I can't eat. I was afraid to drink the juice at breakfast since the seal was open. And the water from the fountain grosses me out. It smells like maybe it's not really for drinking, and I can't drink from the fountain without seeing the toilet.

"A lot to take in," she finally says when I sway in my seat. I try to sit up, plant my feet, and refocus, but she's capping her pen. "Enough for today. We can talk again next week after

I've had a chance to review what they've given me so far and make some calls. Assuming, that is, that I'm your lawyer."

"Yes." I don't hesitate. "Please."

"Good." She uncaps her pen and makes some notes on her legal pad. "The agents want to question you again, but they will have to wait until I'm more familiar with the case and we've had a chance to talk further."

"I don't want to talk to them."

"We'll discuss it after I know more. But for now, my focus is on looking at the evidence and finding out the government's position on jurisdiction and transfer. And in the meantime, don't talk to anyone about anything except the weather. Not about your life. Not about your family. Not *anything* about this case. Nothing. Understand?"

I nod and swallow, because who would I talk to, Taggert?

She is looking at me, thinking. I can practically hear her thinking.

"Bex," she says, leaning forward slightly, "your mother will be coming to see you."

"She's out?"

"Yes."

"What about my dad? Uncle Skip?"

"Your uncle has been released, but your dad has not."

Thank God. Uncle Skip.

"When your mother comes to see you," she says, "please remember that she can be compelled to testify against you. Anything you say to her can be used against you in court. And . . ." She pauses, rethinks what she wants to say, and then tries again. "Your mother's world has been turned upside down. Her husband and both of her children are in custody. Her home is a crime scene. . . . She may not be thinking clearly." She waits for me to say something. When I don't, she says, "She may not understand the legal implications of everything she, or you, knows. Please do not discuss the case with her."

But she's my mom. She can tell me what's happening. Where Mark is. And Dad, and . . . everyone.

"Bex," she says. "Until we understand the evidence and potential charges better and can sort out some things. Please."

I don't answer. I can't. This woman is a stranger who's paid by the government. Even if she means what she says, she's still employed by them.

Mom will tell me what's going on.

CHAPTER 25

"Oh, thank the Lord," Mom says, rushing at me and pulling me into a hard hug. I look behind her, but no one else is here.

I've never been in the family visiting room before. There are tables, with bolted-down seats. Like sometime there must have been a brawl. Then again, how many kids are in here because of their crappy families? Better not to have weapons for those visits—even chairs.

At least it's cooler in here. It's hot in my cell. The walls sweat. The jumpsuit itches where it sticks to me, but it's all I have to wear except for the T-shirt under it.

"I came as soon as they let me." She leans back, holding my face and looking at me. "Are you okay?"

I nod because it's what she needs.

"Your father and I have been so worried."

"He's home?"

"Not yet. But soon, we hope," she says. "He told me to tell

you he loves you. And to be strong." She looks like she wants to say more, but her lips are pulled in tight. "Be brave."

We sit down at the table, but Mom won't let go of me. "Are you really okay?" she asks again.

"I guess," I say.

We sit in silence.

"What's going on?" I whisper.

She shakes her head, looking away. "I was questioned. They kept me for days. The attorney finally made them let me go."

"You hired an attorney?"

"Your uncle Nathan did." She looks down at her hands clenched in her lap. "For me."

Of course. Not for me. For me he sent Aunt Lorraine to tell me to confess. For Mom he hired a lawyer.

"Dad? Uncle Skip?"

"Skip's been released, too."

"Where is he? Can I see him?"

"I don't think they'll let you see him. Just immediate family, I think. But I can ask. . . ."

"Where is he?"

"Staying with a man named Heinman."

Oh. Good. Mr. Heinman is good people.

Mom digs into her pocket and pulls out a tissue. She

wipes at her eyes. The dark, puffy circles under her eyes look like bruises.

It hurts, the way she's looking at me.

"What?"

She shakes her head, dabs at her eyes, but she's not crying. Her eyes are dry and hard and scared, or not scared—worried, or angry, or like she's scared of me, like she thinks I did something bad. Like after she found out about the pipe bomb, only worse. Much worse. Like she thinks that they had a reason to arrest me. She thinks this is *my* fault.

"I swear, I didn't—"

"Bex!" Mom shouts, holding up her hand. "Not a word. Don't tell me anything." Mom reaches for my hand and then pulls back before she touches me. "It doesn't matter. Not right now. What matters now is keeping you safe. Keeping you *all* safe. Your lawyer, Ms. Bryant—and Mark's—they both said we shouldn't talk about the specifics of the case. There'll be time for that . . . after."

After. I can't even think of after, of what after might be. After what? When is *after*?

Mom finally pulls my hand in closer. "Anything you say, to us, to the government, to *anyone*"—she looks at me—"*anything* you say can be used against both of you, *all* of you." Her stare bores into my skull. "You, Mark, and your father. Do you understand?" she asks, stroking my hand. "The attorney Uncle Nathan hired said there's a good chance that as a juvenile, you won't be facing much of anything. Maybe not even a criminal conviction."

My stomach churns.

"Mark's nineteen," she says, staring down at my hand, clasped in hers like she's praying over it. "An adult. And your father . . ."

I don't understand. I look at her stroking my hand, like she used to when I was a kid.

"They're adults," Mom says, eyes hard and clear when she looks up at me. Determined. She's here with a purpose. Not to see me, or not *just* to see me. "Mark's in with the adult men. Criminals." She takes a deep breath and leans closer until her face is almost touching mine. "You are a juvenile. But he's an *adult*."

Oh.

"Do you understand?" she asks.

Yes.

She's trying to protect Mark. Wants me to help protect Mark.

"Just think real hard before you say anything, to anyone. Please."

She holds the look, won't look away until I nod.

"Family," she says. "We take care of each other. No matter what."

No matter what. No matter that he went crazy and could have killed me. Or that I could have killed him. Family.

She tries to smile, but it doesn't work. "My good girl, it's going to be okay. I promise. This is all a big, big mistake. And it's going to be okay."

She hasn't called me her "good girl" in years, but lying to me, and to herself, is nothing new. It probably won't be okay, but she doesn't have to worry about me. I won't betray them.

I didn't do anything, and I won't help them prove whatever Mark did. Not because we're family, but because I'm not a snitch, or a collaborator. Because something made him paranoid or high or terrified.

Someone could be setting him up, setting *us* up.

Something made him lose it and that almost made me shoot him.

I've been planning and training and begging and trying to save them, all of them—even Mark—for the past year. Longer. I may not be able to save them, but I won't help anyone hurt them.

CHAPTER 26

Someone is crying. Someone new, not the Cryer: she's at the other end.

It's not close, and I only hear it in brief snatches of sound, maybe when a door is swinging closed behind a guard. Or maybe when the ventilation shuts down for a second. But someone new is crying.

After more than eight weeks, I'm all cried out. Couldn't cry if they paid me. Maybe not even if they beat me.

Solitary will do that to you.

I try to remember how to breathe. Slow, deliberate breath in. Hold for a few seconds, as long as I can, and then out. For hours. Too exhausted to move. Straining to make sense of it all. Trying to wake up. Because this can't be real.

It's freezing in the hole now. Outside, it still looks like when I came here, not even really like fall yet, at least for the one tree I can see through the slats of my window. But over a couple of days, it went from hot to okay to cold. My body can't catch up. I can't get warm. I've started sleeping with my socks over my hands and my T-shirt wrapped around my head.

Last night I thought I would die I was so cold. And it's not even winter. How bad will it be in winter? Will I still be here in winter?

This morning I woke groggy and cold and queasy. Breakfast didn't help.

Joan is coming today. I need to be more than awake.

I do my morning workout—sit-ups, push-ups, stretches, jumping jacks—until I have to lie down again. Eight weeks and I'm weak. I'd never be able to sprint for three minutes now.

I jump at the sound of keys in the lock. I stand and keep my hands in sight, waiting to see which one it is.

Gage doesn't work on Wednesdays, so another of the regular guards and one I haven't seen before take me down. The new one's almost polite.

Joan smiles at them. I'm beginning to understand her smiles. That one is meant to soothe.

The new guards always seem surprised when they first see me. I have no idea what they were expecting, what is being said about me out there.

Once the guards are gone, Joan stays standing, looking me over.

Joan never asks how I am. It makes me want to like her. I can't like her. We're not friends. Even when she's making sense, I need to remember: she gets paid by the government. I need to stay focused. Like in the woods. Move slowly. Act deliberately. Cautiously.

But I also need to know what's happening. "My mom said that my dad's out. And that Mark might be coming home soon, too," I say.

"Yeah," Joan says. "Maybe. His lawyer is arguing he be released with an ankle monitor." She shakes her head, like she doesn't think his lawyer will win. "Parts of the case are starting to look shaky."

"When can I get out?"

"The case against *you* isn't that shaky. But there's movement. They're . . . refocusing the investigation. They want to interview you still."

"Tell them no."

"You know the drill," she says. "I can't stop them from trying, just advise you not to answer, at least not yet."

"I'm not talking. Ever." I cross my arms over my chest. Dad's out. They might be letting Mark out. If it's shaky enough that Mark might get to go home, then everything's going to be okay. They can't release him and hold me.

"You need to start telling me what you know. And where you were. The timeline," she says.

We've been here before. The timeline. Always the timeline. Joan's code for her wanting me to snitch. She watches my face when she says stuff. Sometimes I think about other things so I can't accidentally give something away.

"They've searched the Clearview grounds again. Took out more materials and samples. *They're* cooperating." Of course they are. I've had enough time to think to realize Riggs could have ratted them out, even if he didn't set them up. Riggs was asking questions and pushing, and Mark went nuts after talking to him. And now Riggs is cooperating. But what about everyone else? Cammie and Karen and all the rest. Are they cooperating, dissecting everything I've ever said or done and telling the feds? Are they all okay with Riggs hanging us out to dry? Or are they pushing back? Are they all still training, like nothing's changed?

"So, they're all out, or soon to be out, and I rot in here. It's bullshit."

"It's pressure. Leverage. They have hard evidence on you, and they will use it to their advantage."

"No, I mean it's bullshit that the feds think these guys — if they are the badass terrorists the feds say they are — that they would tell me anything, let alone include me in their grand plans. Not even Mark!" I stand up. I need to move. "If they understood them *at all*, the feds would know they'd never let my girl germs anywhere near them." I laugh, but Joan doesn't look impressed. "Like my being included might make their dicks fall off."

"Are you done?" she asks, making some note on her legal pad, or pretending to, like I'm so very boring.

I'm not done. "The feds are morons if they actually think those guys would actually let a girl have any part in their big terrorist plan."

"They don't," she says without looking up.

"What?"

"Or at least they didn't." She puts down the legal pad and looks at me. "You weren't a target. When they were getting warrants and executing the raids, they didn't think you were necessarily part of the conspiracy," she says, holding up her hand to stop my next rant. "Oh, they thought you knew *something*. They were counting on it. They couldn't find Mark, didn't know what he had been up to for several days, and thought he was about to act. They cast a wide net. But if they actually thought at the time of the raids that you were part of a seditious and treasonous conspiracy to shed American blood on American soil—law-enforcement blood—then you'd have been interrogated round the clock for hours, quickly transferred to be tried as an adult in federal court, and immediately whisked away to a secure federal facility." She tilts her head. "Probably a very disorienting and scary facility in Texas that would make this look like summer camp."

"But . . ."

"The government thought the threat was imminent and acted to prevent Mark and the others from carrying out the plan. But, so far, the evidence doesn't support the more serious charges." She leans back and looks at me full on. "Maybe they moved too soon, or maybe, they think, they just haven't found the missing links yet. They now think *you* are one of those links. They are developing new theories about how this went down. Theories that focus more and more on you."

"On *me*?"

"They're analyzing that pipe-bomb video. Looking for more footage or posts. Your search histories from the computer at the station don't help. I assume there will be more on your phone when they turn that analysis over." God. My phone. I try to swallow. I deleted all evidence of Lucy, but what did I leave on there? "If they can make any plausible case that you knew about or were helping—or even planning to help—Mark build explosives, even acquiring the materials, then it's game over. There's still the possibility that they'll charge you as the one who taught him how to build explosive devices."

"But . . . It was just a pipe bomb. Just powder and a pipe. Just to see. And I followed a YouTube video. I didn't 'teach' him!"

"He was there. He did the filming."

"Yeah, but not like, *Why don't you go build some bombs and hurt people?*"

She shakes her head slowly and leans forward. "A case like this, it's about headlines. They made huge, public arrests, and now they need the resulting convictions. It can be Mark, or the others, or you. But they need to convict someone of something significant. And they will use whatever leverage they have to get someone to talk, to give up the evidence that will let them convict *someone* of *something* headline grabbing."

"Won't be me."

"See, that's where you're screwed," she says, tossing her pen on her legal pad. "The evidence against most of them is weak on all but the weapons charges. What they have on you is not."

"I didn't do anything!"

"The concealed handgun, the knife, the stockpile of ammunition you had squirreled away, the pipe bomb." She ticks them off on her fingers. "Even if they never tie you to your brother's plans, your possession of the weapons and ammunition, and other activities, could very well support violations of state and federal law leading to a delinquency finding, sufficient for the government to at least argue for confinement until you turn twenty-one, if not a transfer to adult court and worse."

There's pounding in my ears and hands. "You're supposed to be on my side. Fighting for *me*!"

"I am," she says. "But you're not giving me much to go on. Certainly not being smart or helping yourself. You're pointedly *not* telling me anything, and I have to believe you can. You can tell me things that will help me prove you were not a part of a murderous terrorist plot! You can give me information that will help me get you the best deal I can."

"But you said . . . innocent until proven guilty and, and . . ."

"No matter what I do, I can't make it all go away. The only questions are where you will go, when you will get out, and with what long-term repercussions."

The room spins and everything goes cold.

"The disposable cell phone they found in the trunk in the barn," she says, "and the information on cell-phone timers, with your fingerprints all over everything, coupled with your search history, has them looking hard for more. Testing soil.

It's the only proof of an actual explosive they have, as far I can tell. And state or fed, unless you cut a deal, or can give me some solid evidence to prove, definitively, that you were not involved in the conspiracy, that you didn't help or discuss any of the plans, even with your brother—unless you can do that, you are facing at least several years in a juvenile facility. *At least*. Maybe more. Maybe prison. Fed, state . . . doesn't matter. They've got you."

She waits for that to sink in, like I will suddenly spill my guts.

"Bex." She looks like she wants to grab me and shake me until it all spills out. "Talk to me."

I can't. Just a little bit longer. Mom said Mark will be released soon. They wouldn't be talking about that if they thought they could prove any of this. I just have to keep my mouth shut and wait it out. I can do that. I can handle this a little longer.

CHAPTER 27

"Bex," Mom says, giving me a quick, shallow hug.

She smells exactly the same. But her eyes are sunken and her hair is limp and there are tired lines all over her face that weren't there before.

Her eyes water. "You're so thin." Her hands move over me, and all at once it's too much. I pull back, hands up to block any more touching.

"Sorry, just . . ." I can't explain. Explaining would be worse.

"Come sit," Mom says. "How are you?"

"I'm okay."

"Really?" Her mouth sucks in. "I tried to call Ms. Bryant. She wouldn't return my calls. She needs to talk to me about your case."

"She's not supposed to."

"You are my child."

Her look hits me hard, fierce and protective and not at all embarrassed or ashamed of me. She hasn't looked at me like that in forever. I swallow the lump in my throat. I can't cry. I don't cry anymore.

"Lorraine said I should go to the court and demand that they order her to talk to me, as your mother, but . . . What am I going on for? That's for the adults to discuss. How are you?"

"I'm fine," I say, because there's no point in saying anything else. "Segregation sucks."

"Segregation?" Mom asks.

"Solitary. They call it seg here. And it sucks, but . . ." I shrug, trying not to let her see how much I need to get out of here. I need to get out of here. No, I can handle it. Not too much longer.

"Well, at least you're safe."

"Safe?" I stare at her. She's acting like I've been tucked away, all cozy and comfy. "A girl killed herself last week. She couldn't take seg anymore. She'd been there three weeks. I've been here for months."

Mom pales and swallows. Her hands shake in her lap, then her whole body trembles.

I feel bad as soon as I see her gulp down the sob. She didn't put me here. She didn't keep me here. She couldn't have done anything. She's here, now, for me, and I need to make it okay.

"Sorry. I'm sorry, Mom. How's Dad?"

"Okay," she says, but it's clear he's not. "He's had some . . . health issues, from the stress. But he's doing okay. Wishes he could see you," she says with a forced, watery smile.

They won't let Dad see me, not while we're both still considered possible coconspirators.

"And Mark?" I ask, needing to know what's going on.

"It's not fair," Mom says, the tears finally spilling over. "He's in an awful place. The things that have happened to him . . ."

"So . . . he's still in custody?"

"Yes," Mom says.

"I thought he was getting out. I thought . . ."

"So did his lawyer. But then . . ." She rubs her forehead. "I can't . . . I . . ."

"Is he okay?"

"No, Bex," she says. "He's not okay. His lawyer's been trying to get him released, but . . ." She cries harder.

Cries about Mark. Who's the one who caused this, *all* of this.

"What about me, Mom?"

"What *about* you?" she asks, knife sharp and deep.

"I'm here because of Mark! I didn't do this! Mark did! He's the one—"

"You're the one who dragged him into this," she says. "Always pushing, always trying to show him up, getting him all riled up with your paranoid theories. He never would have been involved in any of this if you hadn't been pushing, pushing, always . . . He never should have been there!" Mom wails. "If it wasn't for you, and your father. Always making him feel like less . . ."

Me, making Mark feel like less. Making him become . . . whatever he is now.

"Mark knows I wasn't involved."

She tries to shush me. "Don't. We can't—"

"He knows I didn't have *anything* to do with . . . *any* of it. And he's letting me rot here." My face feels stretched and contorted. "He could have had me out of here months ago. In five minutes. But he didn't say a word. No one's talking about releasing me. And you're still worried about Mark."

"Maybe he was worried it would be worse for you if he said anything."

"How could it be worse for me? I didn't do anything!"

She looks at me without any of the weepiness or cajoling. "Maybe he thought the best thing he could do for you, to help you, would be to say nothing to the people who were trying to hurt you."

I start to get up and she grabs my arm.

"He can't help you. Prison, Bex," she whispers, like whispering means it can't be used against us. "If he is convicted, he goes to prison. Not juvenile detention. Prison."

Her grip tightens.

"We cannot allow them to send Mark to prison." No tears. Hard. Determined. This is why she's here. "He won't survive prison, Bex. He'll die."

"Why did you even come here?" I ask.

"How can you ask me that?" But she knows I'm not buying this worried act. She isn't worried about me. None of this is about me. She realizes she's still digging her fingers into my arm and lets go, goes back to petting my hand. "I needed to see you, to make sure you were okay." She tries to smile and continues to pet my hand. "And to make sure you know we will do everything we can to help you, to get you out of here, as fast as we can."

Will do. Not *are doing*. They will. After. After I don't talk and they convict me.

"You need to sit tight, for now. Be brave." She smiles again. "Mark hasn't told them anything about you," she says. "He could have told them about things, illegal things. He could have thought, maybe, that you were up to something, all the sneaking around . . . and the gun he removed from your room," she whispers, "to protect you."

She can't really believe . . . "Is that what he said?" My brain feels like it's going to explode.

"Maybe he was just trying to protect you," she says. "That's what family does. They protect each other."

I pull my hand back. This isn't about Mom wanting to see me for me. This is about making sure I don't talk. And letting me know what Mark might say if I do.

"We're family, Bex. Families stick together."

Funny. No one's stuck by me. Except Joan.

"And when this is all over, we will deal with the rest of it," she says with a wave of her hand. Like my being locked up for months because of him is like he broke my toy or hurt my feelings. "The important thing is to get you both home in one piece. Then we can move on. Together. As a family." She must see the look in my eyes, how I will never share a roof with him again. "Or," she says, "maybe just you and I will go to Arizona for a while until things cool down. Wouldn't that be good? Some sun? And peace and quiet? And enough time for people to forget. You'll be older. You can change your hair. Maybe you can go by *Rebecca*. You can blend in there. Go back to school. Maybe community college, since you'll be older . . ." She flashes a too-big smile to try to sell it. "A fresh start. For all of us."

Yeah, I can see it perfectly. Mom's plan to just move, together, and then pretend like nothing's happened.

She doesn't care about me, not compared to Mark. She doesn't even want to know the real me. She's still pretending.

CHAPTER 28

Joan doesn't stand when I come into the room. No friendly talk or concerned once-over. I've never seen her look really angry before.

"What's wrong?" I ask. "Is it Dad? Mom said he'd been sick. Did . . ."

"What's wrong?" she repeats. "What's wrong is that you've been locked up here for *months*, and you haven't told me *anything*, and I have to find out from your cell-phone records that you have an alibi!"

I blink. An alibi? Cell phone? Oh, God.

"You should have told me about Lucy Saunders from the beginning. Immediately. As soon as we started going through the key meetings and events, meetings and events you couldn't possibly have been at because you were with, or talking to, Lucy Saunders miles away."

"She isn't important. She's just a girl. . . ."

"I've read the texts, Bex." My face flares hot. "And the e-mails. So has the government." Humiliation.

"But I deleted them."

She smiles, starting to calm down. "They subpoenaed your cell-phone records. E-mails, texts, the works. And hers."

"They can get that stuff? Even if I delete it?"

"In your case, yes," Joan says. "I just got the records, but the U.S. Attorney has had them, and your phone, for months. A phone and records that show all kinds of information about your calls and texts and whereabouts. And her phone was backing up to the cloud—a gold mine of alibi evidence. Would have been helpful and saved us a lot of time if you had told me what your phone would show. If you had told me about Lucy."

Oh, God. "Can we just keep her out of this?"

"No. She's a witness. An important one, as it turns out. Which is why I needed to know about her earlier." She watches me. "I knew your phone might hold valuable information. I didn't know it holds piles and piles of alibi evidence."

A shiver races up my body.

"Calls. Texts. Apps on your phone pinging cell towers. Times when you were with her, all cataloged from those same texts and calls and pings. Contemporaneous evidence that you were nowhere near some of the key meetings and events at the heart of the conspiracy. A tremendous lack of any texts or calls at all between you and your brother. None."

She smiles a real smile.

"In the weeks leading up to the alleged preparation for this huge terrorist plot, you were either working at your uncle's station, at the club with people not implicated in these events, or off talking with, texting, or actually in the presence of someone not at all a part of any of this. Someone horrified by it all. From the looks of it, you barely had time to eat, shower, and go to the bathroom, let alone be part of a massive criminal conspiracy."

I can't feel my head. It's like it's floating to the ceiling.

"She doesn't want to be involved," I say. "At all. Just leave her alone. "

Joan waits, pen over her legal pad ready to write. She smiles again, this one patronizing, or like she thinks it's cute. I can feel my face get hot. "They've already talked to her. My investigator has already talked to her."

"I didn't say you could—"

"You didn't say anything." She dares me to argue with her. "Bex, this is a good thing. A very good thing."

I could tell her no.

"I don't understand you." Joan leans over the table. "I'm

here telling you that you have an alibi, and you're acting like this is bad news."

"I told her this wouldn't affect her." I told her I would protect her. "I promised her."

Joan stares at me. Then she blinks, leans back, her jaw moving like she's trying to figure out what to say. "Bex, I'm not sure you are understanding the position you are in. " The way she says it already makes me feel stupid. "I keep trying to get through to you that unless you start helping yourself, you are going to prison. Prison," she says for emphasis. "For years. And now I discover you have a very strong alibi, and you're worried about . . . what? Hurting her feelings? Some . . . promise you made, before any of this happened? Where is your head? I'm trying to help you and you act like I'm the enemy. You lie to me."

"I haven't lied."

"Not telling the truth is lying. If you want me to withdraw and ask the court to appoint another attorney for you, then fine. But any attorney is going to use this evidence. She is your alibi."

I can't. I promised her. But they already have the texts and calls. They've already talked to her.

"Now, we are going to go through these key dates and

events, and you are going to tell me everything you can remember. No more stalling. No more bullshit. You will tell me everything you remember. Now."

I can't protect Lucy. And she already knows that I lied to her when I said I could.

"Bex," Joan says. She taps the table and I look up. I can't take how she thinks this is all so cute, that she's won. "I won't need details of anything intimate." Oh, God. "Just times and places. This is important."

Mom's voice screams in my head. Calling me a coward, telling me to be brave. I push on my ears to try to get her voice out of my head.

"Bex?"

Their plan is to let me get convicted. They're not going to help me.

"Bex."

I'm not a traitor. But I can do this. I can talk about Lucy and keep Mark out of it. I don't have to talk about Mark to answer Joan's questions about Lucy. Maybe if I have an alibi it will be enough. They'll have to let me go and stop trying to make me talk about Mark.

I nod.

Joan makes me go through every day—by calls, texts, e-mails, and the absence of them. Where I was, for how long, and did anyone see Lucy and me. I have to talk about Lucy, so I do, but I don't say anything she doesn't already know about Mark.

"Now," Joan says, stretching. We've been at this forever. The closer we get to the end, the more my stomach twists and my head aches. And the more I need to stay focused. Nothing about Mark. "Friday, a week before the arrests, you texted with Lucy earlier in the day about picking you up that night. She sends you a text asking when you'll be done, and then nothing until the next day."

Cammie and Karen at the station, Lucy showing up, and dinner at Lucy's grandparents' house. Home.

Joan makes more notes. Then she reads the list of texts and calls.

"The texts and calls slow down after Friday." She flips back and forth. "A lot. What happened Friday?"

My face flames hottest yet.

"Why did the texts and calls slow?" Joan asks, swallowing the smile.

"Lucy started asking questions, about training. It didn't go over well."

"Did you tell her about training? About Clearview or . . . ?"

"I downplayed it," I admit. "A lot."

Joan doesn't judge me. Much. She writes some more notes.

"Tell me about Tuesday. Four days before the arrests."

"We texted some."

"Yeah, I can see that. But what else?"

I shrug. I try to keep my face blank. Mark, at the house. Those guys and the cooler.

"Whatever you can remember."

I'm not a traitor. "I . . . went to work, probably. I think. I don't remember."

"Think."

I pretend to try to remember. "I don't remember. I mean, I know I went to work. I probably rode home from work with Uncle Skip, had some dinner . . . and . . . went to bed."

"That's it?"

"Um . . ." I pretend to think again. "Yeah, I think so."

She stares. I wait. Keep my face blank. Hold still. She makes a slash on the side of her legal pad, a violent, vicious slash.

Shit. She knows something. But I can't talk about Tuesday, about Mark and them at the house. Mark's crazy eyes, jumping down from the porch. Mark in prison. Adult prison. I can't.

"What about Wednesday?" she asks, her voice tight.

"I worked all day. Saw Lucy that night." Stay calm. Be cool. "She picked me up. At the station."

"Anyone see her pick you up?"

"I don't know."

"How long were you out with her? Where did you go?"

"Not long. We had a fight," I say, nodding at her look, "before we could go anywhere. She took me home."

"She dropped you off at the house? What time?" Joan's voice sounds weird. I look up at her; something prickles at my neck.

I start to shrug and then feel it more. Fight. I have to fight, because there is no flight. This is important. But I need to be careful. Maybe I can say what I need to say without saying anything about Mark. I sit up, try to think. "I don't know. Maybe seven? Seven thirty?"

"Was anyone home? Anyone who can verify what time you got home? Did you go anywhere where people might have seen you? Bex," Joan says, "I need you to focus here. Where *exactly* did you go? Would anyone have seen you between five thirty and when you got home?"

Five thirty. Specific. Joan is staring through my skull. Ready to write. She's trying to hide it, but she's excited. This is more significant than the rest.

And then clarity, something that has nothing to do with Mark.

My mouth is dry. "A sheriff's deputy."

She stops writing. Stops breathing. Neither of us moves.

Alibi. I tell her everything I can remember about the deputy.

"What time was this?"

"No idea."

"Did you get his name or shield number or . . . ?"

I shake my head.

"Did he give her a ticket or . . . What happened?"

I tell her about getting out of the car, about thinking we were in trouble and trying to decide what to do. And his radio going off and him leaving. I describe him as best I can remember. The mole on his cheek. His hair. His height. I don't tell her I was planning to ambush him or run so he'd have to follow. I try not to sound crazy, or like a terrorist.

"What happened after that?"

"Lucy drove away." I wrap my arms around myself to stop the shakes and tell her everything I can remember about the wheres and whens. I try not to hear Lucy's words in my head. Or Mom's. I can't block out Mom's. Adult prison. Careful.

"Was anyone home to see when you got back?"

"No," I lie. If she knows about the deputy, she doesn't need to know about Mark.

She stares at me. She knows I'm lying. I can feel it. But I can't tell her. Not that. Another slash.

She puts her pen down slowly and leans back in her chair.

I curl my toes in my floppy shoes to keep still.

We stare. She works something around her head, or her mouth.

I curl my toes harder, until it hurts.

"Here's the thing," she says. "In addition to your cell records, I got some other discovery that fills in some of the holes." I try to swallow. "Now we know that up until eight days out from the arrests, this is all talk, or mostly all talk, as far as I can tell. That night Mark and one other coconspirator use a copied key to go to your uncle's station, where they use the computer and take some things, oil, gas, some tools and materials. Maybe something else, something they'd hidden there. Who knows? The feds think something more." She waits for that to sink in. "Then something happens between Tuesday and Wednesday that spooks them. Or some of them. Mark, in particular. There's been a lot of big talk, but vaguely in the future, until something makes them, some of them, Mark," Joan says, "think they have to act right away. Now."

Oh, God.

"Or so the feds think. Because the informant, Glenn Stewart . . ."

Glenn? We don't need Glenn.

". . . realizes that things are happening that he's not privy to. Stewart thinks they are moving now. The government thinks he's blown his cover and something's imminent. And they don't know where Mark is. Or Zach. And the feds think maybe they have the explosives Stewart was planning to offer to provide. And there's a big ceremony planned for Saturday to honor first responders killed in the line of duty in the previous year."

Oh, God.

She watches me. Waits.

"That's why the government moves on Friday."

I know this part. They arrest Devon and Neal and another guy asleep in their beds. Find Zach at his girlfriend's. Detain us. Sixteen hours later, they find Mark, in Dad's truck. Mark, who might have been on the run longer if he hadn't tried to call Devon, whose phone was already in the possession of the feds.

I force myself to breathe as regularly as I can with my heart pounding in my chest and jaw and temples.

"Something spooked Mark, or them, and caused them to

cut Stewart out of the loop," she says again. "And I think you know what."

I can't.

"The government's getting restless, Bex. Desperate. They need this win."

I can't.

"And right now, the most solid evidence they have is on you. They're still looking at you. All they have on these guys right now is some weapons and ammunition charges. And talk. They want the bombs, the conspiracy, the headlines. And they think you are the key."

"Why me?"

"They think Mark went rogue, and that he didn't act alone. They think—or maybe *hope*—that you became his new coconspirator, so secret even the others didn't know. They're looking for anything to tie you to him between Tuesday and Thursday of that week. And if they find it"—she leans closer—"if they find what ties you to him between those days, it will be too late to talk deals. If they can prove you two met, and especially if there is any shred of evidence that you were providing him help about explosives or weapons, then you are done." Her stare holds me still. "Unless we can explain your meeting first."

I can't. Mark. Mom. I can't be what sends him to prison. I can't.

"They put you here," she says, leaning across the table. "Your brother, your father, the rest of them." She waves toward the walls. "They may not have done it intentionally, and you certainly did enough to put yourself in here, too. But if not for your brother and his friends, are you detained and searched? Does anyone sweep your home?"

I can't. Not even to her. Not about Mark. They'll never forgive me.

"If they find anything at all that they think can plausibly show you as a link between your brother and his actions that week, they will charge you. I won't be able to keep this a juvenile matter." She waits. Her eyes widen, like she's trying to force me to talk. "Tell me."

"There's nothing to tell."

Joan's jaw tenses. "Fine, then you're going to be here for a while, maybe prison." Her voice is hard, like ice. "Maybe prison for a long time. They may all walk, and you'll spend the next ten years, minimum, behind bars if they tag you with teaching him how to build the explosives."

I stand. I need to move.

"Sit down."

I sit.

"They put you here," she says. "And I can guarantee you that the feds have offered to go easy on you if your father and brother cooperate. I guarantee you that they gave them a chance to help you. And you're still here."

No. Not Dad. He wouldn't just leave me here, not if he could have helped me. Would he?

"You just lied to me. At least twice. I know you did."

I can't look away from her eyes.

"I need to know why. Now. *If* I am going to defend you."

"If? But you said . . ."

"If you don't trust me, if our relationship is compromised so that you won't tell me what I need to know to defend you, then I will ask the court to allow me to withdraw. You can get another lawyer. One you trust," she says. "Or one who doesn't care and lets you throw your life away on some fool idea that you are being loyal to your family."

"You can't."

"I can. I don't want to, but I will. I won't watch you sacrifice yourself for them."

I can't do this without Joan. I can't. The shakes start again.

"If you really weren't part of this," she says, her voice so low I have to lean forward to hear her, "then you need to start telling me everything. I need the details. I need to know the things you most don't want to tell me. I won't tell the government unless you give me permission. But I need to know. To defend you. To help you. Now."

She doesn't look away. I look down. If I tell her, what does that make me? Do I want to be that person? Someone who betrays her family to maybe save herself? A collaborator? Worse?

"You've got to trust me, Bex."

"I do."

"No, you don't," she says. "You don't. And maybe I'd feel the same way. But . . . I can't help you if you don't trust me just a little more. It's time."

The silence is loud, pressing in on my ears.

"Help me convince them that you were not involved. If your brother was actually taking steps to move the criminal conspiracy forward, if that's what you know, then he put himself in this." I can't look at her. "And all the others. If they are guilty, they made the decisions and took the actions that put them there. Even your father. He chose to help your brother when he knew your brother was in trouble. He gave him money and his truck."

Oh, Dad.

If I tell her, she's going to want me to tell the government. I know she will. She'll talk me into it. She won't stop until I do.

I can't.

"I wasn't helping Mark with anything."

"Then why did he have a Bobcat pistol with your fingerprints all over it in his possession when he was arrested?"

Oh, God.

"I can't."

"It's okay to save yourself." Joan touches my hand until I look up. "You have to save yourself." Her fingers are warm. "Because no one else is going to. I need to know what happened that week."

Ican'tIcan'tIcan'tIcan't. The first drop hits the table, then another, then they spread and splatter and then form blobs. She doesn't move her hand away. I don't try to dry them. It's quiet. I'm quiet. Just the barely there sound of the tears hitting the table.

"Let it out," she whispers.

I suck in air, scorching my lungs, clogging my throat. It comes back out as a wail. Choking, snotting sobs.

She lets me cry. She doesn't say a word. Eventually some tissues slide in front of me. She gets up, comes back, and a bottle of water is there.

I start to feel like more than my tears. More than my face. I scrub at it with the rough tissues, until my face feels raw and hot, the rest of me cold. I take a deep breath and it doesn't hitch coming out.

"Tell me about Tuesday. You left work early." How would she . . . ? My texts, to Lucy. My call to Dad. "You saw Mark?" She knows.

"The power went out at the station," I say. "Uncle Skip sent me home." She smiles, like she knew, encouraging me. And picks up her pen, ready. "Before that—a few days before, a week, maybe . . . *before*, anyway—Riggs, Jim Riggs, at Clearview, asked me about Mark. About him not being around as much, and not working for Darnell, one of the men." She doesn't push; she just waits. I tell her everything I can remember about the conversation with Riggs.

"And Tuesday?"

I tell her about the guys, the trucks, and the cooler.

"The cooler," Joan says. "Describe it."

"Orange on the bottom, white top, big." I use my hands. "They each had a handle, and from the way they were leaning over, it looked heavy."

She makes a noise, writes more, looks up at me like she can't believe I didn't say it earlier. But when she finishes writing, she just waits for me to continue.

"What?"

She shuffles through the new discovery file, then looks up at me. "A cooler like that is in evidence. It held several firearms that had been illegally modified. And the kits for additional modifications. And some maps and lists. Of supplies."

Wow. Maybe that's why they were at the station? Did they need tools? Somewhere to work?

"Anything else? Anything at all on Tuesday."

My stomach churns. *You keep your mouth shut.*

"Mark and I talked, for a few minutes. I . . . told him Riggs had asked about him."

"Okay," Joan says. "Wednesday."

We don't need Glenn.

"Bex?"

My stomach turns over. I'm a traitor.

"Wednesday night, when Lucy dropped me off, Mark was at the house."

Joan stops writing. I can feel her looking at me, but I don't look up.

I tell her everything. Everything I can remember.

"I tried to stall. I knew I couldn't outrun him. I didn't know when Uncle Skip or Dad would be home. I tried to find out what he thought I had said." I look up at her. "I didn't know. I really didn't know what was going on."

If you don't tell me . . .

His arm on my throat. "I mean, maybe he would have stopped. I don't know. But . . ." His eyes.

If you don't tell me . . .

"It's okay," she says.

I take a deep breath and try to remember that I can breathe now. "He kept asking over and over what I had told Riggs. He wouldn't believe that I hadn't said anything. That Riggs hadn't said anything, not really. I couldn't tell him anything—he wouldn't believe me."

Joan makes a sound but waves me on when I look at her.

"He knew about Lucy. He said to keep my mouth shut. I threatened to tell Dad or Uncle Skip about his stealing from the station, and being there when he wasn't supposed to, if he didn't leave, but . . ."

"But what?"

"He wasn't stopping. And . . . I got away. Ran upstairs."

The gun, in my hand, ready, tracking him in the hallway.

"I could have killed him." I look at her. "Upstairs. I would have, if he had tried to shove the door open. I told him I had the Remington, to go away."

My hands, shaking, with the Remington pointed at the door. Waiting. Waiting. If he comes near that door. If he . . .

"He just left?"

"His phone rang." I tell her about the call. *She won't. I'm handling it.* "He was freaking out. Said he was sorry, but . . ." *We don't need Glenn.*

"When . . . ?" She clears her throat, swallows. "Did he come back?"

"No. Uncle Skip came home a couple hours later, and then Dad. I pretended to be asleep. I waited until the next morning to move the bureau away from the door."

"What did you tell them about . . . ?" I shake my head. "You didn't tell them? Your mom? Anyone?"

I keep shaking my head. "I thought about it. But he'd found the Bobcat, some of my ammo, some of my money. He took them. Said they were hostages to make me keep my mouth shut. They wouldn't have believed me. He would have lied, and showed them the Bobcat. I needed proof. I needed to know what was going on, so they'd *have* to believe me."

"That's why you were carrying the gun and the knife," she whispers.

I don't have to answer.

She moves her pen toward the page, and then moves it away, shakes her arm, and tries again, actually writing this time. I wait.

"Has he threatened or attacked you like that before?"

"No." She doesn't believe me. "Not like that. Not . . . He was just . . . But maybe he would have stopped." It rings hollow. "I think he was scared."

"Of what?"

"I don't know. As soon as I saw him, I could feel it: something was different. He just . . . He's never been like that." I try to stop my hands from shaking.

She asks questions. I answer. About the station, and seeing Zach's truck there. We go through the fight again.

I close my eyes and answer.

Eventually part of me is answering while the rest just says, over and over, in my head, like a reminder, that I could have killed him. I would have killed him. If his phone hadn't rung. If he hadn't left. If he had tried to get into the room. I would have killed him.

Would he have killed me, if I hadn't gotten away? If I hadn't been able to get upstairs? Would he have killed me?

I've been trying to protect him. For Mom, for Dad, maybe even for him — maybe.

But he could have killed me.

And he left me here.

He's not worried about what's happening to me. Neither is Mom or Dad.

For years, I've been planning to survive. I thought they would come around and I could save them, too.

But I can't save Mark. And he won't save me.

Joan's right. I have to save myself.

CHAPTER 29

I should be thinking about Mark. About what he did to me. About what I did to him. But when I think about Mark, my brain rotates between how it felt for him to choke me and Mom screaming through the phone. *How could you tell them your brother tried to kill you? Why? Why would you do such a thing? Tell them you lied! You have to tell them. . . .*

I don't want to think about Mark. I'm done thinking about Mark. And Mom.

Instead, I think about Lucy. Not about sex. Or her smile. Or her laugh. Not about any of that.

I can't stop thinking about how I am exactly what she was afraid of.

I wonder if they took the skull ring when they raided my room. Maybe. I hate thinking of Lucy's plastic ring in some evidence bag somewhere. But I hate worse thinking of it lost, dropped or thrown away while they took everything else. And then I feel stupid for thinking about the stupid ring at all.

Lucy wasn't the love of my life. That isn't surprising. But I'm not sure I even really liked her, the parts of her that weren't about kissing and fooling around. I didn't even know her, not the real her. She sure as shit didn't know me. I made sure of it. Not the real me. Not the parts of me that are most me.

Even before the fight, I knew I wasn't following her to college. We weren't going to call and text and pretend it was something more. Maybe a weekend hookup, if she was back at her grandparents' next summer, but this wasn't going to be some big long-distance romance. The way she looked at Karen and Cammie. The way she dismissed everything I believe, like she was so much better than us. Maybe I would have tried to see her one last time, maybe, just so it didn't end like that, but it was over.

And then I was in handcuffs and she was the furthest thing from my mind.

Then I was in the hole.

And this is what she feared: that I was some crazy person who could get her hurt or in trouble.

I lied to her and hid who I was because deep down I knew she wouldn't like that person. I knew it was unfair, and I didn't care.

I could have been with her when I was arrested.

They could have thought she was involved.

She's eighteen. She'd have been held in adult jail.

When Joan first started asking questions, I made a pledge to keep Lucy out of this. If I didn't say her name, they'd never know she exists. Just another example of how deep my stupidity goes. Of course they'd be able to find the deleted texts and calls. They'd probably already talked to her by the time I was deciding never to say her name. I told her once I could protect her, that I would put myself between her and danger, and I did the exact opposite.

I have no idea what she might say to them.

My head falls back against the cinder-block wall. I let my fingers trace the painted-over seam between slightly rougher painted-over blocks. What would she say? Would she tell them a distorted version of that night with the deputy? *Would* it be distorted, or was I the one who was seeing it all wrong?

Did she tell them I'm a liar?

I am a liar. I lie a lot. Sometimes without saying a word. How many times did I lie to her so that she would want me? How many times did I keep information from Uncle Skip, or Mom, or Dad, that might have prevented this? What if I'd told Uncle Skip about Mark's being at the station, about them being at the house? What if I'd told Uncle Skip about Mark, about how crazy he was acting?

"Bex, you doing all right?" Ortiz asks through the slot in the door. "Bex?"

I look up, make eye contact, say "Fine" so she'll leave me alone. She probably has to ask me since I flipped out. After I told Joan everything, I flipped out.

Lucy was in this from the beginning. Because of me.

Will she end up saving me, even if I broke my promises to keep her safe?

Would I have seen that Mark was planning something, if I wasn't so wrapped up in her? Balancing so many lies to see her? Would it have mattered?

Mark is going to prison. I'm going . . . somewhere.

Lucy is gone.

Everything's gone.

And Mom will never forgive me.

CHAPTER 30

"'Morning, Bex," Gage says when she brings me breakfast. "Back to normal," she says, like an apology. Now that Christmas and New Year's are past, there'll be no more treats or "special" meals.

Christmas. Mom didn't come. She hasn't called or visited since she heard Joan was talking to the U.S. Attorney.

Joan said the lawyers may have told her not to, but it still hurts.

They won't let Uncle Skip visit. Once I'm out of pretrial limbo, he'll be able to visit, to call, Joan says. But not while I'm here. And I have to be here until the feds give me up to the state or until the case is done.

I would have actually preferred to forget that it was Christmas. I tried to. Kept my schedule as best I could on Christmas and New Year's.

My workout in the mornings—push-ups, sit-ups, lunges, jumping jacks, anything to move—until I'm too weak to do any more.

I've never gone this long without a run, a hike, something fast and hard and exhilarating. What I can do here is a sad substitute. But I can work my heart rate up, a slight sweat, *something* so my body doesn't become entirely useless. So that I can maybe sleep later.

Reading in the afternoon. I never read much before, and I can't say I'd choose it now if I could do almost anything else, but sometimes reading can make the day, the hole, everything fade away for a while. Just a while. Until a sound—yelling, keys, doors—pulls me back to reality.

Someone put lights on the tree by the lot. Like a Christmas tree for those of us on this side of the building. They've taken them down now.

That tree is all that grounds me some days. A few weeks ago, I woke up freaked out, and got it in my head that they had stretched out time—spaced meals and morning and night so that what I perceived as a day was really more than a day. That I'd been here years instead of months. It took all day, counting and obsessing and waiting, to talk myself down. I was so freaked I couldn't eat at all. I wondered if they were drugging me, too. The tree is what convinced me. I look at it every day. The seasons—no one could fake the seasons.

If they ever let me out of here, I swear I will never live in a place with cinder-block walls.

I will sleep with the windows open.

Drive with the windows open.

Maybe a motorcycle. I wished for one when I was little. On a motorcycle, I'd feel everything.

If I ever get free, I want to see the ocean. Both oceans. First one, then the other.

Joan promised to come as soon as she heard from the U.S. Attorney. But it's been weeks since I've seen her.

What if there's nothing? What if I'm in limbo in the dark for years? They could do it, keep me here, try everyone else, leave me to rot. Joan says they can't, but every time there's a delay, I trust that a little less.

She says that if there's a deal, I'll get out of the hole. But there are others down here—how many of them had deals? She can't promise me that. I've been here long enough to know that in here, the guards call the shots.

After lunch I give in, curl up under the blanket, and sleep. Warm and quiet in the afternoon lull. It's not dark like at night. Maybe I can sleep if it's light enough to see what's in here with me.

Heart pounding, I jolt awake, sweat wet on my skin, cooling a trail of goose bumps down my arms, my lungs remembering how to work.

I was running. First through the woods, the old ones, where we camped when I was a kid. The trails marked by yellow slashes on the trees. I wanted to touch them, but they were too high. I climbed. I fell and fell through the leaves and brush and into a building. A maze of cinder-block walls. I couldn't find my way out. Someone was calling my name—Joan, I think, maybe.

She could totally be one of those TV cops or a PI. But not the kind who has some stupid man partner who's always saving her. She wouldn't need saving.

She could totally survive. Lead her own MAG, even. I'd follow her.

Fighting for people who can't fight for themselves, even when guilty—holding the government's feet to the fire. She holds a line against the government every day, more than anyone at Clearview or any backyard brigade ever has. So much better than the idiots like my brother. How many more people are safe and free because of what she does? I'm never going to be a lawyer, but there's got to be loads of stuff between whatever I was before and Joan.

After dinner I try to read the book again, but it's lost its magic. I can't forget it's just a book. That the people in it don't matter. They don't exist.

I sleep off and on, and then it's morning. Another morning. But a shower day. And clean clothes. The jumpsuit is almost scratchy it's so clean, and this one fits better than the last. I comb my uneven, stupid-looking hair over and over so it will dry flat.

"Bex," Shields says, opening the door, "lawyer's here."

I'm glad I got a shower.

When they lead me into the room, Joan's still standing. I study her face.

I can't read her. I sit and brace for the news.

"The U.S. Attorney has interviewed the corroborating alibi witnesses."

"Lucy?"

"Yes. And your uncle, a few others."

"Is she okay?"

"I believe she's fine. Happy she's not going to have to testify." There's more to it.

"There was some press," Joan says. "Her parents were

worried. She's gone home to North Carolina. Until things calm down."

My stomach turns. Exactly what she didn't want—my scary life messing up hers. Sent home, like *she* did something wrong.

Joan has a clean, uncreased folder. She opens it and pulls out some papers. "They will agree to drop the transfer motion and allow your case to proceed as a delinquency matter for carrying the gun and the possession of the ammunition. No mention of the pipe bomb, since it was on private land, no damage to persons or property," she says. "No mention of sales or transfer of ammunition, which will mean no issues for you down the road if you want to join the military, get certain kinds of licenses and jobs, future gun ownership." I hadn't thought about that. "*If* you give a full statement, on the record, answer their questions"—she takes a breath and lets it out—"and testify against any of the defendants, if necessary." She waits a beat and then says, "And your source for the Bobcat and ammunition."

I'm shaking my head before I can even really think it through.

"They already have him, Bex. Wasn't hard to trace the gun and ammunition to him."

"How long?"

"Ultimately, a judge has to approve it. But your maximum exposure is an additional five years, until your twenty-first birthday. I'll argue for much less than five years, and the government will likely agree to less."

"No more seg?"

"Up to the facility, but I'd expect them to move you out of segregation. Part of that would depend on you, on how you do with the other residents."

"Residents," like we're renting apartments or something.

Five years.

"Even if we defeat the transfer motion," she says, leaning closer, "you will be found delinquent. Possibly for the pipe bomb, too. And the judge will likely reduce the time if you cooperate."

"Then why—?"

"Because they want your testimony. Or at least the threat of your testimony. They want you on their witness lists. If you cooperate, the judge will hear about it. It will go a long way to knocking time off that maximum, and maybe even getting you out of a secure facility."

What happens to people who turn on their own family? Turn for getting out a few years faster?

Leverage. Strategy. I'm a pawn. And maybe a traitor.

"Bex?"

I've known for a long time, even before all this, that I might have to act on my own in a crisis scenario.

There was no training for this, but I will fight to survive.

CHAPTER 31

Uncle Skip insists on carrying my duffel upstairs for me. He never would have done that before.

There's not much in it. I gave away most of my stuff before I left the halfway house. I can get more. I don't need much, anyway.

"I tried to put everything back where it was," Uncle Skip says from the doorway.

The bed's different. And there's fresh paint and an area near the closet where the floorboards have been replaced.

"Mike helped, with the floor, the paint," he says. I nod to show I heard him. "And some others, too. Helped."

With the house. Putting it back together after the agents ripped it apart. Because of me. Me and Mark.

"Thanks," I say.

Someone washed the curtains but didn't know to starch them.

The same mirror, except I hardly recognize myself. My hair is short but boring. I've never been this pale before.

"If you'd rather have a different room, you can, but I thought . . . this is your room."

I turn around to face him. "No. It's perfect. Thank you."

"You said that already."

"I mean for coming to get me, letting me come here."

"Oh," he says, taking off his hat and rubbing his neck. "How about I make us some dinner? Are you hungry?"

"Sure." I'm not. I actually don't know if I'll be able to eat with the nerves and tension climbing up my spine and through my limbs. "Can I go for a run first?"

He stares at me, his lips pulled in tight. He wants to say no, but he can't. As of twelve days ago, I'm an adult.

"Not too far."

"I won't."

When I first got to the halfway house, I ran on a track at the nearby school. It was easier, somehow, than being on the streets, where anyone could see me. My muscles were so weak, I could only do half a lap. Then a lap. Then more. The track let me run without worrying about who was lurking in the shadows. I could see everything.

Later I ran on the neighborhood streets, anxiety choking

off my air until I was dizzy, but I kept going until it was just a lump in my throat.

Walking across the backyard toward the barn, I can still see signs of the searches. Boards on the barn that have been replaced. Areas in the yard that are uneven, grassless. We can level that all out again. Maybe plant something. Aunt Gracie had a garden a long time ago. Maybe Uncle Skip liked it. Maybe he'd like one again. It would be something to do.

I can't make myself go past the barn or into the woods. Too many shadows. Too many ghosts. Instead I accept today's limitation, as Dr. K. would say, and run along the edge of the woods and then up the drive. I can run the drive, up and back, and around the house. In the open, where I can see anything coming.

I loop Uncle Skip's new truck and smile at the shiny bumper, so different from his old one covered in dings and dirt.

All this has aged him. Being questioned, being held, being scared he might lose the house or the station. Worrying about me. He looks tired all the time now. And older. But here, at home, he still looks like himself. He doesn't look scared. That's comforting.

After a few laps, I realize that the lump is gone from the back of my throat. And I'm actually, maybe, hungry.

Inside, I wash up enough for dinner and help Uncle Skip carry our plates to the table. New paint in here, too. And a new table. New chairs. New plates.

"Sorry it's not a fancy homecoming meal," he says.

I stop pushing the potatoes and meat around my plate and force myself to take a bite. "It's good. I just don't eat as much."

"Well, you eat what you want. Then stop. There's cake for after—store-bought, but cake."

"Chocolate?"

He looks at me as if to say, *You had to ask?*

He sips his iced tea. "I'm glad you're home," he says.

"Home," I say, like I'm testing the word.

"Home," he says again. "Wherever I am, there will always be a place for you."

Uncle Skip looks at his phone. I still can't get used to him with a cell phone.

"Trouble?"

"Nah," he says. "Just Mike, checking in." Uncle Skip grins, and I feel myself smile. Mike, checking in on me. "Mike, some of the others, wanted to come over here tonight. I thought it might be too much for you. Maybe I was wrong?"

I shake my head. "You weren't."

"That's what I thought." He eats another bite of potato.

"But maybe you could come to the station with me tomorrow. We could stay a few hours, then come home. Something I want to show you."

"What?"

"Just something."

"Okay," I say, but even I can hear the tremor in my voice.

"There hasn't been any trouble at the station in months. Not since the sentencings started. For once the papers got things almost right."

The papers. The articles. About how the whole big grand plan—bombs and killing people and sparking a revolution—was mostly talk, and how the informant panicked. How most of the guys were really only guilty of big talk and having too many of the wrong kinds of guns. Even Mark. At least that's the story they're telling now.

Mom and Dad and his lawyer wanted me to speak at Mark's sentencing, about Clearview, about how we ramped each other up, or so they argue. About the "fight." How I exaggerated the fight, another side effect of my "paranoia." That I'm really the one to blame. Joan finally convinced them that if they called me to testify, it would not go well. But they'll never forgive me.

I didn't put him there, but I'm easier to blame than him. I'm out. And they didn't see him coming. I was the one they thought might do something scary. No one saw Mark coming. Maybe no one saw him at all. All my talk about being prepared, being vigilant, and I missed the greatest threat right under our noses.

It may be true that the informant panicked, embellished, but there was a plan, and I'll never be sure Mark and Zach and maybe the others weren't getting ready to act on it. If Riggs hadn't been suspicious, if I hadn't said something to Mark, if the feds hadn't been watching them and stopped them when they did . . . The papers can all say there was nothing to it, but there was something.

They had the guns. Fully automatic. And plans.

Riggs disclaimed any suspicions, of course. His shocked and tortured face was all over the news. It helped that he was able to say Devon, Neal, Mark, and Zach hadn't been out to the club for "a while." He stretched the weeks to months, but who was going to correct him? And then he doubled down once things fell apart by crowing about the overzealous government, targeting and setting up these young men. Stopping just short of *fine young men*. No one ever mentions me.

"One of those corporate places offered again."

"To buy the station?" The buzzing under my skin feels like panic.

"Decent money. Would pay off the legal bills, leave enough to make a difference."

Legal bills caused by taking us in and trying to help us. Which almost cost him big, more than just legal bills and repairs.

"So you're gonna sell it?"

He plays with his food. "Not today."

I sip my water, icy cold, and look out the screen door at the fading light of dusk.

"I don't think I can work inside, where anyone can come in," I say, staring into my water. "Not yet." I look up at him. I can't say *maybe not ever,* can't admit that's a possibility, or that cinder-block walls make it hard to breathe. But he shakes his head soothingly.

"I have it covered."

"Really?"

"Yeah." He takes a drink. "The job's yours, of course, if you want it back. But . . . it's covered, for now."

Did he hire someone? I'm too embarrassed to ask, since it didn't occur to me to ask before. Dr. K. would say let the guilt go, but it's lodged there in my chest.

Uncle Skip gets plates for the cake.

I pour the milk, then put an ice cube in mine. I need it as cold as I can get it.

"You still want to learn?" He watches me. "Repairs? Rebuilds?"

"Yes." I do. I really do. I need to do something. "But I might not be . . . ready," I say, hearing Dr. K.'s voice in my head, her murmurs telling me to take ownership of how I feel and be clear. "But I want to try."

"Good."

We eat the cake, but I can barely taste it. I force myself to chew and swallow, bite after bite, because he bought it, for me, as a celebration. He reaches over and stops my fork. He doesn't say anything.

Enough.

I sit on the porch and try not to vomit up the too-much food. The air smells like mud and spring. Part of me wants to sleep right here, on the rocker, under the open sky. The part of me that freaks out at being walled in. But it's at war with the part of me freaking out about being this exposed, this open to attack. Ultimately I decide I'm not ready to sleep on the porch, where anyone could get at me, but I'll leave the windows open upstairs.

After a shower, before I get into bed, I pull Joan's business card out of my new wallet. Her cell number is written on the back. *Just in case,* she said, right before she hugged me good-bye. I run my finger over the numbers and then put it away.

I need another pill. I don't like taking them, but Dr. K. says, for now, brave is accepting when I need help.

I made my choices. Now I have to live with them.

CHAPTER 32

"Bex," Mike says, coming around the truck in his bay and pulling me into a hug, a hard one that almost lifts me off my feet, oblivious to how much he's freaking me out. "Look at you." He smiles big like I've been away at college or camp. "You're taller? And skinny. Man, we are going to have to get my sister in here cooking for you." He's so happy. And Mr. Heinman and Mr. Henderson. So happy it's overwhelming. I didn't think anyone besides Uncle Skip would really be happy to see me.

"Come on back," Uncle Skip says.

Mike's grinning like he's in on the joke, whatever it is.

I don't like surprises.

I step out the back of the service-bay doors and stare at the broken-down heap sitting there. "I know it's not much to look at right now," Uncle Skip says, "but it's solid underneath the dings and missing parts. It'll be beautiful when we're done. When *you're* done."

I'm rooted to the ground. But they're all looking at me, so I force myself to walk around the shell of a truck. I thought it would take a year to earn enough money again, months to find something I could afford. They did this for me, so I'd have something to do, something of my own.

"When the weather turns," Uncle Skip says, "if you're still working on it, we'll make room for you inside. But for now . . ." He looks so uneasy. "You said you wanted to be outside. I thought maybe . . ."

"It's great," I get out before my throat closes. I step closer to the truck so he can't see my face, keep nodding so he knows it's okay.

"I already started tracking down some of the parts," a voice says behind me, and I whirl around in shock.

Cammie. Standing in the doorway. Hair back in a ponytail, in jeans and a shirt with the station's name. Holding a stack of papers. Like she belongs here. Like she belongs here more than me.

"Not anything . . . cool," she says. "Just the obvious, like new bumpers. And a door. And . . ." She trails off. "I'll just . . ." She points behind her. "Welcome home, Bex." And then she's gone.

Was she even real? Did they see her, too? I turn to Mike and Uncle Skip, but Mike already went inside.

Uncle Skip rubs at the back of his neck. "She kept showing up. Asking about you, wanting to do something or be helpful. I told her to go away, but she kept coming back."

"So you *hired* her?"

"She was there. After they took down the police tape. After the windows were busted out, both times. After the vandalism. I'd turn around and she'd be there, cleaning up, making calls, getting supplies. She'd show up with food and things we didn't even realize we needed. Said she had to do something. And she kept asking about you, over and over . . ."

I can't feel my feet. Or my hands.

"Eventually, she got it out of Mike, that you'd want this," he says, waving at the truck. "And then she was here even more, with ads and online listings and questions. She was going to do it no matter what I said," he says, looking at me. "So I let her. She found it." He turns to look at the truck.

"I can't let her pay for this."

"Oh, she didn't pay. I paid. Long overdue. And you'll work off the parts," he adds, waving off my objections. "But she found it, made them hold it until we could get there, begged and pleaded and pushed until she got it." He smiles. "Relentless, actually." I can imagine. "And somewhere in all that she started answering the phones and making the coffee. The guys thought she worked here. I couldn't *not* pay her."

I can't reconcile having her here. I thought I'd never see her again, or if I did, it would be bad. Ugly. That she'd hate me. When I heard Clearview continued, I figured they'd bought Riggs's talk and I'd be the only bad guy left, the one who collaborated with the government.

"She looked lost, Bex," he says. "After the arrests. She was worried. About you. And when it became clear that . . ." That I wasn't coming home. "Her grandfather called me. Said she wanted to do something. And . . ." He takes a deep breath and blows it out. "I couldn't do anything for you, but I could for her, who was trying to do something for you."

Uncle Skip goes back inside, and I sit on the picnic table they dragged back here for me and stare at the truck. It feels wrong for her to be here. Wrong to let her buy me off or whatever. It feels wrong to want to accept it. It feels wrong for *me* to even be here.

I feel wrong.

I thought I'd get free, and come here, and it would feel real. This would feel right. The only place I trusted would feel right.

Maybe *I'm* just wrong.

The door opens and closes.

"I thought maybe you could use a pop," Cammie says. She has one for herself, too. "I didn't know what kind you'd want."

There's none of the take-charge Cammie here. I don't know this Cammie. But I don't see pity or fear. And I am thirsty. I take one of the cans. But immediately it feels like being back in the interrogation room. I put it down instead of drinking it.

"I wanted to see you. I tried, but they wouldn't let me," she says. She takes a big sip from her can. "If you want me to go, I will. But this is a coming-home present. Nothing more."

But it is something more. One more person who got caught in the crossfire of this mess. One more person who wants to fix me. And one more person who stood by me, even if I didn't know it.

CHAPTER 33

When Cammie pulls up outside an indoor range sandwiched between a gas station and a plumbing supply store, I start to doubt whether I'm ready.

"It's just like riding a bike," she says. "Or maybe easier. I don't know. I never learned to ride a bike."

"I can teach you to ride a bike."

"I'd like that," she says, and I suddenly want to, and the warm feeling has me confused and squirming and not looking at her at all.

I work on the truck as much as I can, in between days I do real work for Uncle Skip and days when I'm too in my head to do much of anything. Cammie does at least half the haggling and driving to find parts. A lot of hours of the two of us in her car. Even more of Cammie keeping me company while I work. Somewhere in there we became friends for real.

"You have to face this," she says.

I force myself to get out of her car. I wait while she gets her gun case and range bag, trying to make myself breathe slowly.

Inside, I see why she was so sure it would be fine. Randy's working the range check-in. And the way he doesn't react when he sees me, only nods, makes it clear he knew we were coming. I guess he doesn't think I was involved with Mark and them, and doesn't think I'm a collaborator, either. I don't know what the others think. Karen's family moved to Texas soon after the arrests. There's been an exodus from Clearview. No one decent wants to be involved with a place that's had so much bad publicity. Too bad there are three of the wrong kind who want in for every one of the right who wants out. I don't know what happened between Cammie and Karen, but I know they haven't talked since Karen left.

Randy and Cammie talk while he checks us in. Something in the way he acts with Cammie makes me wonder if Randy owns this place. She signs us in, pays, and gets us down the hallway and in side-by-side lanes. The other people in the range are finishing up.

Soon, it's just us. I know Randy's watching from somewhere, but I can't see him. All I can see is Cammie. And the guns.

She places the rifle on the shelf in front of me in my lane, places the ammo beside it, and hands me my earmuffs. She's brought a nice bolt-action rifle — exactly what I would have packed for myself. I didn't know she'd paid attention to what I like.

She doesn't force me or try to convince me. She leaves me to face it myself, loading hers and getting ready to shoot.

"Eyes and ears," she says when she's ready.

I put my shooting glasses and earmuffs on and wait.

Her first shots make me flinch. She reloads and goes again. And again. Until I stop flinching.

And then I'm doing it. Checking the rifle to make sure it's empty. Loading the magazine. Taking sight down my lane toward the target. I can't see her or hear any shots. I know she's waiting, maybe even watching, but it's just me and the rifle.

My hands are shaking, but I steady them and fire. The first. The second. And then the rest of the magazine. Forget accuracy. This is about feel. How it feels. How I feel.

I shoot until I stop thinking about the fact that I'm shooting. Long after Cammie's retreated to the bench behind me to watch.

My accuracy is for shit, but the thrill is still there, under the lingering anxiety, doubts, and fears.

I could be good at this again.

I used to think that if I prepared enough, I could keep bad things from happening. That maybe the preparation itself would be like a barrier, keeping the bad stuff out.

I went to sleep every night knowing—knowing with absolute certainty—that something terrible was about to happen.

And then it did.

And I caused it, at least part of it, by doing the very things I thought could protect us.

I could have killed Mark. He was out of control, but in a way, I was, too.

Dr. K. asked me about why I was so scared, about whether it's possible that what I was really afraid of was me, was knowing, deep down, that what I was doing in the name of that fear was itself dangerous. If maybe something bad happening was inevitable, because I was so focused on something bad happening.

I still don't know the answer to that.

Maybe I never will.

What I do know now is that there isn't enough preparation in the world to control everything. And it can't prevent really bad things from happening. But *thinking* I could control everything was part of the problem.

How many people could Mark have killed if Riggs hadn't asked me about him and I hadn't asked Mark and Mark hadn't panicked? Was it really all talk and one-upsmanship? Or would they have actually tried to go out in a blaze of glory if the government hadn't stopped them? And if they were serious, their big plan was destined to fail. They'd be dead or in prison, and a lot of innocent people would be dead or hurt, and nothing would have changed.

Dr. K. says I'm not responsible for Mark's actions. And I know I'm not. He is. But none of this happened in a vacuum. We started out reading the same sites, watching the same videos. There are some real things to be scared of. But the websites and forums were a rabbit hole that sucked me in deeper and deeper until any crazy theory seemed possible, seemed real. Uncle Skip tried to tell me that, but I couldn't hear it. Maybe Mark's rabbit hole was even deeper and darker than mine. Because someone modified that gun or showed Mark how to do it. Whoever was egging him on, whoever was helping him—did they know what they were doing? Were they looking for guys exactly like Mark, with nothing better to do with his life? Yeah, had Mark gone through with this, he'd have been responsible, but there were other people who would have carried some of the guilt, too.

I've never been more sure that the government doesn't

play fair. I still believe that I have the right to own guns. But if we're down to guns as our weapons, we've already lost. They can't save us from those who lie to us, who preach that we are the front line all the while believing us to be expendable. And if the government ever really turns on us, we'll need something smarter than an AR-15. We'd need an army of Joans. People like Joan. Maybe people like Cammie and me, who have seen both sides.

I still think we're headed to some kind of crisis, eventually, if things keep on this way. But I no longer go to bed every night thinking tomorrow might be that day, or that I might have to fight my way to safety next week. And until that happens, I'm going to have a life worth living.

When I turn around, Randy is waiting with Cammie.

"Accuracy will come with time," he says. "Just give it time."

Time.

The way Cammie smiles at me makes me shiver. And sweat.

Makes it hard to look at her on the walk back to the car. She doesn't try to fill the space, and just walks beside me.

I've been staring at the computer in Uncle Skip's office for an hour, trying to write my last e-mail to Lucy. A short e-mail. Just to say I'm sorry. To say she'll never have to hear from me again, but I wanted her to know that I'm sorry. And to thank her. She helped me, protected me. She was brave. But I can't hit send. It feels unfinished. Like there's something I'm forgetting to say. But I don't know what.

She hasn't answered any of my previous e-mails or phone calls. Last time I called, her father said not to call again or he'd get a restraining order. It's the last attempt I'll make. It has to be right.

"So, the truck's done? Done done?" Cammie asks, leaning around the doorway.

"Except for the last test drive, yeah. I thought you might . . ."

"Cool," Cammie says. "I'll meet you out back in twenty minutes."

The truck starts right away, purring, perfect.

"Have a name yet?" Cammie asks, petting the dash.

"Not yet." I'm not sure I'll name her. I'm not sure I'm the naming-vehicles kind of person. "Feel like a good long test drive?" I ask.

"Yes," Cammie says. "Hell, yes."

"I know a great place for pizza," I say.

We take the extra-long way, just enjoying the ride, the night.

The pizza's as good as I remember. Greasy and cheesy and hot. Cammie drinks pop instead of tea and covers her slice in grated Parmesan, and I'm not at all nervous about being here with her.

Tomorrow I'm sending the e-mail. As is.

Good-bye, Lucy.

CHAPTER 34

"That's it." I toss my backpack behind the seat. "Be right back."

"Hurry up," Cammie says, looking at the map. She's started ordering me around again. I think it means she thinks I'm cured.

Uncle Skip is in his workshop, working on something that is still in multiple pieces. He's been sanding it for days. Maybe he's just playing at building it.

"We're leaving."

He looks up as if he forgot I was here or that I was leaving today. He hesitates before putting down the plane and wiping the sawdust from his hands.

"You've got enough money, and—"

"Yes. I've got enough." Joan got them to give me back my cash by showing them my pay records from the station. Every penny, honestly and legally earned.

"I got something for you." He reaches behind him and pulls out a box. "A little late, but happy birthday."

"We agreed that the truck would cover birthdays and all other gift-giving holidays for a while."

"It's not a big deal."

I take the box. Inside is a cell phone, along with a charger, car charger, and earpiece.

"The kid at the store said it's a good one and explained all the extras. I didn't understand, but I got you what he recommended. He programmed some numbers for you. So you can call if you need to, or want."

"And you can call me."

"Yeah. That, too."

I throw my arms around him and hang on, his hand stroking the back of my head, until I swallow the tears.

"You be careful," he whispers before letting go. "And don't stay away too long."

I walk back to the truck slowly, trying to swallow the lump in my throat. I feel like I should run back and hug him again, hang on until it feels less like saying good-bye. But I know if I do, I might not let go. I have to go.

"Ready?" Cammie asks through the open window.

"Ready," I say.

I start the truck and then search through the stations to find something I want to listen to. Then I put it in drive.

"We are not listening to this crap the whole trip," Cammie says.

"Driver picks the music."

Cammie considers it and then says, "That's fair. Just remember it later."

"You think I'm letting you drive my truck?" I ask.

Cammie smiles and flips her sunglasses down. It's a wicked smile. "I think I can convince you."

Windows down, wind whipping in, sun on my arm, I realize I'm fully warm for the first time in months.

I can't wait to see the ocean.